TAKE CARE

by

DONNA TERRES

PublishAmerica
Baltimore

© 2004 by Donna Terres.
All rights reserved. No part of this book may be reproduced, stored in a retrieval system or transmitted in any form or by any means without the prior written permission of the publishers, except by a reviewer who may quote brief passages in a review to be printed in a newspaper, magazine or journal.

First printing

ISBN: 1-4137-3740-4
PUBLISHED BY PUBLISHAMERICA, LLLP
www.publishamerica.com
Baltimore

Printed in the United States of America

IN MEMORY OF

TERRY LEE TERRES

CHAPTER ONE

Janelle woke abruptly. Her eyes flew open and darted around the room. Her hands tightened into fists on the edge of the sheet, clutching it tight under her chin. Heart pounding, she took a hushed breath and held it, listening intently. The house was silent. The only sound came from the whisper of a summer breeze that filtered through her bedroom window, ruffling the pink lace curtains and gently swaying the sheer, rayon material of the pink and white canopy over her head.

She had not intended to sleep. Time slipped away too quickly when you slept. Her stepfather would be home any minute. She could not let him find her away from her mother.

Pushing back the light sheet that covered her shorts and halter-clad body, she slid her legs over the side of the mattress and crept out of her youth size bed, padding barefoot across the thick rose carpet. Flipping back her thick mane of ebony hair and quietly pulling open the door, she stopped to listen again.

The house was silent and still, as if it, too, slept. The grandfather clock in the living room chimed softly—four musical tolls. It was four p.m.! She had slept for over an hour. Baxter would be home any minute.

She tiptoed silently across the open balcony and peered cautiously over the dark oak railing that decorated the edge of the open hallway.

The rectangular living room below glowed warmly with afternoon sun. A balmy breeze from an open window stirred the fronds of the large, beautiful fern her mother kept in front of the bay windows. No one was in sight. Janelle started toward the stairs.

At that moment the front door slammed and her stepfather's voice called loudly, "Delphine! Where are you?"

Her mother answered from the direction of the vegetable garden at the back of the house, her words clearly audible through the open windows. "I'm in the garden, Dear."

Janelle silently backed into her room. Baxter was now between her and her mother.

A second later the back door banged and Baxter's voice came from the back of the house, "Where are the girls?"

Janelle rushed toward the steps. She could be out the front door and around the side of the house before Baxter came back in. At the curve, where the back door came into view, she stopped and peered around the corner. Baxter was standing on the deck, his hand on the door handle. Janelle backed up quickly. He would see her if she continued to the front door.

"They're taking a nap," she heard her mother say. "They were both exhausted after the late night at my folks and the romping with their cousins."

Baxter's voice sounded pleased, "A nap, yeah, that sounds like a good idea. What time is supper and what did you make? It better be better than that junk you made last night."

Janelle shuddered and tiptoed back up the stairs as her mother's voice continued.

"It won't be ready for at least another two hours. You said you'd be home at six. I put a meatloaf in the oven." Janelle heard the disillusionment in her mother's soft voice. Her mother seemed to crumble whenever Baxter was around. He never stopped criticizing and kind words were not in his vocabulary.

Janelle remembered when her mother had been dating Baxter. She found it hard to believe that the man had once been so kind and nice. She and her sister, Allison, had both liked him and had giggled between themselves, hoping their mother would marry him. They had wanted a father again. A father like their real daddy had been. Janelle clearly remembered her real daddy, who died when she was seven.

"Holler when it's ready," Baxter's voice growled. The hinges on the back door squeaked in protest as he threw it open.

Janelle was frozen with fear. The sun tanned color of her pretty face paled and she stuffed her fist in her mouth to keep from moaning aloud. She forced her stiff legs into motion and ran silently to the end of the balcony, rushing unannounced into her older sister's bedroom. Allison would help her hide from him.

TAKE CARE

Shaking Allison awake, she choked, "Baxter's home and Mom's in the garden." Both girls had steadfastly refused to call him Daddy as he continually insisted.

Allison needed no further explanation. She jumped from her bed and grabbed Janelle's shaking hand. "We'll go out the back door," she promised, her fingers quickly and reassuringly tracing the contours of Janelle's pinched face.

Allison started for the door of her bedroom, pulling Janelle behind her. Her eyes glinted with a spark of determination that her terror was threatening to capsize.

They reached the bedroom door just as Baxter stepped in front of them. Allison stopped so suddenly that Janelle ran into her and stumbled, falling to the floor.

Both girls stared up at Baxter's lazy, sarcastic smile, "Going somewhere girls?"

Janelle scrambled to her feet and backed further into the room. Tears began to stream down her face. Allison stood her ground, but neither girl answered their stepfather.

Baxter reached out a large, calloused hand and patted Allison's dark head. Allison flinched and quickly backed up a few steps. Her big, green eyes darted to her younger sister and her pretty face hardened with a confidence born of desperation. *I won't let him touch her,* she promised herself.

"You go help your mother in the garden, Allison, and remember what I told you." He abruptly reached for Allison's ear lobe. His thick fingers closed over her left ear and he pinched cruelly as he repeated the warning he had already given them dozens of times. "She wouldn't believe you, but if she did, I'd kill all of you. Your mother will be first, so you can watch. And, I'll kill you slowly." Baxter's eyes glowed. "I'll cut off your ears and your fingers, fingernails first. I'll slice you open so you can see your insides." He paused and stared hard at Allison. "Understand?"

Allison's shoulders slumped in defeat. She believed him. Their mother would never believe anyone could be so cruel. She looked at her sister. Her eyes filled with tears and she moaned aloud as she rushed toward Janelle.

Janelle was huddled against the headboard of Allison's bed, her thumb in her mouth; a long-ago habit that had been broken, but which Janelle had started again after Baxter became their stepfather. Allison hugged her sister and hurriedly whispered, "Try not to think. Try to make your mind a complete blank like we talked about. Okay?"

Janelle stared up at her sister. Allison saw the hope drain from her eyes and fresh tears began to course down her pale cheeks.

"Get!" Baxter hissed, coming up behind Allison.

Allison jumped away from Janelle. She wanted to try begging, but she knew it wouldn't help. She had tried before. Baxter had twisted her arm behind her back until she had thought it was going to break. He had snarled another warning, "I don't want to hear another word about either of you not wanting to please your daddy, not now and *never* again. Do you understand? Answer me!"

Allison threw a murderous look at Baxter as she detoured around him to reach the door. She wondered if God could strike Baxter dead. She decided to pray that God would get him out of their lives.

Baxter turned back to Janelle. Allison had been dismissed.

Her steps slow, Allison headed down the hall. Her insides were tight with pain for her sister and fear for them all. Janelle was only twelve, two years younger than she was. She was old enough to understand why she couldn't tell her mother about Baxter, but she was still too young to understand why a man who professed to love them wanted to hurt them.

Allison didn't understand either. She didn't think you could get old enough to understand why there were evil people like Baxter in the world.

He was a very accomplished actor. He had their mother completely fooled. He treated them kindly when she was around. He brought them treats and was always offering to take them places, the zoo, the movies, out to eat, or to the beach. Janelle and Allison always refused his offers unless their mother was included in the plans. Whenever Baxter was around, the girls stayed close to their mother.

Stopping in the kitchen, she tried to control her sobs. She couldn't let her mother see her crying. She knew Delphine would cuddle her and try to coax the reason for the tears from her.

She wet a washcloth in cold water and stood slumped against the sink, holding the cold rag against her reddened eyes and telling herself that Baxter's abuse of Janelle wouldn't go on forever.

Three weeks had passed since Baxter had last taken Allison to his room. The last time had been a Saturday morning when her mother had gone grocery shopping. In the bright light of early morning, Baxter had suddenly noticed the slight puffiness of her slowly maturing nipples and the light dusting of fine hairs that had begun to grow under her arms and in her pubic area. He had backed away from her in horror and then reached out to heartlessly twist the tender, young nipple in his callused fingers. 'What's this?' he had demanded, 'That's disgusting. Get away from me,' and he had given her a shove that had toppled her off the side of his bed.

Allison had jumped to her feet, grabbed her clothes from the floor and hurried out the door; relieved and thankful that Baxter no longer wanted her.

She was halfway down the hall to her room when Baxter emerged from his room and headed for Janelle's room....

Allison had rushed back to him and had caught up to him before he reached Janelle's room. 'No!' she had whispered fiercely. 'You leave her alone! She's only a baby.'

Baxter had stopped short, surprise and amazement had flooded his face. His words had mocked her, 'A baby, is she? She's been sharing my bed just as long as you have!'

Allison had been shocked into silence. She could not believe that Janelle had kept such a vile act a secret from her.

Allison slowly replaced the washcloth on the towel rack above the sink and moved out of the kitchen. Her thoughts tumbled around and around. She and Janelle had since spent hours trying to figure out how to get away from Baxter.

At the back door, she caught sight of her mother heading for the house. Allison's heart melted at the sight of her, while her eyes took in the beauty of her dirt-smudged face and the supple strength of her slender arms and legs. Allison loved her mother more than anyone in the whole world. Her mother was soft and loving, raising her fatherless girls with kindness and patience. Her mother understood their problems and consoled them with unending love and devotion. Tears again rose in Allison's eyes and she hurriedly backhanded them away.

Allison stepped out the door, wanting to divert her mother back to the garden. She couldn't allow her mother to discover what was happening upstairs. "Hi, Mom, I was just coming to help you with the weeding."

Delphine's eyebrows rose in mock surprise, "Of your own free will? Or did your dad send you down?"

Allison swallowed hard and ducked her head. She tried to laugh, but the sound, which issued from her throat more closely resembled a broken sob than a laugh. "He's not my dad," she muttered under her breath. She wondered how her mother managed to appear happy and content in front of her daughters, when Allison knew Baxter no longer treated her good. His name-calling and demoralizing remarks did not stop with Janelle and her. She also knew that Baxter did not go to her mother's bedroom.

Delphine frowned and a comforting arm came around Allison's slim shoulders, "Allison? I know Baxter isn't your real dad, but he's trying real hard to be a father to you. You have to try, too." She stopped and gently lifted Allison's face till their eyes met, "Is something wrong? Have you been crying?"

"No. No, nothing's wrong, Mom. The sun is so bright it's making my eyes water, that's all," Allison lied, turning her face away again, wanting to avoid her mother's sharp eyes. "And I still miss Daddy," Allison added.

Delphine hugged her, seeming to forget her question about why Allison had come to help her, "Of course you do. We all do and we always will." Allison relaxed into the comfort of her mother's arms. "Did you have a nice nap?"

"Yes," Allison murmured, still avoiding her mother's eyes.

Delphine turned back to the house. Allison watched her hand come up and wearily brush back a fallen strand of hair as she started into the kitchen. "Is Janelle still sleeping?"

"Where are you going?" Allison asked, suddenly realizing her mother was going into the house.

Delphine turned back to her and Allison saw the surprise in her eyes, "I have to check on supper, why?"

Allison rushed after her, but she let the screen door come closed as silently as possible. In her haste to cover her fearful and unreasonable question, Allison stuttered, "I..ju..st won..dered."

Delphine pulled two pot holders from the cabinet drawer and turned to open the oven door. Allison watched her long auburn curls tumble forward with her movements.

Her mother pulled the meat loaf from the oven and removed the foil wrap from the top of the loaf pan. The meat was barely brown. Allison gritted her teeth. *Mom wouldn't be worrying about the meat if Baxter wasn't always so critical of everything*, she thought. Hate rushed through her, making her wish she was older and much stronger.

"Did you say Janelle was still sleeping?"

"She was sound asleep when I peeked into her room," Allison lied again. Her mother couldn't go upstairs! If Delphine discovered what was going on in Baxter's bedroom, they would all be killed.

Allison shuddered at the thought of the sharp, curved blade of the knife that Baxter kept hidden under his hankies in the small drawer of his night stand. The memory of the night he had shown it to her still filled her with horror. He had laughed, seeming to lap up the fear in her eyes. 'Nice, huh? It's for emergences, such as talkative little girls. It's very sharp,' and he had rubbed his thumb lightly across the blade to illustrate his meaning.

Allison had been firmly convinced that she couldn't tell her mother, but she had developed fantasies about using the knife on Baxter. As much as she hated the man, she was sure she couldn't cold-bloodedly cut his throat while he slept, and she knew she did not have the strength required to attack him while he was awake. What could she do?

Delphine's sigh brought Allison back to the present. "We'll give her another half an hour and then I'll go wake her up."

"I'll wake her up," Allison quickly offered as they walked hand in hand to the garden.

Delphine smiled and ruffled Allison's jet-black hair, "Thank you, Allison. You're a very good helper. I am so lucky that God gave me two such sweet, wonderful girls."

Allison bent her head, fell to her knees and hurriedly began to pull weeds. She didn't feel sweet and wonderful. She felt dirty and worthless. And she was sure the God she had believed in all her life had abandoned her and her sister. Baxter had stolen their innocence and forced them to become accomplices to his crime, even denying Allison the opportunity to help her sister.

Baxter reached out and took Janelle's hand, "Come along, sweetheart." He pulled her from Allison's bed and dragged her along to his bedroom. Janelle held back with all her might, but this time Baxter seemed to ignore her unwillingness to accompany him. The last time she had resisted him, Janelle had a swollen ear lobe for a week. She had worn her long hair down around her face so her mother would not see the bruised ear.

In his room, Baxter pushed her toward the bed. Janelle lost her balance and fell on the floor. Terror filled her at the sight of Baxter's king size bed. She quickly crawled toward the window and curled into a ball beneath the open window. She wrapped her arms tightly around her bent legs, shuddering with fear. No matter what, she wasn't going to help him. She would never willingly climb on his bed.

The window faced the front of the house and Janelle could hear a car slowly cruise past, but she gave no thought to calling for help. If her sister couldn't help her, neither could a stranger. And their lives depended on her silent endurance of Baxter's unspeakable torture.

She watched her stepfather close and lock the bedroom door. When he turned toward her, she squeezed her eyes tightly closed. I won't think. I won't think at all, she chanted to herself. I'll pretend I'm still sleeping in my bed.

Baxter reached down and grabbed her around her waist. Lifting her effortlessly, he dropped her on his bed and knelt beside her. His blunt fingers hooked themselves under the elastic waistband of her shorts.

Immediately after Baxter said she could go, Janelle rushed to the bathroom and washed her mouth out with soap before she climbed into the shower and scrubbed her body raw with a small vegetable brush. But she still felt dirty and nauseous.

When Janelle returned to her bedroom, after her horrible hour with Baxter, she found Allison waiting in her room. "No more," she said. She was past the point of dreaming about running away and she was tired of trying to convince Allison that she should come with her. Last night their whispered discussion had turned into an argument.

"I'm not waiting any longer," Janelle urgently whispered, her voice thick with emotion.

"But Janelle, you're almost thirteen. I started to develop when I was thirteen and a half. You know Baxter won't want you anymore then and he'll leave you alone."

"Mom says she didn't start to develop until she was fifteen. I asked her. If I take after her, I'll have to suffer through another two years with Baxter! It's already been almost a year. I'm not going to do it," Janelle flatly stated. "And what if I get pregnant? What then?"

"You can't get pregnant, Janelle. The hygiene teacher says you have to have had your period before you can have a baby," Allison reminded her. "And anyhow, what would we do? Where would we live and how would we pay for our food?"

"I don't know and I don't care. This kind of life is not worth living." Janelle's eyes fell to the floor and then slowly she raised them back up to lock with Allison's. Her left hand toyed with her still sore ear and her right thumb went in her mouth. "I don't want to live anymore...not like this," she whispered past her thumb. Her eyes begged Allison to understand her complete and desperate despair.

Allison couldn't answer her. Her throat closed with emotion and her eyes widened in fear as she stared at her sister in horror. Could Janelle be thinking of killing herself?

"I've been saving my allowance and I've got almost fifty dollars. We'll think of something," Janelle continued. "You'll go with me, won't you?"

"I'd never let you go alone," Allison promised. "I've got about seventy dollars. What about Mom? Are we going to tell her where we're going?"

"We can't! We'd have to tell her everything and she won't believe us. You know she won't. Mom has never seen any of the things Baxter does. He's so good at pretending, he should have been an actor! She thinks he really loves us."

"Mom will be worried sick if we just disappeared," Allison moaned in pain.

"I know, but we can't tell her." Janelle began to sob, but she remained unyielding. "I'd rather have her worried than have Baxter find out she knows."

Allison was silent. She couldn't argue with Janelle's reasoning. For the hundredth time she wondered if they should tell their mother about Baxter. She was sure that Delphine no longer loved Baxter. Would she believe them?

Of course she would, Allison chided herself, *she doesn't know we lie*. But what could she do? If Mom told Baxter that she knew what he was doing, he would kill them all.

Was it possible she was staying with him for their sake? Baxter was still nice to them when Delphine was around, a lot nicer than he was to her. Or maybe it was because they were Catholic and there is no divorce for a good Catholic.

Both girls had steadfastly disguised their hate of the man, fearful that Delphine would discover their secret and Baxter would carry through with his threats. Lately, Delphine had seemed to become curious why the girls stayed so close to her, making them work harder than ever to convince her that he was a good man. Once or twice, Janelle had even called him dad, making Delphine smile, the relief plain on her face.

"Allison? Are you going to pack?" Janelle asked, her eyes pleaded with Allison to hurry. "I'm leaving now, tonight." She got up from her bed and dragged her small overnight case from her closet. Quietly opening her dresser drawers, she began to pack only what she considered the bare necessities.

For a few moments Allison silently watched her. *I'm not going to be able to talk her out of it,* she thought, *but do I really want to?* Gathering her courage, she straightened her back and murmured, "I'll get my clothes."

A half hour later the two girls slipped out the front door and started for the highway.

"Where should we go?" Allison asked. She turned and looked back at the large white house where they had been so happy, until Baxter's arrival on the scene.

"Let's hitchhike to Minneapolis. No one will ever find us there and we can get jobs." Janelle had always been the planner and instigator of the two, while Allison was a peacemaker, a follower. Janelle had been begging Allison to leave with her for almost a year, since right after they had discovered that Baxter had been molesting both of them.

"Janelle, you're not going to be able to get a job. Even if you lie about your age, they won't believe you. You look even younger than thirteen."

"If I can't get a real job, I'll baby sit. I'm more than old enough for that." Janelle frowned and then said, "Do you think we could both work at night and go to school in the daytime?"

"I hope so," Allison said. "I wanted to go to college, too."

Janelle didn't miss the longing in her sister's voice. Both girls shared the love of learning that Delphine had instilled in them at a very young age. "Allison, you don't have to go with me. Baxter doesn't bother you. I'll be all right and I can come back when I start to develop," Janelle offered, praying Allison would refuse to let her leave alone. She wanted to go, but she was even more scared to leave alone.

"I'm going with you! Let's not argue about that," Allison said. They walked in silence for a few minutes before Allison suddenly stopped and added, "We can both go back when you start getting breasts. Maybe Baxter will even leave if you're not there. He never goes to Mom's bedroom. If he doesn't want her and he doesn't have you, maybe he'll leave." Hope filled her and she hugged Janelle. "Everything's going to work out fine. We can call Mom in a couple weeks. Maybe he'll be gone."

Janelle didn't answer. They started walking again. *How can everything ever be fine again?* she wondered. *Baxter has ruined both our lives.*

At the highway, they nervously stuck out their thumbs. Both girls were terrified of hitchhiking. All their lives they had been warned repeatedly not to talk to strangers and never to go in a stranger's car.

"What if the person who picks us up turns out to be a rapist or a murderer?" Allison muttered, her voice squeaky with fear.

TAKE CARE

"We could take a bus," Janelle said.

"We only have a hundred and twenty bucks. The bus would probably take more than half of that."

"I know, but we'll get jobs right away." Janelle wearily pushed her long black hair over her shoulder and wondered if her confident words would come true. "Did you remember your social security card?"

"Yes."

At that moment, a car pulled over to the side of the road and the driver stuck her head out the window. "Want a ride?" she asked.

Janelle and Allison both breathed a sigh of relief. The driver was female. She looked like a respectable woman and she wore a tailored suit. *We have nothing to fear from a girl, do we?* Janelle wondered as they ran toward the car.

The door of the red Pontiac opened as they reached the car. The lady driver was smiling as she called, "Jump in." The girls both scrambled into the front seat. "Where are you headed at this late hour?" the woman asked as she signaled and pulled back into the lane of traffic.

Janelle shoved her right hand behind her back and quickly crossed her fingers, she hated all the lies she and Allison had been forced to tell. "We're going to our grandma's in Minneapolis. Our stepfather is drunk again and we decided we weren't going to stay around for him to beat us again." She sneaked a look at Allison, hoping her sister wasn't going to contradict her swiftly made up story. *If only the story was true*, she thought, *having been beaten would be infinitely better than having been molested.*

The lady's face hardened and her eyes flashed with quick anger, although her voice remained soft and gentle, "Where's your mother?"

"She ran away about a month ago," Allison put in, there by corroborating Janelle's lie. "Our stepfather was beating her, too."

The woman shook her head and muttered under her breath. Both girls heard the exclamation, though it was low voiced. They looked at each other in fear, wondering if the woman was swearing at them. Her next words put them at ease. "Well, you hit it lucky. I work in the Cities and I'm just on my way back down there. Where does your grandmother live?"

"In Minneapolis," Janelle said quickly.

The lady's smile was patient, "Where in Minneapolis?"

"Close to the Mall of America," she answered, hoping there were houses close to the huge mall that they had never visited.

The lady frowned and glanced quickly at the two girls, "I know that area.

What's her address?"

Her mind a blank, Janelle looked to Allison. "We don't know, but we know what her house looks like. It's big and green. We'll recognize it," Allison said, throwing a quick look at the woman. "You don't have to take us to the door. You can just let us out when you reach your house. We'll find the way to Grandma's."

Janelle could have kicked herself. *Why didn't we get a story all made up ahead of time?* she fumed to herself. *The lady's getting suspicious; she'll probably make us get out again.*

The lady suddenly pulled over to the side of the highway and Janelle's heart fell. She was right; the lady was going to kick them out. And after they had been so lucky and found a really nice woman.

The lady turned toward the two girls, putting her arm on top of the seat. "You don't have a grandma in Minneapolis, do you?"

Allison and Janelle hung their heads and didn't reply.

"Tell me the real story, girls. I'll do whatever I can to help you, but I have to know the truth."

Janelle reached for the door latch, "We don't want to get you involved in our mess. We'll get a ride with someone else." She pushed the door open and started to get out.

"Wait! I really want to help you. You don't realize what you're getting yourselves into. Minneapolis is a hard place to be homeless in, even in the summer. There are all kinds of creeps who will take advantage of you; maybe even force you into becoming prostitutes."

Allison grabbed Janelle's arm and pulled her back into the car. "Let's tell her, Janelle. Maybe she can help us," she whispered.

Janelle cupped her hands and spoke directly in Allison's ear, "She might take us to the police! And then they'll call Mom and the whole truth will come out! Baxter will find out before we can help Mom."

Allison turned back to the woman and asked, "You won't take us to the police, will you?"

The woman pulled back slightly and Janelle saw the sudden suspicion in her eyes. *Now she thinks we're criminals,* Janelle thought.

The woman asked, "What did you do?"

"We didn't do anything," Allison said. "It's our stepfather."

"And he's been beating you?" the woman visibly relaxed.

"Will you take us to the police?" Allison asked again.

"No. Not unless that's where you decide you want to go," the woman promised.

Janelle tugged on Allison's arm, trying to get her to leave the car. Allison ignored her and said, "He says he'll kill us if we tell what he's done to us."

"I can help you," the lady encouraged. "Tell me the whole story."

Allison hesitated, looking at Janelle. Janelle sighed in defeat and then nodded in agreement. Allison quickly related the basics of their life since Baxter and their mother had married.

Janelle was silent while Allison told their story. Her eyes searched the dark area around the car, trying to pick out places to hide from the woman if she insisted on calling the police.

A long silence followed Allison's horrifying story. Janelle sneaked a look at the woman. She was surprised to see tears flowing freely down the woman's face.

"Oh, you poor kids!" The woman reached out and wrapped her arms around the two girls. "I'm so sorry."

Janelle looked at the woman in surprise and confusion, "It wasn't your fault."

The woman sniffed and then dug in her purse for a Kleenex and blew her nose. "I know. I just feel so sorry for you." The three of them sat in silence for a long time.

Suddenly, the woman straightened up, "I've got an idea. Why don't I call your mother and pretend to be a friend of hers from high school. I'll convince her to come and meet me and then we'll tell her the whole story. We'll go to the police and they will arrest your stepfather. What do you think?"

"You're going to call at this time of night and say you're an old friend?" Janelle asked. "Mom won't believe you."

"All I have to do is give her an excuse for the late night phone call, something for her to tell your stepfather. We could even tell her the story on the phone—that is if she goes in a different room from your stepfather—and then she could come and meet us or we could go pick her up."

"Baxter won't hear the phone ring. They have separate bedrooms and there's no phone in Baxter's bedroom," Janelle said.

"That's even better," the woman said. She looked at the two girls, "What do you think?"

Janelle and Allison looked at each other. Janelle shook her head. "I don't want to go back there as long as Baxter is still there. We have no way of knowing for sure if he'll wake up or not. He might hear her on the phone, wait until she hangs up, and then kill her before we can get there."

"Okay, I can understand your fears. We'll get your mother to come to us," the lady assured her.

Janelle and Allison looked at each other for a long moment before Janelle said, "What if Baxter does wake up? If he discovers we're gone, he'll know something is up."

The lady frowned, "That's a good point, ah...what's your name?"

"Janelle," Janelle said.

"And Allison," Allison put in.

"I'm very glad to meet you," the lady smiled, solemnly shaking each girl's small hand. "Okay. What if we go to the police first? Then we'll all go to the house and the police will arrest your stepfather."

"What if the police don't believe us?" Allison asked.

"They'll believe you, Honey," the woman's voice was soft and caring. "In fact, you're already talking to the police. I'm Dena Lark, a policewoman. I'm sorry I lied to you, but I've found that young runaways will not confide in the police. And I have to admit that in some cases the kids are right to mistrust the police, because the police are only as good as the system."

"Why?" Janelle and Allison asked together, forgetting their fear of the police in the face of the woman's kindness.

"Because the police are only as good as the system, and because sometimes the system does not always work the way it was intended to work. Sometimes the runways are hurt more by the system than they were by their parents...." She paused, silently contemplating the many cases she had been involved in that had gone wrong for just this reason. She remembered with horror a recent case where the court returned a young child to her alleged abusive father because there was no one else to care for her: no foster homes available. Shaking her head in anger, she continued, "Well, what do you say? Should we get some officers over to your house and arrest your stepfather?"

"Are you sure they'll believe us?" Janelle asked.

"I believe you, they will, too. I'm very hard to convince."

Allison and Janelle slowly nodded their heads. "I think it will work," Allison whispered to her sister. Dena smiled as Allison gave Janelle's hand a reassuring squeeze.

"I do, too," Janelle agreed, hope coming alive on her pinched face. "It would be wonderful if we could just go back to Mom and not have Baxter there."

Allison sighed in relief and nodded happily.

Officer Dena Lark put the car in gear and headed for the next exit. "I work at the downtown Police Headquarters and I just got off duty. There are some very good men on duty right now. We'll go over there."

Officer Lark took Janelle and Allison to a small break room and bought them each a soda pop and a candy bar. "You girls wait here and I'll go talk to the Lieutenant. We'll make short work of having your stepfather behind bars," she promised, giving each girl a quick hug.

Twenty minutes later Dena returned to the girls, accompanied by three policemen and the Lieutenant. "We've decided, if you agree, to take both of you with us when we go to arrest your stepfather. You'll have to wait with me, a short distance away, until the officers have your stepfather in custody, but then you will be able to go to your mother. She's going to need to see you right away when she finds out what has been going on." Both girls nodded and Dena softly asked, "Ready?"

They arrived at the Perry house at one thirty a.m. They heard quick steps coming toward the door and then Delphine Perry's voice called out, "Who's there?"

Dena Lark answered, "Police."

The door cracked open. Delphine Perry stared at the officers. Her face first registered shock and then on the heels of that, fear.

Baxter Perry stumbled down the steps before the officers had a chance to explain their presence to Delphine. "What? Who's there?" he shouted angrily. Seeing the officers, his tone changed and he stuttered, "Wh...what's wrong?"

The officers stepped forward and one man asked, "Baxter Perry?"

"Yeah, I'm Baxter Perry." Baxter straightened his shoulders, pushed out his chest and pulled the belt of his bathrobe tighter around his trim waist.

"You're under arrest on suspicion of child molestation. You have the right to remain silent...." Baxter's mouth dropped open in shock as the Officer moved behind him and handcuffed him while he spoke the words of the Miranda.

"What are you talking about?" Baxter demanded, his voice high and suddenly jittery. "You're crazy! I didn't do anything." His eyes slid to the open balcony above the living room as if he expected to see Janelle and Allison standing there, ready to accuse him.

Delphine stared open mouthed at the officers, her eyes wide with shock.

"Your stepdaughters say differently, Mr. Perry, and we believe them," Dena said, stepping in the door with Janelle and Allison right behind her.

"They're lying! I didn't do anything. They're lying I tell you. Ask my wife, she'll tell you," Baxter screamed while the officers forced him out the door and pushed him toward the waiting patrol cars.

Janelle and Allison rushed around the policewoman and threw themselves at their mother. Delphine stared at them in disbelief. Her eyes showed her confusion as they flicked to the balcony, where Janelle and Allison's closed bedroom doors were plainly visible. "I don't understand. I thought you were in bed. You were with the police?"

"We had to run away, Mom...," Janelle began, her voice cracking.

Allison silently raised her face to Heaven and said, *Thank You, God, for getting Baxter out of our lives. Thank You! Thank You!*

"Run away?! But why?" Delphine was in a state of shock. The words she had heard had not registered. She wrapped her arms around the girls and led them to the couch. In the back of her mind the ugly word 'molest' lurked, waiting to pounce if she let it, but she had pushed it away from her conscious thought patterns. Gently pulling the girls down on the couch, she said, "Okay. Tell me. What's going on?"

Allison began with the early part of the ghastly story and Janelle took over the later part. Delphine didn't interrupt. She didn't say a word, but tears of grief ran down her face and her arms tightened protectively around the shoulders of the two girls.

"She's the one who picked us up," Allison pointed to Dena Lark.

Officer Dena Lark moved forward and shook hands with Delphine. Formal charges would have to be filed, but there would be no harm in their waiting until morning. She handed Delphine her card and whispered, "Please call me tomorrow."

"Of course, Officer Lark, I don't know how to thank you for helping my girls," Delphine said, swallowing over the lump in her throat.

"I'm glad I happened to be in the right place at the right time, Mrs. Perry," Dena smiled.

Delphine shuddered with revulsion, "Please don't call me Mrs. Perry. As soon as this is all over, I'm going to have our names changed." Delphine looked at Allison and Janelle, "For now, will you please just call me Delphine?"

Officer Lark nodded and raised a hand in farewell. With a sad, gentle smile, she turned and went out the door, softly closing it behind her.

Delphine, Allison and Janelle talked long into the early morning hours. Delphine was beside herself with grief and remorse. She shook her head sorrowfully, "I should have known. I knew something was wrong with the way Baxter treated me, but I had no idea he was after you two. God forgive me...."

"How could you know, Mom? We didn't want you to find out," Janelle sobbed. "We did everything in our power to keep you from finding out. We were scared Baxter would kill us. He said he would."

"Thank God you were lucky enough to run into Ms. Lark," Delphine said, trying to wipe away the tears that continued to flow swiftly down her face.

"We almost ran away from her, too," Janelle moaned in anguish. "I was sure Baxter would somehow find out what we were up to and he would kill you before we could get back here with help."

"Nobody's going to get killed, Sweetheart, Baxter will go to jail for a very long time." Delphine prayed he would never be released again, but she knew this was too much to ask for in their country. She knew Baxter well enough to realize that he was vindictive, his hate and desire for revenge would make him a very dangerous enemy. She pulled the two exhausted girls to their feet, "We have to get some sleep. Tomorrow will be an extremely difficult day for us." She wanted to warn the girls there would be many bad days to come, but she felt the two had been through way too much already. She dreaded the thought of the examinations at the hospital that the court would force them to have. Her heart ached for the loss of innocence her two little girls had had to suffer.

Tomorrow the pain will have started to dim slightly, tomorrow they would be better able to handle the continuing pain and fear that would plague them for many, many days to come. Delphine began immediately to plan the steps she would take to protect her daughters from any future vengeance Baxter would try to impose on them and she would do everything in her power to restore them to good mental health.

When both girls had finished changing back into their pajamas, Delphine hugged them close and said, "Come on, we'll all sleep in my bed." She couldn't bear to be separated from them right away. She needed the warmth and security of having them close to her, safe and loved, and she knew they needed that same warmth and security.

The bond that extends from a deep and everlasting love silently wrapped its protective blanket around the mother and her two young daughters.

CHAPTER TWO

Janelle eased her foot off the accelerator and the eighty thousand pounds of steel and cargo that followed behind her began to slow. Her sharp eyes picked up the sign on the side of the road that read, Rest Area, ¼ mile. She sighed in relief, downshifted smoothly, slowing the heavy rig more, and flipped on her right turn signal. By the time she reached the blue Exit sign, she had the nine-speed transmission of the big rig shifted down to the required 25 MPH.

The lights of the huge rest area were a welcome relief to Janelle. She and Ross, her boyfriend of two years, had changed drivers on the road and she had to go to the bathroom when he called her, an hour ago.

The power steering of the big silver CH Mack responded easily as she turned onto the exit. She followed the curved road around to the back of the rest area where the truck area of the parking lot was completely full of eighteen-wheelers. She drove slowly along the long line of trucks, hoping against hope there would be a space open for her.

Janelle groaned in exasperation as the entrance ramp to the freeway came into view ahead of her. If she wanted to take her potty break she was going to have to park along the ditch of the deserted ramp. She hated being so far from the lights and the building, especially since she would be walking back to the building alone. Ross had been dead tired when he had climbed into the sleeper, and Janelle was sure he had gone out like a light.

She pulled the two hundred and sixty inch long tractor with its fifty-five foot trailer as far off the tar as possible, eased it out of gear and set the air brakes; hating the loud hiss of releasing pressure that seemed to thunder through the quiet, cozy cab. She turned in her swivel seat and peeked around the closed leather curtain, hoping the noise hadn't wakened Ross, but at the same time wishing he would wake up.

Ross lay curled on his side in the big, comfortable bunk of the two-bunk sixty-three inch custom made Aerodyne sleeper. He was sound asleep. Janelle watched the slight rise and fall of his chest and willed him to wake up. She had always hated the dark, isolated loneliness of the night and she really didn't want to walk back to the bathroom alone. But she knew she would never be able to wait until the next rest area to go to the bathroom, and besides, it was one a.m., the next rest area would more than likely be full, too; forcing her to park just as far away as she was now.

Ross didn't move and Janelle reluctantly closed the curtain, zipping it shut to minimize the sounds of her leaving the cab. Digging in her big, shoulder strap purse, she located the extra key for the truck and pushed the solid door of their ninety-two, conventional Mack open. She stuck one slim jean clad leg out the open door and then hesitated briefly before she slowly climbed down the steps to the ground, locking the door behind her.

Janelle knew that the roar of the engine would drown out any sounds from outside the truck. Ross would never hear her yelling, no matter how loud she called. She was on her own. She turned back and already had the key in the lock before she decided she was going to have to quit being such a big baby and letting her fear control her actions.

She smiled nervously as she recalled the happy days when her father had gently explained to her that the dark in its self held no threat for her. 'The darkness will not hurt you, Honey, just be cautious of the areas of darkness where you choose to walk,' he had said. 'I don't want you to be afraid of the dark, but I do want you to understand there are some places where it is unsafe to be after dark.' He had hesitated, while his gentle hands rubbed her back, then he had smiled warmly and added, 'But your bedroom is not one of the unsafe places.' He had smoothed her tangled hair and laid her back down on her pillow, 'Go to sleep, Sweetheart, Mommy and I are right next-door. I love you.' Janelle could still see the tender look on his face and she could still feel the warmth of his gentle touch. Her father had had no idea that Janelle's bedroom, with the onset of Baxter in her life, was to become one of her most feared places.

She quickly pulled the key free of the lock and determinedly turned toward the lights of the far away bathrooms. At twenty-seven, she knew her fears were illogical—and she did manage to keep them at bay most of the time—but she was sure this setting was one of the places her dad had warned her about. A large rest area, in the middle of the night and so far from the buildings, would probable fall in the number two place on her father's list of unsafe places. A large city's dark streets had to be number one on the list.

She walked down the center of the deserted roadway, not wanting to pass too close to the boxed in trash barrels that stood just off the tar to her left. She eyed the up and down slatted boards with distrust. It was even too dark inside the enclosure to see the bright aluminum of the garbage cans that she knew were hidden there. An opening of about two feet circled the bottom of the ten by twelve foot wooden structure. Her vivid imagination pictured someone hiding there, ready to reach out and grab her ankle as she passed.

Quit that! she ordered herself, *you're always letting your imagination run wild. Nobody's there! The first thing you know you'll have yourself so scared you'll be running back to the truck screaming bloody murder. And then you won't get to go to the bathroom.*

Janelle tried her best to control her fears, but her steps quickened in spite of her resolve. Fifty yards to her left, her eye caught the movement of a person between two of the huge trucks parked at the end of the truck parking spots. As the person moved into view, she realized there were two people, a man and a woman, pressed close together. The man had a firm grip on the girl's arm, dragging her along, and the girl was struggling wildly against his superior strength. Their voices carried clearly over the still night air.

"I changed my mind!" the girl hollered, fear thick in her voice. The girl's red hair was long and stringy with dirt. Her face was so pale that the light of the last street lamp at the edge of the lot made it look white.

"You're too late, Whore. You already have my money." The man's voice was very deep and it sounded to Janelle like he was either a heavy smoker or had a very bad cold.

Janelle watched out of the corner of her eyes as she hurried toward the restroom. The man dragged the girl up the steps of the last truck in the row and pushed her through the open door. Janelle saw the man turn slightly and catch sight of her walking past. He stared darkly at her, smirked, and then followed the girl into the black Freightliner. The company name, SAI Trucking, was printed in large letters on the door of the truck.

Janelle shuddered, the man was grubby looking, downright filthy looking! His black hair and beard looked as though they hadn't been washed in months. She broke into a run, her face flushed with embarrassment at the thought of a woman making her living in such a degrading manner.

Seconds later she was running full blast up the small rise to the large building that housed the restrooms. Her breath came in gasps as all the terrors of her childhood returned to threaten her every pounding footfall. She could still see herself being forced into her stepfather's bedroom, while he laughed at her pleas to be released and left alone.

Janelle was out of breath when she entered the welcome doors of the modern rest area and crossed to the ladies room. She shook her thick, ebony hair off her shoulders and forced the horrible memories of her unbalanced stepfather from her mind. She was surprised the memories had returned at all. She seldom—if ever—thought about her stepfather, but the man beside the black Freightliner had slightly resembled him.

She put a hand to her breast, feeling the wild pounding of her heart, and stared at herself in the mirror. Consciously blocking out thoughts of her stepfather, she fervently promised herself again that she was going to cut down on the cigarettes. *I shouldn't be out of breath after that short distance, she thought, I'm only twenty-seven, not seventy-seven! If I keep smoking at the rate I have been, I won't be able to make it around the bases if I ever hit a home run again!* She smiled at the thought; softball was one of her favorite past times.

Janelle turned to the bathroom with a sigh of relief. The pause that refreshes, she chuckled to herself. Finished, she washed her hands, left the bathroom and started across the open area of the building where maps and pictures of the area lined the walls. One corner held a group of vending machines that offered candy, sandwiches, coffee and pop. Janelle hesitated and then turned to the row of machines. She purchased a chocolate bar and a can of pop while she promised herself she was going to walk sedately back to the truck, giving herself time to enjoy the balmy beauty of the early June night.

As she reached the door of the building, a small door to her right opened with a screech of un-oiled metal against metal. An overweight man in his late sixties shuffled into the large entryway. Janelle jumped in panic and screamed. The man's face fell and he quickly apologized, "Sorry, Miss, I didn't mean to frighten you."

"It's all right, it wasn't your fault," Janelle breathed softly, trying to still the shaking of her small hands while she bent to retrieve the candy bar that had slipped from her nerveless fingers. "I'm always jumpy when I'm alone in these places in the middle of the night."

"You're all alone?" the caretaker asked, glancing toward the men's rest room.

Janelle hesitated. The man looked harmless enough, but that didn't mean he was harmless. "My husband's smoking a cigarette outside the door," she lied, quickly looking away from the man. She didn't want him to see the telltale blush that always crept up her neck when she told a lie. Even small, innocent lies brought the blush rushing to her tanned face. Ross teased her constantly, saying she had to be the world's worst liar. *Or the world's best*, she thought, remembering how she and Allison had kept their mother from finding out about Baxter. Janelle felt her face harden with remembered fury and horror. *I must not have blushed in those days,* she thought.

Janelle pushed open the heavy glass door and murmured over her shoulder, "Good night."

"Take care," the caretaker responded, smiling kindly.

'Take care?' Janelle fretted to herself. Why 'take care', why not 'have a good night', like most people said. She threw a quick, small smile at the man and hurried out the door, already dreading the long walk back to the safety of the truck.

Janelle managed to walk sedately along the lighted cement walk that led past the row of tourist cars parked in the lot. She could see people sleeping in the cars and the sight of them gave her a feeling of security.

As she started across the roadway, her eyes strayed to the black Freightliner that still stood at the end of the long line of trucks. The truck 'looked' deserted, but Janelle was sure the man and the prostitute were still in it. She looked away quickly, not wanting to take the chance of having to meet the eyes of the cruel looking man again.

The outskirts of the rest area's lighted area were just ahead of her now and Janelle tried to hold on to her courage, but as she approached the slatted wood structure that held the trash barrels, she broke into a panicked run.

When she reached the truck, her fingers were shaking so bad she had trouble inserting the key in the lock and then couldn't get the door open fast enough. She threw herself into the cab so fast that she bumped her knee on the steering column and winced in pain. Muttering to herself, she slammed the door shut and quickly locked it.

Behind her, she heard the leather curtain being opened and Ross stuck his head out of the sleeper. "What's wrong?" he asked sleepily.

"Nothing, but I did manage to scare myself again," Janelle explained. "I'm sorry I woke you."

"It's okay. You should have called me. I would have walked with you," Ross said.

"I know you would have, Honey, but I didn't want to bother you." Janelle put her pop in the holder and opened the broken candy bar. She held it out to Ross, "Want a bite?"

"No thanks." Ross wrinkled his nose at the thought of sweets when he was half asleep, although he was as crazy about candy as Janelle when he was fully awake.

Janelle put the truck in gear and released the air brakes.

"Wake me up the next time, I don't mind and I don't like the idea of you being alone out there. A lot of these places are not safe for a girl alone," Ross murmured.

"Thanks, Honey, I will. Good night. Sleep tight," Janelle replied warmly. *I really love that man*, she thought, a contented smile curving her full lips. *How did I ever get so lucky as to find him?* She smiled at the thought of his soft blond hair and the enchanting way it fell in a loose wave over his forehead. He kept his handsome, appealing face clean-shaven and his thick, brown eyebrows topped his large, dark brown eyes to perfection.

He towered over her five feet four by seven inches and although Janelle knew his five foot eleven was not considered tall, she had always regarded his height over her as an added security and she felt doubly protected when they were together. The muscles of his upper arms were thick and strong, his belly flat and taunt with hidden muscle and she knew he was stronger than his appearance implied.

She took the Mack smoothly through the gears and entered the freeway. They were still about two hundred miles short of Cincinnati, Ohio and Janelle finished her candy, deftly poured herself a cup of coffee and lit a cigarette. She knew the coffee would make her have to go to the bathroom again by the time she reached Cincinnati, but it also kept her awake. As she bounced along the dark freeway, she let her mind wander to her favorite daydream.

Back at home, in Duluth, Minnesota, she was writing her first novel. She had always been an avid reader and Ross had encouraged her to try her hand at writing. To her great surprise, she had found she loved creating her own story. She had saved her money until she could buy a computer, printer and the WordPerfect program and then she taught herself how to use the program, glorying in the ease with which she could write on the computer in comparison with handwriting.

She had always loved truck driving, but now she found herself wishing she could spend all her time at her computer.

She had been delighted to discover that the words poured out of her almost automatically. A month ago she had watched a television special where three famous authors explained their method of writing and one of them had stated she always made an outline of her story before she started a new novel. Janelle didn't know from one page to the next what she was going to write, but the words just kept flowing out of her.

Now, as she barreled down the lonely highway, her daydreams pictured herself as a published author, which would allow her to stay at home and write all the time. A sad smile crossed her lovely face; she knew she was going to miss the truck driving, if her dream came true.

Janelle couldn't wait until her book was finished. She already had a manuscript of nearly ninety thousand words and she was coming to the end of her plot.

She didn't try to plan the way she was going to end the novel, because she knew that wouldn't work for her. The only time the free flowing words came to her was when she was actually sitting at her computer, writing the novel. She remembered the famous author she had seen on television and her advice about making an outline. She wondered if her inability to plan her words ahead was a bad sign. *Oh well,* she thought, *I'm not going to worry about that now. What will be, will be*!

A rest area sign came up on the side of the road and Janelle was reminded that her bladder was full again, but she decided she could wait until she reached Cincinnati.

Most truck stops were a good source of directions to their drops; if the employees of the truck stop didn't know where a factory or warehouse was located, another truck driver could usually give them good directions. In fact, they usually asked the truck drivers first, since four wheel drivers frequently didn't understand the room needed by semis and many times you were directed down a road where it was impossible to make the turn they had specified or where a low underpass would stop you in your tracks.

Ten miles down the road, she maneuvered the huge rig onto a service road that led to the vast conglomeration of buildings and eighteen-wheelers that was one of Cincinnati's largest truck stops. Here she knew she would receive correct directions to their unloading place. She hated using the CB radio for directions because she always had a hard time understanding the person she reached. Besides, the guys out there usually had some smart remark to make in reference to the fact that she was a women and Janelle didn't like their insinuations.

The truck stop was full of every kind of tractor and trailer imaginable. The four a.m. loneliness of the freeway was definitely not in evidence here. Truckers and service people were moving in all directions, although there was little evidence of patrons other than truckers. The place was like a small city, bustling with activity.

Here Janelle felt safe, although she knew this feeling as a false sense of security, brought on by the reassuring sight of people everywhere. What could happen with all these people around? she asked herself. But she knew what could happen. She had heard the stories, too. There had been numerous tales of crimes and abductions, even murders, happening at truck stops around the nation.

Janelle glanced at her watch, it was going on five a.m. and the appointment time for their drop was seven a.m. She climbed quietly down the steps of the gleaming silver Mack and locked the door behind herself.

Hurrying into the fuel station, she showed the girl behind the counter the address of her drop. The girl was friendly, not like some people you ran into in truck stops. She pointed to her left and said, "You're almost to the place. Take the first right off this street out here and it's about two miles down on your right. You can't miss it." She smiled at Janelle and added, "You're not alone, are you?"

"Why?" Janelle countered, thinking of the caretaker at the rest area.

The girl leaned her elbows on the counter, smiled and said, "I was just curious. I really envy you girls who drive the eighteen-wheelers, but I wouldn't want to be out there alone. It's too dangerous for a girl alone. But I do wish I could learn how to drive one of them things. I don't think I ever will though, because I'm scared to death of how big and heavy they are!"

Janelle smiled back at the vivacious young girl; she liked this girl. "No, I'm not alone. I feel the same way you do. It's too dangerous for a girl alone. But it isn't as hard as you might think. I went to a driving school when I was twenty-two and they helped me get a job in my home state, which is Minnesota. I didn't start going over the road until I was twenty-five and met my boyfriend. We bought a truck and we've been trucking together for the last two years. We just traded off our first truck for a brand new CH Mack," Janelle added proudly, her eyes sparkling with excitement. She loved their new truck and she also loved the free life of the open road.

"How much does it cost to go to driving school?" the girl questioned with obvious interest.

"Mine was fifteen hundred," Janelle answered.

"Oh," the girl's smile faded. "I could never save that much money."

"Sure you can," Janelle encouraged. "You just have to make up your mind that you really want to be a truck driver."

The girl studied Janelle's tired face, "I also don't know if I can handle the long hours you guys put in."

"I've only been driving for the last five hours, but I *am* tired. Ross loaded in Toledo at twelve o'clock and he was going to drive down here, in fact he drove the first little bit, but he has been trying to shake a bad cold and he's been more tired than usual, so he woke me up after I had only had two hours of sleep. If I hadn't managed to scare myself at that big rest area outside of Toledo on seventy-five, I might have decided to sleep a little bit there. I'm glad I didn't though," she added, "I might have slept too long and we could have missed our appointment here."

A truck driver on the other side of the counter, whose patience had run out, called to the girl and she jumped guiltily. She turned away quickly and flung a breezy farewell over her shoulder, "Have a good day. Nice talking to you."

"Same here. Bye." Janelle turned away and headed to the bathroom, thinking about all the friendly people you met when you traveled all over the United States. *People are the same everywhere you go,* she mused , *some good and some bad. We've been lucky; we've met significantly more good people than bad people.*

Back at her pride and joy, Janelle climbed into the comfortable driver's seat and headed for their destination. *Might as well grab a couple hours sleep before they unload us,* she thought, *I'm sure I'll wake up when they drive the fork lift into the trailer.* Janelle had always had a hard time sleeping when the truck was shaking from the fork lift or moving down the road, but with their new air ride Mack, they had also purchased an air ride trailer and now she could—at least once in a while—sleep through the loading or unloading process and, unless the road was very rough, she was able to sleep while Ross drove.

She reached the packing company and backed the truck into the only open dock, being careful not to hit the dock with a bump that would wake Ross up. When they started to unload their truck, Ross would be out there helping; making sure nothing had been damaged on the trip down. Some dockworkers accidentally dropped boxes or pallets and if the driver wasn't watching, they made a habit of trying to blame the damage on the trip or the way the load was loaded.

Janelle checked the doors to be sure they were locked, quietly climbed into the second bunk and was instantly asleep.

Two hours later she awoke to the sound of someone knocking on the door of the truck. She reached down and shook Ross awake. "Someone's at the door," she told him. "They must be ready to unload us."

"Okay. Go back to sleep, Honey," Ross mumbled as he jumped out of his bunk and hurried into the cab of the truck. "Be right with you," Janelle heard him say as she drifted back to sleep.

The next thing Janelle heard was the closing of the door as Ross got back into the truck. She reached over and pulled the curtain of the sleeper open. "Are you done unloading already?" she asked in surprise.

"What do you mean, already? It's nine o'clock," Ross responded.

"Oh...it seems like you just crawled out," Janelle smiled.

"Want to get some breakfast?" Ross asked.

"Sure."

"We'll be reloading about five miles from here and we have to drop in Kansas City, MO tomorrow morning at six a.m., so we have plenty of time."

"Good." Janelle was relieved, the last few days had been tough and they were both ready for a small break.

"Did you see anyplace to eat, that looked good, on your way in?" Ross wanted to know.

Janelle climbed out of bed and pulled the blankets up over her pillow. She sat on the bigger bottom bunk and began to pull on her scuffed cowboy boots. "I stopped at a big truck stop to get directions and we're only a short distance from there now. Take a left out of here and a left on Travis Road. It's a block down on your left," she directed.

"Okay. Boy, I'm starved. Was the place clean?"

"Looked real good to me." Janelle grinned as she moved to the rider's side and slumped tiredly into the air ride bucket seat that wrapped comfortably around her. "I slept good, but I'm still tired," she yawned.

"Well, you can crawl back in after we're done eating. I'll take the first lap to Kansas City."

"Good. How's your cold?"

"It's finally letting go. I feel twenty times better today than yesterday."

At the truck stop, Ross backed into an empty parking spot and they held hands as they strolled toward the door to the fuel and supply area. "Let's look at their boot supply," Ross said. "Mine are pretty near shot."

"Good idea. Maybe they have that light gray color you've been looking for," Janelle readily agreed.

The restaurant windows they walked past showed the happy pair that there might be a little wait before they would get served.

"Boy, are they packed," Janelle exclaimed.

"Good," Ross remarked happily. "Means the food must be good and I don't mind waiting if I get good food."

Ross and Janelle spent more than fifteen minutes looking at the boots, but they were out of Ross' size in the gray boots and he decided he'd wait until they could find the time to stop at a different place.

"That's what you always say, Ross. That's why your boots are so worn out," Janelle laughed. "Why don't you just get a pair of brown ones?"

"Because," Ross lightly tweaked her small nose and smiled, "I want gray this time. And a gray that as closely matches the silver of our prize Mack as I can get."

"But Ross, gray is so popular. We may never find your size."

"Then we'll just keep looking until we do," Ross promised.

As they passed the check out counter, the girl Janelle had talked to at five a.m. waved and beckoned them to come over.

"Hi," the girl's voice was subdued, but Janelle sensed an excitement in it, too. Something was wrong. She immediately thought of her mother. *Had something happened to her? But no, this girl doesn't even know my last name. No one can contact us through her or this truck stop. Mike, our dispatcher, would have told us if something had happened,* Janelle reminded herself as relief flooded her body. "Did you guys listen to the news this morning?"

Janelle shook her head and Ross looked totally confused. "Do you know this girl?" he whispered in Janelle's ear.

Janelle shook her head again and laughed, "We talked a little this morning after she gave me directions." She turned back to the friendly girl and asked curiously, "What was on the news this morning?"

"That rest area you were at, the one by Toledo? There was a murder there last night!"

"You're not serious, are you?" Janelle's reply was flippant, but she felt herself go cold with dread.

"Yes! And it must have happened right around the time you were there. The caretaker found the body when he dumped some garbage about three a.m."

"Oh, no!" Janelle had turned white as a sheet. A perfect picture of the man with the beard and the girl with the bright red hair flashed into her mind. Her voice shook when she asked, "What did the girl look like?"

"She was small, or I should say short and thin. About seventeen, they thought. Here, here's the story," she reached under the counter and pulled out a newspaper that was folded back to the second page and pointed to the article.

Janelle and Ross bent over the counter to read the column that the girl was pointing to. Their bowed heads, the ebony black of Janelle's hair and the blond brightness of Ross', made a striking contrast.

"I saw that girl, Ross!" Janelle breathed in horror.

"What? Where?" Ross was shocked. He stared at Janelle's terror stricken face.

"A man was forcing her into his truck at the rest area. I was just heading up to the bathroom. They were getting into a black Freightliner." Janelle was shaking now and her smooth face was white and pale. She twisted her slim hands together in agitation.

"How can you be sure it's the same girl?"

"The red hair...the girl was a redhead, and the time, the caretaker found her shortly after we left," Janelle's face was filled with dread. "I should have done something! I knew the guy was forcing her. I heard her say she had changed her mind, but the guy called her a whore and said she was too late. He said he had already paid her."

"You couldn't have stopped the guy, Janelle. And how could you know what he would do?" Ross was trying his best to soothe her.

"I should have told someone. The caretaker. I saw him while I was inside, but I figured it was just sex. I didn't know he was going to kill her!"

"But, Honey, like you said, you couldn't know he was going to murder the girl," Ross protested.

"That man was forcing her! He didn't have any right to force her." Tears were sliding down Janelle's pink cheeks and her green eyes were huge with panic. "I should have done something. Seventeen...she was only seventeen."

"Honey, you couldn't have known. There's no way you could have known. If you would have said something to the caretaker and he had gone out to check on the situation, he probably would have found them having sex. Or maybe the man would have attacked the caretaker, too. The caretaker might have been killed, too. It's not your fault."

The girl behind the counter had been listening to everything Janelle and Ross said. Other people were waiting to be waited on, but the girl was too shocked by what Janelle had seen to even care about her duties.

"I have to go to the police, Ross. I have to tell them everything I can to help them catch that madman."

"Okay, Honey. You're right," he put an arm around her shoulders and drew her away from the counter and the line of irate customers that had bunched up behind them. He led her over to the telephones. "We can't take the truck to the police station, so the police will have to come to us. I'll look up the number for you."

Ross opened the front page of the telephone book and the local police station's number was on the back of the front cover. He dialed the number and gave the phone to Janelle while he pointed out the sign over the bank of telephones that gave the truck stop's address, East Side Truck Plaza, 11246 Turnbull Rd, Cincinnati, OH.

Janelle jumped slightly when an impersonal and harassed voice came on the phone, "Cincinnati police station. How may I help you?"

"Ye...s," Janelle stuttered, her mind suddenly blank, "I...um...I have some information for you about the murder in the rest area by Toledo."

"I see. What is your name, please?" the voice was now more personal and definitely more interested.

"I'm Janelle Richardson, from Duluth, MN," Janelle responded, her voice slowly gaining its usual confidence.

"What information do you have, Janelle?" the voice was again bored and distracted.

"I saw the murderer and the girl who was murdered by Toledo," the horror was back in Janelle's voice.

The voice immediately lost its bored tone, "Okay. We'd like to talk to you, Janelle. We're located at 5568 Vermont St. Will you come in and talk to one of our detectives?"

"I can't come down there, we're here with our truck, an eighteen wheeler," Janelle explained.

"Oh...okay, we'll come to you. Where are you and how will the detectives recognize you?"

"We're at the East Side Truck Plaza on Turnbull Rd. and we'll be in the restaurant. We'll sit in the trucker's section. I'm wearing a pink blouse and blue jeans and I have black hair. My boyfriend has on a red shirt and he has blond hair."

"Okay, Janelle, someone will be there shortly. Thank you very much for your call and your time. See you soon."

TAKE CARE

"Good-bye," Janelle said to the phone that had already gone dead. She turned to Ross, oblivious of the many people who moved past and around them. In a quivering voice that was close to tears, she admitted, "I'm scared, Ross. What if I get in trouble for not telling someone right away? What if it's like a traffic accident, when the first three cars have to stop at the scene? Do you think I could be fined for leaving the scene of a crime?"

CHAPTER THREE

Ross gently led Janelle to an empty booth in the far corner of the trucker's section. "You're letting your imagination get the best of you, Honey. No one's going to blame you for anything. Now please quit worrying and let's order breakfast. I'm starved and the cops won't be here for a little while. We should have time to eat before they get here," he smiled reassuringly and patted Janelle's cold hand.

Janelle nodded and smiled wanly. "I know you're right, Honey, but I can't help worrying. And I just thought of something else. What if they want me to go to Toledo and look at the girl's body?" she shuddered and covered her face with her hands.

Ross hesitated before he spoke sadly, "I think there is a pretty good chance you may be right about that last thought. They're going to want to know if the girl you saw is the same girl that was murdered. Did you say you saw the guy, too?"

"Yeah. He was dirty, filthy. He had a black beard...," she broke off as the waitress arrived with a pot of coffee and two cups.

"Coffee?" she asked indifferently.

"Yes, please," Ross answered.

She plopped the cups on the table with a crash and slopped coffee over the tops of the cups as she filled them. Not bothering to apologize for the spills, she dropped the menus in the middle of the table and left.

"Boy, why do we always have to get the worst waitress in the whole place," Ross complained without rancor. He picked up the menus and handed one to Janelle. "Let's decide what we want before you continue. I'd like to be done eating before the police get here."

"Okay, but I'm not very hungry anymore. This whole situation has really upset me."

"I know it has, Honey, but you'll feel better after you eat something," Ross encouraged kindly.

"Okay. I'll order something." Janelle bent her dark head over the menu and studied it for long moments before she looked up. "I'll have an order of toast and orange juice."

"That's not enough to eat, Sweetheart. You're going to need your strength to get through the ordeal of talking to the police," Ross objected.

"Okay. I'll have some bacon, too," Janelle smiled with a small portion of her old spirit.

Ross grimaced, "Well, I'm going to have pancakes, two eggs, ham and hash browns. And orange juice, too."

They placed their menus at the edge of the table and looked around for their waitress. The girl was standing behind the counter flirting with a lone truck driver, completely ignoring Janelle and Ross. They waited impatiently for about five minutes and then Ross got up, his face beginning to tighten with anger.

He approached the girl and she glanced up at him, anger washing over her face. Ross waited another forty-five seconds for a break in the engrossed couple's conversation, which centered around the guy's trying to pin down a time and place for the two to meet. Suddenly, Ross was angry, too. He broke into the animated conversation. Sarcasm hung heavy in his voice as he said, "Miss, if you don't mind, if you can possibly tear yourself away, we would like to order."

The girl gave Ross a dirty look and stalked toward the booth where Janelle sat watching the exchange. "What's it going to be?" she asked sourly, the anger evident in the bright flush of her face.

Janelle and Ross looked at each other in exasperation, gave her their orders and watched as she wrote it all down. Finished, she turned around and stomped away without even a thank you. Slapping the order on the counter in front of the cook, she returned to her friend at the counter.

Ross sighed, "I don't usually like to do this, but I'm going to tell the manager about this one. She doesn't deserve a job, not with her attitude. There are plenty of people looking for jobs that could do better than she is without half trying. Did you see her name?"

"Yeah, Chris," Janelle answered, hiding her wavering smile at Ross's unusual irritation. She knew that the murder she had nearly witnessed was heavy on his mind, too. She supposed he was probably frightened out of his wits by the fact that she might have been the murderer's victim. That horrible thought had crossed her mind, too. What if she had reached the rest area a few minutes earlier? Could the murderer have been searching for a victim, any female victim? Or maybe he had been looking for a prostitute and the redhead had done something he didn't like that set him off.

"Are you going to go with them to Toledo if they want you to?" Ross changed the subject.

"I don't know. What do you think?"

"I suppose you should, but it's going to make it hard on us."

"Will you go with me?" Janelle asked faintly, hope for a positive answer raising her full eyebrows.

"I'd have to ask Mike if he can change our delivery time, but I'll go with you if I can," Ross promised, happy that she wanted him with her. He studied Janelle's pale face. She was usually quite strong and very independent, but he could tell she was very disturbed about this terrifying affair.

His glance turned toward the cook's counter top and saw their plates of food sitting there waiting for the waitress to pick them up. His mouth tightened and he stared hard at the waitress, who was still talking to her attentive friend, trying to penetrate her subconscious mind, willing her to look their way. He waited one full minute, which felt more like an hour, and then slid quickly to his feet, deliberately walked to the cook's counter and retrieved the plates himself.

The waitress was so absorbed with her apparent conquest that she did not even see Ross go behind the counter to pick up the food. The man at the check out counter, whom Ross assumed was the manager—since he wore a white shirt, a multi-colored dark, attractive tie and well creased dress pants—did notice Ross' actions. The man must have been watching the waitress for quite some time, because he crossed the restaurant and beckoned her to follow him. Ross carefully hid his smile of satisfaction.

As the man passed their booth, Ross and Janelle caught sight of the nametag he wore; Fred Reece, Manager.

At the end of the counter, far enough away from the man the waitress had been flirting with that he would not hear their conversation, the man from the check out counter spoke softly to the waitress. Her face fell and tears came to her eyes, she opened her mouth to argue but, presumably changing her mind, she closed her mouth in a tight line, removed her tiny apron, stalked into the kitchen and out of sight.

Ross and Janelle had started to eat, but they had watched the exchange between the incompetent waitress and the manager out of the corner of their eyes. "Best thing he could do for his business," Ross whispered to Janelle.

"Yeah," Janelle murmured, losing all interest in the scene with the waitress as her eyes met the keen eyes of a middle aged man dressed in a dark suit, who was advancing toward their booth.

The manager from the check out counter and the man in the dark suit arrived at their booth at the same time. The manager apologized, "I'm terribly sorry about that. I've spoken to another waitress and she will be right over to help you with anything else you need." He smiled and moved around the dark suited man with a look of curiosity.

"Janelle Richardson?" the tall man asked politely.

"Yes," Janelle responded shakily.

"I'm Detective Chet Archer. I'm sorry to interrupt your meal."

Ross stood up and extended his hand, "I'm Ross Taylor, Janelle's fiance and business partner."

"Pleased to meet you, Mr. Taylor," the detective replied, shaking Ross' hand firmly.

"Ross is good enough," Ross smiled.

"Thank you, call me Chet," the detective returned Ross' smile and as if by magic a small dimple appeared on his left cheek. He turned to Janelle, "May I call you Janelle?"

"Sure."

His eyes on Ross, Chet continued to smile as he added, "My partner, Jud Rafferty, is on his way in. You two go ahead and finish eating, we'll wait for him."

A new waitress appeared at the table, she handed a menu toward the detective with a cheery, "Good morning."

Chet shook his head at the offered menu and his clean brown hair bounced with the motion, "Just coffee for me, please. In fact, bring two cups. We have one more joining us."

"Yes, Sir." She turned to Ross and Janelle, "How are you two doing? Can I get you anything?"

"We're fine, thank you for asking," Ross smiled warmly.

"I'll be right back with your coffee, Sir," the girl grinned at the detective. The detective was a very handsome man, although his face was slightly craggy and his nose a hair bit too big. *I'd be interested, too, if I didn't have Ross,* Janelle thought. The detective and the waitress looked to be close to the same age, which Janelle guessed to be about forty.

At that moment a black man who was all of six foot six arrived at the booth. He greeted Ross and Janelle, "Good morning. I'm Jud Rafferty, Chet's partner. I don't stand on ceremony, so please call me Jud." Graceful, in spite of his huge size, he slid into the booth beside Chet and shook Ross' extended hand.

Janelle and Ross had both finished eating when the waitress returned with two full cups of coffee and another pot, filled to the brim with steaming hot black coffee. She whisked away their dirty plates and left them alone.

"If you're ready, Janelle, we're anxious to hear what you saw up by Toledo," Chet encouraged gently.

"I didn't see much," Janelle apologized. "I was walking from our truck up to the bathroom when this man and woman came from between two trucks. The man had a hold of the girl's arm and was pulling her along. He pushed her into a black Freightliner on the end of the line. It was about an eighty-five model and I assumed it was his truck. The name on the truck was SAI Trucking, which I've seen before. It stands for South American Inc. I didn't see the name of the town.

"I heard the girl say, 'I changed my mind!' and the man said, 'You're too late, whore, you already have my money.' The girl sounded scared."

"What did they look like?" Chet asked, taking notes in a small wire bound notebook.

"The girl had red hair and she was wearing black shorts and a black halter top. She had big brea...I mean, she was big busted." Janelle's face turned a deep red and her eyes quickly fell to the table top.

Chet nodded, his thoughts going to the pictures of the naked girl that had been faxed to their precinct. Her small face had been a mass of ugly black and blue bruises. Large, purple bruises, in the shape of fingerprints, circled her neck where the murderer had strangled her. Chet felt sick as he threw a quick, warning look at Jud. There was no reason for Janelle to see that gruesome photograph. They had others that showed only the murdered girl's face and hair. They could use those for identification purposes.

"Anything else?" Jud questioned.

"She was short. Or maybe the guy was real tall." Janelle's brow puckered as she pictured the couple next to the black Freightliner. "No...I think he was tall, but not as tall as you are Mr. Rafferty."

"Jud," the detective reminded her. "Maybe about six one or two?"

"Yes, I think so. But the girl was short, because the top of her head didn't come close to reaching the bottom edge of the side mirror on the truck."

"What about the guy? What did he look like?" Chet asked.

"He had black hair, although not as black as mine, and a reddish, curly beard. He was dirty. In fact, I would say he was really filthy. He was wearing a red, plaid shirt, blue jeans and cowboy boots," she stopped, something was bothering her. "There was something...about his face.... Oh! I know! His nose was crooked, like he had broken it at one time or another."

"Thank you, Janelle. You're very observant. We have a couple of pictures of the girl. Would you look at them, please?" Chet wondered.

Janelle nodded slowly and fearfully, already anticipating that the pictures would be a grisly sight.

"It's not a pretty sight, but violent deaths usually aren't," Jud smiled grimly. "We see far too many of these and I still can't seem to harden my heart against the sight of them." He shook his head sorrowfully as he pulled the pictures out of the large brown envelope he had brought with him and laid them in front of Janelle.

Janelle gasped at the ghastly sight and tears of sorrow came to her eyes. She nodded slowly and whispered, "And she was only seventeen. The poor kid."

"Yes, seventeen," Chet repeated. "Is that the girl you saw?"

"Yes. That's the one." Tears trickled down her fair cheeks and she wiped them away with the back of her hand, like a small child who doesn't have a Kleenex. Her tortured eyes met Ross'. He pulled his hankie out of his pocket, handed it to Janelle and covered her small hand with his rough and calloused, but compassionate grip, squeezing tenderly. "I should have done something," Janelle moaned in despair. "I should have told the caretaker."

"That might have helped.... But if the caretaker had tried to interfere on his own, he may have gotten hurt, too. Of course, he could have called the police, but most men don't think of that. We tend to think we should be able to handle most situations on our own," Chet remarked, sounding bitter. "How old a man was the caretaker?"

"Probably about sixty, maybe sixty five or seventy," Janelle guessed.

"At that age, he might have decided to call the police, but you never know," Jud said.

"Really, I thought it was just sex. It was none of my business." Janelle began to sob. "I never thought he was going to kill the girl!"

"I'm sure you didn't, Janelle. I think you're the type that would have done anything to help if you had thought he was going to hurt the girl," Jud's smile was comforting.

"Thank you for saying that," Janelle sniffed and wiped Ross' hankie across her wet eyes. "I really feel guilty."

"There's no reason for you to feel guilty," Chet said kindly. "You were just an innocent bystander, but because you happened to be there, we stand a good chance of catching this guy."

"Would you be willing to come down to the station and go through some mug shots?" Jud asked.

Janelle smothered a sigh of relief. She had been anticipating him to ask her to come to Toledo with them. She looked at Ross and he nodded. "I'll come. Can Ross come with me?" she asked, again sounding and looking like a small child.

"Sure." In spite of the gravity of the situation, Jud grinned at the look on her face, "Are you ready then?"

"Yes, I just want to stop at the restroom," Janelle replied.

They slid out of the booth and the men moved to the check out counter while Janelle headed toward the bathroom. When she emerged from the bathroom, the men were waiting by the door for her.

They were silent as the four of them walked through the glory of the June morning to the waiting police car. Janelle and Ross were ushered into the back seat while Chet and Jud crawled into the front of the new Ford LTD. Chet started the car and then turned to the young couple in the back seat with a whimsical smile, "Don't mind the wire divider, we'll be sure to let you out whenever you want out."

Janelle glanced at the door and noticed there were no handles to reopen the solid door. She hadn't felt trapped until Chet mentioned the wire divider, but now she suddenly realized what it would feel like to be the prisoner of these two men. Her cold fingers searched for the reassuring warmth of Ross' hand and she snuggled close to him.

"It'll all be over shortly and we can put it out of our minds," Ross whispered.

Janelle tried to smile in return, but she was too tense and nervous. Her stomach felt like a hundred butterflies were playing jump rope in it and her heart was beating with the speed of a freight train.

Chet drove smoothly and competently across the city to the headquarters of the Cincinnati Police Department. Fifteen minutes later they were seated in a small room waiting for Jud to return with the mug shots of known criminals.

TAKE CARE

"Would you like a cup of coffee?" Chet asked.

Ross and Janelle both shook their heads and murmured, "No thank you."

Jud entered with a large stack of photograph books. He placed the heap at the edge of the table and handed the one with the most current offenders to Janelle.

"We'll start with this one," he said, "and work our way backwards."

The room was silent, except for the frequent interruption of the P.A. system, while Janelle slowly flipped the pages of the books; stopping occasionally when one of the men closely resembled the man she had seen. Thirty minutes slid by, then thirty more. She was on the sixth book when she suddenly stopped and pointed at the picture of a man who was wanted for rape and murder, although Janelle was not aware of this fact as the charges were not listed with the pictures. Beneath the picture there was only an identification number.

"That's him!" she exclaimed.

Jud moved to the table, "Number 666." He turned to the long row of file cabinets that lined one complete wall of the room and flipped through the contents of the second drawer from the top of the file. Pulling out a thick folder, he laid the pile on the top of the file drawers and quickly thumbed through the papers.

Producing four large photographs of the man—a left profile, a right profile and two straight away pictures—he laid the pictures in front of Janelle. "Take a close look," he instructed. "We don't want to make any mistakes."

Janelle's skin crawled as she closely examined the photos. The enlarged photos clearly showed the man's previously broken nose, plus, at this close range, Janelle could make out the scars of a past case of either chicken pox or acne. His lips were thick and his coloring dark; suggesting a slight amount of either Negro or Spanish blood. A deep scar ran from his nose to the bottom of his upper lip. The man at the rest area had had a beard and a mustache and the man in the picture had only a beard, but Janelle was sure they were both the same man. "It's him. I'm sure. They were real close to one of the bright lights at the rest area and I got a good look at them."

"Good. Very good, Janelle. We'll round this guy up and then we would like to have you return and identify him in person."

Janelle's face filled with fear, "I don't want him to see me!"

Chet was quick to reassure her, "He won't see you. You'll be behind a one way glass." He didn't mention that if they found the guy—and it was a big if, since he had been on the wanted list for more than two years—whose name was, Jack Thomas Huxley, she would be a key witness in the prosecution of the man. Janelle Richardson could not be scared off at this early stage in the case.

"Good. I couldn't handle having him see me again," Janelle shuddered.

Jud grew very still, "You mean the guy," he did not mention the man's name, "saw you?"

"Yes," Janelle confirmed. "I was about fifty yards away and more in the shadow than he was, but he looked right at me and sneered. That's why I figured it was just sex, the dirty sneer he gave me."

Chet and Jud exchanged a quick, worried look that Janelle and Ross both missed as they looked again at the pictures on the table.

"Did he see your truck?" Jud asked. All commercial truck lines were required by law to have their company's name and city of origin prominently displayed on both sides of the cab.

"I don't know," Janelle looked up, suddenly worried again. "I don't think he saw where I was coming from and I didn't see him or the girl inside the truck when I returned. I figured they were in the sleeper...," she blushed a bright red.

"Okay. Can you think of anything else?" Jud changed the subject slightly.

"No...nothing else."

"You've been very helpful, Janelle. I realize we've put you behind schedule, so we better get you back to your truck. There's just one more thing. Will you please write down your home address and the address of the trucking company you work for? We'll let you know when we catch the guy."

"What's the guy's name?" Ross asked, speaking for the first time since they had arrived at the police station.

Chet seemed to hesitate and then, perhaps deciding they would hear the name on the news anyway, told him. "Jack Thomas Huxley."

"Where is he from?" Ross wanted to know.

The hesitation was longer this time, but Janelle was sure her involvement in the case gave them the right to know. "His home state is Minnesota.... He was born and raised in Minneapolis."

Janelle's mouth dropped open and Ross frowned.

"We've been searching Minneapolis and the area surrounding it for over six months." Chet said. "We have a man watching his parents home around the clock. There's been no sign of him."

"What are the other charges against him?" Ross wanted to know.

"He's wanted for rape and murder," Chet said slowly. "With the information you've given us, we'll get him. It's just a matter of time now and we'll have him back in custody."

"Back in custody?" Ross questioned.

"We arrested him back in the last part of December ninety-one on suspicion of murder. On the way back to New York, which is where he committed his last alleged crime, he escaped. He was also in prison two years for rape, back in eighty-nine and ninety. He was released on patrol in late ninety."

"How many people has he murdered?" Janelle whispered, the revulsion hitting her stomach like a lead ball.

"He is alleged to have raped and killed five women...," was Jud's obviously reluctant response. "But he has never been convicted of any murders. He was tried on a murder charge, but the evidence was only circumstantial and he was acquitted. We've never had a witness before."

Janelle and Ross were silent, staring at the detectives in horror. Janelle pushed the finished addresses toward Chet Archer and rose unsteadily to her feet. Ross quickly followed suit, anxious to be out of the police station and back in their truck.

"Thank you very much for your help, Janelle. We'll be in touch with you," Chet said as he and Jud dropped Janelle and Ross off at their truck.

"Guard this address with your life, Chet," Jud shook the piece of paper with Janelle and Ross' address as they pulled out of the truck stop. "If she's right, if it really was Jack Thomas Huxley she saw, and if our suspicions about him, and the ring of perverts he seems to be connected with, are right, that girl and her boyfriend are in grave danger."

They were back in their truck, out of Cincinnati and twenty miles down interstate seventy-one before either Ross or Janelle spoke again.

As if on signal, they both spoke at once.

"Why...," Janelle started.

"We'll...," Ross said.

The thick tension was broken and they laughed long and a bit too loud.

"Go ahead," Janelle said, when she could speak again.

"No, you first."

"Okay. I was going to say that I wished I would have told the police that I don't want my name mentioned on the news," Janelle voiced her fear. "What were you going to say?"

"I was going to say that we'd have to make sure we watch the six o'clock news on a television in one of the truck stops." Ross said, slowly adding, "Are you worried this Jack guy will come after you if he hears your name on the news?"

"Yes," Janelle tried not to whimper, but her voice felt scratchy with fear. "I'm not only worried, I'm scared to death. If I was in his shoes—and thank God I'm not!—I'd go after the only eye witness in the case, wouldn't you?"

CHAPTER FOUR

Baxter Perry sat in the comfort of his air-conditioned office and watched the activity in the hot, dusty yard below. Three eighteen wheelers had pulled into the yard in the last hour. Each driver had immediately come to Baxter's office to report on his cargo. Among the three drivers, they had delivered seven new children to Baxter.

Baxter had been on the phone to his many contacts and five of the new kids were already spoken for. The contact he hadn't yet been able to reach, a man from New York who now made his home in Honolulu, Hawaii, had been interested in two small white blond boys between the ages of two and three. Baxter had put out a special order for the two white blond boys and it had taken his driver three weeks to find exactly what the contact was looking for.

The three trucks were now backed up to the loading docks at the warehouse, but Baxter knew the kids had not been removed from their cells in the trailers. They would remain locked up until his delivery girls arrived, which should be within half an hour.

Each girl would take the child that was assigned to her and leave immediately for different airports. One child was being delivered to China and that flight didn't leave until late tonight, but the other four were consigned to different points in the United States. Baxter had easily secured tickets for the delivery girls and their 'daughters.'

After being in the truck trailers for close to a week, the children had already cried themselves out and, except for the most sensitive ones; they would do what the delivery girl told them to do.

Baxter rubbed his hands together in anticipation of the fee required to obtain the special order boys. *Twenty thousand for each regular order plus fifty thousand for each special order kid,* he thought, *a cool million, on just three trucks!*

Baxter had ten trucks on the road. This week alone would bring in close to five million. *Of course that's before expenses*, he thought, *but I should clear over four million.*

Baxter smiled; his black eyes glittered with greed. He had been running this business for two years and he had salted away over a billion dollars. *I really should quit while I'm ahead*, he mused.

His house on the outskirts of Miami was a huge mansion, more than forty rooms of luxury, well staffed and very comfortable. *Well, it will have to be sold*, he reminded himself. He had already reluctantly included this in his future plans. He couldn't stay in a house with a staff that knew him to be a divorcee without children. He needed a new location, a new name and a new staff that would be told he was a widower with two or three kids, depending on the number of girls he finally decided to 'adopt'.

Baxter had been very careful whenever he brought kids home. He always arrived home in the middle of the night and carried the child into the house in a large suitcase. Not wanting the large suitcase to arouse questions or suspicions in the minds of the staff when he returned the girl to the warehouse the next morning, he invented business trips; dropping small hints, such as 'I won't be able to be reached today, I'll be out of town.'

The servants' rooms had been conveniently—as specified in Baxter's house plans—placed on the fourth floor and in the back wing of the mammoth house. After eleven p.m., the door connecting the two separate wings was locked until six a.m. the following morning. As a further precaution, Baxter had had the wall between the wings, and his bedroom walls, soundproofed.

Of course there was always the slim chance that one of the servants would go out for the evening and be returning home at the same time Baxter arrived with his girl; hence the suitcase, with the girl firmly bound and gagged.

Yup, I should retire. In fact, I will retire! Last night's fun and games had turned into a bad circus show. The four-year-old girl he had taken home with him had been one of the prettiest girls he had ever had. The girl's eyes had been the bluest he had ever seen. Her blond hair had been so many different colors that he had gotten completely lost in the rare beauty of it. Her skin had been soft and silky, unmarred by birthmarks or scars of any kind. And she had been small boned and very petite. Her nose turned up appealingly.

The problem was, the girl had not stopped screaming from the first moment he had begun to remove her clothes. The crying and begging had gotten on his nerves and he had done something he had promised himself he would never do...he had beaten the girl. Once started, he didn't stop until the child was unconscious.

Disgusted with his foul loss of temper, Baxter had immediately turned off the video camera that he had had installed in the ceiling of his bedroom to record his romping. He had quickly rewound the tape inside, not wanting to give himself time to change his mind. Turning the camera back on, he had flicked the switch that replaced the sliding section of ceiling that completely hide the camera from view and restarted the recording, blacking out the movie he had made of his performance with the girl. He wanted no reminder of the way he had beat the small girl, but he had been disappointed to lose the earlier pictures of the girl's perfect features.

Baxter had been undecided what to do with the girl. Her face had swollen and parts of her body had turned black and blue from his beating. Faced with a child who could not be returned to the warehouse and sold, he had taken the girl out of the city and carried her unconscious body into the ditch on a deserted stretch of road, intending to leave her for someone to discover at a later date.

Looking down on the small child as she lay in the ditch, he had felt sorry for her. He didn't want some pervert to find her and he didn't want her to die.

He had hurried back to the city and stopped at a pay phone on a busy street. He had placed his hankie over the mouthpiece and dialed 911.

Clearing his throat, he had pitched his voice high, trying to give the impression of a girl's voice. 'There's a little blond girl lying in the ditch off Highway 27; about a mile north of where 27 and 41 connect.'

"Is she alive?" the operator had asked. Baxter had replaced the phone without answering. He had felt better then. They would find the girl and take her to the hospital.

Baxter had been almost back at his house before he had remembered that the police could trace semen as well as fingerprints. He had sworn violently and banged his fists on the steering wheel, but the deed had been done.

I'm getting too old for this, he thought. *I'm getting soft in my old age. The girl should never have gotten on my nerves the way she did, but after I lost my temper and made all those ugly bruises on her, I should have had the guts to kill her.*

Baxter frowned. He didn't care for the terror that each new child displayed. He wasn't like some of his contacts; he didn't enjoy torturing and killing kids. He wanted the kids to love him, come to him with their troubles, and admire him. He wanted the unconditional love children gave their fathers. But the kind of trust and love he wanted would take too long to cultivate in these scared kids. He needed younger kids, ones that would grow up loving him.

His plans, his retirement plans, included his abduction of two or three girls that looked very much alike. His new neighbors and friends would be told they were his daughters. He wanted the girls to be no more than eighteen months old.

His craggy face grew thoughtful and he ran thick fingers through his graying black hair. He knew he couldn't leave any witnesses to his lucrative business. Witnesses could mean blackmail; or, worse than that, an attack of conscience on the part of one of his former employees could mean he, Baxter Perry, would spend the rest of his natural life in prison.

Baxter was taking no chances. He had devised a foolproof plan that would wipe out all the witnesses, ten truck drivers—plus any girlfriends that rode with them—eight delivery girls and the office help, in one big sweep.

The warehouse doors looked like any other warehouse doors, they opened easily from the inside even when they were locked from the outside, but Baxter had cleverly installed hidden locks that could be locked with a key, leaving the doors unable to be opened from the inside or the outside.

Baxter's retirement plans called for a meeting of the whole group, with the meeting-taking place late at night in the warehouse. He would claim to have forgotten his list of new orders and would leave the building, making sure the doors were all locked with his special key. Once outside, he would set fire to the building. *Presto! All my witnesses disappear together,* Baxter had laughed to himself while making the plans; pleased with his foresight.

At five p.m. the delivery girl for the two white haired boys arrived to pick up her charges. With the boys out of the way, and the warehouse empty, Baxter decided to close for the day.

Calling together the three drivers that had arrived that day, Baxter informed them of a change in plans.

"I have a very big order coming up," he lied smoothly. "I'm going to need every available truck and driver to deliver on this one. It's big, very, very big. Our plans will need to be extremely well organized in order to extract the largest possible profit. There will be a bonus for each of you at the end of this job, the amount of which will depend on the success of our mutual efforts.

"In the meantime, there will be an unavoidable delay. As soon as I know the arrival time of the last truck, I will schedule a meeting that will include everyone, the delivery girls, too. I'll call you when the meeting date and time is set. If you're not going to stay home, have your answering machines on. I'll use the normal code."

Baxter looked at each of the drivers in turn, none of whom had women with them, and then asked, "Any questions?" When there was no answer, he added, "Okay. Goodnight."

As he walked away, the men eyed each other with curiosity. One man, a tall, sandy haired man in his late thirties, said, "An unplanned vacation, huh? Let's go have a beer at Duke's and talk this over. I, for one, don't trust that little creep."

The other two mumbled assent and the men headed for their cars, leaving their trucks parked where they were, against the docks of the warehouse.

The six p.m. news came on as Baxter made himself comfortable in front of the television with his after supper cup of coffee and a rich Havana cigar. His housekeeper placed a fresh bottle of Jack Daniels whiskey and a clean glass on the oak end table at his elbow and left the room, softly closing the door.

Baxter's study was a very large, but cozy, room. The windowless room was dominated by a sixty inch TV screen on the far wall, which Baxter kept covered with red velvet drapes. No one had ever seen him use the enormous TV screen, but the housekeeper could testify to the fact that it was used often, since Baxter often neglected to close the concealing drapes. She could not say what tapes, if any, he watched. A large brown box—that looked about the right size to contain videotapes—was stored in an oak cabinet below the giant television screen. The box was kept locked.

The housekeeper knew it was always locked, she checked it each time she cleaned the room. And each time she muttered to herself, "Curiosity killed the cat!"

Rich furnishings were scattered randomly around the huge room, creating warmth, which did not harmonize with Baxter's sneaky and forbidding character.

The news about Jack Thomas Huxley was the third item on the evening news, being preceded by news of the latest hurricane that was brewing in the Atlantic and heading for the Florida coast and the finding of an unconscious child in a ditch off Highway 27.

The story of the child was covered extensively. Baxter watched closely as a videotape was played, showing the spot where the child was found and a picture of the hospital bed where the child lay.

In spite of the announcer's years of experience with violent crime stories, his voice held more than a trace of horror as he relayed the story to the public. "The three year old child, who has yet to be identified, was badly beaten," the newscaster continued. "During a news conference, a hospital spokesman reluctantly admitted that the child was also raped. The police are looking for the anonymous caller that reported the child and are checking the files of the FBI's missing persons reports. Police Chief Byron Avery is asking the public for help. If you, or anyone you know, saw anything that will help the police in their search for this perverted attacker, please call the Miami Police Department at 813-333-1111 or this station at 813-333-2121. No further details are available at this time."

Baxter sat back with a sigh. He was glad the child had been found, but at the same time he was worried about the semen specimen the police now had in their hands.

A picture of Jack Thomas Huxley appeared on the screen, causing Baxter to sit up with a jerk, which splashed hot coffee on his lap. He swore under his breath and pulled the hot fabric of his pants away from his leg, but kept his eyes and ears glued to the TV.

"This man, Jack Thomas Huxley, is wanted for questioning in the death of a young girl in Toledo, OH. The girl, whose name is being withheld until relatives are notified, was strangled and left in a dump cart in a rest area just south of Toledo.

"A trucker from Duluth, MN, Ms. Janelle Richardson, identified the suspect, Jack Thomas Huxley, from mug shots. Ms. Richardson alleges to have seen Jack Thomas Huxley with the dead girl in the rest area near Toledo. Mr. Huxley was seen entering a black Freightliner with the name SAI Trucking on the door. SAI, or South American Inc., is a local trucking company, which is, based right here in Miami. The FBI is asking anyone with information on Jack Thomas Huxley to please call area code 813-332-1040."

Baxter stared at the TV as a commercial replaced the newscaster's face. "I knew it! I just knew that loser would eventually leave a witness to his stupid shenanigans!" he exploded in fury. "Thank God I did not let the drivers put the real name of my company on their trucks."

Baxter jumped to his feet and began to pace the large room. "I don't want to go to Duluth! I don't have time to go to Duluth." He was speaking aloud, knowing that the sound of his own voice had always calmed him when he was upset or nervous.

"If I know that dumb Huxley, he'll go looking for this girl and get himself in more trouble." Baxter suddenly collapsed on the couch.

He knew Huxley. If the police should catch Huxley in the process of wiping out this Janelle Richardson, Huxley would try to make a deal with the cops, hoping he would get less time in the pen. Since Huxley and his creepy girlfriend, Ivy Muir, were always complaining Baxter didn't pay them enough, Huxley would take great pleasure in spilling the beans about Baxter's business in Florida. He was glad the rest of his drivers had never pulled any of the stunts Jack and Ivy had. He had many times contemplated killing Jack and Ivy, but he had never had the stomach for cold-blooded murder.

He stood up and stomped off to his bedroom. The big meeting at the warehouse and his retirement were going to have to wait. The guys he had already told about the meeting wouldn't mind sitting around for a while; they knew what his bonuses were like. He would leave a note at the warehouse, explaining he was unavoidably called away and the returning drivers should leave their cargoes on their trucks until he returned. Baxter didn't plan to be gone more than one or two days.

But he was definitely going to Duluth. He was going to make sure the police didn't get the opportunity to talk to Jack Thomas Huxley.

At five o'clock, Janelle pulled into a truck stop on the west side of Evansville, Indiana. She had tried hard to fall asleep after the long night and their grueling experience with the police, but she had been too keyed up. *Nervous and scared*, she thought, hating the weakness in her character that let her fear get the best of her. Finally, at two p.m., she had crawled back out of her bunk and relived Ross at the wheel, but not before they had found a rest area and walked to the bathrooms together. Janelle didn't think she would ever be able to walk alone in a rest area again; especially not at night.

She parked behind the restaurant and then woke Ross. "Honey? Come on. Let's get something to eat. I'm really getting hungry now. I guess we should have stopped for lunch."

"Okay," Ross mumbled, turning over and immediately falling back to sleep.

Janelle smiled and watched as his eyes closed again. She knew he was beat, but he would never forgive her if she went to eat alone. And besides, they both wanted to catch the six o'clock news. She reached out and shook his shoulder gently. "Come on, Hon. We have to hurry a little if we want to see the news."

Ross sat up quickly as memory poured the events of the day over him. "Yeah. I'm coming."

He pulled on his boots while Janelle took out her make-up kit and smoothed on a light coat of glossy peach lipstick. Ross quickly brushed his teeth at the tiny sink in the sleeper and joined Janelle. He knelt on the floor between the two seats and pulled her into his arms.

"Everything is going to be alright, Honey. This will all pass and we'll view it as a forgotten nightmare." He hugged her close and planted a soft kiss on her forehead. "Let's go eat."

Janelle forced a grin, "Sounds good to me. And I'm sorry I've been such a baby about this."

"No apology needed, Sweetheart, you haven't been a baby. You've handled everything very well." He smiled into her eyes and opened the truck door for her.

They climbed down the gleaming wide steps of the truck and headed toward the enormous restaurant, hand in hand. Glad to be together and out of Cincinnati.

After a delicious supper, they walked up the stairs to the trucker's lounge, happy to find the place deserted at this early hour of the evening.

A local station announced, "The six o'clock news is next." Ross and Janelle made themselves as comfortable as possible in the deep plastic covered chairs that lined the slightly shabby room, while the television station finished five commercials in quick succession.

"Our top story tonight is the murder of a seventeen year old girl in a rest area south of Toledo. The girl, whose name is being withheld until relatives have been notified, was found by the night caretaker in the waste container at the rest area. She had been strangled to death.

"A trucker from Duluth, MN, Janelle Richardson, saw the girl being forced into a black Freightliner by the alleged murderer; Jack Thomas Huxley. Ms. Richardson was able to make a positive identification from mug shots she was shown by the Cincinnati Police Department. Ms. Richardson also gave the police a detailed description of the alleged murderer's truck and pertinent information on the trucking company he drives for. Ms. Richardson and her fiancé, Ross Taylor, drive for the Garvey Truck Lines, which is based in Duluth, MN.

"In Evansville last night...."

"No...no...no!" Janelle had started moaning in terror at the first mention of her name and had slid down in her chair while her eyes darted to the open door of the lounge.

"It's okay, Sweetheart, he'll never find us! He has no way of knowing where we're headed. He doesn't know what we look like or what kind of truck we drive," Ross consoled her.

"We won't be able to go home, Ross. He has only to look in the Duluth phone book to find out where we live. And we have Lars' wedding coming up. Your brother will never forgive us if his best man doesn't show up."

"I know, but we still have eight days before the wedding."

"But our vacation starts the sixteenth."

"Yeah," Ross murmured. He was silent so long that Janelle pulled back from his embrace and stared into his face.

"Ross?"

"Do you think we could stay with your mother?" he asked.

"Mom! I have to call her. If she's heard about this, she's going to be worried sick." Janelle jumped to her feet, almost tipping Ross over in her haste to reach a phone. She grabbed Ross' hand and hurried into the hall outside of the lounge, where the walls were lined with telephones.

She dialed quickly and as the phone started ringing, crossed her fingers in hope that her mother would answer. The phone was answered on the third ring and Janelle knew without asking that her mother had heard the news. "I thought I better call you," Janelle whispered sadly.

"Janelle!" her mother cried. "Are you alright?"

"I'm fine Mom, but I'm scared silly."

"Of course you are. Who wouldn't be," Delphine Kipp exclaimed.

"Ross and I were just talking about it. We won't be able to go to our apartment until they catch that madman. Do you think we could stay with you when we get back?"

"Of course! Don't give it a second thought. I'd love to have you. I don't get to see you near enough anymore." Delphine was obviously delighted at the prospect of her daughter's proposed visit.

"Thanks, Mom, we'll let you know when we get back. And don't worry, Ross will take good care of me. I love you. Good-bye."

"I love you, too, Janelle. Take care."

Janelle turned to Ross hopefully, thinking about his solution. "She had already heard about it and she'd love to have us," she reported. "And you're right, he'll never be able to find Mom's place because her name is different than mine. After Baxter was sent to jail, Mom changed all our names to Richardson; after her grandmother and grandfather. She thought Baxter would try to find us when he was let out...."

"And did he?" Ross interrupted.

Janelle shook her head, "I don't know. He may have looked, but he didn't find us, because we never saw or heard from him again. Thank God! Anyway, Mom married Frank Kipp when I was twenty. You met him, didn't you?"

"No. He died a few weeks before we met. I remember you talking about him."

"I wish you could have known him. He was a wonderful man, just like my Dad." Janelle smiled weakly, "Mom didn't have the best life."

"She had you and Allison. Two daughters any mother would be proud to have. And she had the happy years with your father and a short time with Frank Kipp," Ross reminded her.

Janelle nodded. "You're right. I just wish we had never lost Dad. He was so wonderful—and we all loved him," she sighed, "Anyway, I'll feel a lot safer at her house."

"Right. Besides, the police will catch Huxley real soon with all the information you gave them. I'm sure they'll have him in custody before it's time for our vacation, much less the wedding date." Ross smiled down into her eyes, "Everything will be alright, you'll see."

"Thank God the news media didn't have a picture of me. I'd really be scared then." Janelle followed Ross down the hall to the stairs, gripping his hand tightly as they started down the steps to the main floor.

"I have to stop at the bathroom before we take off," Janelle said.

"I figured that," Ross laughed.

"Don't laugh! I told you we should have ordered the tractor that had a bathroom. And now I'm never going to walk to the bathroom alone again. You won't be laughing when you have to get up and go with me every time," Janelle chided him.

Ross immediately sobered, "You're right. Not about my minding having to go with you, but I know when this is over and forgotten, you'll get brave again and I don't want you walking around alone; especially at night. Hang the extra weight. We'll order that toilet stool setup as soon as we get home again."

Janelle sighed with relief and wrapped her arm around Ross' slim waist, "Thank you, Honey. That's a relief. Then all I have to do is take an exit where I can reenter right away again and pull over on the entrance. That'll be great.

And what we lose in weight, we can make up with saved time."

Ross put his arm around her shoulders and hugged her close, "I couldn't stand it if anything happened to you, Janelle." He solemnly looked into her big green eyes, "I wonder if you really know how much I love you? You're my whole life. I would cease to exist if I ever lost you."

Janelle was deeply touched by his obvious sincerity. Her eyes misted over with tears of happiness and she let her cool fingers trail lightly down his handsome face, "I love you, too, Ross Taylor."

Ross unlocked the truck and Janelle climbed over the driver's seat to the shotgun seat. He started the truck and then jumped back out to kick the tires and check the load. Janelle slumped down in her seat, suddenly more tired than she had ever been in her life.

Her eyes were heavy and she felt completely drained, as though her muscles had turned to liquid. Ross returned, glancing at her with concern etched on his face, "Are you alright?"

"I'm so tired, so ungodly tired," Janelle mumbled sleepily.

"Off to bed with you then. Do you want me to help you?"

Janelle straightened up with an effort and turned to the sleeper, "No, I'll make it. When you get tired, pull over. We have plenty of time, but don't forget to set the alarm." She had reached the bunk and sat on the edge looking at her cowboy boots, wondering if she had the strength to pull them off.

Ross was suddenly beside her. He pulled off her boots, tipped her legs into the bunk and pulled the cover over her. Her eyes closed immediately and Ross bent to place a gentle kiss on her lips. She moaned softly and was instantly asleep, her breathing slow and even.

Ross smiled down at her, restraining himself from brushing her fine hair off her forehead. *My poor little sweetheart*, he thought, *why did this have to happen?*

He turned the air conditioning in the sleeper down to low and closed the heavy flap of the curtain; zipping it tight. He sighed as he climbed behind the wheel. *What have I gotten her into?* he wondered, *why didn't I just let her keep her old job? She was so much safer with the local driving. But no, I wanted her with me all the time. Why couldn't I have been satisfied with just the weekends?*

But Ross already knew the answer to his questions. He couldn't stand being away from her. His love for her took first place in his life. She had filled his life with a happiness he had never thought was possible to find, not on this earth.

Janelle had told him about her stepfather's abuse and he had cried in sorrow for the innocence that had been stolen from her. Her mother had put both her and her sister, Allison, in therapy as soon as she had found out about the abuse and Janelle had seemed to work out all her terrors and hatreds. To Ross, she seemed well adjusted, happy and content with her life. She had accepted the fact that there was no changing what had happened and she had gone forward bravely, one day at a time, putting the past behind her.

Night had fallen before Ross reached the outskirts of Kansas City. He was tired, but not extremely tired. He had decided he would sleep better if they were already at their next drop, instead of somewhere out on the highway; out in the boondocks, as Janelle would have said.

He followed the directions their dispatcher, Mike, had given them and drove right to their destination; a grocery warehouse on the west side of the city. He backed into a place in the line of trucks that were already there waiting to be unloaded and set the air brakes.

The weather was hot and muggy and Ross decided to leave the truck running so they could leave the air conditioning on. He pulled off his boots and crawled into the top bunk, careful not to disturb Janelle. Seconds later he was sound asleep, the truck and the air conditioning making a constant pleasing hum that would cover any noises from outside the truck.

They left Kansas City at noon, with breakfast behind them and a load of plastic cartons that they would deliver in Los Angels. They would each drive for four-hour periods and their meals would have to be quick ones, but they could make it if they kept the hammer down.

At eight a.m., Ross called Mike to report they would arrive at their destination with about an hour to spare.

Mike whistled, "Good job. I knew I could count on you guys."

He had a load ready for them to pick up in San Bernardino, CA, that delivered in Duluth on the sixteenth. "You guys can be back by the fifteenth." They would be dead tired, but this past week would pay very well and Mike said they could start their vacation two days early. Ross didn't immediately reply and Mike seemed to quickly realize the reason for his hesitation. The TV and radio news had been full of the reports about Janelle's involvement with the murder in Ohio.

"I can give you a couple of short runs if you want," Mike offered. "Keep you busy right up to the day of the wedding if that's what you want."

"No...it's all right. I think we'll just take our time coming home. This load doesn't have to be there until the sixteenth, which is the first day of our vacation. Maybe they'll have that guy before we get back. We're more than ready for a vacation, Mike. We've decided to stay with Janelle's mother until that guy is caught. Have you heard anything more about it?" Ross was glad Janelle had gone to the bathroom while he made the call to Mike. He knew the murder was always in the back of her mind, but he didn't want to talk about it. He tried to keep it hidden from Janelle, but he was very worried about this guy, this Jack Thomas Huxley. Janelle was right; they wouldn't be too hard to find if someone put their mind to finding them. And he was just as sure as Janelle that Jack Thomas Huxley was going to put his mind to finding them.

"They haven't found him yet, or at least there's been no announcement to that effect on the news," Mike reported.

Ross shook his fair head, "When we get back we're going to report Janelle's mother's address and phone number to the Cincinnati police, that way you won't have to worry about giving our address to anyone. I wouldn't put it past that guy to call you and say he was the Police or anyone else that would sound convincing, hoping you would tell him where we are."

"Don't worry, Ross. I won't give out your address to anyone and I won't tell anyone else here at the office where you're going. That way we won't have to worry about someone slipping up and giving out your address." Mike sounded pleased with himself for thinking of this possibility.

"Good. Thanks, Mike. I have to get going now, Janelle's on her way over here. Talk to you later." Ross returned the phone to the hook just as Janelle reached him. "Ready to go?" he smiled.

"Ready," Janelle confirmed.

"Mike has a load ready for us in San Bernardino that goes to, guess where?" he teased.

"Minneapolis?"

"Nope. It goes to Duluth."

"You're kidding! That's great," she enthused. "Boy, we're piling up the money this week."

Ross laughed, "And we're going to turn around and spend it on a potty."

Janelle frowned and a shadow crossed her delicate features.

Ross' face fell, "I'm sorry, Honey. I was just teasing. I didn't mean to remind you." He took her arm gently and led her toward the door. "Let's get going. We've got a long many mile ahead of us, but at least this time we get to take our own sweet time."

The next five days were spent leisurely traveling toward home. They stopped to see a few tourist sights on the way and their meals were two hours affairs instead of the quick half hour they usually spent. The Black Hills delighted both of them and they spent more time there than they had planned, making the last part of their trip a rush and leaving both of them tired out again.

"But it was worth it, wasn't it?" Janelle smiled at Ross.

Ross agreed, "It was very beautiful and educational."

Janelle and Ross were glad to be back in Duluth. They questioned Mike about Jack Thomas Huxley and were disappointed to learn that the man had still not been caught.

Although they both loved to visit Janelle's mother, they were lonely for their own home. Disheartened, they called Janelle's mother, told her they were just going to stop at their apartment to shower, pick up some clean clothes and they'd be there soon.

"Don't make supper, Mom, we're going to take you out to eat."

"You don't have to do that, Honey, I've got some steaks in the freezer and they don't take long to thaw. Besides, you must get tired of eating out," Delphine continued.

"You're right, Mom. You talked me into it. Anyway, you make the best steaks east of the Mississippi," Janelle complimented truthfully. She looked at her watch, "See you about five thirty."

"Flattery will get you everything," Ross teased as she hung up the phone.

"Yeah, Janelle, he's right. But I bet your mom loves it anyway," the secretary in the small office behind them yelled.

Janelle laughed; Erica heard everything that went on in the small group of offices. "See you later, Erica. Don't take any wooden nickels."

"Have a nice vacation," Erica called as they headed for the door.

"Thanks. See you in four weeks," Janelle called back, to which she vaguely heard Erica respond, "Lucky dogs!"

They arrived at their silver Mazda just in time to see their new Mack leaving the yard. Both Ross and Janelle stared after it; looking as though they had just lost their best friend.

"Are you sure Carl Tate is a safe driver?" Janelle worried, watching their 'baby' turn the corner and head toward the downtown area. Carl was the driver who was going to keep Ross and Janelle's truck on the road while they were on vacation.

"I'm sure, Honey," Ross said. "He's been driving for twenty years and the only accident he ever had was years ago and was not his fault."

"Did you ever get a chance to check out the inside of his truck?"

"I just looked at it a few minutes ago. It was neat and clean. No spots, no cigarette burns, no garbage, and, the windows were clean. Satisfied?" Ross laughed.

"I guess so...but I still wish we could have just let the Mack set until we got back," she sighed. "I know! We'd lose too much money if we let it set for a month. Are you sure he won't wreck the transmission?"

"Nobody can be sure of that, Sweetheart, but it's still on warranty and Mike assured me that the company hasn't had any trouble with any of the different trucks Carl has driven." Ross turned his back on the disappearing sight of their truck and begged, "Let's go home. I'm beat."

"Me, too," Janelle groaned as she slid into their comfortable car. "I still don't think it's a good idea to even stop at home. We could wash our clothes at Mom's."

"I don't think we have to worry about Jack Thomas Huxley in the middle of the day, Honey."

"But he might be watching our place. He might follow us to Mom's."

"We'll go in the back way. And he doesn't know our car or what we look like. We'll be fine," Ross' voice was reassuring and Janelle did want different clothes to wear while they were on vacation.

"Okay. Let's not forget our swimsuits. I wish we could just stay home. I'm too tired to be good company for Mom," she complained.

"Me, too," Ross mimicked as he pulled unto the freeway, taking the long way around, but knowing they would reach their cozy little apartment sooner this way than going directly across town.

"Darn! I forgot to call Chet Archer in Cincinnati."

"You can call him from home, while I'm in the shower," Ross crowed.

Janelle was as anxious to shower as Ross and she usually went first since her long hair took so long to dry. She laughed, "Well, if you're not done by the time I'm done calling, I'm going to join you."

Ross leered at her, "I was planning on a very long shower."

Janelle snuggled close to him, glad they had decided against the Mazda with the bucket seats, "Good. I'm glad to hear that." Her finger tickled his firm thigh and Ross' free arm came around her shoulders, pulling her closer yet.

As they pulled into the big parking lot of their apartment building, they both looked over the parked cars as Ross drove to their appointed spot. No one sat in any of the cars and nothing looked out of order. No one stood outside the apartment building door and no one stood or roamed aimlessly along the sidewalks. Ross and Janelle stayed in their car for long moments, searching the whole area with worried eyes.

They looked at each other and smiled, both of them were feeling a little sheepish for their anxious vigilance. Ross searched out and squeezed Janelle's hand warmly and murmured, "Let's go home, Sweetheart."

Home at last, Ross unlocked the door, held it open for Janelle and pushed it closed again, not stopping to lock it. The thought that there could be someone in their apartment never entered either Janelle or Ross' mind. The door had been locked, they were safe. They were home.

They carried their dirty clothes from the trip into the laundry basket in the small fold-away-doors laundry room that was located in the short hall that led to their bedroom and the bathroom.

Janelle hurried to the phone in the kitchen, while Ross—striping as he went—headed for the shower. She dug out the phone number Chet Archer had at the last minute remembered to give her and quickly punched out the eight hundred number.

Chet picked up the phone without thinking about the action. "Detective Archer."

"This is Janelle Richardson."

Chet's jerked his feet from the top of his desk and slammed them on the floor with a bang; his chair sprung quickly to an upright position, "Yes, Ms. Richardson. Is anything wrong?"

"I thought we were going to use first names?"

Chet laughed, now relatively sure that Janelle was not in trouble, "Of course, Janelle. What can I do for you?"

"Did you catch Jack Thomas Huxley yet?"

"No.... But he was sighted in South Carolina. At least we were quite sure it was him. But before the police could get to the place where he was reported to have been seen, he was gone. The bartender was shown Huxley's picture and he said he thought it was the same man, but nobody had dared to follow him when he left the bar. Nobody even knew which way he had headed, if he was on foot or had transportation," he sighed disgustedly. "It's extremely aggravating to come so close and not get him. But we'll have him soon. His picture has been televised and with everyone looking for him, it's just a matter of time."

"Oh.... Well Ross and I are back in Duluth and we're afraid to stay at our apartment after you broadcast our names," Janelle's voice was suddenly sharp with anger.

"I'm terribly sorry, Janelle. That information, including your place of employment and your city of residence, was not released to the press from our office, but somehow they found out anyway. The only thing I can think of is someone at the truck stop must have overheard our conversation," Chet apologized. He hoped he sounded sincere. They needed Janelle's continued cooperation.

Chet did not tell Janelle the truth. He was sure it had not been at the truck stop. Their names had been mentioned during the introductions, but there had been no mention of their home state, town or the company they worked for. The leak had to have come from the Cincinnati Police Department. Now days, there were too many 'loose lips' in police departments across the country. The press paid good money for tips.

"Oh...anyway, we're going to stay at my mother's. She remarried after her divorce and our last names are different. I'll give you her name, address and phone number, but you have to make sure it doesn't get out." Janelle didn't feel it was necessary to mention that her mother had remarried twice after her father died.

"I will, Janelle. I'll be very careful. And you're right. It's not a good idea for you to even go to your apartment at all. Where are you now?" he asked.

"At our apartment," Janelle said. "We discussed the possibility of Jack Thomas Huxley watching the place, but we decided that we'd be safe in the middle of the day and we needed some clothes."

Chet was silent as long moments passed.

"We checked out the parking lot. Everything looked fine." Janelle said.

"I'd hurry," Chet said, his voice grim. "And make sure you aren't followed when you leave. Remember, Huxley will be hard to spot. He's had a lot of experience keeping out of sight."

Janelle had moved from the kitchen with their cordless phone and her eyes wandered down the short hall to their bedroom door. She gasped and stopped in her tracks, staring at the door.

The door was closed, but not tight, and neither she nor Ross had been in there yet.

She could see the frame of the doorway through the tiny crack. Was it that way when they came in? Wouldn't she have noticed it if it had been? She always closed the door tight, even when they weren't going to be home. She insisted that keeping the door closed was much safer in case of a fire and it also kept the flies and mosquitoes out. It only took one fly or one mosquito to keep her awake until she was forced to get up and kill it.

Janelle suddenly felt lightheaded with fear and her heart began to hammer painfully.

"Hold on, Chet," she stammered, dropping the phone on the table—unmindful of the crash that sounded along the lines and painfully pierced Chet's eardrum—and rushing toward the bathroom.

"Ross! Ross!" she screamed in fear, tearing into the bathroom and propelling the door closed behind her.

The splashing water in the shower came to an abrupt halt as Ross slammed down the knob and threw back the curtain, throwing water all over the Janelle and the bathroom floor.

"What?! What happened?!"

Janelle threw herself into Ross' arms and tried to explain, her words falling over themselves, "Chet said we shouldn't have come home.... That murderer might be here! And the bedroom door isn't closed tight!"

Ross knew Janelle's compulsion to keep the bedroom door closed at all times. He hadn't looked at the door when they were putting their clothes in the hamper, but he was sure Janelle had closed it tight before they left. His mind held a vivid picture of Janelle closing the door. He remembered waiting for her to go back and close it after he had left it open again. She had closed it tight, solid against its frame.

He gasped in spite of himself and attempted to untangle Janelle's clinging arms. "Why didn't I think to look through the apartment?" he berated himself. He pulled at Janelle's terror tightened arms, "Let me go, Honey!"

"No! What if he's out there?"

"We can't just stay in here," Ross argued, finally managing to pull away and reach his robe. "Stay here!" he ordered as he started for the closed bathroom door.

"No! I'm not staying here alone!" Janelle was very nearly hysterical with as yet unfounded fear. She locked her hand in the thick terry cloth at the back of Ross' robe and followed him out of the bathroom.

Ross detoured to the wall of the living room and grabbed the poker from the bucket by their fake fireplace. He raised it over his head. Janelle whimpered in terror and threw a frantic look over her shoulder toward the bedroom door.

Ross advanced on the bedroom, his face grim and determined, but scared, too. They reached the door and Ross stopped, staring at the small crack. He glanced back at Janelle's terrified face and his own face softened briefly in a look of love. Suddenly he raised his foot and with a swift kick slammed the door open. It smashed against the inside wall with a terrifying crash, making Janelle shriek in fear.

Ross reached back with his free hand and tried to break her hold on his robe, "Stay back."

But Janelle would not relinquish her grip on Ross. She moaned, but clung tightly to him as he moved slowly into the bedroom. A blackout shade, with thick maroon drapes pulled over top of it, made the room nearly as dark as night. Ross flipped on the light switch as he moved through the door.

The large room was suddenly filled with brilliance. Their eyes quickly scanned the area, nervously jumping from the queen size water bed with a thick black and rose quilt neatly covering it, to the tall oak chest of drawers, to the handsome twelve drawer dresser with the wide, tall mirror...and then locked as one on the closed closet door.

Ross crept slowly to the closet door, hesitated for a brief second, and then abruptly jerked it open, jumped back and pushed Janelle back with him as the door banged against the wall. He sighed with relief when no one attacked them. More relaxed now, sure that if someone had been in the closet he would have charged them when the door was opened, Ross brushed aside the hanging clothes. No one was there, in either side of the long closet.

"Look under the bed," Janelle whispered, still unconvinced no one was in the room.

"A man wouldn't be able to fit under that bed," Ross whispered back, pulling away the bedspread as he spoke and kneeling beside the bed to peer under its low side. "Nothing," he confirmed his prophesy.

Janelle had surrendered her hold on his robe when Ross bent to examine the floor under the bed, but as he straightened up she again locked her hand in the thick material of his robe.

"There's no one here, Honey," Ross murmured, breaking her tight grip and putting his arms around her.

"We didn't check the kitchen." She locked her arm around his waist and held on tight.

"I didn't lock the door when we came home," Ross suddenly remembered. "He could have walked right in while we were in here!"

Ross turned and headed back to the small, cozy living room. With Janelle still close beside him, he reached to lock the door and suddenly noticed that it wasn't closed tight. He frowned and whispered, "I closed this tight. I know I did!"

Janelle stared at him with horror while Ross locked the apartment door and turned toward the kitchen. More leery than ever, his eyes traveled around the living room as he moved and he suddenly stopped. Their long couch. It was so long that it filled one complete wall and stuck out into the opening to the kitchen. *A man could easily lie hidden behind that length,* he thought, wondering if he was getting as paranoid as Janelle was. *But I did close that door tight*!

He moved to the kitchen opening, keeping as long a distance between them and the couch as possible. He stopped just short of the back of the couch and craned his neck to see behind it. The carpeted floor was empty and nothing could fit under the couch, not even a small child.

They advanced slowly to the kitchen doorway, poking their heads into the bright, cheery room. Janelle immediately screamed, causing Ross to jump with alarm. "What?!" he hollered, shaking in spite of himself.

"The door! The glass in the door is broken." She pointed to the sliding glass door that led to a small balcony and a fire escape. They turned together, their eyes going to the only place left for a man to hide; the small pantry across from them. "It's the only place left, Ross," Janelle whispered.

Ross started toward the closed door, the poker again raised over his head. This time Janelle hung back, sure that Jack Thomas Huxley was hiding in the closet. She didn't want to be in Ross' way if he needed to swing the poker. Her hand fell to the silverware drawer next to her. She jerked it open and pulled out the large butcher knife she used to cut bread and roasts. Holding it up, pointed forward like a dagger, she bravely stood ready to back Ross up.

Ross turned the doorknob silently and then with a jerk threw the door open, jumping back as he did so. One glance assured them the closet was empty. Ross sighed deeply and his shoulders slumped with relief. Janelle began to sob with reaction.

They looked at each other for long moments before Ross held out his arms and Janelle rushed into them; still holding the butcher knife.

"Whew!" Ross whistled softly.

Janelle pulled out of his arms and hurried back to the phone. Before she reached it she could already hear Chet's voice calling her.

"Janelle! Janelle! What happening?! Pick up the phone!"

"Chet? I'm sorry. I guess I panicked. I thought someone was in our apartment," Janelle hurried to explain.

"Why did you scream?"

"The window in the kitchen is broken. I think someone was in here," she shuddered as she thought of the broken window and the two doors that had been closed tightly. "He may have still been here when we got here. He could have slipped out the door while I was on the phone in the kitchen or when I went to get Ross out of the shower."

"No. No, I don't think so, Janelle. If Jack had been there when you got home, he wouldn't have run off again," Chet said. Jack Thomas Huxley would have killed both Janelle and Ross if he had been there. The man would have been able to overpower both of them, although Ross was stronger than he looked. Still...Ross did not have the killer instinct that Jack had.

"Why do you say that?" Janelle asked fearfully. "When we came in Ross closed our apartment door, tight. He's sure he closed it tight, and then when we got done searching the bedroom, it was open a tiny crack." She pulled Ross to her side and collapsed against his firm strength.

"That's strange...but I still don't think it was Jack. Jack is desperate. But we don't need to go into that now. I think you should leave there as soon as possible. Go to your mother's and don't tell anyone of your whereabouts."

"We already told our dispatcher," she admitted. "We didn't want someone in the office to accidentally say where we were, so we told him and asked him not to tell anyone else, even if the person who asks says he's a policeman."

"Good. Why don't you call him, after you get to your mother's, and tell him that if anyone wants to reach you, they should call me. That way we won't have to worry about Jack finding out where you are."

A sudden soft knock at the door caused Janelle to yelp in alarm. Ross stiffened.

"Someone's at the door," Janelle whispered into the phone.

Chet swore softly, "Don't answer it."

"But what are we going to do?"

"Quickly and quietly go out the back door," Chet instructed.

"But Ross isn't dressed!" In her fear and nervousness, a wild giggle rose in Janelle's throat, threatening to break loose and expose their presence in the apartment. She could not picture Ross walking out to their car in his short bathrobe.

At that moment a familiar voice called through the door, "Ross? Janelle? It's Homer Zeke. Are you there?"

Without further delay, Ross hurried to the door.

"It's the caretaker of our building," Janelle said to Chet, slumping into the recliner.

"Wait! Don't answer the door. He may not be alone," Chet commanded.

Before the words were out of the detectives' mouth, Ross had the door open. Janelle screamed for him to stop, but it was already too late. The door was open.

CHAPTER FIVE

Outside the door stood meek little Homer Zeke. At sight of Ross' stricken face, he stepped back, "Is something wrong?"

Ross stuck his head out the door, hurriedly glancing both ways. "No, nothing's wrong," he breathed in relief. "Hi, Homer. What can I do for you?"

Behind him he heard Janelle's breath escape in a sigh as she told Chet that there was no one at the door but the caretaker.

"Did you notice the broken window yet?" Homer asked.

"Yes. We did. Did someone break in?"

"No. It was Bobby Norton from across the alley. He has a heck of an arm for a kid of seven," Homer bragged. "They were playing catch, him and a couple other kids. He's been waiting anxiously for you guys to get back. He saw your car pull in and came to ask me if I'd retrieve his baseball."

Ross laughed out loud, feeling the tension drain from his body. Behind him, Janelle laughed, too, and reported to Chet. Ross went to the kitchen and there, in the corner under the table, was Bobby's baseball. He was still laughing as he handed the ball to Homer. "Tell Bobby the next time he has to come and get his own ball."

Homer laughed shyly, "I'll do that. I called the repair shop and they'll be here tonight to repair the window. Sorry it happened." Homer peered timidly around Ross and said to Janelle, "That was real brave of you to go to the police about that murder in Toledo, Janelle."

"Thanks, Homer, but I didn't consider it brave, I felt it was my duty," Janelle smiled at the man they had known for over two years. Homer was a small built man of about five nine. Although he was only in his middle thirties, he was almost entirely bald and what little hair was left was a mixture of red and gray. His nose was too big for his small face and his green eyes were large and expressive. His teeth were oversize and very white for his small mouth, but his lips were thick; giving him the look of a chattering monkey.

"I guess I'd have been worried about that murderer coming after me," Homer admitted, his small face reddening with embarrassment.

Janelle threw a quick glance at Ross, "He'd be a fool to come looking for me. The police would know who it was if anything should happen to me." Her voice was firm and her words were bold, but inside, Ross knew, Janelle was shaking with just such a fear; a fear that a moment ago he was sure had materialized into fact.

"But that wouldn't help you. I mean if you're dead...umm...a...but...," Homer stopped, as if suddenly realizing he would scare Janelle. His eyes dropped to the floor as he mumbled, "Sorry."

"It's all right, Homer, I know what you meant," Janelle's smile said she understood.

There was an embarrassed silence before Ross injected, "Anyway, Homer, the broken window wasn't your fault and there's no hurry to have it fixed because we're leaving again anyhow. Thanks for telling us."

"You're leaving again so soon? You just got home."

"I know, but that's the way the trucking business is." Ross decided to let Homer believe they were leaving on another run in the truck. He had no desire to let anyone else know where they were going or whom they would be staying with.

"Yeah, I guess. Well, see you later, have a good trip." Homer waved and started down the long hall to the stairs. Ross closed and bolted the door.

Janelle was again serious and still very frightened. She had hung up the phone and she was stuffing clothes helter skelter into the small suitcase they had just emptied. "Chet says we should get out of here as soon as possible. Hurry and get dressed. I'll shower at Mom's. He also said to be careful we aren't followed." She looked up at Ross, misery and fear making her face crumble into tears again, "Ross, was the bedroom door opened or closed when we first came in?"

Ross frowned with concentration and slowly shook his head, "I don't know. I didn't notice it at all, but I'm sure I closed the outside door when we came in. I think someone was in here. Maybe a robber?"

Janelle's eyes widened in surprise, "Sure. If it was a robber we surprised, that would explain why he snuck out again. I wonder if he took anything."

"We're not going to check now," Ross said. "We've got to get moving."

"What did I get us into?" Janelle moaned. "Oh why didn't I just leave it alone! They would have caught Jack eventually!"

"But this way they'll catch him sooner, Janelle, and maybe he won't get the chance to kill anyone else," Ross consoled her.

"He might get us!" Janelle wailed, avoiding Ross' comforting arms. "Hurry, Ross. I want to get out of here."

"Okay, I'm hurrying." He threw on some clothes and grabbed their toothbrushes while Janelle finished packing their clothes. Five minutes later they were rushing out the door and running down the stairs to their car.

Ross threw the suitcase in the back seat and they both jumped into the car, Janelle immediately pushed the automatic door lock.

"You watch for anyone to follow us," Ross said, backing from their private parking spot.

Janelle didn't want anyone to see her keeping such a close watch on their back trail, so she adjusted the power mirror on her side of the car so she could see the road behind them. If someone did follow them, it would be better for them if that someone didn't know they knew they were being followed. "Nobody's there that I can see," she reported to Ross.

"I haven't seen anyone either, but I'm going to circle a few blocks just to be sure."

"Good idea," Janelle said, beginning to slowly relax.

Ross circled around and around before he finally turned in the direction of Janelle's mother's. They pulled up in front of Delphine's house twenty minutes late, but Janelle knew her mother. Delphine liked her steaks medium rare and she had taught Janelle to like them that way, too. 'Never put the steaks on the grill until you see the whites of their eyes', Delphine had always said; meaning that whoever you were cooking for could wait the few minutes it took to grill the steaks, but the steaks would get too done if they had to wait for the people.

"Maybe we should put the car in Mom's garage. There's room and if we unload our suitcase here, the neighbors will see us."

"I really don't think it matters if the neighbors see us or not, but if it makes you feel better, we'll park in the garage." He pulled out onto the street again and went around the block to the alley.

Delphine's house was in the middle of the block, with two empty lots behind her land. Janelle had mixed feelings about those two connecting lots;

in the daytime she loved them, but at night she hated them. In the daytime you could play ball there—if you didn't mind a few trees in the way—or miniature golf or any one of a dozen different yard games, but at night, those same trees that were in the way in the daytime caused the vacant lots to be filled with shadows. The eerie shadows could hide a lot of terrors, or produce imaginary, unfounded terrors. Janelle had always used the front door of the house at night. Tonight, even though it was still broad daylight, her eyes were drawn—as if by a magnetic force field—to the tall trees. Shadows from the sun were already there, but in the daylight they looked completely harmless. *Still*, Janelle thought, *the trees are tall, with thick trucks that could easily conceal a man; even a large man.*

"Ross?"

"What, Baby?"

"I'm sorry, but could we go back to the front? I don't like those empty lots. I've always hated them. They scare me. I always used the front door at night. I don't know how I could have forgotten that," Janelle was close to tears again.

"But it's still daylight."

"I know, but we might decide to go somewhere after it's dark and then we'll have to come out here."

"Okay, Honey, don't cry. Please don't cry. I hate seeing you unhappy, especially when there's nothing I can do to help. This whole thing has us both upset, Honey. We'll go back to the front. No problem."

Janelle cuddled close to him and tried to stop her tears as he drove slowly down the alley, past Delphine's house, around the block and back up to the front of the house. They pulled into the driveway and ascended the gradual upgrade to the front of the garage.

Delphine opened the front door while they were still climbing from the car. At her side stood her miniature toy terrier, Muffy, barking ferociously. Janelle called to the dog cheerfully and she quieted immediately, running down the steps and jumping around Janelle's legs with joy. Janelle knelt down and ruffled her ears playfully.

"Why did you do that?" Delphine called, "Is someone following you?"

"No, Mom. At first I wanted Ross to park in the garage, but I changed my mind."

Delphine's smile was sad as she came forward to take her daughter in her arms, "The vacant lots?"

"I hate to admit it, but yeah, the vacant lots." Janelle hugged her mother, perhaps a little tighter than she had intended, because Delphine winced.

"Hi, Ross," Delphine smiled sorrowfully. "Heck of a mess, huh?"

"Yes...but Janelle would never have forgiven herself if she hadn't done everything she could to help."

"I know. My good Samaritan daughters. Allison is the same way." Delphine's blue eyes sparkled with love. "Well, you'll both be safe here. Come on in. I put the steaks on when I saw your car out here the first time and they're almost done."

"I suppose I don't have time to shower first, huh?" Janelle asked, teasing her mother.

"Definitely not," her mother scolded, glancing at Janelle and then laughing at the impish look on her daughter's tired face. "You wouldn't want your steak well done would you?'

"No," Janelle admitted, laughing. "I was teasing you, Mom. I'll gladly wait until after supper."

"I know you were teasing, you little rascal." Delphine reached out and gave Janelle a quick hug.

They moved into the house and Ross dropped their suitcase by the open door. The June evening was beautiful; warm and scented with summer flowers. Delphine had a big vase of cut flowers on the sideboard, which Janelle knew would be placed back on the center of the table after their meal.

Janelle longed to close and lock the door as they entered the house, but she realized that she was getting very paranoid. Jack Thomas Huxley would never find them here, if he were in fact looking for them. She was inclined to believe Ross' theory about the person they both were sure was in their apartment. And Chet Archer's portrayal of Jack Thomas Huxley led her to believe that Chet was right, Jack Thomas Huxley would not have snuck back out of their apartment. They were safe here, just as her mother had said they would be.

Delphine Kipp's house had the comfortable, warm feeling of an old shoe, although the house was anything but old. Two years ago, Delphine had had her small four-room house demolished and replaced with a new house built to her specifications. Her taste ran to modern furniture, but with the old fashioned look. The large living room was furnished with beautiful matching hardwood trimmed recliners and a super long sectional couch with a queen size hide-a-bed hidden in the center section and the same rich oak trim as the chairs. A long, low oak coffee table, with a real oak top that shown with a deep, luxurious shine, stood in front of the couch. The live cut flowers that graced the beautiful table gave off a delicate, fresh aroma, which was very pleasing to the senses. Off setting the old fashioned look of the furniture was the presence of an oval skylight. With the help of the curved bay windows, the skylight gave the room nearly as much light as being outside. The field-rock fireplace in the far corner of the room had an oval, braided rug in front of the hearth and a grouping of comfortable chairs, with a love seat, surrounding it.

They moved from the spacious entryway to the kitchen and Delphine quickly removed the steaks from the grill while Ross and Janelle hurried down the short hall to the bathroom and washed their hands.

Until this moment, Janelle had loved the openness of her mother's new house. She glanced around on the way back from the bathroom, now seeing the rooms in a very different perspective. Outside of a half wall between the kitchen and the entryway, the area was actually one big open room. If someone broke into the house, a person would have to run for the open staircase that led to Delphine's bedroom and the two enormous guest rooms on the second floor or for the other open staircase that led to the huge recreation room in the walk out basement. In either case, a person would be exposed to the sight of the intruder for long moments. *More than enough time for someone to pull the trigger of a gun,* Janelle worried silently.

Supper was delicious and both Ross and Janelle complimented Delphine on it. When the dishes were done, Janelle and Ross asked to be excused, pleading exhaustion, which was the absolute truth.

Janelle was embarrassed to be going to the same bedroom as Ross; seeing as they weren't married yet. Her mother had taught her that marriage came before sex and, although she didn't show her disapproval, Janelle was still uncomfortable with the situation.

Janelle had sanctioned her actions by telling herself, 'Everyone does it', but she knew that that didn't make it right.

Janelle cuddled close to Ross, but they were both too tired to make love. The horror of Jack Thomas Huxley, combined with the hard running of the last four days, had taken its toll. They kissed each other softly and fell asleep immediately.

It was ten thirty a.m. before either Ross or Janelle stirred again. Janelle could smell coffee brewing as they dressed quickly. "Your mom's up," Ross commented, passionately eyeing Janelle's beautiful body as she donned her bra and underwear. Janelle smiled coyly at him and shook her head.

"Mom's probably been up for hours. She's a real early bird."

They hurried down the carpeted stairs and out to the kitchen, sniffing appreciatively. "Umm. That coffee smells real good, Mrs. Kipp," Ross said.

"What's this Mrs. Kipp bit? I thought we knew each other better than that," Delphine said, fixing Ross with a haughty look.

"Sorry. Delphine," Ross quickly corrected himself, smiling warmly.

"That's better," Delphine teased.

"Sorry we're so late getting up, Mom. Have you listened to the news yet this morning?"

"I knew you were both dead tired. I expected you to sleep in. And yes, I listened to the news at six o'clock. There was another murder, but I don't remember where."

"In Duluth?" Ross asked.

"Yes. Somewhere over by the lake," Delphine replied.

"It's almost time for the five to eleven news, do you mind if we listen to it?" Janelle questioned.

"Of course not. There wasn't anything about that murderer, Huxley, though." She reached over and clicked on the under the counter radio. "Any preference to which station?"

"No," Janelle and Ross said together. They laughed, said, "Jinx!" to each other and Janelle added, "Whatever you have on is fine, Mom."

The announcer's voice filled the room as Delphine turned the volume on the radio up. "The time is ten fifty five and here's the news. Raymond Thayer Lock, a repairman for Brewer Construction Co., was murdered last night as he attempted to repair a broken window at 1286 Bradley Street West. Police have discovered no motive for the brutal slaying and are asking anyone with information to please call the Duluth City Police Station."

The voice continued to other topics of interest, but Janelle and Ross heard no more. "That's our apartment!" Janelle exclaimed in horror. The blood had drained from her face and she reached blindly across the table, to lock her fingers with Ross'.

"No! You must be mistaken!" Delphine realized at once the significance of the murder.

Janelle shook her head sadly, "It was our apartment, Mom, and it had to be Jack Thomas Huxley who murdered that repairman. He probably thought the repairman was you, Ross!" She shuddered and tears slid down her pale cheeks. "Oh God! Thank God we weren't there."

Ross stared at Janelle, his face stricken with guilt. "We should have warned Homer. We should have told him what was happening. Maybe if they had gone up there together, whoever...and I'm not saying it wasn't Jack Thomas Huxley, but we don't know that for sure, whoever it was," he repeated, "it's possible that he wouldn't have murdered the repairman if two guys had been there."

There was a long moment of silence, broken only by the radio announcer's voice giving the weather, which none of the three people at the table in North Duluth heard. Ross and Janelle stared at each other in horror and sorrow.

"You aren't trying to say that any of this is your fault, are you Ross?" Delphine asked.

Ross dropped his eyes to his and Janelle's locked fingers and didn't reply. His actions spoke volumes.

"No!" Delphine spoke sharply. "It was not your fault. Either of you. Not you for not warning Homer, Ross, and not you for becoming involved with this affair in the first place, Janelle. How could you know that madman would even show up at your place, much less murder an innocent repairman? You couldn't know," she answered herself.

"No...we couldn't know for sure," Ross said sadly. "But if we had warned Homer of the possibility that this killer might show up at our place, the repairman might not be dead."

"But last night you said that the detective from Cincinnati said you shouldn't tell anyone where you were going. I assume he meant he wanted the whole thing kept quiet," Delphine said.

"Maybe he did, but I still think we should have warned Homer," Ross murmured.

"Homer did know about the case, Ross," Janelle put in. Ross didn't answer.

Delphine was silent, privately wishing her daughter had not gone to the police with a description of the man and his victim. *I know I'm being illogical,* she reasoned with herself, *because I'm the one that impressed on her the need to tell someone in authority when you believed something wrong was done to yourself or someone else. If I had taught her that earlier, maybe Baxter might not have gotten the opportunity to molest her.* Delphine's warm blue eyes hardened and her lips pinched together with the onslaught of the horrid memory. She wondered again how on earth a horrible thing like that could have happened without her knowledge.

"I'm going to have to call the Duluth police and tell them about Jack

Thomas Huxley," Janelle sighed.

Ross and Delphine both nodded slowly. "I know you have to, but I wish you didn't," Ross said. He hoped Janelle would want him to go along. He didn't like the idea of her being alone, but he knew Janelle liked her independence.

"You know you can't call from here," Delphine warned. "The police will know where the call came from and then there's the possibility of the information leaking out to the press."

Janelle looked up at her mother, "I never thought of that." She hesitated and then continued, "We could go to the mall, but I wouldn't have much privacy there."

"You might as well just go to the police station," Ross commented. "They'll have a million questions and I would think it would be easier to talk to them in person."

"You'll come with me, won't you?" Janelle pleaded. "I hate to put you through this again, but I really want you with me."

"Of course I'll come. I just didn't want to pressure you. If you had wanted to go alone, I wanted you to know it was alright with me," his eyes were warm with love and support. "And I don't mind, so don't even ask," Ross silently signed with relief.

"How did you know I was going to?" Janelle's eyebrows rose questioningly.

"I know you better than you think," Ross teased back affectionately. He was glad to see that Janelle was able to tease about this horrifying crisis. In spite of her obvious fear, he knew she had strength of will and she was scrupulously honest; with her own feelings and everyone else's. Although he was sure the thought had crossed her mind, Janelle would never hide from what she felt were her obligations as a member of the human race.

"Well, I suppose we better get it over with," Janelle sighed, pushing back her chair.

"You have to eat first. I made some pancakes and I have bacon ready to fry. It won't take but a minute."

Janelle slumped back down, relieved at the postponement of the ordeal ahead of her. She watched while her mother plugged in the large griddle and spread slices of bacon on it. Her eyes turned to Ross and she smiled sadly while she got to her feet and moved to the sink for a dishrag to wipe off the table. "I sure got us into a mess," she said.

Ross shook his head, "There wasn't anything else you could have done, Janelle. I just wish you hadn't stopped at that particular rest area. This whole thing is getting more and more involved and more and more dangerous. I really didn't want to believe that man would come looking for you. I was hoping against hope they would catch him before he even made it to Minnesota. With his picture on all the TV stations all over the country, you would think they'd have him by now."

Delphine turned from the griddle, the pancake turner in her hand, "I think so, too. Look at all the people who know what he looks like and what he's wanted for. Surely someone must have seen him somewhere."

"He was spotted in South Carolina," Janelle told her mother. "But before the police got to the bar where he was seen, he was gone."

"I didn't know that," Ross said, giving Janelle a questioning look.

"I'm sorry, I forgot to tell you. Chet Archer told me about it when I called him from our apartment. After he said we should get out of there as quick as possible. And then I noticed our bedroom door and I forgot all about it."

"What about your bedroom door?" Delphine asked in surprise.

"I was on the phone, talking to Detective Archer, when I noticed that our bedroom door wasn't entirely closed. I thought maybe that man was hiding in there," Janelle shuddered and Delphine gasped. "After Ross searched the bedroom and we were on the way to search the kitchen, Ross noticed that the apartment door wasn't closed tight and he's sure he closed it tight when we got home. Detective Archer said he didn't think that Jack Thomas Huxley had been in our apartment, because he would never have snuck back out," she shrugged her shoulders in an expression of indifference, but the horror in her eyes told Ross and Delphine a completely different story.

"And I still think that bedroom door was closed tight the first time I looked at it, because if it hadn't been, I would have gone over to close it."

Delphine dropped the pancake turner on the counter, for once not worrying if the pancakes burned, and rushed over to her daughter, pulling the shaking girl into her comforting arms, "Oh Sweetheart! You must have been terrified."

"I was," Janelle admitted, tears coming to her eyes. "I still am."

"Don't worry, Honey, it'll be alright. That horrible man will never find you here," Delphine hugged Janelle tight and kissed her cheek. "The police will catch him real soon, especially since he broke into your apartment and killed that poor repairman."

Delphine released her daughter and hurried back to the pancakes, murmuring in disgust when she found them darker than she had wanted. She was about to throw them away and start over when Ross noticed what her intentions were.

"Whoa! Don't throw them away. I like my pancakes dark, Delphine."

"Well, I know Janelle wants them light. I'll fry some more."

"That's all right, Mom, I'm not very hungry anyway," Janelle protested quickly.

"You have to eat, Honey. I know how you are when you're worried about something, but food will give you the strength you need to face this ordeal."

Janelle resigned herself to the unpleasant thought of a full, nervous stomach and finished setting the table in silence.

Her fingers shook as she lit another cigarette. Ross caught her eye and patted his leg, motioning her to sit on his lap. Janelle wiped her eyes as she moved toward him and sat down gingerly, afraid her weight would be too much for him. Ross pulled her close and whispered in her ear, "I love you."

"I love you, too," she whispered back. Smiling bravely at him, she laid her head on his shoulder, cuddling as close as possible. The clean smell of shampoo and after-shave filled her nostrils and she smiled contentedly. "I wish we could just forget this ever happened," she whispered.

"I do, too, Honey," Ross murmured. "But you did the right thing when you went to the police; even though we don't like the consequences. That's one of the many things I love about you, you have a good sense of right and wrong and you always do the right thing, no matter how tough it will be on you."

"I love you." Janelle kissed his cheek and then reluctantly rose to help put the food on the table. She poured fresh coffee for all three of them and orange juice for herself and Ross. Replacing the orange juice in the refrigerator, she took her mother's homemade maple syrup from its place in the storage area of the door and carried it to the table.

Delphine brought the bacon and pancakes to the table and sat down. She passed the full plate to Ross, "Be careful at the police station. There was an article in the paper a few months ago about policemen who give the press tips about arrests and other police business. The press pays for the tips and since the police are underpaid, it's tempting for them."

Janelle and Ross nodded solemnly. "We'll be careful, Mom. Don't worry, we'll be real careful after the way my name was released to the press in Cincinnati."

Janelle and Ross turned into the parking lot at the police station and Ross parked between two patrol cars. They were silent as they climbed out of the car and headed up the wide cement walk to the imposing front door of the station. The day was warm, with temperatures predicted to reach the upper eighties, and the door to the station was closed. Janelle pulled it open and stopped, staring at the line of people waiting to talk to the officer at the front desk.

She looked back at Ross and whispered, "What can they all want?"

Ross shrugged his shoulders and placed a firm hand on the center of her back, giving her a gentle push into the air-conditioned room. "Quit stalling," he taunted her softly.

"I'm not."

"Yes, you are." Ross took her arm and led her to a place in the line, which had shortened only slightly. "I know you're worried about this, Honey, but we might as well get it over with."

Frowning, Janelle conceded, "I know. I know. I'm going." She leaned closer to Ross and whispered softly, "I'm afraid they're going to make me give them Mom's address. And what are we going to do about a phone number where they can reach me? If I give them Mom's number, it will only take them a matter of minutes before they know where she lives and figure out that we're staying there. We can't trust the confidentiality of the police after what happened in Cincinnati."

"Give them the number at Garvey's. Mike can call us," Ross suggested.

"Good idea," Janelle gave him a relieved look.

Ten minutes later they were facing the tired look of the desk officer. "Can I help you?"

"I need to talk to one of the detectives," Janelle requested politely.

"And what is this about?"

Janelle looked at the man behind Ross and lowered her voice to a near whisper, "It's about the murder last night."

"Pardon? Could you speak up please?" the officer's voice was polite, but his attitude was rude.

Janelle was immediately defensive; she did not want the whole room to know their business. She decided to be forceful, "My business is private. Please call a detective for me."

The officer's eyebrows rose in surprise and a small amount of respect came into his eyes, "Have a chair over by the wall. I'll call someone, but it may take awhile." He pointed in the general direction of a line of straight-backed chairs that sat along the cement block wall. The line of chairs was nearly full and there was no place left where Janelle and Ross could sit together; they moved to the end of the line and leaned their shoulders against the cool wall.

Ross smiled, "Kind of hard on him weren't you?"

"He deserved it. Not everyone that comes in here is a criminal. And I won't be treated like one," Janelle retorted.

"Okay, okay. Simmer down," Ross laughed.

They were kept waiting for almost an hour before a tall man in a striped gray suit approached the line of waiting people. He stopped in front of the couple that stood next to Ross and Janelle and looked back at the desk officer. The officer shook his head and signaled the man to move to his right.

The man turned to Janelle and Ross, "Are you the couple who wanted to talk to a detective?"

"Yes," Janelle answered for both of them. Ross smiled. Janelle could be very independent one minute, almost aggressive, and the next minute be unsure, scared of her shadow. He liked a girl who was dependent on her man at times, but very independent at other times. He liked a girl with spirit.

The man looked them over and then said, "I'm Detective Ken Osmond. I understand this was a private matter, please come in to my office." He led the way through the maze of desks and files to a small cubical at the far end of the large room. Holding the door open, he motioned Ross and Janelle into the room.

"Have a seat," Detective Osmond said. When they were seated in front of his desk, Detective Osmond moved around to his large swivel chair and sat down. He leaned back and asked, "What can I help you with?"

Janelle was tempted to say that it was they who were going to help him, but she restrained herself. "The apartment in south Duluth where the murder took place last night? That was our apartment. We think we know who the murderer was." She had decided not to mince words.

Detective Osmond sat up quickly and his chair hit its restraints with a bang. His mouth opened and then closed again. He seemed to be at a temporary loss for words.

Janelle smiled, "Sorry. I didn't mean to startle you. I'm Janelle Richardson and this is my fiancé, Ross Taylor." She gestured toward Ross.

Detective Osmond's eyes widen with comprehension. "The murder in Toledo, Ohio," he flatly stated.

"Yes," Janelle confirmed.

"And you think the murder here in Duluth was committed by Jack Thomas

Huxley. That he was after you."

"Yes," Janelle repeated.

Detective Osmond rubbed his face with the palms of his hands, he looked tired. "Please tell me about it."

"We came back yesterday...."

"Yes. That's right. You're truck drivers. The caretaker, Homer Zeke, said you were gone in your truck," Detective Osmond interrupted.

"That's what we wanted him to think," Janelle replied, thinking the man could learn some manners and not interrupt. "Anyway, we came back yesterday and went home to change. I called Detective Archer in Cincinnati from our apartment." Janelle went through all the details of her conversation with Detective Archer, their panic when they thought someone was in the apartment and Homer Zeke's report about the broken window and the expected repairman. "We're staying with friends," she didn't elaborate on the subject of their whereabouts.

Detective Osmond shook his head, "You've had a pretty hard few days. Now I understand your anger at the desk sergeant and also your desire for privacy. It's regrettable that your name and home town was released to the press...."

"It wasn't released," Janelle interrupted, angry all over again at the breach of confidentiality in Cincinnati. "It was either overheard or someone on the police force in Ohio is a snitch for the press."

Detective Osmond scratched his thick dark hair, "I'm sorry to say that things like that do happen." He didn't say that the snitch idea happened all too often. Some underpaid officers filled their pockets by selling information to the press. These unscrupulous officers are fired immediately if they are caught, but it was a known fact that few are caught. Rumors of an officer of that caliber were at that moment circulating the offices of the Duluth Police Force. "But we will need an address and phone number where we can reach you."

"We've decided not to take any chances. We're willing to give you the phone number at the company where we work. If you need to talk to us, call our dispatcher. He'll call us and we'll call you."

"Okay. It's irregular, but I understand your feelings and I'm not sure but that I don't fully agree with you. But if we knew where you were staying, we could put a watch on your house. Maybe we'd catch Huxley and maybe we'd prevent him from getting to you. What do you think?"

"No! If someone lets it slip where we are, Huxley will find us!" Janelle cried.

"Okay. We'll do it your way. Oh, I also agree with Detective Archer in Cincinnati, stay away from your apartment. The information you've given us will be on the six p.m. news and I'm sure we'll spot this Huxley soon. Thank you very much for your help and good luck to you," Detective Osmond smiled.

Janelle and Ross said goodbye and left the station.

Detective Osmond moved to the small window in his office and watched as Janelle and Ross climbed into their silver Mazda and backed out of their parking spot. He wrote down the license number. When they were headed toward the exit of the parking lot, with their backs to the door of the station house, he rushed out of the station and jumped into his private car. Hastily starting his old brown Chevy, he pulled out behind them.

"Sorry, Guys," he muttered out loud. "I'll be real careful with the information, but we need to know where you're going to be. This may be the only chance we have of catching Huxley."

CHAPTER SIX

"He seems like a nice enough guy, doesn't he?" Janelle asked Ross.

"Yup. Real nice. I was surprise that he understood about us wanting to keep our place of residence a secret."

"So was I." Janelle nestled close to Ross, "Let's stop at the shopping center. We need some shampoo."

"Do we have to? We could use some of your mom's."

"I know we could, but we're taking advantage of her as it is. I don't want to use up her soap, too."

"Okay, you're the boss," Ross agreed good-naturedly. He signaled and changed lanes, preparing to exit into the crowded shopping mall on the next block.

"How long do you think it will be before they catch Huxley?"

"I wish I knew," Ross squeezed her shoulders. "But I really don't think we have to worry about it as long as we stay at your mother's." He signaled again and pulled into the parking area of the mall. They walked hand in hand to the drug store. Neither of them noticed the brown Chevy that had followed them into the mall area; parking two cars down from their car.

Ross and Janelle pulled into Janelle's mother's driveway and Ross opened the automatic door of Delphine's attached garage with the control box Delphine had given them that morning, saying, "You might as well park in the garage, there's plenty of room. It's not good for your car to set out in the sun and Janelle won't have to worry about the deserted lots if she's getting into the car while it's still in the garage."

They climbed out of the car just in time to see the brown Chevy pass in front of the house, but they didn't give it a second glance.

Delphine was lying down and the house was quiet, except for the hum of the large fan that Delphine kept running in her room when she napped. The whirring noise of the fan covered the noises from outside of the house and allowed her to get a peaceful nap. Ross yawned and suggested, "Let's us take a nap, too."

"Good idea. This whole thing is beginning to wear on my nerves. It's nice to sleep. Your mind turns off and then you don't have to be thinking and worrying about everything." Janelle headed for the stairs and then whispered, "You did say we were going to sleep, didn't you?"

"Well...," Ross grinned at her.

Janelle smiled back, her eyes gentle and full of love. She couldn't resist a small dab of ribbing. "It's a good thing Mom's bedroom isn't right under ours, because then we'd have no choice but to abstain."

They tiptoed up the steps and turned slowly into their bedroom. Their progress was delayed greatly by the tangle of their legs as they kissed each other ardently. Ross reached behind himself to quietly close and lock the door.

When they reached the bed, Janelle pushed Ross backward and then allowed herself to fall on top of him. As his hands found the buttons of her blouse, Janelle sighed with contentment and surrendered all her thoughts to her love for Ross and the deep feelings that were pouring over her senses.

At supper that evening, Janelle filled her mother in on the events of their trip to the Duluth Police Station, "The guy we talked to, Detective Osmond, was real nice, but the guy at the front desk was a real loser."

The small television that Delphine kept on the counter in the kitchen announced the approaching six p.m. news and the room were abruptly silent. An enlargement of Jack Thomas Huxley's picture flashed on the picture tube and the announcer reported solemnly, "This man, Jack Thomas Huxley, is now wanted in connection with last night's murder of a Duluth man, Raymond Thayer Lock, which occurred on the south side of Duluth. Lock was a repairman for Brewer Construction Co. of Duluth and had been retained to repair a broken window at 1286 Bradley St. South. The residents of the apartment were not at home at the time of the murder. Jack Thomas Huxley is the same man that is a suspect in the murder of a seventeen-year-old girl in Toledo, Ohio. The girl has been identified as Penny Davis, from Toledo, Ohio. Police received information about the murder in Duluth from an unknown source; one, which we have been told, is very reliable. We will keep you updated on this bulletin as we receive further information."

Janelle sighed in relief, "At least they didn't give out our names again. The less we're connected to Jack's crimes, the better I feel."

Ross and Janelle cleaned the table while Delphine loaded the dishwasher. "We have to go over to Lars' place tonight, Mom. There are still a lot of small details to clear up about the wedding and Lars and Kate want us to help them put the finishing touches on the bouquets for the bridesmaids."

"Sure, you go ahead. I have some bookwork I need to finish up. Before I got into this business, I never would have guessed the real estate business involved so much bookwork. But I love it all."

"And it shows, Mom." Janelle looked around her mother's beautiful house. "Look what you've done for yourself in only two years. I bet you've got this place all paid for, don't you?"

Delphine laughed, her face showing her pleasure at Janelle's compliment, "Not quite."

"Anyway, see you later."

"You've got the key I gave you?"

"Yup." Janelle held out her hand to expose the key she held in her palm and then reached out and kissed her mother on the cheek. "Bye. Don't work too late."

"I won't. Have a good time," Delphine said as Janelle pulled the door closed.

They covered the short distance to Ross' brother's house in silence, until Janelle noticed that Ross was paying more attention than usual to the rear view mirror. She turned quickly and asked fearfully, "What's wrong?"

"Nothing. I thought maybe we were being followed, but the car is gone now." He squeezed Janelle's suddenly cold fingers, "I'm sorry I scared you. Guess I'm getting paranoid."

"Like me," Janelle said as she looked behind them again. "There's a car behind us now, is it the same one you saw?"

Ross glanced in the rear view mirror, "No, the one I saw was a brown Chevy, an old one. The one that's there now just came around the block."

"Oh." Janelle slid closer to Ross, her eyes worried, "You don't think that Huxley guy found out where we're staying, do you?"

"No, I don't. How would he find that out?" Ross' voice was strained and his anger was evident.

TAKE CARE

"I don't know, but you're the one who thought we were being followed." Miffed at his sudden anger, Janelle moved away from Ross and straightened in her seat.

"I'm sorry, Honey, I didn't mean to bark at you. It's just that I'm worried about you and mad at myself for worrying. I couldn't stand it if something happened to you. You know you're my whole life, don't you?"

"I'm sorry, too. I love you, Ross. I guess we're both a little on edge." Janelle cuddled back against Ross' muscular side and pulled his arm tight around her shoulders. "Let's make it an early night, okay? We can go back tomorrow night if we need to."

"I'm all for an early night. I can't wait to get you back to bed," he leered at her playfully and Janelle sighed with contentment.

"You're not the Lone Ranger with that idea," she laughed happily and reached up to caress his cheek with her mouth, leaving a trail of moist kisses across his cheek and down the open area above the buttons of his casual shirt.

When she stopped kissing him and leaned her head back against his arm, Ross whispered, "Don't stop now. I know a few good parking places that are not too far away."

"Ross! It's broad daylight."

"The better to see you with," he growled animatedly.

"Forget it! I don't want to be arrested for indecent exposure," Janelle laughed.

Ross sighed and then laughed with her.

At Lars' cute little bungalow, which he and Kate had purchased three weeks ago, they pulled into the driveway and shared a long, gentle kiss before they climbed from their car and hurried up to the door. Ross rang the doorbell and kissed Janelle quickly, just as the door opened and his brother greeted them with a warm smile for Ross and a quick hug for Janelle.

Janelle was still not comfortable with the easy, free way Ross' family hugged and kissed each other each time they met or parted, but she tried not to let it show, knowing the family didn't give the hugs or kisses a second thought. To them, it was a form of greeting; one that Janelle favored and was trying hard to accept as a way of life.

"Hi! We thought you'd never get here. My fingers are already sore from struggling with those small flowers," Lars greeted them.

Kate's amicable voice called from the kitchen, "Come on in you guys. This is fun." Lars' eyebrows rose in mock contempt as he led the way to the kitchen.

As they passed through the living room, Janelle's eyes roamed the room. She loved Kate and Lars' cute little house and wished that she and Ross were this close to getting married and having a home of their own. Kate and Lars were already making plans for their first child.

The living room was just big enough for a reclining love seat—with individual seats—and a short couch across from the consul television set, VCR and stereo hi-fi set that graced the shelves of a beautiful oak entertainment set. The carpet was a lovely mixture of light and dark blues and was plush enough to use for a bed. The first time Janelle and Ross had been invited over to see the house, Lars and Kate did not have any living room furniture except for the entertainment set. The four of them had lounged on the carpet, listening to music, eating popcorn and playing scrabble.

Janelle suddenly felt a deep ache for that evening, before their last trip to Ohio. *Why did I stop at that miserable rest area!* she cried silently, wishing with all her heart that the terrifying events of that trip had never happened. She turned her eyes back to the kitchen and firmly pushed the horrible thought of Jack Thomas Huxley from her mind; determined to have a good time.

The combination kitchen and dining room was larger than the cozy living room and the sliding door that led to a small rock patio gave the room an airy, comfortable feel; with enough room for Kate's mother's wedding gift, an exquisitely beautiful oak table, with leaves that could make room for at least eight place settings.

Kate had temporally covered the table with a white plastic tablecloth and the entire surface was covered with silk flowers.

Janelle raised her eyebrows in mock surprise, "I thought you said the finishing touches?"

"It is," Kate assured her. "We've already finished five of them and there's four to go."

Ross and Janelle enthusiastically joined Kate and Lars, carefully forming the dainty flowers into bouquets. The four of them bantered back and forth—Lars and Kate graciously refraining from any mention of Jack Thomas Huxley—and the evening passed more quickly than either Ross or Janelle had anticipated.

"It's eleven thirty already," Janelle exclaimed in surprise, putting the finishing touches on the last of the bouquets. "We've got to get out of here, Ross."

"It's early yet," Kate objected. "I have a pizza in the freezer and I don't know about you guys, but all this work has depleted all my energy and I'm famished."

"Yeah, good idea, Sweetheart," Lars put in. He gathered together the flowers while Kate headed for the stove to preheat the oven.

Ross and Janelle looked at each other questioningly. "It's up to you, Hon," Ross said.

"Are you hungry?"

"For pizza? Any day!" Ross said.

"Okay with me, too," Janelle replied. Lars carried the flowers to the spare bedroom and Kate went down in the basement for the pizza.

"I thought you wanted to get back early...," Janelle whispered.

"I did, but we missed early by over an hour and besides, I enjoyed myself; didn't you?"

"Sure. It was fun. That's why we both forgot the time," Janelle teased.

Ross and Janelle arrived back at Janelle's mother's house at one a.m. The house was dark, except for a small light that Delphine had left burning by the door that led into the house from the garage. They were both relaxed and tired as they pulled the car into the garage and Ross switched off the car's motor. They had forgotten to watch for anyone following them and the murders were far from their minds as they approached the lighted door.

Janelle silently turned the key in the lock and swung open the door. They turned off the light, locked the door and slowly made their way toward the stairs to the second floor.

"We should have left the light on until we had the light by the stairs turned on," Janelle whispered.

"I'll go back and turn it on," Ross offered quietly.

"No, it's okay, I'll find the way." Janelle took three more silent steps and abruptly collided with a chair that was not pushed all the way under the table. Suddenly the shrill barking of Muffy, coming from Delphine's bedroom, startled both of them. Janelle gasped in fright and then laughed at her jitters.

"Janelle? Is that you?" Delphine called.

"Yes, Mom, it's us. Sorry we woke you."

Delphine emerged from her room pulling on her robe and quieting Muffy with a pat on the head and a few soft words. "I would have been upset if you had made it all the way through the house without Muffy hearing you. I rely on her to warn me if someone should break in.... Speaking of break-ins, a funny thing happened tonight."

"What?" Janelle breathed in fear.

"After you left, I sat outside on the deck for a little while and this car kept driving past the house. I know it was the same one every time, because it had a big dent on the driver's side and a splash of white paint on the other side. You can't see the deck very well through the trees and I don't think they knew I was out there."

"What kind of car was it?" Ross asked.

"A black Ford. There were two men in it. It kind of bothered me. I'm not usually so jumpy, but with this murderer on the loose...."

"I'm so sorry, Mom. I didn't mean to get you mixed up in my troubles," Janelle sadly hugged her mother.

"Nonsense! What are mothers for if not to help out their kids when they can? I'll be all right...it was just strange," Delphine straightened her shoulders and laughed softly.

"They were probably just people admiring your beautiful house or out for a joy ride." Janelle wanted to put her mother at ease and besides, she was sure—she was sure, wasn't she?—that Jack Thomas Huxley would never find out where she was.

CHAPTER SEVEN

On the south side of Duluth, in the very back row of a junky, third class truck stop, sat a black Freightliner tractor, its trailer dollied down behind it. The eighteen-wheelers that surrounded it were old, giving the false impression that they were no longer in use. It was the perfect place to park a truck and not worry about someone wondering why the truck was there longer than was to be expected. The perfect hiding place.

The truck stop itself was large and well filled with eighteen-wheelers of every description. The food in the restaurant was good and it was cheap, drawing a large and continuous number of truckers and town folks as well. Picky patrons found it hard to ignore the general dirtiness of the place, the sloppy appearance of the waitresses and the sometimes-dirty dishes that their food was served on. These people did not return.

Ten blocks from the truck stop, a run down old motel was built back from the road. Tall Norway pines concealed the dilapidated row of individual small cabins, but the dingy office was noticeable from the road...if a person looked closely.

A man and woman who were in the midst of a roaring argument occupied number eight. The man stood nose to nose with the woman; although the woman was stretched to the very tips of her tiptoes and the man was slump shouldered, his back bent.

Jack Thomas Huxley and Ivy Muir were at it again.

He rubbed his bearded face with his grimy hands, "You stupid broad! Why didn't you just take care of them yourself?! God only knows where they've gone to and now we have another murder that the pigs are looking into. One day our luck in going to run out and the cops are going to come up with something we missed, some proof that will link us to the crime." He glared at the woman, "Think you're going to keep your lily white hands from getting dirty? Is that what you think? Well I'll tell you something, girl, you're as much a part of this as I am. You were the one who held down that girl while I raped her and strangled her. And you enjoyed every minute of it, too!

"And in Montana, you were the one that coaxed that girl into the truck. If we get caught, you'll be doing time for murder, too. And that's if we're lucky. If the Boss finds out we're having little parties on our own, we'll be dead!"

The girl propped her small clenched fists on her slim hips and shouted back, "There were two of them in that apartment. And don't you call me your family's names. I may be strong for my size, but I'm not stupid! Her boyfriend is young and built very good." She sneered at the man, her look saying that he was old and extremely out of shape.

The sun broke over the horizon and filtered through the thin drapes that covered the grimy windows, lighting the man's face. Five a.m. He was tired, it had been a long night. A stupid window repairman was dead for no reason and they hadn't found the witness.

He pulled his bulk up, straightened his shoulders and thrust a meaty finger in her face, "Don't give me that story, Babe. You could have taken on three of them if you had wanted to. What did you want, a little longer game? You wanted to play with them, didn't you?" He stared at her and his face broke into a malicious smile, "You wanted us both to play with them, didn't you?"

The girl's face turned red and she angrily shook her head full of dirty blond hair; ashamed of the fact that after all they had been through together, he could still make her blush. She admitted to herself that he was right. She had had a vague plan of returning that night with Jack and making it with both the man and the girl. They were so good looking, both of them. She thrilled at the idea of seeing them naked, naked and terrified.

She and Jack together would have stripped them naked...tied them one at a time, spread eagle on the bed, with the other one tied where he or she could watch every move on the bed. Ivy's body smoldered with heat at the thought. And afterwards, maybe Jack would have let her decorate their bodies with her small, wickedly sharp dagger, before she slowly cut their throats. In the couples' apartment they wouldn't have had to worry about spilling blood all over, like they did in their truck. Their truck was different; they couldn't leave evidence of their crimes in their truck. But cutting a person's throat was much more fun than strangling them. And the blood...the blood gushed out everywhere.

Her silence and her expressive face gave her away. Jack Thomas Huxley suddenly wrapped her in a hard bear hug and laughed loudly, "It's okay, Baby, maybe we'll still get our chance. We'll find them. Don't worry, we'll find them; one way or another."

He flopped on the bed, closed his lids over large black eyes, and was silent for so long that Ivy Muir thought he had fallen asleep. She stood looking down at him, clenching and unclenching her hands until her long, knife-like fingernails drew blood. "Well? What are you planning, Lover?" she asked impatiently.

Jack's eyes slowly opened and a lazy smile softened the lines of his fierce looking face, "In time, Sweetheart, all in good time. Let me think about this for a while. We both need some sleep anyhow. Two long nights of watching their apartment have drained me. How about you?"

Ivy shrugged, "I suppose I could sleep for a while, but I'm anxious to get my hands on those two."

"I know, Baby, I know, so am I." Jack turned on his side and seconds later Ivy heard his harsh snores. She pivoted to the shabby couch and dropped down on the sprung cushions. She turned a few times, trying to find a comfortable place among the wires sticking from the pillows, and then joined her comrade in sleep.

The short man in the back of the black limousine was holding binoculars to his small, black eyes. His thick, bushy eyebrows were furrowed in a deep, menacing frown. He already regretted the use of the limousine. The car was too visible, it stuck out too much. He didn't want people to remember him or his vehicle.

A quick call to his contact on the Duluth Police Department had immediately told him where the witness to Jack's murder was. "What's the story?" he had asked his contact.

"A window repairman was killed in the girl's apartment last night and she came in to report that she was sure the murderer had been Jack Thomas Huxley. She explained who she was, the girl who saw Huxley with the murdered girl in Ohio, but she wouldn't say where she was staying. Detective Osmond followed her when she left the station." The contact knew better than to ask questions as to why this man, code name Florida, wanted to know where the witness was.

Baxter Perry grinned, *money moves mountains*, he thought. "There will be a deposit made to your account. Stay handy, I may need you again," he had told the contact, hanging up without another word.

The witness' mothers' address was easy to find. He spotted the deck at the side of the house and the powerful glasses easily picked out Delphine's slim figure sitting behind the concealing branches of the wide spread oak tree that shaded the graceful lines of her house.

Baxter's breath caught in his throat and he stained to get a better look at the woman on the deck, but the car had already moved too far past the house. He lowered the binoculars, "Go around the block to your left," he ordered the driver. When they were on the next block and directly behind the house he had been observing, he said, "Stop here and wait for me." The driver pulled the car over and Baxter got out quickly.

He frowned as he entered the vacant lot behind Delphine's house. *It couldn't have been her,* he thought, shaking his head, *it's just too much of a coincidence.* Standing behind a tree, he trained the glasses on the deck again. *It is her! How lucky can a guy get?* He moved the glasses to the girl in the other deck chair. Janelle! So she was the one, the one who had witnessed Jack's murder of the little red haired prostitute in Ohio.

Baxter Perry lowered the binoculars and hurried back to the limousine. "Back to the hotel, Driver," he ordered, his voice harsh with barely suppressed excitement.

Unbelievable, he thought. *She was right here in Duluth all the time, with a new name. No wonder I didn't find her when I got out of prison. She changed her name and moved across the city.*

Baxter laughed aloud, making the driver eye him curiously in the rear view mirror. Baxter pushed a button and a bulletproof tinted glass panel silently closed the car into two separate compartments.

But you won't escape me this time, my darling ex-wife, not with the connections I have now. Money buys anything, even a cop who used to be honest. Oh how I'm going to enjoy this job. In Delphine's case, murder will be a pleasure. And to think I didn't want to take the time to come up here. He laughed again, ignoring the driver's eyes in the rear view mirror.

Suddenly the smile left his face and his lips tightened in fury as he thought about his ex-wife and his two stepdaughters. He wondered if both girls still lived with their mother.

He had never forgotten the velvety feel of Janelle and Allison's small bodies. He had been disgusted when Allison developed early in life. His enjoyment of her had come to an abrupt end, but Janelle had still had her immature body; even at the end of the long trial. If it had not been for Delphine, he could have continued to ravage that exquisite beauty until Janelle started to develop.

The little girls he took now had never compared to the thrill of having his own little harem available whenever he wanted them. Of course having his little harem had cost him the revulsion of having to put up with Delphine's body for three long weeks.

Baxter shuddered at the memory. He had had to drink himself into near oblivion before he had been able to pretend she was a young undeveloped girl, not a woman. It had been the last time he had touched an adult female body. But he had been willing to pay the high price for the enjoyment he received from Allison and Janelle. His only regret was that the girls had been too old when he and Delphine married. They had never learned to love and trust him like a real father.

Baxter's lips tightened, Delphine had been the sole reason his fun had abruptly been terminated and he had spent five long years locked behind bars. Baxter didn't want to remember that the girls were actually the ones who had brought the cops down on him. He was fueling his hatred for Delphine.

Suddenly Baxter smiled. The jail stint had been bad, but he had made some very lucrative friendships while on the inside. *My present business could never have been founded without the connections I acquired in the pen,* he thought. *And through those first most important connections came the connections that located the witness to Jack's crime. Little did I know that the witness was going to turn out to be my own little Janelle.*

The limousine pulled up in front of the hotel. Baxter's face hardened as the doorman opened his door. *Now she was going to pay, and pay dearly, for those five long years she took from me,* Baxter promised himself. He wondered how he had ever managed to put her out of his mind for so long. He had spent the first six months he had been out of prison searching for her; with no success. *Too bad that back then I was so full of hate that I didn't think of using my prison connections.* He shook his head at his own stupidity, *Delphine and her brats would have been out of the picture a long time ago if I had only used my brains!*

Well, first things first, he thought. *I have to locate Jack and his whore before they find Delphine and Janelle. Jack is good at snatching kids, but when there's murder involved, he and his whore get carried away. Better all around if I send them back to Florida and make sure he and his whore attend my big meeting. I'll take care of the witness myself.*

He dismissed the limousine driver and walked into the plush hotel lobby. "Call Rent a Car and have a gray or white Pontiac ready for me in an hour," Baxter instructed the desk clerk, dropping a ten in front of the man and never even thinking to say please or thank you.

"Would you like that put on your credit card or added to your bill here, Mr. Howland?" the clerk asked.

"Put it on my bill," Baxter told the man. Baxter laughed to himself. *Sure, put in on my credit card under my real name. Might just as well call the police and tell them I'm in town.* His lips tightened in anger as he thought about the restraining order that forbid him to set foot in the city of Duluth.

He returned to his room, pulled out the heavy Duluth phone book and began to make a list of the names and addresses of all the truck stops in and around the Duluth area. If Jack were in the area, as Baxter was sure he was, he'd find him. Jack and his little plaything had to be detoured back to Miami before the cops got to them. He couldn't have Jack singing to the cops about him.

And then he'd put an end to Delphine and her girls, with Jack Thomas Huxley as the immediate suspect for their deaths.

Daybreak had just found its way through the mini blinds of the bedroom, where Janelle and Ross lay sleeping, when Janelle sat up with a start. Her sharp moan pierced the stillness of the newly begun day. Ross turned over and stared up at Janelle, his eyes heavy with sleep.

"What? What's wrong?"

Janelle shuddered and goose bumps suddenly appeared on her soft bare flesh. Ross could actually see her heart hammering with some unknown fear and her breath came in short, wild gasps. Her fright seemed to have stolen her voice and her fingers clutched her throat.

Ross sat up, fully awake and startled by the panicky look in Janelle's usually soft eyes. He wrapped his arms around her shivering body. "You must have been dreaming," he cooed soothingly, trying unsuccessfully to pull her back into the warmth of the bed covers. "It's just a dream, Sweetheart. Everything's okay. I'm right here. I won't let anything happen to you."

"Ross...Oh Ross! What's happening? I just had the most awful feeling. My throat felt weird. I thought I was dying!"

"It's okay. It was only a dream," Ross murmured, tightening his arms around her and kissing her chilled forehead.

She shuddered again, threw her arms around Ross and spoke haltingly. "It didn't feel like a dream. My throat felt like it must feel to have your throat slashed. I could feel the blood running out of my body, flowing through my fingers. My life was slipping away...." She shook her head, "It wasn't a dream...it was more like a feeling...a premonition."

Ross did not believe in premonitions or anything else supernatural. He held her away from him, staring into her distraught face. "It was a dream, Honey. It had to have been. You don't really believe in premonitions, do you?" Alarm tingled in his fingers and raced up his arms, making him unable to stop his gasp of fright. "You must have been thinking about that maniac—that Jack Thomas Huxley—when you fell asleep." He pulled her still shaking body back into his arms, holding her as close as humanly possible. "It was only a bad dream, Honey," he repeated. "You're alright. Oh, Janelle, I love you so much, more than you'll ever know. I'll never let anything happen to you, I promise."

Janelle slowly shook her head from side to side; not knowing what she believed. Seeking reassurance, for herself and Ross, she forced herself to believe Ross' explanation, "You must be right. It must have been a dream. A terrible nightmare. At least I've never had anything even close to a premonition before, so you must be right. A dream...only a dream."

She felt Ross relax and breathe an almost silent sigh, full of relief. He drew her down in the bed and pulled the covers back over their naked bodies. They were silent, holding each other tight and trying to go back to sleep.

Janelle watched the blinking digital clock beside their bed, counting the seconds that slipped quickly away. Five minutes later Ross was asleep again, but Janelle continued to stare at the clock.

She tried to remember the time immediately preceding the terror she had felt when she had sat up in the bed. Had she been asleep? Was it only a bad dream?

She moved her head slowly on the feather pillow. *I was awake*, she thought in terror, *I remember looking at the clock just before that horrible feeling came over me. It was five-o-three a.m. I'm sure. I wasn't sleeping.*

Janelle moaned softly and cuddled closer to Ross' warm, relaxed body. *If it wasn't a dream, if it really was a premonition, what did it mean? Is Jack Thomas Huxley going to murder me? Is he going to cut my throat? Am I going to be his next victim? And because I had this feeling, this premonition, does that mean that there is no escaping my destiny? Does it mean that no matter what precautions we take, I'm going to die?*

Tears filled her eyes and slowly rolled down her cheeks to plop unheeded on the whiteness of the feather pillow she lay on. Then suddenly the fear receded and a strong determination filled its place.

I'm going to have to try and find him on my own, she thought. *I can't rely completely on the police. I'm just one more person on their busy rosters. Maybe that's why I had this sign. Maybe I was being forewarned.*

The clock read five fifty six. She turned over, pressed her back into the warmth of Ross' body and began to count sheep, picturing them jumping a fence, one by one; minutes later she drifted back to sleep.

When Janelle awoke again, it was already nine a.m. She jumped out of bed and headed for the shower, throwing her light summer robe on as she walked. She adjusted the water temperature and stepped into the warm spray. As the water rushed over her head and cascaded down her neck, she suddenly shuddered with reaction over the early morning episode she had experienced. *I won't think about it until after the wedding,* she thought, her hands wrapped protectively around her throat, *there's too much to do. I don't want the thought of Jack Thomas Huxley to ruin our fun at the wedding.*

She began to make a mental list of the things left to do. There was the final fitting of her bridesmaid gown, Ross' tux had to be picked up, she had volunteered to decorate a box for the wedding cards, Ross wanted to give their silver Mazda a good wash and wax and they were picking Allison up at the airport in Minneapolis at four p.m.

Darn! Why didn't we get up when I first woke up, she worried. *It's three hours to Minneapolis. We'll never get everything done.*

She shut off the water and reached for the soft, large towel that hung over the top of the shower rod. Briskly drying her firm body, she hurried out of the tub and quickly threw on her clothes. She ran a comb threw her damp hair and hurried back to their bedroom.

Ross was up and dressed in old shorts and a tank top. "Good morning, Sweetheart." He pulled her close and kissed her lips softly.

Janelle smiled warmly and hugged him, whispering, "I love you."

"I love you, too." Ross held her away and looked deeply into her eyes. "Are you alright?"

"I'm fine. I've decided to put all thoughts of Jack Thomas Huxley out of my mind until after the wedding."

"Good," Ross murmured, pulling her close.

A blaze of desire flowed through her and Janelle regretfully whirled away from Ross' embrace, "We have an awful lot to get done today."

"Yeah. I'll start with the car and when you're done with everything you have to do you can come and help me put the final touches on it. Okay?"

"Fine. I'll go for my fitting—I'm supposed to be there at ten—and then I'll pick up your tux. I'm sure Mom won't mind making breakfast alone and I should be back by ten forty five at the latest. The box for the cards won't take long. What time do you want to leave for the Cities?"

"If we leave by one or a little after, we should have plenty of time."

"Okay. We should be able to make that. We can have supper on the way back. I can't wait to see Allison! It's been more than six months since I saw her."

Ross smiled. Janelle's enthusiasm to see her only sibling again was touching. He kissed her cheek, started for the door and then stopped, "Are you sure your mom isn't going to mind your using her car?"

"I'm sure."

"Okay, see you later." He left the room and bounded down the steps.

Janelle applied a light coat of make-up, drew a faint line of lipstick across her lips and hurried after Ross.

Delphine was in her study, curled in an easy chair studying a long list of homes for sale. She looked up as Janelle peeked into the room, "Off for your fitting?"

"Yup. I'm picking up Ross' tux, too. I should be back by ten thirty or quarter to eleven."

"Okay, I'll have brunch ready. The car keys are hanging by the garage door. Drive careful."

"Yes, Mother." Janelle ran across the room and kissed her mother's cheek. "See you later."

"Goodbye," Delphine responded.

She watched her youngest daughter hurry out of the room and her eyes went to the window. Across the street and half way down the next block, the black Ford that had been parked there all night was gone. She had watched it pull away about an hour after sunrise.

Before dawn, in the dark of her bedroom, Delphine had spotted the car that was just visible behind a short lilac hedge. She had used her powerful binoculars to study the car and its occupants; sure that the car was the same one she had seen the night before as it cruised slowly past her house. The binoculars had not been able to pick out the features of the man and women in the car, but Delphine had been able to see that it was a man and a woman and the man's hair appeared to be very dark, while the woman's was lighter. Perhaps blond or a light brown.

She had watched them sipping on covered coffee cups and munching on sandwiches. She was positive they had been watching her house. She had called the police and five minutes later a patrol car had stopped by the black Ford.

The patrol car had not stopped for more than a fraction of a minute and then had continued down the street, turning away from her house; not even passing in front of her door.

The taillights of the patrol car were still in sight when the sharp ring of the phone by her bed had caused Delphine to jump in fear, but the precinct officer had reassured her that the black Ford was stationed at her house to protect them from a possible attack from Jack Thomas Huxley.

"But how did you know where I lived? How did you find out my name? My daughter did not tell you where she was going to be."

"I'm sorry, I don't know the answers to your questions. I was only told that the black Ford was definitely police officers on stakeout. I'll have the Captain call when he gets in."

Delphine hesitated and then relented, "Okay. Thank you. What time will that be?"

"He's usually here by seven a.m."

"Okay. Thank you again." Delphine hung up the phone and sat wondering how the police had found Janelle. Janelle had been very definite when she had told Delphine that she did not want the police to know where she was because the police in Ohio had somehow let the information regarding her place of employment and her home state and city slip to the press. Jack Thomas Huxley would not have had the slightest idea where to find Janelle and Ross—indeed he would never have found out their names—if this information had not somehow leaked out.

At seven ten a.m. a Captain Art Johnson called. Delphine grabbed the phone after one ring, hoping Janelle and Ross would not hear it. Captain Johnson had turned the phone over to a Detective Ken Osmond of the Duluth homicide squad and Detective Osmond explained that he had followed Janelle and Ross after their visit with him at police headquarters.

"We understood Janelle's reluctance to have her whereabouts known, but I felt that we could better protect her if we knew where she was. And we may be able to apprehend this murderer on his way to your house. I hope Janelle will be able to understand my side of this thing."

Delphine though about his words and then replied, "I saw your car cruising past yesterday and I told Janelle about it, but I have decided not to mention that it was the police. She's hoping it was only sightseers. I'm sure she would be very upset if she knew the truth."

"Thank you, Mrs. Kipp. We'll try to keep our surveillance most subtle. You can be sure we'll do everything in our power to protect you, your daughter, and her fiancé. Thank you again for understanding. Goodbye."

Delphine hung up the phone with a sigh. She wasn't sure if she felt better that the police knew where Janelle was or not. Since the police had found her so easily, what about Jack Thomas Huxley? Was there something they had overlooked? Would he be able to find her, too?

CHAPTER EIGHT

Jack Thomas Huxley awoke at eleven a.m. He turned on his back and hooked his hands behind his head. He slowly reviewed the few facts he knew about Janelle Richardson.

She was a truck driver; her home base was here in Duluth; she and her boyfriend drove for the Garvey Truck Lines out of Duluth.

He stopped. Garvey Truck Lines. He knew where they were located. He had picked up a load that was consigned through them and he had had to pick up the paper work at their office.

He thought a minute. Ivy had not been with him on that trip and her face was not plastered all over the local and national news. As far as he knew, the cops knew nothing about Ivy. He would send her to Garvey Truck Lines with a cover story. What? What reason could he have Ivy give that would convince them to give out the place where this Janelle Richardson was hiding?

Suddenly he sat up. *That's it!* he thought. *Ivy can say she is an old high school friend of that girl's and that she is only in town for the day and wants to see her old friend. She can say she went to the girl's apartment and she wasn't there. She can even give the address of Janelle's apartment; that will convince them that she really knows Janelle.*

He jumped from the bed and shook Ivy awake, "Hurry, I have a plan, but you have to get cleaned up. Get in the shower. I want you to be at the trucking company where this Janelle works at lunchtime. I hope you have some clean clothes along."

Ivy frowned at him, "Why at lunch time? What have you got planned?"

Jack roughly pushed her toward the small, grimy shower stall, "Hurry up! I'll explain on the way."

Ivy rubbed bar soap into her lank hair, uncaring of the residue that would remain to dull the finished product.

"Hey, Stupid, can't you even once do a good job on yourself?" Jack thundered as he passed the shampoo bottle to her.

She glared at him through the clear glass of the shower stall, but took the bottle and redid her hair, mumbling through the splashing water, "What's so darn special?"

Jack was throwing clothes out of their suitcase, growling his displeasure at the grime that coated the majority of the articles. He ignored Ivy's question as he searched, finally finding a pair of Ivy's jeans at the bottom of the case that were at least passably clean. The blouses she had along were in worse shape than the jeans. They were clean, or as clean as he could expect from the way Ivy washed clothes, but they were terribly wrinkled. "How do you figure you can present yourself as a decent person, and at a decent place, in these rags?" he shouted, holding out one of the offensive blouses.

Ivy had just stepped from the shower, "Throw it in the clothes dryer for a little while. That'll take the wrinkles out."

Jack stormed out the door, shouting, "You better be ready when I get back. And do something decent with that mop of hair."

Ivy dressed in the jeans he had laid out and took the hair dryer to her hair. The hot wind fluffed the hair and made it look almost stylish. She didn't have a curling iron, but she didn't look too bad.

Jack was back in five minutes. He looked Ivy over and growled, "Put on a bra."

"Why? I never wear one. They're uncomfortable," Ivy protested.

"I said you have to look decent. Now get it on," he ordered.

"Okay, okay." Ivy donned her ragged bra and slipped the thin material of the pink blouse Jack held out to her over her head.

"Come on, come on. Let's go. I've got a cab waiting."

Ivy looked at him, surprise in her eyes, "A cab?"

"We don't have time to walk back to the truck stop," Jack shouted. "And I don't want that truck to be seen either."

They hurried to the waiting cab, Jack keeping his head down, concealing his looks, and climbed into the back seat. Jack gave the driver an address that he hoped was no more than a block away from the Garvey Truck Line; still keeping his head ducked. "And turn on the radio. Country western."

"Right oh," the driver said, pulling away from the motel and turning the dial on the radio at the same time. As the music came on, Jack ordered, "Turn it up. I like that song."

Under cover of the music, Jack whispered his instructions to Ivy as they sped toward their destination, "Now, if you can't get someone to give you the address without making a fuss, then just leave again. We don't want someone to put two and two together and get four. They'd have the police on us before we could get two blocks. I'll wait down the block."

"Why?"

"Because, Idiot, they might recognize my face from the TV news," Jack snarled under his breath.

"Okay, okay," Ivy's dander was up. "I told you not to call me by your families' names. You sure don't mind them seeing my face."

"Keep your voice down," Jack ground out softly. "No one knows anything about you."

"You sure seem bound and determined to let them know who I am," Ivy complained.

"I'm just trying to find the girl," Jack consoled her.

The cab swung around a corner and pulled to the side of the street in front of a dingy, dilapidated apartment house. Jack was relieved, he had been afraid he might have given an address that was a vacant lot or something else just as bad. The driver would be sure to remember a fare like that and he didn't want to be remembered.

He shoved a five at Ivy, "Pay the man."

Ivy ripped the five from his fingers and shoved it at the driver, "Keep the change."

"Gee, thanks, Lady," the driver sneered, totally discussed. The fare had come to four seventy-five. He stared after the couple as they started up the crumbling walk to the apartment house. *Now why would anyone want to go to an apartment building that was scheduled to be demolished?* he wondered.

"Is he gone yet?" Jack asked, not turning around.

Ivy turned and gave the staring driver a dirty look. He quickly put the cab in gear and roared away. "He'll remember me for sure," she complained again.

"Doesn't matter. He wouldn't know you from Adam. Or should I say Eve." Jack turned and started back down the apartment walk. He grabbed Ivy's arm and pulled her after him. "Now remember what I said, don't make a fuss. If this doesn't work, we'll figure out a different way to find the girl."

They reached the end of the block and Jack sat down on a bus stop bench,

"Get going."

Ivy turned away without a word. Knowing Jack was watching her, she let her hips sway more than normal, grinning to herself at his expected reaction. *Jack may be tough,* she thought, *but he can't keep his hands off me. I have him wrapped around my little finger!* She laughed out loud and turned to give Jack a burningly coy look. He gave her the finger and shook his fist at her.

Entering the Garvey Truck Lines office, Ivy approached the only person that seemed to be in the room. Jack was right. The lunch hour was the perfect time. There would be only one person to identify her and the girl was frantically busy with incoming calls.

Another phone rang in the distance as Ivy smiled at the girl and waited while she finished the call and returned the already ringing phone to its cradle. The girl smiled apologetically at Ivy, picked up the phone and said, "Will you hold, please?"

When she looked up again, Ivy grinned brightly and said, "Good morning."

"Good afternoon," Erica replied with an answering smile.

"Is it that late already?" Ivy let her face fall. "I'm looking for Janelle Richardson. I've been to her apartment but she's not home. Are she and Ross gone on the road?"

"No, they're home. Or I should say they're in Duluth."

Ivy let her face light up again, "Janelle and I went to high school together. I moved to California three years ago and we haven't seen each other since. I called to tell her that I was making an unexpected trip home, but there was no answer." Ivy let her statement hang for a long moment and then sorrowfully added, "My grandfather died Tuesday and the funeral is tomorrow." *Jack hadn't thought of this dig for sympathy,* Ivy thought smugly.

"I'm sorry to hear that," Erica said.

"I hate the idea of having to leave again without seeing Janelle. Can you tell me where to reach her?"

"Sure." Erica pushed around some papers on the desk and came up with an address book. She flipped it open to the R's and frowned. "Guess Mike didn't write down her mother's address, but her name is Kipp. Delphine Kipp. She lives on the north side." She flipped through the small book some more, searching for the K listing. "Oh, here it is. That Mike. He's supposed to put relatives names in the same section with the employee's name. Janelle's mother lives on North St. Number 718," she smiled up at Ivy as another phone line rang. "You're lucky I just happened to overhear Janelle saying they were going to be staying at her mother's."

"Thanks! Thanks a lot. If you should talk to Janelle, don't tell her I was here. Now that I'm here in town, I want to surprise her," Ivy waved cheerfully and left the office. *I'll surprise her alright,* she thought with glee.

Erica returned the phone to her ear and glanced at the large round clock on the wall. Twelve forty five. *Mike should be back in a few minutes,* she thought, feeling the hunger pangs in her stomach.

The back door opened and then closed again with a bang. Mike walked into the room and Erica immediately got up from his desk. "Am I glad to see you," she said. "I'm starved and my appointment at the dentist is for two o'clock. See you Monday."

"Right. Any messages?"

"They're all right here. I swear everyone in the country called while you were gone. I don't know what's been happening in Bruce's office, but the phone has been ringing off the hook there, too."

"Thanks. See you later," Mike said as he crossed the room to Bruce Tucker's office.

Erica gathered together her purse and some papers she was taking home to work on over the weekend and quickly left by the back door. She was in her car and halfway to the restaurant she favored when she remembered the blond girl who had asked for Janelle. She shrugged her shoulders and dismissed the occurrence from her mind. Mike wouldn't care about the girl; she had nothing to do with business.

Ivy puffed up with self-satisfaction as she told Jack, "Got it! They're staying at the girl's mothers. 718 North St."

Jack's smile was wicked, "Tonight's the night, Baby."

Ivy's eyes glittered with excitement as she rubbed her body against him, "I can think of an interesting way to pass the time."

"Food first. I need my strength," Jack leered at her as they made their way back toward the truck stop.

"We're not going to walk all the way, are we?" Ivy pouted.

"Do you see a phone to call a cab? Got a better idea?"

"We can hitchhike."

"Sure, and maybe attract a pig," Jack berated her.

It took them an hour to reach the truck stop, where Jack sent Ivy in to get some food.

"Why can't we just go in and eat?" Ivy demanded.

"Because we're too close. I don't want to mess up our chances of getting that girl. Why can't you just do as you're told?"

"You're not my boss, Jack Huxley! I do as I please."

"Alright. Have it your way," Jack smirked and made his voice sound like a young, polite girl, "Will you please go and get us some food?"

Ivy jerked the money from his hand and headed for the restaurant. *One of these days,* Jack thought, his mean eyes following Ivy's progress to the restaurant, *one of these days I'm going to have to get rid of her.*

CHAPTER NINE

Ross and Janelle finished waxing their car and hurried upstairs to clean up for their trip to the airport. A half hour later they were back downstairs.

"Are you ready, Mom?" Janelle called excitedly.

"Ready," Delphine said from the study. "Be right with you. Do you mind if we take my car? There's a lot more room and I know you don't smoke in your car."

"Fine with me," Janelle glanced at Ross, knowing he had wanted to take their new car.

He smiled at her, "Fine with me, too." Delphine went to make sure the back door was locked and he whispered, "Then we can smoke, too. And we can show off our car when we get Allison home."

"You're so sweet. I love you."

"Same here," he said softly.

The trip to the Minneapolis, St. Paul area was full of fun. Ross drove, with Janelle beside him and Delphine in the back seat. They had all put Jack Thomas Huxley from their minds and they sang old songs, Ross' baritone making a perfect blend with the girls' soprano. They laughed at their mistakes and made up words for the words they didn't remember.

The airport was busier than usual with visitors arriving for the upcoming fourth of July holiday, but Allison's plane landed right on schedule.

Janelle ran forward when she saw her sister emerge from the plane. They threw their arms around each other and both girls broke into tears of happiness.

Janelle pulled Allison with her as she headed back to their mother and

Ross. Allison hugged her mother and then kissed Ross' check.

Ross smiled at the vivacious girls and marveled again at the likeness of the sisters. *If I didn't know better, I'd take them for identical twins*, Ross thought. *Janelle's eyes may be the tiniest bit bigger than Allison's and her nose a smidgen shorter, but the resemblance is nothing short of remarkable. Allison's hair is short and she wears it curled in the latest fashion, but if her hair were long like Janelle's, no one would be able to tell the two girls apart, especially not me.*

"I saw the news about that murder you witnessed, Janelle. I've been scared to death ever since!" Allison burst out.

Janelle's smile disappeared immediately, "We're worried, too. We're staying at Mom's."

"Why did you go to the police? You should have been thinking about your own safety," Allison accused.

Janelle sighed, "I had to, Allison, and you would have, too. I'd never have been able to live with myself if he had murdered some other young girl. The worst of it is that I'm responsible for the death of that repairman. If I hadn't gone to the police in the first place, that man wouldn't be dead!"

Ross took Janelle's shoulders and turned her toward him, his eyes full of misery. "That was not your fault, it was mine. I should have warned Homer."

"It was neither of your faults! You did the right thing by going to the police and you know you did," Delphine exploded. She turned to Allison, her eyes sad with unwanted memories, "You would have done the same thing, Allison. I was late with my teaching, but I taught both of you to go to the proper authorities when you need to."

"I'm sorry. You're right, Mom, I would have done the same thing. I shouldn't have brought up the subject at all. I'm sorry."

The three linked arms and headed for the baggage department.

"Have you two set a wedding date yet?" Allison quickly changed the subject.

"Not yet," Janelle smiled at Ross and winked. "I think Ross has gotten cold feet."

"Not me, Sweetheart. But you know we wanted to get a good share of our truck paid off before we start on bills for the big wedding you want."

"*I want!* I thought you wanted a big wedding, too."

"Well, I do want to be able to invite all our friends, but I don't relish the idea of standing in front of everyone to say our vows. I know I won't be able to remember a thing the priest tells us and I'll look like a fool," Ross blushed at having admitted his fears in front of Janelle's mother and sister.

"The priest will say the words first, Ross, and all we have to do is repeat what he says."

Ross gave her a long look, but didn't reply. He turned to Allison, "What about you, Allison, any special man in your life?"

Why did I say that, Janelle thought, angry with herself for making Ross feel stupid. He KNEW he wasn't going to have to remember the words of their vows.

"No...but I haven't been looking. My job has been taking most of my time."

"I'm sorry," Janelle whispered in Ross' ear. But Ross turned away without acknowledging her apology. Allison pointed out her suitcases and Ross quickly grabbed the bags off the revolving carousel when they reached the point where they stood waiting.

"Let's go out the back door. We'll be closer to the car," he said, leading the way through the throngs of travelers. A wary silence fell over the group as the women followed him. Janelle knew her mother and Allison could sense Ross' anger.

They had reached the car before Janelle broke the silence. "When are you coming back to Minnesota for good, Allison?"

"When a job opening as good or better than the one I have turns up," Allison said promptly.

"Are you looking for one?" Janelle exclaimed, climbing into the front seat while Allison and Delphine slid into the back seat. Her eyes followed Ross' stiff back while he put the suitcases in the trunk and returned to the drivers' seat.

"I've been keeping an eye on the market since I left. I wanted to surprise you and Mom, if and when I find an opening. Texas is so lonely without both of you," Allison admitted.

Delphine reached over and put her arms around Allison, "We've missed you, too, Honey. It's been two long years."

"Oh, I can't wait! I wasn't going to tell you until it was more sure, but I just can't wait," Allison's usually light voice was deep with suppressed excitement. Janelle dragged her thoughts away from Ross' hurt and anger and turned in her seat. "I sent my resume to Computers International in Minneapolis two weeks ago and I received an answer last Wednesday."

"What? What did they say?" Delphine broke in excitedly.

"I have an interview on Monday and, from the sounds of the phone call from a Mr. Nathan Orrin, I have high hopes of being offered the position," Allison announced triumphantly.

"Wonderful!" Delphine exclaimed.

"Great!" Janelle said. "Isn't that wonderful, Ross?" *If I can get him talking again, he'll soon forget his anger*, she thought. *That's one of the many things I love about Ross. He doesn't hold a grudge.*

"That's fantastic, Allison," Ross murmured.

Allison's face fell and she faked a pout, "You could sound just a little more pleased, Ross."

Ross smiled at her in the rear view mirror, "Sorry, my mind was busy with all this traffic. I'm happy for you, Allison, really I am."

"That's better. Now I feel welcome."

They arrived back in Duluth at eight thirty. Ross parked Delphine's car in the garage and Janelle and Ross hurried toward their car. "We might be pretty late, Mom. Everyone wants to go out after the practice and we won't have to get up too early because the wedding isn't until three o'clock. Want to come along, Allison?"

"No thanks. I'm beat, I'm going to turn in early."

"Okay. See you tomorrow. Bye." Janelle kissed both Delphine and Allison's cheeks and ran to the car.

"Good bye. You have your key, don't you?" Delphine called.

Janelle patted her jeans' pocket and waved, "Yup. See you later."

Delphine unlocked the door and watched as Ross and Janelle backed out of the garage. When they were clear, she waved and pushed the button to close the heavy, wooden overhead door.

She and Allison entered the silent house. Muffy immediately began yipping excitedly from the laundry room and Delphine hurried to let the small dog outside. Delphine changed her routine and took Muffy to the front door instead of the back; wanting to see if the police car was on surveillance, but not wanting Allison to know what she was looking for. Her eyes raced to the spot where the police car had sat the night before, but the spot was empty. She looked around, wondering where they could be.

No one was there. No strange cars. A few neighbors sat on their porches or walked along the sidewalk, enjoying the beauty of the early evening. The sun was falling toward the horizon in a red ball of glory and the day had cooled to a comfortable seventy-eight degrees.

"Mom? What are you looking for?" Allison asked, coming up behind

Delphine.

Delphine jumped guiltily and quickly turned back to her daughter, "Nothing. I was just enjoying the beauty of the sunset."

"Should we sit outside for a while?" Allison wondered.

"Let's. But let's sit on the deck. The mosquitoes won't bother us there," Delphine said. "Want something to drink?"

"Sure. Have you got a Pepsi?"

"Yup," Delphine reached in the refrigerator and retrieved a Pepsi, filled a glass with ice, got herself a cup of coffee and followed Allison out to the screened in deck. *It's still daylight,* she told herself, *that's why the police aren't there. Oh God, I'll be so glad when they have that madman behind bars.*

Delphine and Allison made themselves comfortable on the padded lawn chairs and settled in for a good catch-up visit.

When the phone rang a few minutes later, Delphine moved to get up, but Allison jumped to her feet and hurried toward the door, "I'll get it, Mom."

Delphine smiled softly; Allison had always loved to be the one to answer the phone.

Delphine sat up when she heard Allison's annoyed voice say, "Hello? Hello? Who is this? Hello?" Allison came back carrying the portable phone in her hand, a mystified look on her face.

"Have you been getting prank calls, Mom?" Allison looked worried.

"No...."

Allison shrugged, "Probably nothing important.... But whoever it was stayed on the line until I hung up, but didn't say anything."

CHAPTER TEN

Jack Thomas Huxley replaced the phone and grinned at Ivy, "They're home. The girl answered the phone."

"How do you know it was the girl?" Ivy asked, excitement gathering strength in her voice.

"Because I've listened to the old woman's voice on the recording often enough to know it wasn't her, Dummy. Who else would answer the old woman's phone but her daughter?"

"Don't call me names!" Ivy exploded angrily.

"Okay. Okay," he was silent for a long moment. "We need a car. We can't take the truck or a taxi to the scene of a crime. Especially not a crime we plan to commit and get away with," Jack roared with laughter at his crude joke.

Ivy did not laugh. She was in a state of high agitation. Her body was consumed with desire at the thought of getting her hands on Janelle and Ross.

"Where are we going to get a car?" she demanded loudly. "We can't just go and buy one, even if we had the money. They'd want your driver's license."

"Did you just figure that out? How smart of you," sarcasm dripped from his voice.

Ivy ignored the mockery, "Well you can't, can you? Even if you give them one of the fake licenses, what about your picture?"

"Oh for cripes sake, Ivy! How can you be so stupid? Next thing you'll be saying we could rent a car," he laughed again.

But this time Ivy didn't ignore his jeers. She was jittery with excitement and her anger exploded abruptly. Her hand streaked to her boot top and the slim, sharp point of her dagger was suddenly under Jack's chin.

Jack choked off his laughter and his eyes narrowed dangerously as he stared Ivy down. He knew better than to let even a small trace of fear show in his black eyes. Ivy feasted on fear, even the thought of it turned her on. Jack slowly rose to his feet and Ivy backed off a step, letting the knife fall to her side.

Suddenly Jack's hand flew out and he smacked her across the face, knocking her to the floor with the force of the slap. His voice was hard and flat, "That's twice you've pulled that knife on me and it better be the last time. If there's a next time, you better use it fast, because if you don't, you're dead. Understand?"

Ivy dropped the knife to the floor and threw herself against Jack's mammoth frame, "I'm sorry, Jack! But you make me so mad. Why do you always make fun of me?"

Jack violently pushed her away, his voice hard and menacing, "I asked you a question."

Ivy's face went blank, "What?"

"You will never pull that knife on me again, understand?"

"Yeah, yeah." She stooped to pick up the knife and Jack brought his knee crashing into her unprotected stomach. Ivy abruptly dropped to the floor, curled in a ball and gasped for breath.

"Now, tell me again. Do you understand?" Jack rasped.

Ivy choked and suddenly vomited tumultuously. Tears ran down her cheeks and she rocked slowly back and forth, holding her stomach with one hand while she wiped the back of her other hand across her mouth.

"Well?!" Jack unrelentingly demanded again.

"Yes! Yes!" Ivy gasped, anguish twisting her voice.

Jack turned away and reached for an open bottle of whiskey that sat on the small round table in the corner. He tipped it up and poured three long swallows down his throat. *I better plan on getting rid of her real soon,* he thought, watching Ivy writhe on the floor, *she'd be just stupid enough to attack me while I'm sleeping.*

Slamming the bottle on the scarred night stand next to the bed, he ordered, "Now let's get back to business."

Ivy clawed her way to the bed and pulled herself painfully up. She dropped onto the dingy, rumbled sheet and slowly raised her eyes to Jack. "If you ever hit me again I'll use my knife on you!"

Jack laughed, his voice thick with scorn, "The next time that knife of yours' will be turned on you."

Ivy dropped her eyes. She knew Jack was too strong for her. The only way she'd ever be able to get the best of him would be when he was sleeping or if she caught him by surprise, from the back.

Ivy considered the consequences. Jack gave her the excitement she needed and wanted. The excitement she was not willing to live without. Where would she find another guy that would help her kidnap, rape and murder people? She thought of all the bodies; girls, guys and kids. She licked her narrow lips and smiled greedily.

The girls were the most fun. They screamed, kicked and fought furiously for their virtue and their lives. Ivy loved the wild fear in their eyes. It really turned her on.

The guys were fun, too, but only when there was a girl with them. Their eyes were so full of pain while she and Jack tortured and raped their girlfriend or wife. Ivy loved that pain in their eyes. She always hated it when they were finished with the girl and started on the guy. The pain in their eyes turned to fury and then fear. The fear was exhilarating, but the fury made her mad, too. It took away the excitement and filled her with such rage that at times she had not been able to resist the forces of that rage and had ended the man's life before she had a chance to enjoy the fear that always followed the fury.

The kids were the Boss' thing...and Jack's...sometimes. Once in awhile they were fun, but most of the time she wasn't interested in them. Ivy had at times even felt sorry for the kids.

But the Boss, he was the one who *really* wanted the kids. Jack didn't touch the ones that they kidnapped for the Boss and he very seldom wanted to keep one for himself, but when he did, Ivy often felt sorry for the kid. At times she had even left the room or the truck, not wanting to watch the cruel way he raped them. Once, with a cute little girl who was only about two, Ivy had begged Jack to turn her loose when he was done with her. 'She's too little to tell what happened or what we look like,' Ivy had begged. 'Let's just drop her off on a back road. Please?'

Jack had not even dignified her humanitarian plea with an answer. He had turned his anger on the little girl, viciously snapping her neck, rolling down the window, checking for passing cars and tossing her body out the window like a bag of garbage, where it splashed into a rain filled ditch.

When Ivy hadn't immediately started the truck, he had barked, "What are you waiting for? Get moving."

Ivy knew the Boss was making tons of money selling the kids all over the world. He had often shown them the customer's written description of the child he or she wanted and one description she had seen had been from China. But the share the Boss gave to her and Jack was not enough. Not for the chances they took. She wanted more and someday she would figure out a way to get it.

Ivy shook her head in resignation. She needed Jack. She would probably never find another guy as good at the kidnapping as he was. This was the first time, in dozens of times, there had ever been a witness and she would never make it to the witness stand.

"Just don't ever hit me again," she muttered and quickly changed the subject back to the car. "Where are we going to get a car?"

"Steal one of course, what else?"

Ivy brightened and took a deep breath. Her eyes fell on the mass of vomit on the floor. She wrinkled her nose at the smell, "Let's get a different room, closer to the girl's mother's house. Then we won't need a car."

Jack eyed the vomit with disgust as he quickly changed into a black long sleeved knit shirt, "We could get a different room, but we'd still need a car. We have to get back to the truck." He moved to the door, stopped and turned back to Ivy, "We don't need a room. Pack up while I get a car. When we get done with the girl and her boyfriend, we're getting out of this stinking city anyhow."

He opened the door and then closed it again. "Think I'll get us a different truck, too. That girl gave too good a description of ours." He looked at his watch, angrily wondering why he was wasting time by filling Ivy in on all the details, "It's nine o'clock. I'll be back by ten or ten thirty, be ready."

"And then we're going to the mother's house, right?" Ivy's pale blue eyes sparked with hope and excitement.

"Right," Jack grinned at her and disappeared out the door.

Delphine and Allison stretched out on Delphine's comfortable, padded lawn chairs, sipped their drinks, and talked about the six months that had passed since they had last seen each other.

"No interesting men in Texas?" Delphine asked.

"No.... Well, maybe a few. There's a guy I work with that's real nice, but....," Allison shook her head slowly.

Delphine laughed, "But just not the guy, right?"

"Right. I went out with him a few times and he's lots of fun, but just as a friend."

"Good. If you had found a guy down there, you probably would never have wanted to move back to Minnesota."

Allison smiled, "I didn't want to move to Texas, Mom, but there were no job openings here."

"I know," Delphine looked at her beautiful daughter. "What ever happened to Curt Dempsey?"

Allison's smile softened and her eyes turned misty. Delphine suddenly realized why there had been no special man in Texas. "He's in Minneapolis. He works for Computers International."

"The place where you have an interview on Monday!" Delphine exclaimed.

"Yes. He's the one who told me about the job opening. We have been keeping in touch with each other."

"I see," Delphine smiled.

"I couldn't get him off my mind, Mom. I was angry with him when he wouldn't consider moving to Texas when I got that good job down there, but now I realize how he felt. He had no job waiting for him and he wasn't about to live off me.... He's too proud for that," Allison smiled and her eyes softened with love.

"Sounds pretty serious to me."

"It is. We want to get married next year," Allison admitted, her smile broadening.

"That's wonderful! I've always liked Curt. I suppose you'll live in Minneapolis?"

"Yes. Curt has convinced me to marry him even if I don't get the position at Computers International. He says there will always be other openings that are just as good paying and as prestigious, but in the mean time we are letting our lives slip past."

"You're only twenty seven, Allison. That isn't exactly ancient you know," Delphine gently reminded her.

"I know, but we want to be young enough to enjoy our kids. We want to be able to run and play with them, even when they are teenagers, like you did with us."

Delphine laughed, "Sounds good to me. How many kids are you planning on?"

Allison giggled in embarrassment, but then admitted, "I told him once, in front of his mother and dad, that I was going to have a dozen kids and he was outrageously shocked. His eyes got as big as saucers and he said, 'Not with me, you're not!' His folks thought that was very funny," Allison laughed at the memory. "But I really do want a bunch of kids! We finally agreed on a half dozen."

"Great! I'll love it," Delphine enthused excitedly. Suddenly her face fell, "But I won't get to see them very often."

"You can move down to Minneapolis, Mom. There's lots of real estate down there," Allison exclaimed.

Delphine smiled. Allison seemed to have been thinking about her moving to Minneapolis. She thought about it for a minute. "It's not impossible. The winters aren't quite as harsh down there either."

"Right," Allison hid a yawn behind her hand and glanced at her watch. "Think about it, Mom. We'd love to have you close. Well, it's almost ten o'clock and I'm beat. Do you mind if we call it a night?"

"Of course not. You go ahead; I'm going to sit awhile yet."

Allison rose gracefully and hugged her mother, "I love you, Mom. Goodnight."

"I love you, too, Sweetheart. Goodnight. Sleep tight and don't let the bed bugs bite."

Allison laughed, "You've said that since Janelle and I were babies!"

Delphine smiled as Allison disappeared into the house. She'd never forget the joy of her two sweet babies. She closed her eyes and pictured them as they were at three and one. She could remember chasing them around the yard, Allison screaming with joy while Janelle tried her best to toddle after them.

Her eyes moved to the side as a car slowly cruised past. Suddenly she remembered Janelle's horrifying dilemma and she sat up quickly. She searched the side roads for a sign of the unmarked police car she had seen that morning. Nothing.

Somehow, she was relieved. The absence of the police seemed to diminish the threat. Maybe they had caught the guy and there was no longer any need to guard Janelle.

Delphine picked up her empty coffee cup and slowly moved into the house. She closed and locked the sliding door behind her, automatically placing the wooden rod Ross had made for her between the frame and the movable part of the door.

She let Muffy out the back door and watched as the small dog happily sniffed around the back yard. Her eyes lifted, wandering over the darkness of the vacant lot behind her yard. The shadows moved softly in the slight breeze that had sprung up.

Delphine shivered, a chill of apprehension running down her spine. She called softly to Muffy and when the dog was in, she quickly closed and locked the steel door.

Shaking her head at her foolishness, she gathered Muffy into her arms and climbed the steps to her room.

Allison's door was closed and no light shown under it. *Sleeping already*, Delphine thought, *she really must have been exhausted*. She moved into her room, closed the door and quietly prepared for bed while Muffy settled herself on the foot of the bed.

Delphine glanced at the clock on her nightstand, eleven p.m. She had been in bed for almost forty-five minutes. She groaned, *why couldn't I get to sleep?* Reaching out, she switched on the bedside lamp and picked up her book and her glasses. *Might as well read if I'm not going to sleep*, she grumbled.

Five minutes later Delphine was sound asleep; her glasses still on her face and the light still softly illuminating the silent room.

Jack left the motel and walked slowly down the street. *There'll be no problem with the car,* he thought, *most people are in bed by this hour and there will be no alarm raised until at least morning. Maybe no alarm will be sounded for a week or longer, if I manage to find a car that isn't used every day.*

But the truck.... If he took one that the guy was in a restaurant eating, he'd only have a matter of a few minutes, or at best an hour, before the cops were alerted. And to take a chance on a truck in which the driver was probably sleeping in the sleeper left him with the possibility of being overpowered by a man who was bigger and stronger than he was. And he knew that some drivers slept with a tire iron next to them in the sleeper.

No, Jack decided, *I'll wait for a driver coming from the restaurant; I'll have less chance of having to confront two drivers, too.* He couldn't eliminate the possibility of a co-driver. But most important, Jack liked to judge his opponent's size and strength ahead of time.

He headed for the truck stop. Their truck still stood where they had left it two days before. Jack walked along the line of trucks, none of them looked familiar. He reached the dirty black Freightliner, unlocked the door and climbed into the driver's seat. He started the truck, waited for the air to build up, and moved the truck over one space. He would need a free shot at his trailer.

He grinned wickedly at the thought of the special accommodations in his trailer. The front of the trailer had four small, closed in rooms built into it. Each room was carefully vented to the bottom of the trailer, where the vents would not be seen. The rooms contained a small bed and a covered bucket served for a toilet. Heavy padlocks secured each door and stout bars closed off the vents, although their 'passengers' were always securely tied and gagged. They could not have the 'passengers' calling through the vents for help. And they had not thought of a way to make the rooms sound proof and still provide fresh air.

The back of the trailer was loaded with Styrofoam plates and cups. He had papers saying the load originated from a factory south of Chicago and he occasionally changed the destination according to the route he decided to take. Most often the destination read Miami, Florida, but for this unplanned detour he had changed it to Duluth, Minnesota.

Turning off the truck, he gathered all his and Ivy's personal items and anything else that might identify them to the police. Using a grease rag, he carefully wiped every surface inside the truck and then moved outside; keeping an eye out for any observers. Ignoring the cab itself, he concentrated on the doors, windows and the hood.

Finished with the time consuming job, he climbed back in the driver's seat and waited. Fifteen minutes passed, forty five minutes. And then he saw a lone truck driver moving toward the parked trucks in the back row of the lot. The man was small, not much taller than Ivy. Jack grinned. This would be a cinch.

He climbed from his truck and casually made his way toward the approaching driver. He nodded to the driver and asked, "Are you familiar with the Duluth area?"

"I've been here a lot of times. What are you looking for?" the driver smiled and lit a cigarette.

"Keefe Brothers Warehouse. It's supposed to be in Arnold, just north of Duluth."

"Yup. Arnold's only fifteen, twenty minutes north, that is after you get through Duluth. Keefe Brothers is on the main road into Arnold, on the right hand side of the road. You can't miss it."

Jack was irritated by the driver's use of the overused cliché, 'you can't miss it'. He wondered how often those same words had been said and how often the looker did not find the place 'he couldn't miss'. "What's the road number?" Jack asked, barely keeping his aggravation out of his voice.

"Let's see, what was that road number?" the driver wondered.

"I left my map in a truck stop back in Montana," Jack explained. "I should know better than to take it along in. That's not the first time I lost one that way."

"I've got a map in my truck. Let's go look it up," the driver offered helpfully. He turned and started toward his truck. Jack smiled and followed him.

"You drive alone?" Jack asked, managing to say the words conversationally.

"Yup. How about you?"

"I'm alone, too. Couldn't stand having another person along. Makes for problems about where you should stop to eat and which route you should take. Not to mention the snoring." Jack laughed, letting himself relax, now that his prey was within reach.

The driver unlocked his truck, climbed in and leaned into the sleeper to retrieve his map. "Come on up," he called, his back to Jack.

Jack was already in the truck. He pulled the door closed, extinguishing the overhead light. He wasted no more time. Reaching up, he locked his strong, bull like fingers around the small man's throat.

Anticipating very little fight, Jack was not prepared for the battle the man put up. His grip was broken and the driver was suddenly on top of him. Jack grunted in pain when the man's fist connected with his chin, but the blow was not strong enough to disable Jack. He expertly found the driver's throat again; this time using all his bullish strength. The driver's frightened eyes bulged out and his face reddened.

Jack kept squeezing, while the driver clawed impotently at his locked fingers.

Ten minutes later Jack dragged the body to the dead man's trailer. He opened the doors and was relieved to see the trailer was empty. Grunting, he heaved the body into the trailer and closed the door. Returning to his own truck, he took a heavy padlock from the sack containing his and Ivy's things.

A sudden voice at his elbow made Jack jump in alarm, "Hey, Buddy, you got a match?"

Jack quietly let out his breath and handed the man a full book of matches, "Keep them, I've got more." He turned his back to the man and climbed into the black Freightliner, closing the door in the man's startled face. The occasions were rare when a trucker wasn't willing and eager to share a few words with another trucker. The long haul could be a very lonely job when you drove alone.

Jack started his truck and watched the guy amble slowly across the lot and disappear into the second line of trucks.

Moving quietly and leaving his truck door open, Jack sprinted along the back of his line of trucks. He was in time to see the man climb into a bright red Mack and start the engine. He waited. He wasn't going to take the chance of the guy watching him in his mirrors.

When the truck slowly began to pull out of the lot, Jack returned to his chore. He locked the dead driver's trailer, dollied down its legs and pulled the sleek, light blue Kenworth out; backing it under his custom made trailer. He quickly switched license plates from the black Freightliner to the Kenworth and flung the Kenworth's plates into the sleeper of the Kenworth. Grabbing the bag full of personal belongings from the Freightliner, he locked the doors and climbed into the beauty of the ninety Kenworth.

"Full of fuel, too," Jack grinned broadly and pulled out of the truck stop. He headed for the North side of Duluth, looking for a place where there was room enough to park his newly acquired rig. Spotting a large grocery warehouse, he pulled around the block. The loading docks were empty and no one was in sight. He parked in the large truck waiting area and jumped from the truck; locking the doors and leaving the engine running. Carefully noting the address of the warehouse and looking for landmarks to guide him back to the Kenworth, he quickly walked away.

Six blocks from the warehouse, he found what he had been looking for. The house had the look of an older couples' home. A handmade, braided rug graced the doorway of the front door and two small, well cared for gardens of mostly decorative flowers adorned the well manicured front lawn. The unlocked garage door concealed an older model Oldsmobile.

He quickly hotwired the car, rolled quietly out of the garage and got out to close the door. With luck the car would not be missed for several days. Singing with glee, he headed back to pick up Ivy.

Ivy stood outside the door of their motel room, dressed in black jeans and a long sleeved black shirt that matched Jack's clothes. She had no desire to remain inside with the stench of the vomit. Her eyes moved back and forth along the road and every few seconds she checked her watch again. Eleven o'clock! Where is he? Her eyes narrowed. He wouldn't have deserted me, would he? No, of course he wouldn't, she reassured herself quickly. She lit another cigarette and forced herself to remain calm.

By twelve a.m., Ivy was frantic with worry. *He has deserted me!* she fumed. *What am I going to do now? No money and no transportation.* She thought of the money they had hidden away in a savings account in Florida. Jack had put the money in both their names, but he had the only card with which to draw on the account.

I'll go to a bank on Monday morning and see if they can help me, she planned, *but what am I going to do in the meantime? I don't even have money for food.*

She turned back to the motel room and picked up their packed suitcase; her face twisted with hate. *First I'll check out the truck stop. If he's not there, at least I'll be able to make some money screwing the truck drivers,* she consoled herself.

She started the long walk to the truck stop while her thoughts went back to the first time she had met Jack Thomas Huxley. She had had a whole truck stop to herself—having beaten and threatened every prostitute who entered her territory until no one bothered her—and Jack had been just another customer until she had had sex with him.

Jack had tied her in the sleeper of the black Freightliner, stuffed a dirty rag in her mouth and stripped her. Using a small dagger—the same one Ivy now carried in her boot—he had slowly craved her body full of tiny scratches, making her skin tingle with pain and become slippery with blood.

Ivy had been terrified at first and sure she was going to die. But somewhere in the midst of what started out as an ordeal, her terror had turned to excitement; an all-consuming excitement which Ivy had never felt before. She had been beside herself with passion and when it was over, she had decided that it would be more fun to stay with Jack than continue to work the truck stop.

Ivy's face softened and she laughed faintly. *And that's how I discovered the ultimate in thrills,* she remembered, *although I have to admit that it's much more fun to torture and cut someone else than to have myself cut.* She switched the heavy suitcase to her other hand and trudged on, cursing Jack for insisting they take a motel at least ten blocks from the truck stop.

Her face darkened, the rage returning with a rush. *And how am I going to find another guy like Jack?!* she wondered.

She looked up as a car pulled to the curb in front of her. "Jack!" she cried, as her eyes identified the man behind the wheel of the strange car. Joy and rage battled inside her, "Where have you been?"

Jack smiled cockily, hearing the happiness in her voice, "I knew you couldn't live without me, Darlin."

Ivy threw the suitcase in the back of the brown Oldsmobile and jumped into the front seat, throwing herself into Jack's waiting arms. "What took you so long?"

"I had a lot to do," Jack grinned with pride. "I got us this car and a real nice truck."

Ivy was not interested in the car or the truck, "Let's get going. I can't wait to get my hands on that girl."

"Don't you want to see the truck? It's a Kenworth with a big aerodyne sleeper."

"I'll see it later," Ivy impatiently replied. "Right now all I can think of is that girl."

Jack circled the block where Delphine lived, carefully checking the area. Delphine's house was dark and silent, as were all the other houses on the block except the one on the far end. "Looks good to me," he commented.

They left the car directly behind the house, where an empty lot was all that separated them from Delphine's house.

"Smear some of the dirt from the gutter on your face," Jack ordered Ivy. "You're too white." Ivy fumed inside at the tone of Jack's voice and the order, but she decided not to challenge his assumed authority.

Using the tall, thick trees to cover their approach, they moved through the shadows as silent as stalking panthers; their dark clothes making them nearly invisible.

Angling around the house to their right, they crouched beside the hedge of the house next to Delphine's. Ivy nudged Jack and whispered, "I didn't see that light on the second floor."

"Neither did I, but it's no big deal, we aren't going to make any noise going in. If need be, we'll take out the old one, too." He pointed and whispered, "The deck. Those sliding doors pop open with little or no noise or effort."

Ivy nodded silently. A stray shaft of silvery moonlight caught her eyes, illuminating their gleam of exhilaration and growing need. They moved forward slowly.

CHAPTER ELEVEN

Ross and Janelle were seated with Lars and Kate at Jerry's Bar in the middle of Duluth. The rest of the wedding party had finally called it a night and headed for their respective homes.

"It's late, we better head for home," Janelle said.

"Let's have one more for the road," Lars suggested. "It's not that late. It's only twelve o'clock."

Ross laughed, "You're going to have a pretty full day tomorrow, Brother. Sure you don't want to pack it in?"

"Right after this one," Lars smiled at Kate. "Tomorrow will come sooner if we can sleep right up till the time to get dressed for our wedding."

Kate's look was full of love. She reached over and kissed Lars on the cheek. "Most guys would be crying about their last night as a free man," she murmured softly. Janelle and Ross smiled, having caught every word she said.

"If I had wanted to stay a free man, I wouldn't have asked you to marry me, Sweetheart." Lars kissed Kate full on the mouth and Ross and Janelle applauded softly.

The jukebox was playing a sentimental song from the groups' high school days and Janelle couldn't resist the urge to dance to the hauntingly beautiful melody. "Want to dance?" she asked Ross.

Ross took her hand and pulled her to her feet, "With you? Any day, all day, everyday."

Janelle smiled, knowing that if the threat of Jack Thomas Huxley wasn't hanging over her, she would be the happiest girl in the whole world. "I love you too," she whispered.

They moved out onto the crowded dance floor and let the music fill them. Out of the corner of her eye Janelle saw Lars and Kate join them on the floor. *Darn I envy them!* she thought. *I wish we could have made it a double wedding.* She laughed to herself, wondering if it was possible that only a short two years ago she had made up her mind to stay single. She had not wanted to be tied down to any one man. At least that was what she had told herself. In her heart she knew that she was afraid of marriage and having kids. What if the guy she picked pulled what her stepfather had? Would the kids tell her? Would she believe them if they did? She had heard of cases of child abuse where the mother didn't believe her husband would do anything like that and the abuse had continued for years and years.

What if she herself abused her kids?

She shuddered and Ross' arms tightened around her. "Honey? What's wrong?"

"Nothing. I just had a chill. They've got the air conditioning turned pretty low." Janelle hadn't told Ross of her hidden fears and she didn't think she ever could. What would he think of her? Could he continue to love a woman who harbored such dreadful thoughts as hers'?

On the way back to her mother's house, Janelle cuddled close to Ross and asked, "What was your childhood like?"

Ross frowned at her question. "What do you mean? I've told you almost every detail of my childhood." They had spent many, long happy hours reminiscing about their childhoods while cruising down the highways and byways of the United States.

Janelle hesitated, wondering how to vocalize her fears, wondering if she should say anything at all. "I don't know. I guess.... Well, did you have any real bad experiences?"

"You mean like yours," Ross said softly.

"Yes...," Janelle haltingly admitted.

"No, Janelle, nothing like that ever happened to me, thank God. My father and mother may not have been the picture book perfect parents, but Lars and I loved them and they loved us. Why are you asking?"

"I don't know...I just wondered." Janelle shook her head dismally, wondering why she was bringing this up now. Was she getting cold feet? Was she worried about Ross? Or was she really worried about herself? Would she abuse her kids? Would she follow in her stepfather's footprints?

Ross suddenly thought he knew what was on her mind. He had heard the statistics on sons and daughters following in their abnormal parents' footprints. Anger made his words harsh, "What are you suggesting, Janelle?"

Janelle sat up quickly. Ross' voice did not conceal his obvious anger and hurt.

"Nothing! I'm not suggesting anything, Ross."

Determined to have this out in the open, Ross asked, "You were wondering if Lars and I were abused because you're afraid if we were that I'll abuse my children. Isn't that right?"

Janelle slumped down on her side of the seat. She didn't deny Ross' accusation. "The one I'm really worried about is me, Ross," she murmured softly.

Ross was shocked by her answer. He pulled the car to the side of the street. His anger evaporated as quickly as it had risen. He wrapped his arms around Janelle and pulled her close.

"I've heard of the many cases where kids who were abused end up abusing their own kids, Ross. I don't want to be one of those parents. I can't stand the thought of hurting my kids the way I was hurt." Janelle broke into sobs and pulled away from Ross. "Maybe we shouldn't get married, Ross."

"Janelle, we are going to get married. That's final. No ifs, ands or buts about it. Okay?"

Janelle sniffed back her tears and nodded, vastly relieved by Ross' trust in her. She had finally faced her fears and shared them with Ross. They didn't seem as bad now and Ross still loved her, still wanted her.

"I'm not one bit worried about you abusing our kids, but if you're still having these fears, why don't you go back to your councilor?" Ross suggested.

"Maybe I will, but I feel a lot better now that I've admitted all this to you. I was scared to death if you knew I doubted myself, you wouldn't want to marry me."

"Honey, you could never talk me out of marrying you. We may have our disagreements, and maybe even a few knock down fights, but I will never stop loving you," Ross promised. He put the car in gear, pulled out into the street and headed for Delphine's house. Janelle cuddled close to him and silently wished this feeling of doom she was having would go away.

Baxter Perry pulled into the fourth, and last, truck stop on his list. At the last minute he had decided to include any large warehouses in the area. Jack just might be smart enough to stay away from truck stops, especially since the cops knew the crime had taken place in a black Freightliner. What better place to park a seventy-foot long rig than a truck stop? The cops were sure to be checking the truck stops.

He had checked three different warehouses along with the three truck stops.

The third warehouse had presented a disturbing problem. With the amount of business being transacted at all hours of the day and night, with trucks going in all directions, he had had to drive around the lot for too long a time; making sure he had checked all the trucks. The dock foreman had stopped him and had asked for his identification and his reason for being there. Baxter had had to show the man his fake driver's license, showing his name to be a Mr. Alan Howland from Miami, Florida.

"What are you doing here, Mr. Howland?" the foreman wanted to know.

Baxter thought quickly, "I'm on vacation. I'm a dispatcher in Miami and one of our drivers was supposed to deliver here. I was hoping to catch up with him, he's a good friend of mine."

The foreman frowned, looking closely at Baxter, "We don't get much freight from Florida and I'm sure we aren't expecting any today."

"Oh, the load isn't from Florida, it's from Chicago," Baxter quickly amended his story.

"Oh. Yes, we have a number of loads from Chicago being unloaded right now. What kind of tractor does your friend have?"

Baxter was getting nervous. The guy was sure to remember him if there were any questions later. He glanced down at his list of warehouses and then pointedly looked at the name of the warehouse he was at. "I'm at the wrong place! No wonder I couldn't find him. Thanks anyway. Sorry I bothered you." Not waiting for the foreman's answer, Baxter quickly put the car in gear and headed for the exit. Watching the foreman in his rear view mirror, he saw the man write down his license number.

Swearing aloud, Baxter had decided to forget about the warehouses.

He wrinkled his nose at the sight of the dirty, unpaved lot of the truck stop and the cruddy looking restaurant. *Just the type of place Jack would pick*, he thought. He drove slowly along the long lines of trucks, stopping at every black truck and checking the license plate. Baxter did not know the difference between a Freightliner and a Mack.

At the back of the lot he came across the black Freightliner with no license plate. He stared at the truck, matching the name on the door with the name he knew was on Jack's truck. *It's his. I'm sure it's his,* he thought.

Baxter got out of his white Pontiac and moved slowly over to the truck. He tried the doors. They were locked. And no trailer, he thought. He's dumped it! Jack has gotten himself a different tractor.

He turned the car around and slowly started for the exit. Suddenly he noticed the trailer without a tractor. He nodded, *that's where Jack got his truck. I'd be willing to bet the driver of the missing tractor is in that trailer, deader than a doorknob.*

Baxter slowly headed back to his hotel. As he passed the Glensheen mansion, he shook his head. He had been lost so many times and had covered so many of Duluth's streets, that he was beginning to feel like the native he had been years ago. It was after midnight and he was beat.

He thought about Jack and Ivy. If they had switched trucks, they would be ready to make their move against Janelle. Baxter wouldn't see them again unless they managed to completely elude the police and were ready to start bringing kids to him again.

Baxter wanted them back in Florida, but *before* Jack attempted to wipe out Janelle. He needed Jack for a decoy, someone Janelle and Delphine's murder would be blamed on.

And he didn't want Jack to pick up any more kids. Baxter was very superstitious. He had not thought of retiring before the night he left Miami for Duluth, although he had years ago made plans to insure the complete disappearance of his illegal business and his employees when he did decide to retire. Now he was sure that his thoughts of retirement meant that his luck had run out and if he continued with his business, the police would catch up with him.

Baxter had pulled into the parking lot of the hotel when a sudden thought struck him. He hadn't been able to find Jack and Ivy, but if they had discovered where Janelle was staying, his best bet was to catch them at Delphine's house. If they didn't show up, he'd take care of Delphine and Janelle and head back to Florida. Jack would hear about the witness being murdered and he'd guess who the murderer was. He'd come back to the warehouse.

Baxter parked and quickly went to his room to change shirts, collect a lightweight jacket and his gun with the silencer. He'd wait in the vacant lot behind Delphine's house until close to daybreak. If Jack showed up, he'd detour him back to Miami while he, Baxter, took care of the witness *and* her mother. This was one task he felt he was going to thoroughly enjoy.

Jack took the small crowbar from his back pocket and inserted it between the sliding door and the doorframe of Delphine's house. He pried gently and the door gave slightly but did not open. Jack sworn under his breath and Ivy whispered urgently, "Hurry up. I can't wait."

"Shut up," Jack ordered as he pried harder. The door lock had snapped easily with the first thrust, but the door refused to budge. Jack eyes fell to the inside of the door's slide area.

"She's not so dumb," he whispered. "She's got a rod holding the door closed."

Ivy peered over his shoulder, "Well, use your glass cutter." At the sound of a car, she checked the street. "Get down!" she warned. They fell flat on the deck as a car rolled quickly past. When it was gone, Jack rose to his feet and backed away from the sliding door.

"Use your glass cutter!" Ivy's fierce whisper cut the darkness.

Jack grabbed her sleeve and pulled her off the deck, "That door has double glass, Stupid."

"Don't call me names," Ivy warned, her voice rising with anger.

"Shut up! Come on, we'll try the back door." They quietly made their way back to the rear of the house and crept up to the back door.

Jack ran his fingernails over the door, "It's a steel door and this side window is double glass, too."

"Let's go to the front door."

"No. Too much chance some neighbor who can't sleep'll spot us. We'll have to go through a window." He bent and examined the double hung window close to the back door. "Too small," he muttered.

"I can get through there," Ivy offered.

"No. We go in together. If you trip on something and wake the dames up, they'll have the police on the phone before you can let me in."

Ivy didn't reply. She started for the side of the house opposite the sliding door that had fouled up their plans. Jack followed her. "Here! An open window."

"Good," Jack snickered. "Makes getting in easy as pie." The open, crank out window was large enough for a man to pass through without too much trouble. Jack quickly cut the screen and moments later the two were on the basement floor of the three story house. Jack pulled out a small penlight and they moved soundlessly across the plush carpet of Delphine's recreation room to the stairs that led to the main floor.

"Stay to the edge of the steps. We don't want them to squeak and give us away," he mumbled quietly.

They made it to the main floor and moved silently through the openness of the kitchen, dining room and living room area, searching for the bedroom. They passed the first floor bathroom and approached a closed door.

Jack gripped the door, keeping pressure against the hinges, and slowly eased it open. The door moved silently on well-oiled hinges. The bedroom was empty.

They slowly backtracked to the stairs that led to the second floor. Jack inched along the wall, testing each stair before putting his full weight on the step, ascending at such a slow rate that Ivy wanted to push him quickly forward. Her breathing quickened until she was panting and she could barely contain her elevated excitement.

At the top, Jack shown his light on the four doors that faced them; two were open, one showing it to be another bathroom. He signaled Ivy to stay where she was and he moved to the second open door. It was another bedroom, with a suitcase on the cedar chest at the end of the bed. No one was in the room.

Jack backed away and approached the first closed door. He gave Ivy a black warning look and slowly turned the doorknob. The door swung silently open.

Allison was sleeping soundly on the bed. Jack grinned, thinking he had found his witness, completely unaware of the fact that he had found Janelle's sister, not Janelle. He signaled Ivy and when she reached him, he whispered in her ear, "Keep her quiet."

Ivy moved toward the sleeping girl, a wicked grin lighting her face.

Jack moved more quickly now. He was sure the house was empty except for the woman and her daughter. He wondered briefly where the boyfriend was, but it didn't matter. The boyfriend hadn't seen him, just the girl.

He opened the second closed door with a confident flourish and jumped with surprise when Muffy jumped to her feet and set up such a wild commotion that Jack was sure the noise would wake all the neighbors within a five-block radius.

Delphine sat up with a start, knocking her book to the floor. At the sight of Jack, she screamed in fear. Jack was on her in seconds. His beefy right hand slammed across her head, momentarily stunning her and causing her to fall back on the pillows.

Muffy continued her savage barking until Jack clubbed the small dog with his crowbar. Muffy abruptly slumped to the bedspread and blood immediately began to drip from her open mouth. Her eyes slowly glazed over.

Delphine had recovered quickly and she opened her mouth to scream again. Jack instantly shoved a balled rag into her mouth and grabbed her hands, rapidly securing them with a thin nylon rope he had pulled from his pocket.

Ivy had reached Allison's bed before the noise from Delphine's room could awaken her. She clamped a small hand across Allison's mouth and held her dagger to the girl's throat, stabbing the skin painfully as a warning to Allison to remain silent.

Allison's eyes widen in terror as she stared up at Ivy's dirt smeared face and crazed blue eyes.

Ivy pulled a dirty rag and a length of nylon rope from her pocket. She forced Allison's mouth open and pushed the dirty rag deep into her throat. Allison was terrified at the small women's strength when she pulled her arms in front of her and tied them tightly with the nylon rope, breaking the tender skin with the tautness of the rope.

Allison's eyes rolled in fear as her mother's scream cut through the riotous noise of Muffy's barking.

Ivy pulled the girl to her feet and pushed her through the door toward Jack. She held the dagger in her hand and prodded Allison with it when she hesitated outside her bedroom door.

Jack signaled Ivy into the older women's room. "Where's your boyfriend?" he demanded of Allison. Allison shook her head in confusion and mumbled behind her gag.

Delphine's eyes widened with fresh horror. She knew now who the man was and why he looked so familiar. She had seen his picture on TV many times.

"It doesn't matter. You're the one who saw me; I'd recognize you anywhere, even with the shorter hair. Your boyfriend didn't see me. Throw her on the bed," he told Ivy.

Allison abruptly realized that this man must be the man Janelle had seen in the Ohio rest area. He must think I'm Janelle! Allison was suddenly sure that she and her mother were both going to die.

Ivy pushed Allison down on the bed. Jack looked at Ivy, "We're going to have to skip all our little fun and games, Darling. With the noise that yapping dog made, it's best we make short work of this and get out of here. Slit their throats and let's go."

"But Jack, I...," Ivy whined.

"Do it, Ivy! Let's move," Jack barked, taking a step toward her.

Ivy turned back to the two terrified women. Allison could see by the women's dispassionate eyes that their time on this earth was over. Both women closed their eyes and began to pray....

Baxter Perry stood next to a tree in the deserted lot behind Delphine's house. He had arrived just in time to see Jack and Ivy disappear into the open ground floor window. *How did they find out where the girl was staying?* he wondered, thinking of the time he could have saved by just staking out Delphine's house.

He moved quickly across the alley and silently entered the house by the same window that Jack and Ivy had used. He carefully removed his gun from his belt and screwed on the long, black silencer while his eyes adjusted to the difference in darkness from outside. He was part way up the first flight of stairs when Muffy's wild barking broke the stillness.

Now he had the cover of the noise from upstairs to conceal any noises he made. He hurried toward the sounds, anxious to have this whole business over with and be clear of the house.

Baxter swore under his breath, Delphine's dog is making enough noise to wake the dead! He had no desire to be returned to prison. Jack must not talk to the police.

Mounting the second flight of stairs, he saw Ivy and Jack through the open door at the end of the hall. Baxter recognized Delphine as Ivy moved around the bed and grabbed her by her hair, forcing her head back. Delphine jerked to the side and tried to roll away from Ivy's advancing blade. Ivy cackled loudly, the sound a perfect mimic of a TV show's caricature of a witch, and easily pulled her back. Delphine's terror stricken eyes rolled back in her head and she crumpled to the bed unconscious.

Baxter hurried forward and called out softly, "Ivy! Jack!" He did not want his vengeance denied him.

Ivy dropped Delphine's limp head back on the bed and spun around in stunned surprise.

Jack turned to the doorway, his mouth open in shock. Immediately recognizing Baxter standing in the shadows, he stammered, "Wh...what are you doing here, Boss?"

Baxter entered Delphine's bedroom, casually keeping his gun ready, but down at his side. Jack did not have a gun. "I heard about your bit of fun in Ohio," Baxter said, his eyes swept over Allison and Delphine before returning to fasten on Jack, "and the witness you left behind. I came to make sure the witness was silenced."

Allison's eyes gave away her terror, but Baxter wasn't looking at her.

Baxter Perry! What was he doing here? she screamed silently. Of one thing she was sure, he wasn't here to help her or her mother.

Jack had seen the recognition in the girl's eyes. He frowned when she cringed and backed slowly away as Baxter entered the room. Where did this girl know Baxter from? Jack quickly turned his attention back to Baxter, "That's what we were just going to do, Boss."

"So I see. But it turns out these two ladies have a special place in my heart. We happen to be well acquainted. I want you and Ivy to get your butts back down to Florida. There's going to be a big meeting as soon as everyone gets in. Lots of money, big bonuses for everyone." Baxter kept his cold gaze leveled on Jack and continued, "No shopping on the way, just get back to the warehouse as quick as you can. I'll take care of your witness and her mother. Do you understand?"

Jack glanced at Ivy, "Fine. The bonus sounds good. We're on our way. See you back at the warehouse." He turned and started out of the room. Ivy followed him, throwing deadly looks in Baxter's direction.

Baxter ignored Allison and Delphine. He watched as Jack and Ivy headed down the stairs. Silently falling in behind them, he observed their exit out the back door. Jumping down the rest of the steps, Baxter slipped up to the window beside the back door. His black, broody eyes followed them as they hurried through the vacant lot and disappeared down the street.

Allison's eyes were wide with terror. Her mother had not moved. She scrambled to the side of the bed and pulled the gag from her mouth, hoping the added oxygen would help to revive her.

Praying she would reach the phone and be able to complete her call for help before Baxter returned, Allison veered to the nightstand beside Delphine's bed. With her hands tied in front of her, she easily dialed 911.

Janelle and Ross drove into the driveway at Delphine's house. "Since you didn't want to take the opener, are you going to open the garage?" Ross teased Janelle.

"Let's leave it here," Janelle said, yawning tiredly. "Mom's light is still on. I bet she fell asleep reading. If we open the garage door, it'll wake her up again. Nobody is going to bother it in this neighborhood and I'm beat."

"Fine with me," Ross said, opening the car door. They stepped from the car and hurried up to the front door.

Baxter had reached the top of the steps from the recreation room when he heard the car doors slam. He stopped in his tracks and listened intently. Seconds later he heard the key in the door.

Suddenly Baxter panicked. He didn't know who to expect at the door and he didn't want to take any chances on being returned to prison.

He bolted down the steps and was half way down to the recreation room when Janelle stepped in the door, Ross close behind her, and flipped on the light.

Janelle immediately saw and recognized Baxter as he turned the corner to the basement recreation room. Her heart flew to her throat and she instinctively pulled the door closed again.

"It's Baxter!" she shouted in horror.

Ross was shocked. He had seen the man on the stairs, but he hadn't known who he was until Janelle told him. Seconds rushed by as he stared at Janelle uncomprehendingly. Baxter Perry: the man who had violated Janelle and stolen her happy childhood.

He reached around her, trying to reopen the door.

But Janelle fought against Ross' struggles to reopen the door, holding the steel door closed with all her might. "No! You can't go in! He went down into the basement and I saw a gun in his hand," she cried.

Ross recoiled from the door at the mention of a gun. He hadn't gotten that good a look at the man and he hadn't seen the gun. He grabbed her hand and pulled her toward the neighbor's house; intending to use their phone. "Hurry! We've got to call the police," he whispered.

"Wait," Janelle's voice had also dropped to a whisper. "There's a phone in the garage." She took the key she still held in her hand and shakily tried to insert it into the lock.

Ross took the key from her trembling hand and quickly unlocked the door. The phone hung right next to the door. He grabbed it up and dialed 911 before he realized that there was conversation on the line.

Allison's voice was shouting, "Hurry! Please hurry. He'll be back in a minute and he's going to kill us!"

Ross didn't wait to hear more, he didn't want to slow down the proceedings Allison's call had put into motion. He returned the phone to the hook and told Janelle, "Allison's calling 911."

"What should we do?" Janelle was sobbing.

"I'm going in there. You stay here," Ross said.

At that moment they both heard the sound of approaching sirens. Seconds later the sirens were right on top of them. They both rushed out the garage door and were met by two police cars; four officers jumped out and ran toward them.

Janelle didn't wait for their questions, "There's a man with a gun in the house and my mother and sister are in there!"

The officers slowed, pulled their weapons, and cautiously started for the house; directing each other with silent arm and head movements. Ross and Janelle trailed behind them, disregarding the danger that still lurked inside the house.

Two officers circled the house and approached from the rear, while the other two waited briefly for the men to reach the back of the house and then entered the front door, calling loudly, "Police!"

They ducked in the door and slid quickly to the sides, looking for cover of any kind. The room was wide open; the only available cover was the kitchen counters and the living room furniture.

Suddenly Allison's voice came from the top of the stairs, "Up here!"

Both officers ducked at the sound of her voice and pointed their guns toward her.

Allison backed away and threw her hands up, "I don't know where he went."

"He's not up there?" one officer asked.

"No, he followed the man and woman that were here and he never came back," Allison's voice was squeaky with fear and anguish.

Janelle was right behind the officers, "I saw him go down into the basement, but I don't know if he stayed there. When I saw the gun, I pulled the door closed again."

"Good move. Did you see anyone leave the house?" the officer asked

Janelle.

"No," Janelle replied, "If he left the house, he didn't come around this way."

Allison called from the stairs, "Can I go back up by my mother?"

"Sure, but don't come down until we're sure the house is clear. I think the man's gone, but we have to make sure," the heavyset officer said. The two men made a quick search of the main floor and then started cautiously down the steps to the recreation room.

Janelle and Ross had stopped just inside the door, but suddenly Janelle couldn't wait another minute to make sure her mother was all right. "Is Mom okay?" she asked Allison, who still crouched on the stairs, sobbing with reaction.

"She's fine. She fainted, but she's going to be alright," Allison said and Janelle felt lightheaded with relief. Her breath escaped in a deep sigh.

Delphine appeared behind Allison, her face pale and drawn. She was unsteady on her feet and Allison hurried back up the steps to take her arm.

"We have to stay here until the police are sure Baxter and those other two are gone," she told her mother, helping her to sit down on the top step.

Delphine gasped. "Then it was Baxter I saw!" She moaned, "When that girl was coming after me, I saw someone moving in the hallway. I thought it looked like Baxter, but now, when I came to again, I was sure I had imagined seeing him because I was so frightened."

"It was him. He was here," Allison confirmed.

"I thought my mind was playing tricks on me, too," Janelle whispered.

Delphine looked at Allison; when she spoke, her voice was weak and full of remorse, "I'm sorry I fainted. I left you all alone to face those bastards." Delphine seldom swore, but the danger they had encountered seemed to have left her with no words strong enough to suit the crisis they had faced.

"It's okay, Mom, you couldn't help it," Allison stopped and then added, "I think your fainting saved your life."

Delphine's eyebrows went up questioningly.

"That girl, Ivy, seemed to be feeding on our terror," Allison tightened her grip on her mother. "Her face, I can't describe the look on her face when she was coming toward you. When you fainted, she seemed...I don't know...disappointed, like she had lost something. She hesitated for a fraction of a second. That fraction of a second was when Baxter called out their names from the hallway...."

The police returned to the main floor and reported to Ross and the three women. "No one's in the house. There's a cut screen in the basement, looks like that's how they got in. The other two men are checking around outside, but I think they're gone."

The officers turned to Allison and Delphine. Both men climbed the steps. The younger one of the officers helped Delphine down the steps while the heavy set man-made a quick search of the upstairs.

In Delphine's bedroom he came across Muffy's body and shook his head sadly. *I think we have four very lucky people here,* he thought, as he clumped back down the steps.

The two officers from outside entered and the heavyset man took out a small notebook. Janelle put on the coffee pot and got cups from the cupboard, knowing her mother could use some coffee, but was not up to making it.

The two officers that had searched the outside of the house moved to the door, looking at the heavyset man. The heavyset man nodded and the two officers silently left.

"Why don't you keep an eye on the outside, Rusty, I'll get the report," the heavy set man told the young officer. He turned to Delphine as Rusty hurried out the door, "I'm Sterling Templeton, Madam. Do you feel well enough to tell me what happened?"

Delphine slowly nodded, "I don't know where to start." She glanced at Janelle and then turned back to the police officer.

"Start at the beginning," Sterling gently encouraged.

"Okay. It all began with my daughter, Janelle," she pointed to Janelle, "seeing a murderer in Ohio. His name is Jack Thomas Huxley...."

"Whoa!" Stunned, Sterling turned to Janelle, "You're Janelle Richardson?"

Janelle nodded and lowered her head. She was now sure she would never report something she had seen to the police again; at least not unless she herself was directly involved in whatever had happened. She shuddered. Her mother and Allison might have been killed! Ross' hand came down on her shoulder and squeezed gently. She was sure he knew what she was thinking.

Sterling Templeton stood and moved to the kitchen phone. "I better get the Chief and the detectives." He made his calls and returned to the table. Slowly settling in a chair, he wrapped his big hands around the mug of hot coffee Janelle placed before him. "We might as well wait for the detectives or you'll have to repeat your story. They'll be here in ten, fifteen minutes."

Janelle couldn't wait. "Jack Thomas Huxley was here?" her voice caught on a sob. "I was so sure he wouldn't find us."

Delphine looked at Janelle, her blue eyes full of despair, "Jack Thomas Huxley and a girl named Ivy."

"Oh no," Janelle moaned in terror. "Thank God you two weren't hurt." She looked at Ross, confused and frightened. Turning back to Allison, she whispered, "I wonder why Baxter was here? Why would he show up after so many years?"

"Baxter must be Huxley's boss. At least, Huxley called him Boss," Allison said.

Sterling looked from one to the other. He had no idea what was happening here. He knew only that Jack Thomas Huxley was wanted on suspicion of murder; the murder in Ohio, which Janelle had witnessed, and other reported murders in which he was the prime suspect.

There was a quick knock at the door and the officer who was keeping guard outside stuck his head in the doorway. "Detectives are here, Sterling," he reported.

"Thanks, Rusty, keep your eyes peeled out there." Rusty left the door open and went back outside.

Sterling lumbered to the door. Three detectives came into the room, among them, Dena Lark. She motioned for the two men with her to search the basement.

Delphine quickly got to her feet. She stretched her arms out to Dena and nearly fell into her arms. "Dena. I was hoping and praying you would be assigned our case."

Dena Lark gently patted Delphine's shoulder and soothed, "It's alright now. Everything's going to be alright."

Allison looked at Janelle, her eyes wide with surprise. She had had no idea that their mother and Dena Lark had become such close friends in the years since Dena had been the one to pick them up on the highway when they had decided to run away from Baxter.

In spite of the grave circumstances, Janelle smiled at her sister and whispered, "They've been good friends for a long time now. I see her every once in a while. You didn't know that she had made detective a few years ago, did you?"

Allison shook her dark head as both girl rose to their feet and went to shake hands with Dena, sharing a closeness with the woman which was unwarranted by the small amount of time they had spent in each others company.

Dena ignored the two girls' outstretched hands and gave each of them a warm hug, "It's nice to see you again. I wish it could have been under happier circumstances." She smiled again, "Your mother keeps me updated on both of you. Congratulations on your upcoming marriage, Janelle. Is this the lucky man?"

Janelle introduced Ross to Dena. Dena nodded, saying, "Nice looking guy, and your mother tells me he's a good man. Lucky you."

Janelle's face turned a bright red, but she smiled with pride at Ross. His face was as red as hers, but with a slight smug look hidden behind his embarrassment.

After a short period of small talk, Dena said, "Well, should we try to get to the bottom of this mess?" She turned to Sterling, "Want to see if you can turn anything up in the bedrooms?"

He nodded and headed for the second floor.

Dena held out a tape recorder and asked, "Any objections to my taping your report?"

Everyone nodded their consent.

Dena started the recorder; stated everyone's names, the date and the crime being investigated and then turned to the group, "Okay. Janelle, why don't you start?"

"Well," Janelle started hesitantly, "you have my report on what happened in Ohio, don't you?"

"Yes, we reviewed it on the way over here. Was Jack Thomas Huxley the man that was here?" Dena asked.

Delphine answered for Janelle, "Yes. It was him. Janelle didn't see him because he left before she got home, but I've seen his picture on TV a dozen times and it was him."

Dena frowned and turned as Sterling came down the stairs, "See about getting some road blocks set up on the main routes to Florida, will you? Pay particular attention to tractor-trailer trucks."

Sterling nodded and spoke briefly into his two-way radio.

Dena waited until he was finished and asked, "Did you find anything upstairs?"

"No, but I only gave it a quick going over."

Dena nodded, "Okay. Let's start with when they first got here. How did they get in?"

"There's a cut screen on a window in the basement recreation room and dirt from the flower bed on the carpet," Sterling said.

Dena turned back to Delphine, "When did you first know they were in the house, Delphine?"

"Muffy," Delphine stopped and her face crumpled with pain. When she continued, her voice was choked, "Muffy woke me up when the man, Jack, was just opening my bedroom door. I screamed and he hit me across the head. And then he hit Muffy with some kind of bar.... I was going to scream again when he shoved a filthy tasting rag in my mouth and tied my hands up.

"Then the woman, Jack called her Ivy, came in with Allison. Jack asked where Allison's boyfriend was and that's when I realized the man was Jack Thomas Huxley and he thought Allison was Janelle." Delphine stopped and shakily tried to wet her mouth with coffee too hot to swallow.

Janelle jumped up and got her a cold glass of water. Delphine thanked her and took a big swallow before continuing.

"Then Jack told the girl they were going to have to hurry, because of the noise Muffy made, and she should cut our throats." Delphine shuddered and lowered her head to her hands. She didn't continue. Tears filled her eyes.

Allison took up the story, "The girl—Jack had called her Ivy and she had called him Jack, I guess they didn't plan on us being around to repeat their names—went over and grabbed Mom by the hair. She laughed as she wrenched Mom's head back, but the laugh sounded more like a witches' cackle, and Mom fainted. Just when the woman was lifting the knife to cut Mom's throat, Baxter called to them from the hallway. Ivy dropped Mom." Allison's voice suddenly halted, she swallowed hard and took a deep shaky breath. She took a swallow of Delphine's water and cleared her throat.

Janelle was standing against the counter with her hand clamped over her mouth and her eyes wide with shock and terror. Ross stood beside her, his arm firm around her waist, his face unbelieving of the horror story being told.

Allison slowly continued, "They were both surprised to see him. He told them he wanted them to go back to Florida and no shopping on the way."

"Shopping?" Dena asked, frowning in thought.

Allison shrugged, "That's what he said, no shopping on the way. He said there was going to be a big meeting at the warehouse, lots of money and big bonuses for everyone. They said fine, they'd see him in Florida and they left. Baxter waited until they were down the steps and then he followed them, I suppose to see if they really left. As soon as they were gone, I called 911. I was still on the phone when I heard Janelle holler, 'It's Baxter' and the front door slammed." Allison stopped and looked at Janelle.

Dena nodded at Janelle, "What happened then, Janelle?"

"We had just come home from Ross' brother's stag party. When I opened the door, Baxter was on the steps to the basement. I saw the gun in his hand and I slammed the door closed again. Ross wanted to go after him, but I wouldn't let him. We went in the garage to call 911, but Allison was already on the phone to them. We were trying to figure out what to do when the patrol cars arrived."

Everyone sat silent for a short time and then Dena asked, "You're sure it was Baxter?" She looked from Allison to Janelle.

They nodded. "Positive," Allison said. Janelle nodded again.

"He didn't say where in Florida?" Dena directed her question at Allison.

"No."

"And he didn't mention the name of the warehouse?"

"No," Allison repeated.

Dena looked at her notes and turned to Janelle, "The police in Ohio have discovered that name on the black Freightliner is out of date. SAI, which stood for South American Inc., has been out of business for over two years. They had their home base in Fort Myers, so that's where the FBI has concentrated their search, but they are making inquiries all over Florida."

The two officers appeared from the basement and shook their heads at Dena's questioning glance. She nodded, "Okay. You can go." They turned and left the house. Sterling stood up and Dena nodded again. He followed the officers out the door.

Dena turned off the tape recorder and looked at Delphine. "You better all come with me. I don't think it's going to be safe to stay here. We'll put you up in a hotel with a guard."

"Do we have to?" Delphine asked, exhaustion was clearly stamped on her face and her voice came out weak and defeated. "Can't you leave a guard here? I want to bury Muffy."

Janelle and Allison went to their mother and stood behind her chair, their hands gently caressing her shoulders.

Dena shook her head, "I'm sorry, Delphine, but it would be too hard to guard this place properly. You'll be a lot safer in a hotel. Would you like one of my men to bury Muffy?"

"Thank you, Dena. That's very kind of you, but I'd like to do it myself."

Dena's eyes filled with compassion, but she shook her head, "It wouldn't be safe for you to go outside, Delphine. They have weapons and may even have night vision scopes. I'm sorry."

Delphine sighed in resignation, "Okay, Dena. I know you're right. I'll just say good-bye to her." She pushed herself to her feet, "Can we take some clothes along to the hotel?"

"Sure, I'll wait outside with Rusty. Take your time."

Ross and the girls trudged tiredly up the steps and Dena went out the door to look for Rusty. She stood for a minute on the steps, giving her eyes time to adjust to the dim light of the street lights and then moved slowly toward the deck. There was no sign of Rusty.

Continuing around the house, she began to get nervous. She knew Rusty; he would not abandon his post. He was a good man, sharp eyes and a sixth sense about impending danger. Dena was considering putting in a request for him to join the detective squad, although he was still a rookie.

Dena circled the house slowly, the bad feeling in her gut causing a sour taste to invade her mouth. She slipped her gun out when she was half way around the big home and a moment later took out her two-way radio and called for a back up team. There was no sign of Rusty.

CHAPTER TWELVE

Baxter slipped out the basement window and walked quickly to his rented car. Can't run, he cautioned himself, running draws attention to you. Getting in the car, he started the motor and slowly pulled away, leaving his lights off. When he was out of sight of Delphine's house, he turned on the headlights and drove—carefully within the speed limit—toward his hotel, cussing steadily. Three blocks from Delphine's house, he changed his mind and doubled back to within a block and a half of the house. Sirens split the night silence, but Baxter ignored them.

If he was going to put Janelle out of commission, tonight might be his only chance for a long time to come. He'd wait until the police had left and then he'd go back in and finish the job he had started.

Putting his gun, with the silencer carefully attached, in his pocket and his binoculars around his neck, he quietly left his car in the parking lot of an all night cafe and circled back to within sight of the vacant lot behind Delphine's house.

He hugged the ground next to a thick lilac bush across the street and a little to the right of the vacant lot and watched as the police searched around the house and in the vacant lot. One man crossed the street and walked along the sidewalk, shinning his flashlight into the darkness between the houses.

Baxter came close to panicking again, but he knew that he wouldn't make it clear if he ran now. There were too many cops and he was too close to them. He was relieved that his choice of clothes had been a dark blue pair of jeans, a black long sleeved shirt and black sneakers. He squeezed as close to the bush and the ground as possible and held his breath while the cop walked slowly past him, not more than fifty feet from him.

He breathed a sigh of relief when the man crossed back to the vacant lot.

When the men returned to the front of the house, Baxter trained his binoculars on the house. The men entered the house. Baxter could see them clearly through the un-shaded windows of the kitchen. They spoke a few words to a fat guy sitting at the table and left again. One man stayed on guard outside and the other two drove away.

Another car pulled up in front of the house and three more cops emerged. Baxter gritted his teeth and held his position. *Maybe I was wrong, maybe it wasn't a good idea to come back,* he thought, then quickly discarded the thought. *I may not get another chance.* He prayed the cops wouldn't be smart enough to take Delphine and her brats into protective custody.

He watched as the new group began to search the house for clues. A woman seated herself at the table and took notes while Delphine, Allison and Janelle told their story.

Baxter adjusted the fine-tuning on the binoculars and looked closely at the two girls. With their black hair and green eyes, they had always looked a lot a like, but now he couldn't tell them apart. He shrugged; he'd just have to get rid of both of them. It wouldn't hurt his feelings any. If those two little witches hadn't run away and gone to the cops, Delphine would never have found out about him.

Every fifteen minutes the man left on guard outside made a slow trip around the house; always starting from the east side. Baxter smiled and watched as the officer began his trip; creatures of habit deserved to have their habits broken. The man was cautious, and alert for danger, but Baxter could sense his apprehension slowly evaporating. The officer was becoming convinced that the fugitives had left and wouldn't be back.

Switching the glasses back to the house, Baxter saw the two officers who had been searching the house return to the kitchen. The woman officer said a few words to them and they left. He watched them climb into their car and drive away.

Two officers left, Baxter mused, *and one's a woman. Time to move.*

He left the cover of the lilac bush and quickly crossed the street. Darting in next to Delphine's house, he secreted himself behind the tall, full blue spruce tree that decorated the steps to the back door and found a spot where he would be able to see the young officer come around the corner of the house.

The officer had finished his last round of the house almost fifteen minutes ago and Baxter was sure he would be standing close to the front door, checking his watch to see if it was time for another inspection. Baxter waited patiently, his eyes glued to the corner of the house.

The officer rounded the corner; he was looking out toward the street. Baxter shifted his glaze to the street and was surprised to see a car rolling slowly past. He had been concentrating so hard on the officer's appearance that he had not heard the car approaching. He was glad the officer had chosen to stop and watch the car until it disappeared down the street. A witness would have spoiled his plans.

When the officer started forward again, Baxter's hand tensed on his gun. He waited until the officer was less than five feet from him before he took careful aim and pulled the trigger. The shot made no more sound than the plop of an apple falling from the tree that grew it.

The bullet hit the officer in the front of his neck, slicing his throat as neatly as a knife. He dropped to the ground without a sound, blood gushing from the fatal wound while his arms and legs moved spasmodically as the life flowed from him.

Baxter calmly pulled the man to the side of the house and pushed his body under the thick branches of the pine tree. He inspected the sight where the officer had fallen, noticing that in the darkness, the blood was barely discernible.

Circling the house, he moved into the shadows of the neighboring house and watched while the woman officer completed her questions. When Delphine, Allison, Janelle and the boyfriend started up the stairs and the woman officer moved toward the door, Baxter quickly hid behind the hedge that separated the two houses.

Cussing silently, he wished that he had returned to the back door and the pine tree. He was too far away now. With the glare from the window hitting him in the eyes, he might miss his target.

He knew the woman would look for the officer who was left on guard. She would circle the house and he would have been in a good position to dispose of her, too, had he returned to the pine tree.

He considered his options. If the woman didn't find the officer right away, she might call for more help. And she might even get a shot at him if he moved now. Baxter decided to drop her when she passed through the light from the window.

But the woman moved around the house to the West, reversing the male officer's surveillance route. As she disappeared around the corner, Baxter considered trying to beat her to the back of the house, but decided it was too risky. He shook his head. He'd wait until she reached the lighted window.

He heard her voice before he saw her and realized a second later that she was already calling for help.

"Rusty has disappeared. Send a back up unit right away," Baxter heard her say. His face hardened with determination. He had very little time in which to accomplish his mission.

He leveled his gun on the corner of the house and as Dena Lark's dim shape came into view, he pulled the trigger. The bullet whizzed past Dena's head and she immediately threw herself to the ground behind the corner of the house.

Baxter slipped silently along the hedge until he was opposite the corner of the house, but the woman was nowhere in sight. His eyes searched the shadows next to the house and he thought he saw a slight movement close to the same pine tree he had hid behind. He threw two quick shots at the movement and was rewarded with a grunt of pain from the woman. Lowering the level of his gun, he squeezed off two more shots.

Suddenly a bullet plunged into the ground next to him and the night was shattered by the loud blast of the detective's gun. Baxter rolled to his left and threw two more shots just above the level of the cement steps next to the pine tree.

A bullet suddenly cut through his lower arm and a split second later the sound of the shot echoed through the night. Baxter winced in pain and stared in disbelief at his wounded arm. A light came on behind him; the neighbors had heard the detective's shots.

Knowing he was playing a losing game, knowing that more police would arrive on the scene within minutes, Baxter rose to a low crouch and raced along the hedge to the street. Cutting across the street to his left, he kept the concealing leaves of the hedge between himself the hidden position of the woman. There was no sound of pursuit. Baxter circled around and reached his rented car seconds later. He was glad he had left the car as far away as he had. There was no chance of the detective seeing him or the car unless she had followed him and Baxter was sure she hadn't.

Starting the engine, he pulled out of the restaurant parking lot and drove back to his hotel, pressing his wounded arm tight against his body as he drove.

The back parking lot at the hotel was nearly empty as Baxter pulled into it. No one was in sight. He pulled his jacket off the seat and hung it over his arm, carefully making sure none of the blood on his shirt showed.

In his room, Baxter cut the sleeve of his shirt away from the wound and carefully examined the ugly hole the bullet had made. He was surprised to see that the wound was really no more than a deep scratch.

Relief washed over him. He wouldn't need a doctor. He put on a clean shirt, a scuffed up pair of slippers he was fond of and messed his hair up. Checking his appearance in the large floor length mirror, he was satisfied he looked like he had been in bed.

He went down to the main lobby and asked the desk clerk, "Is there an all night drug store close by? I can't get to sleep and I want some sleeping pills."

"Yes Sir, there's a drug store half way down the block and across the street that's open twenty four hours a day," the clerk smiled.

Baxter thanked the man and quickly left the lobby, trying not to favor his wounded arm. At the drug store he first purchased the sleeping pills to corroborate his reason for wanting a drug store and then added gauze and disinfectant for his wound, telling the clerk that he had stepped on a piece of glass and cut his foot.

Satisfied he had covered his tracks, he returned to his room and carefully dressed his wound before he gave his mind over to the problem of determining how he was going to get to Janelle.

Cursing to himself, he suddenly realized that it was not only Janelle now. Allison and probably the boyfriend—whose ever boyfriend or husband he was—had seen him. It was no longer a matter of just wanting revenge on Delphine. Janelle—*or was that Allison in the room with Delphine?* he suddenly wondered—he shrugged. It didn't matter if it was Janelle or Allison, both girls had been there before he left. Both girls had seen him and whoever the one upstairs had been, she had overheard his conversation with Jack Thomas Huxley and she could testify to that fact, which could be disastrous to Baxter if his current business activities were ever discovered by the police.

With Jack wanted for rape and murder, Baxter didn't like his odds. For all he knew, Jack could at this very minute be leading the police right to his warehouse. He had to clean up this business in Duluth quickly and get back to Florida to see to his retirement.

Baxter was sure the police would now take Delphine and her family into protective custody. *I can't involve any more people in this mess,* he thought, *and that leaves only one alternative; a disguise.* He mused over the many possibilities and finally settled on the only disguise really feasible in this situation. A smile began slowly, but grew rapidly until he was grinning from ear to ear.

TAKE CARE

A policeman. Baxter would become one of their guards.

Laughing out loud, he removed his clothes, took two sleeping pills and sprawled on the king size bed. Janelle and her family would soon be history.

Delphine was shaking with shock and exhaustion. Janelle wrapped an arm around her mother's waist and supported her as they climbed the stairs to the second floor, Ross and Allison trailed behind them. Ross went to his and Janelle's room to retrieve their suitcase while Allison went to her room and repacked her case.

"I'm so sorry, Mom," Janelle moaned, her shoulders slumped in remorse. "I never should have involved you in my troubles."

Delphine sadly shook her head, "I was involved long before you had any say in the matter, Janelle. Baxter Perry is behind this, I know he is."

They reached Delphine's bedroom and Janelle led her to the bed, where Delphine sank down beside Muffy's still form. Her hand stroked the dog's soft hair and tears of sorrow ran down her face. "I'll miss you, Muffy," she whispered.

Janelle watched Delphine lovingly smooth Muffy's hair and her eyes brimmed with tears. Unable to stand her mother's sorrow, she turned away, guilt heavy on her soul. She moved to the closet, pulled Delphine's overnight bag from the shelf and began to pack a change of clothes for her. "I'll pack a few things for you, Mom, and then we can come back tomorrow and get whatever else you want," she murmured.

Forcing her mind away from her mother's grief, fear once again besieged her. Frightening questions without answers flew around in her mind, but she kept them to herself. Her mother was too exhausted to cope with the problems now. Tomorrow would be soon enough, when they were safe, a police guard at their hotel room door.

The sound of distant sirens brought Janelle to a standstill, her head lifted to listen intently. Delphine straightened and cocked her head. "It sounds like they're coming this way!" she exclaimed in fright.

"Stay here, Mom, I'll go see what's happening," Janelle said as she rushed for the bedroom door. She met Ross and Allison in the hall and all three raced down the steps.

They had just reached the bottom step when the loud blast of a gunshot cracked through the night. They froze in their tracks and stared at each other in shock.

"A gun shot...," Janelle whispered, her eyes wide with fright.

A minute later another shot charged through the still air and Janelle ducked down and covered her head with her arms. Allison and Ross ducked down beside her and all three of them waited silently, fighting the panic that threatened to send them flying for cover.

The minutes stretched out slowly, silent and terrifying. Suddenly Janelle could no longer stand the suspense. She jumped to her feet and ran to the front door, "I have to see what's happening!"

She reached for the latch and Ross grabbed her wrist, "Wait. We can't go out there! If Baxter or Jack has come back, they'll be after you. You said yourself he had a gun."

Janelle's hand fell from the door latch as if she had been burned and she backed quickly away. Her eyes flew to Ross and then to the un-shaded windows that surrounded them. Seeing the point of her fear, Ross reached out and turned off the light in the entryway while Allison hurried to the kitchen and shut off the lights in there.

Silent and listening, the three young people stood without moving in the entryway.

The sound of voices came indistinctly through the closed door. A sudden loud rap at the door caused everyone to jump in fright. Ross called, "Who is it?"

"Detective Lark."

Ross reached forward and opened the door, a question out of his mouth before Dena could speak, "What happened?"

Dena was agitated, she ignored his question, "Did Officer Rusty Simon come inside?"

Janelle and Allison quickly shook their heads and Detective Lark turned back to the door, "You better stay in here. Something has happened to Officer Simon, he's disappeared. Keep the lights off and keep your eyes and ears open. Don't walk in front of the windows." She stepped back out the door, while the three young people looked at each other in fear.

"I'm going back up by Mom," Janelle announced, forcing her shaking legs to obey her command.

"I think that's a good place for all of us," Ross said. Allison nodded and followed the other two up the steps. They all went to Delphine's room and closed the door behind them. Delphine's eyes filled with dread when Ross barricaded the door with her heavy chest of drawers and flipped off the light.

Janelle hastened to reassure her, "We'll be safe in here, Mom."

"What happened?" Delphine whispered, her face pale in the dim light from the street lamp.

"They don't know yet," Allison said, sitting beside her mother on the bed and hugging her arms tightly around her chest, "but the officer, Rusty, who was left on guard outside, has disappeared."

Delphine gasped, "Do they think Baxter has come back?"

"They don't know, Mom," Janelle said, her voice shaky. Guilt hung heavy on her slim shoulders and she sagged down on the other side of her mother. *It's all my fault*, she moaned silently. *I never should have gone to the police. Jack Thomas Huxley wouldn't have come after us if I hadn't gone to the police. And Jack must be the one who led Baxter to us.* She frowned. What was the connection between the two men? What kind of business did Baxter run that Jack had called him Boss?

Remembering Baxter's treatment of them and his subsequent jail term, Janelle was sure his business could not be a legitimate business. In what legitimate business would the boss come after an employee with a gun and order him back to his home state for a meeting?

Ross went to the window. Staying to the edge of the glass, he tried to see down into the dimly lit yard. No one was in sight. He looked at the three women on the edge of the bed and a lump formed in his throat as his eyes fell on Janelle. He could see her despair in the slump of her proud shoulders and he guessed at the thoughts that were running through her mind. His heart ached for her. Tears saturated his eyes, but he forced them back. Janelle needed his strength. She didn't need to see him in a state of despair, too.

Heavy steps sounded on the stairs and Ross moved to the door, putting his ear against the solid oak wood. A light knock came and he asked, "Who is it?"

"Detective Lark."

Ross recognized the woman voice, "Just a minute." He pushed the cumbersome chest away from the door and pulled it open. Detective Lark looked in at them and then flipped on the light. Her eyes were red and looked like she had been crying and she held her arm tight against her side, where a faint trace of blood had soaked through her light jacket. "We found Officer Simon," she sadly reported, "he was murdered and his body concealed under the pine tree by the back door."

The women gasped in sorrow and dismay and Ross' face hardened. "It had to have been Baxter," he stated flatly.

"We don't know that, Ross, but I'd say that's a good guess," Dena Lark said. "I called for another back up unit and an ambulance is on the way, but we have to get you guys out of here. Whoever was out there seems to have left now, but we can't be sure of that. Are you ready?"

"Ready," Ross said, stepping forward and gathering up Delphine's overnight bag. The women got slowly to their feet, Janelle and Allison reached to support Delphine, but she gently pulled away.

"I'm not decrepit yet, but I do feel the day isn't far off," she sighed and smiled fondly at her two wonderful, supportive girls.

"We weren't trying to imply you're feeble, Mom, but it's been a very bad night and it's late," Janelle apologized.

Delphine smiled, but said nothing more as they trailed Dena Lark down the stairs and out to her car.

They were given adjoining rooms in a towering downtown hotel. The rooms were large and expensively furnished. The beds were immaculately clean and smelled fresh. Each room had its own private bathroom with a tub and a shower.

Police guards were posted at each room's door and Dena explained that the guards were scheduled to be relieved every three hours. "You don't have to worry about the men falling asleep on the job," she reassured them. "And the windows are a straight drop to the ground, six floors down." She carefully checked the rooms over and turned to leave, "You'll be safe here. I'll see you in the morning about ten a.m. Goodnight."

Janelle and Ross took one room, while Delphine and Allison shared the other. They said goodnight and Ross softly closed the connecting door, leaving it unlocked.

Janelle turned off the bright overhead light and moved to the window. Ross said nothing as he watched her silhouette.

Her worried eyes searched the dark windows of the tall office building directly across the street. The building rose to a height of fifteen stories.

"Remember that movie we saw about the girl that was being watched through a telescope from the building across from her apartment?" she asked.

"I remember, Janelle, but I'm sure the police have thought of that. Anyway, all we have to do is keep the drapes pulled."

Janelle pulled the drape and turned from the window. "I wish our room was windowless, like Mom and Allison's is." She flipped on the bedside lamp. A warm glow spread through the comfortable room. "But you're right. We'll be perfectly safe here. No one can get in.... It's like a jail, no one can get in and we can't go out." She suddenly broke into sobs of despair and crumpled to the wide bed.

Ross recognized her compulsion to reassure herself and her need for physical relief. His heart went out to her. She grieved over the desperate situation they found themselves embroiled in, through no fault of their own. He sat on the side of the bed and pulled her up against him, murmuring senseless comforting words and rocking her gently.

When her sobs died, he held her away from him and gave her a sad, tired smile, "Let's get some sleep, Sweetheart. You want the bathroom first?"

Janelle shook her head, gave Ross a small smile and hiccupped softly, "You go ahead."

Fifteen minutes later they were curled close together in the big bed. "Hold me, Ross. I'm so scared; for all of us," Janelle moaned.

"It's going to be okay, Honey, try to sleep. You're exhausted. Things will look brighter in the morning." He turned off the lamp and the room was plunged into darkness. Outside the door, the guard's chair creaked as he either changed positions or moved from the chair.

CHAPTER THIRTEEN

Jack Thomas Huxley and Ivy Muir had been arguing since Baxter had ordered them back to Florida. They stopped at a small truck stop in Rice Lake, WI and continued to argue after they were seated in the restaurant.

"I'm telling you," Ivy said, keeping her voice to a low growl, "you're the one whose head is on the block. If Baxter Perry doesn't get rid of that girl, you could go to prison for life!"

"Baxter will take care of her," Jack repeated, "He has a lot to lose."

"How are you going to be sure? If we're back in Florida, the news of a murder in Duluth might not be important enough to be reported on our stations. We should go back and make sure for ourselves. We can make sure Baxter doesn't see us," Ivy did not want to give up. She stood up and leaned over close to Jack's face, "Think about that, Big Boy! I have to go to the can." She gave Jack a haughty look and stomped off.

Ivy fumed inwardly as she made her way to the bathroom. Jack was being unreasonably stubborn. She still wanted to get her hands on that girl and her boyfriend. If the sister and mother were handy at the time, they would be an added bonus. Her fingers and toes tingled at the thought and her stomach suddenly felt light and bouncy.

Jack watched her walk away, her hips swaying suggestively. He was beginning to wonder if she wasn't right.

Jack knew the girl had recognized Baxter. He had seen the recognition and fear come into her eyes when Baxter walked into the bedroom.

If Baxter hadn't killed them before he left the woman's house, the girl would have described Jack, Ivy and Baxter to the police. And the girl already knew Jack's name. She knew he was the one who had murdered the red head in Ohio. She knew too much. Jack sworn silently and gritted his teeth in anger.

He didn't think Baxter had accomplished his mission. He and Ivy had listened to a radio station from Duluth for the three hours it took them to reach Rice Lake and there had been no mention of a double murder, although the radio station had had an update on the murder of the window repairman in Janelle's apartment.

It was also possible Baxter had been apprehended while he was in the process of killing them, but again, there had been no mention of this on the radio.

Jack frowned and ran his dirty fingers along the thick mustache that completely covered his upper lip. Would he hear about it in Florida? If the police discovered who the killer was, and if they knew Baxter's home base was in Florida, then the news might be reported in Florida, but if the police decided to keep their information quiet until they had caught Baxter, nothing would be on the radio or television.

If the police don't catch Baxter in the act, they will probably blame the murders on me, Jack seethed silently. *They know she was the only witness to my crime in Ohio. Either way, I'll be targeted by the police.*

Suddenly a new thought came to him. Was this Baxter's plan? Did Baxter want to have the pleasure of murdering the two women and getting off scot free, knowing the murders would be blamed on Jack Thomas Huxley?

Well, he isn't going to get away with it! Jack decided. First they were going back to Duluth and make sure the girl was dead and then he would find a way to lead the cops to Baxter.

Jack suddenly smiled with glee. He and Ivy didn't need Baxter anymore. Now that they knew the business, they could set up their own little ring of kidnappers. Buyers wouldn't be that hard to find. A few ads in the right kind of magazines would have buyers coming out of his ears. He would be the boss and take in piles of money like Baxter had been doing.

Baxter awoke early, refreshed and impatient to be about his business. His arm felt better than it had the night before, but a dull ache still pulsed in the gunshot wound. He showered and carefully changed the bandage, applying fresh antiseptic to the long gash, steadily cussing the policewoman while he worked.

He checked his watch, eight a.m. Picking up the phone, he dialed quickly. A deep voice answered on the third ring.

"Bob. Florida here. I need more information on that witness," Baxter said. Wasting no time on amenities, he asked, "Where did they take her and how long is each guard on duty?"

Bob Kelly smiled, more money, and a lot sooner than he would have guessed. He was well satisfied with the past deposits this contact had made to his savings account, in a large Duluth bank. The account had been opened under a false name and had been started for just this purpose. He had never seen the man that called himself Florida and he didn't want to see him. The less he knew about the man, the less chance the man would someday decide to eliminate his services...and him along with it. He did not underestimate the danger this man represented if crossed.

Bob Kelly was a patrolman at the Duluth Police Department, where he had worked for the last twenty-five years. As a young man, he had been a completely trustworthy, gung ho officer, but his eagerness and hot, uncontrollable temper had defeated him.

Some twenty years earlier, he had been one of the officers called to a gang fight involving Negroes and Asians. During the battle that ensued, Bob had let his temper overrule his common sense and the battle had suddenly become a personal attack on Bob's integrity. The gloating of one Asian, along with the youth's unarmed, but violent, attack on Bob, had enraged Bob to the extent that he had used his blackjack on the boy's head with excessive force. The thirteen year old Asian had died from the blow and Bob's high, ambitious plans to become the youngest Chief of Police that Duluth had ever had, had died with him.

Two years later, Bob had embarked on his unsavory specialty, which had started as a harmless—or so he told himself—leaking of classified information to the press. He had never discovered how men like Florida obtained his name, but his indiscretions had gradually become more and more damaging to the police department and the public.

"She's at the Claremont Hotel, right downtown, and the guys are on three hour shifts," Bob replied.

"Do you have a shift?"

"Tonight; from twelve to three."

"Good. A man will be taking your place early, at two thirty. Is there more than one guard at a time?" Baxter wanted to know.

Bob hesitated. Someone was going to take his place? That would never work. There would be no way to explain it to the Captain. "Two guards at a time. Our positions are around the corner from each other. We change spots every hour. There are two adjoining rooms, the girl and her boyfriend are in one and the mother and the other daughter are in the other."

"Okay. How far apart do you sit?" Baxter swore silently. Two guards made the job a little tougher, but the corner, which obstructed vision from one guard to the other, was a definite plus.

"There's about fifteen feet between us," Bob answered.

"Alright. Make sure you're the closest one to the stairs at two thirty. Starting at the one o'clock switch, tell your partner you're not feeling well. Between one thirty and two, you leave to make the presumed telephone call. At the two o'clock switch, tell the other guy you're leaving early and you called for a replacement. Is there someone on the force that the other guy doesn't know by sight?"

"Yeah. There's a new guy, hired last week, Sloan Berg, that neither of us has met yet," Bob said.

"Good. Tell him your replacement is the new guy. The guy I'm sending over," Baxter was careful not to say he was going to be the guy, "will use the stairs. Do you have keys to the rooms?"

"Yes..," Bob's voice was slow and unsure, "But if you're talking about murder, I don't want to be involved in any kind of violent crime."

Baxter was suddenly angry. This dip-head was questioning him. He kept his voice gentle, "Don't worry. I only want my man to scare the witness." He heard Bob's slight sigh of relief. "She'll only be beat up a little. Only enough so she'll decide she didn't see anything." He paused and then added, "A very sizeable deposit will be made to your account."

Bob opened his mouth to object again and suddenly saw the money slipping through his fingers. His mind raced furiously. There was no way this could be kept a secret from the Captain, especially after the girl was beaten. He could insist that he had called Sloan Berg, but Berg would deny it. What then? Say Berg was lying? Accuse Berg of being the person that beat the girl? It might work. Bob was a trusted employee, a long time employee. Berg was new, no one knew him. Would the Captain believe him or Berg? *Me*, Bob decided, *and if the Captain is the least bit suspicious, we'll pack up and leave real quick. In fact... I won't wait to see if the Captain is suspicious, we'll leave tomorrow. It's time to quit anyway, before I get caught. Ellen and I will hop the first plane to Europe. They'll never find us. I can have my money wired to wherever we decide to go.*

The phone clicked in his ear. Florida had hung up. The deal was made;

there was no backing out now. Bob knew he would rather have the cops after him than this man called Florida.

Baxter listened to the long silence, knowing Bob Kelly was having second thoughts. *I've got to have his help and cooperation,* he thought, *or I'm not going to get close to Delphine and her girls.* Baxter abruptly hung up the phone, giving Bob no further chance to argue or back out. Bob would carry through with the deal. He wouldn't dare back out now. The man would be very familiar with the consequences involved in a double-cross.

Baxter was feeling good. In spite of the change in his original plans and the added expense of having Bob's help, his new plan was going to work out perfect. There was no worry about the other guard seeing him enter the room and luxury hotels had good thick walls, he wouldn't have to worry about the silenced gunshots, or better yet, a knife. He thanked the good Lord he had had the foresight to include a bottle of ether in his suitcase when he left Florida. With two people in each room, the need for a quick, silent execution was a necessity.

Baxter called a costume rental business and learned that they carried a large number of different sized police uniforms.

The clerk laughed, "We have a big call for people, girls and guys alike, who want to be a police person. What size do you need?"

Baxter told the man his size and requested him to wrap the uniform and deliver it to the hotel. "Leave it at the desk. Make sure it's wrapped. Some of the people going to the party are staying at this hotel and I don't want them to see it. I'll be out most of the day, but I'll leave your money with the clerk." He didn't like having to explain his reasons to anyone, but he didn't want that uniform delivery to become common knowledge.

"That's not necessary, Sir. We can bill you."

"No, I'm leaving town tomorrow and I won't be back for two months. I don't like to keep people waiting for their money." *Why doesn't the jerk just do what I say?* Baxter fumed silently at the further explanation.

"Okay," the clerk agreed. "We'll deliver it about one p.m. Will that be all right?"

"Fine. Thank you," Baxter consented. Everything was going even better than he had expected. All he needed yet was a mustache and a beard. Those would only take a few minutes. He had the rest of the day to rest and relax. He crawled back in bed with a book and was asleep a short time later.

At noon he rose, washed and left his room. Stopping at the desk, he told the clerk to expect a package for him and gave the man the money to collect it. *Now for a big breakfast*, he thought with delight.

Delphine and Allison were up at eight a.m. "Do you think we should wake Janelle and Ross up?" Allison asked her mother.

"Let's let them sleep another hour. You should have slept longer, too. You guys are going to have a full day today with Lars and Kate's wedding."

"I couldn't sleep any longer. I was awake at seven and that was late for me. I'm used to getting up at five thirty when I'm working and on the weekends I'm usually up by six thirty. Aren't you going to the wedding?" Allison asked.

"No, I don't know them very well. I've only met them a few times. They did invite me, but it's just because of Janelle and Ross."

"But what are you going to do all day? You can't sit around here all by yourself," Allison said. "You should come along."

Delphine looked sad, "Don't you think Dena will let me go home?"

Allison shook her head, "I don't know, Mom. Do the police know about the wedding?"

"I don't know. I didn't say anything. I didn't even think of it last night." Delphine shuddered as the memory of how close they had come to being murdered flooded over her.

Allison saw the look on her face and wrapped her arms around her mother, "I know how you feel, Mom. I've never been so scared in all my life. Not even when Baxter took me in his room the first time...."

Delphine shuddered again and beseeched her daughter, "I still don't see how that could have happened without my suspecting something. How could I have been so blind?"

"We told you, Mom. We worked real hard at keeping it a secret. Janelle and I didn't even know that he was doing it to both of us until he didn't want me anymore.... I can still see that day as clear in my mind as if it were yesterday. When Baxter started toward Janelle's room, I thought I was going to die." Allison's eyes had filled with tears and her face had that lost little girl look.

Delphine was angry with herself. She didn't know why she had brought this up again, except that she still felt guilty. It had been years since they had talked about Baxter's inhuman treatment, but at the time they had talked it out many times. She had thought she was over the guilt.... "I'm sorry, Sweetheart, I never should have brought this up again," Delphine moaned.

"You didn't bring it up, Mom, I did. And really, I don't think about it anymore. And neither Janelle nor I blame you, not the least little bit. It's just seeing Baxter again.... I'm surer than ever that if you had found out about him before the police were involved, Baxter would have killed you. I'm sure he plans to kill all of us now, because we all know he's involved in this deal with Jack Thomas Huxley."

"We have Dena Lark to help us. I'm sure she won't let anything happen to us," Delphine promised.

"I bet she isn't going to want us to go to the wedding," Allison said.

"I don't think she will either," Delphine agreed. "I don't think it's a good idea to go. How can they guard us at a wedding?"

"Ross will never miss his brother's wedding," Allison predicted.

"I don't think he will either," Delphine agreed. "And I really don't blame him."

There was a light knock on the connecting door and Janelle poked her head in the door and whispered, "You awake in there?"

"Come on in Janelle," Delphine called.

"Shh, Ross is still sleeping," Janelle said as she entered the room and softly closed the door behind her. She joined her mother and Allison at the small table in the corner of the room and Allison poured her a cup of coffee. "What are you guys talking about?"

Delphine and Allison glanced at each other and both started talking at once; neither of them wanted to hurt Janelle's feelings.

"We were...," Allison said.

"The sun's out...," Delphine's voice trailed off to silence. She knew she wasn't fooling her daughter with a lame attempt at casual conversation.

Delphine cleared her throat, "We were just discussing whether Dena was going to allow you to go to the wedding."

"Allow?" Janelle asked, her tone sharp with alarm. "We're not prisoners."

"No, but it's going to be dangerous, Honey," Delphine soothed. "I don't know how the police will be able to guard you when there are so many people around."

"But we have to go," Janelle insisted. "Ross is Lars' best man."

"I know," Delphine said. "Maybe Lars and Kate should consider rescheduling the wedding till a future date. With the threat of Jack and Baxter hanging over us, it will ruin everything for all of you."

Janelle was stunned by her mother's suggestion, "They can't do that, it's too late. How would they get a hold of everyone?"

"It would be hard, but your life is at stake, Sweetheart. All of our lives are in danger. I'm sure Lars will not want to take on that responsibility," Delphine reasoned.

Janelle was heartsick, this was all her fault. Why oh why did she have to be the one to witness Jack forcing that poor girl into his truck? And why did she go to the police? This whole thing wouldn't be happening if she had just kept quiet. "You're right, Mom. I'm going to wake up Ross and see what he says." She rose slowly to her feet and walked with her head down as she crossed to the adjoining room.

Delphine felt tears well in her eyes as she watched her daughter. Janelle was taking all the blame for this horrid situation. She failed to see that she was not responsible for the evil Jack and Baxter had caused.

Delphine wondered how she could ever have thought Baxter was a kind, loving man. How could she have so mistaken his intentions? Why hadn't she seen the sinister side of his character?

She remembered the loneliness she had felt when Allison and Janelle's father had died of leukemia. She had longed for adult companionship. She had wanted someone with whom she could share the precious happenings of her day with the children; someone to share the long evenings.

She had met Baxter at a church meeting four years after Fitzpatrick Lanley's death and had gone out with him for more than a year before she married him. She could not remember one thing that would have led her to believe he was not exactly what he portrayed himself to be. Except...she had never had to fight off any advancements in the love making department, at least not on his side of the arrangement. She had wondered about that...but had dismissed her small tinges of worry, deciding that Baxter was only being considerate of her reputation.

She had slowly fallen in love with him; not the wild, consuming kind of love she had felt for Fitzpatrick, but what she felt to be a mature love on which they could build a solid future.

Thinking about it now, Delphine felt the rise of bile in her throat and she swallowed convulsively and turned back to Allison's worried look.

"Mom? Are you alright?"

"I'm fine. I was just wondering how Baxter managed to completely pull the wool over my eyes when we were dating."

"I bet that's why it took you so long to say yes to Frank Kipp, isn't it?"

Allison asked.

"I suppose it is. But also, I wasn't about to take the chance of putting you and Janelle in any danger again."

"I know. We were both gone from home by the time you married Frank. Janelle finally moved out because she suspected you wouldn't marry Frank until she was gone. We know you better than you think, Mom."

Delphine looked shocked, "I didn't know I was that transparent!" Allison laughed, breaking off at the look on Janelle's face as she reentered the room.

"I told Ross what you said, Mom, and he agrees with you. He's calling Lars and Kate," Janelle told them. Her eyes lingered on the cup she cradled in her hands as she spoke again, "I really wish I hadn't gone to the police."

Delphine reached out and gripped her hand, "Janelle, look at me." She waited while Janelle reluctantly raised her eyes to her mother. "You did the right thing, Honey. You know that the police have a much better chance of catching Jack now than they did before you reported his actions in Ohio. In fact, they may already have him in custody. Remember? Dena had a road block set up."

"I know, Mom, and I hope they did get him, but now Baxter's after us. Not just me, but all of us. And it's all because I went to the police," Janelle's voice broke and tears rolled down her cheeks.

"It's not your fault things turned out the way they did," Delphine reasserted. "You couldn't know your name and address was going to be put on television. If you hadn't gone to the police, Jack might have murdered another young girl by now. They'll get him, Honey, and they'll figure out what Baxter's part in this is. Don't worry, everything will be alright."

"I hope so. I pray none of you will have to pay for my going to the police," Janelle's voice was low and shaky.

"The police will guard us," Allison put in. "I'm sorry I said you shouldn't have gone to the police, Janelle, but really, I would have done the same thing if I had been in your shoes. You did the right thing."

Janelle looked from Allison to her mother, her beautiful eyes brimming with tears. She pushed back her chair and knelt on the floor between Allison and Delphine, putting her arms around them and hugging them tight. "Thanks for sticking behind me," she groaned.

"We'll always be behind you, Janelle. No matter what happens or what you do, we'll always be behind you. We love you." Delphine ached with fear for all of them, but Janelle needed their courage and love. The fear had to be hidden away for the time being. Delphine didn't want Janelle to carry around a load of guilt for doing the right thing. She wanted Janelle to be free to seek help again if the occasion ever arose that she needed help in the future.

If only I had taught them to seek help earlier.... Delphine shook away thoughts of Baxter's abuse. That was in the past. There was nothing that could be done about it now.

Ross knocked lightly and opened the door at Delphine's call. His sad eyes touched on each of the three women as he crossed the room and joined them at the table. "Lars agrees with you, Delphine. He's sure it will be much too dangerous for any of us to attend the wedding and he's going to postpone it. Of course, he's disappointed, but that's to be expected. I just hope we will be able to reach the nearly two hundred invited guests. "He and Kate are on the way over here with the wedding list. He asked if we would mind helping them make the calls."

"Of course we will," Delphine and Janelle said together.

"It will help to pass the time," Allison put in. "I wonder if I should call Curt and tell him not to come. He'll be leaving about nine."

Delphine glanced at her watch and was surprised to see it was only eight thirty a.m. She smiled softly at the look of longing in her daughter's emerald green eyes, "It can't hurt for the police to have one more of us to keep track of."

Allison's eyes lit up and she smiled gratefully, "Thanks, Mom. I really want him to come. I was just concerned about putting him in danger, too."

"The police will keep us safe," Delphine said, including Janelle in her look of love.

"I have to call him and tell him where we are. May I use the phone in your room, Janelle?" At Janelle's nod and smile, Allison hurried off, softly closing the door between the two rooms. When she returned, her eyes spoke volumes of her love for Curt. "He'll be here about ten thirty or eleven."

Janelle's nerves were strung as tight as fiddle strings and the knock at the door caused her to jump in fear. Ross went to the door and the guard asked if they were expecting visitors. "Yes," Ross said. "My brother and his girlfriend are coming."

"Okay. We just wanted to be sure. They asked your room number of the desk clerk," the guard said. "I'll tell the clerk to send them up. Why don't you stay here and identify them for me?"

"Sure," Ross agreed.

"I'll leave the door open, but you wait inside the door. I don't want anything unexpected to happen," the guard instructed.

Ross stepped back in the open doorway and glanced at Janelle. She had heard every word the guard said and her face was anxious and worried, "Back up more, Ross," she pleaded. "It could be Baxter claiming to be your brother."

"No one else knows Lars and Kate are coming," Ross reasoned, backing up a few steps anyway.

The elevator opened and Lars and Kate moved toward the room. The guard politely asked them to stop and hold their hands out in front of them. Lars and Kate looked at each other nervously, but did what the guard said.

The guard kept his eyes on the two while he spoke to Ross, "Take a look, Sir."

Ross stuck his head out the door and nodded, "That's my brother."

"Good," the guard raised his voice. "You can come in." He motioned Lars and Kate into the room, but kept his eyes on the deserted hallway. The guard was glad that the hotel graciously accommodated police situations such as this by not renting rooms in the wing where the witnesses were secluded unless the hotel was overflowing with guests. It made his job a lot easier. He hated to think what it would be like if there were strangers moving up and down the halls at all hours of the day and night.

Lars and Kate discussed the problem with Delphine, Ross, Janelle and Allison. They decided to tell everyone only that there had been an emergency in Lars' family and the wedding was being postponed for three weeks. Lars called the priest, explained the situation and the priest confirmed an opening on Saturday the eleventh of July. The group divided up the list of guests, taking their individual list with them to the extra phones the hotel had furnished for them. They included the future date and time in each phone call, which would save them the expense and trouble of making and sending new announcements.

Kate's face was sad as she started making her phone calls. She realized that the danger to Janelle, Ross and Allison was very real and she and Lars could not ask them to expose themselves to such danger, but this fact did not keep her from feeling depressed about the postponement of their wedding. Her eyes met Lars' and he smiled sadly, winking at her to keep her courage up. His lips silently formed the words, "I love you" and Kate blew him a kiss in answer.

At ten a.m. Dena Lark knocked on the door.

"Oh, I'm sorry. I forgot you were coming," Delphine apologized. "Did we mention that we were supposed to go to a wedding today?"

"No, you didn't," Dena laughed. "But I think your minds were on another track last night." She glanced at the extra phones in the room. "Why all the phone calls?"

"We're postponing the wedding," Delphine explained.

Dena's pretty face sobered and she looked at Lars and Kate, "Are you two the ones...?"

Lars nodded and Kate murmured, "Yes."

"I'm sorry it turned out like this, but you were smart to postpone it. It wouldn't have been a good idea for any of you to go." She paused and then added, "We didn't get Jack in our road blocks. He must have been out of the area before we got them set up. Or it's possible he didn't leave town at all.... There's been no sign of Baxter, but we're still searching the hotels and motels."

Janelle gasped and the blood drained from Delphine's face.

"Don't worry, they won't find you here," Dena assured them. "Go ahead with your calls, I'll come back later. Maybe I'll have better news for you then."

At ten fifty the guard again knocked at the door and asked if they were expecting anyone. Allison happily told him about Curt. The guard insisted on the same routine they had used when Lars and Kate arrived.

Two minutes later Allison was flinging herself into Curt's strong, comforting arms. She turned, with a happy smile, to her mother, "You remember Curt, don't you, Mom?"

"Of course. How are you Curt?" Delphine rose and shook hands with her future son-in-law.

"I'm fine, Mrs. Kipp, how are you?"

"I could be better," Delphine admitted. "But at this moment, I'm very thankful to be alive."

Curt nodded, "Allison told me what's been happening here."

Allison pulled Curt over to Janelle and Ross, "You know Janelle and this is her fiancé, Ross Taylor."

Curt kissed Janelle's cheek and shook hands with Ross. Ross smiled. He was going to like this man. His handshake was firm and he looked you directly in the eyes. Ross had a thing about people who never looked directly at the person they were conversing with. Or people who looked at you briefly and then let their eyes slid away.

Allison turned to Lars and Kate, "And this is Ross' brother, Lars, and his fiancée, Kate." She looked up at Curt while the men shook hands. "They're the ones who have to postpone their wedding. You can help us make phone calls, if you want."

Curt pitched right in and by twelve o'clock the unhappy chore was finished, the wedding officially postponed until July 11th.

Delphine invited Lars and Kate to stay for lunch, but the couple declined with thanks. They hugged Ross and Janelle, pushed away their repeated apologies, and left. Delphine ordered lunch delivered to their room.

There was little conversation while they ate and soon after the meal, Delphine suggested a nap. "Last night was awfully long and late." Suddenly she slapped her head, "I forgot, we don't have a bed for Curt. I better call the manager."

She put down the phone and explained, "There aren't any adjoining rooms that have three bedrooms, but there's an empty room right next to these rooms."

"We'll take that one," Allison put in quickly, her face turned a bright red when she realized that she was admitting to her mother and sister that she and Curt were intimately involved.

Delphine laughed at the look on her daughter's face, "It's alright, Allison, this is the nineties. The desk clerk said she would have to okay the room with Dena and she'll let us know."

Dena Lark came back at seven o'clock, bringing with her a couple decks of cards and a variety of different board games. She shrugged her shoulder and said, "It will help to pass the time."

"Thank you, Dena," Delphine smiled. "Did the desk clerk tell you about the extra room we need?"

"Yes. I instructed the guards and we put another guard on the door. Be sure to alert the guards when you and Curt are ready to go to your room, Allison."

Allison nodded.

"Have you found out anything new?" Delphine asked.

Dena frowned, "Both Jack Thomas Huxley and Baxter Perry seem to have disappeared into thin air. We've been running down every possibility, but we've come up with nothing."

The room was silent while this news was digested, then Delphine looked up, "Can we go back to my house and get some more clothes?"

"I'm afraid not, Delphine. It would be way too dangerous, but I could stop and pick up whatever you need."

Delphine nodded and gave Dena her house key, "Thanks, Dena. I'll make a list for you."

"Will tomorrow be soon enough?" Dena wanted to know. "I have something to take care of yet tonight."

"Of course," Delphine agreed.

"Good. I'll be going now. See you tomorrow," Dena waved and left.

By ten p.m. the group was ready to call it a night. Allison and Curt left for their room and Ross and Janelle turned to their room, softly closing the door behind them.

Left alone, Delphine showered, put on her pajamas and crawled into bed with her book. She had profound confidence in the abilities of the police guards posted outside the doors. Within minutes she was deep in sleep.

Janelle and Ross showered and sat Indian style on bed, talking over the day.

"Do you think Lars is mad at me?" Janelle asked.

"No, he's not mad. Neither is Kate. They were both disappointed, but they understood the need for caution."

"Kate told me she was kind of glad it was postponed," Janelle confided. "She said there were some things she had wanted to finish for the wedding, but she hadn't had time. She probably just said that to make me feel better."

Ross smiled, "Kate would do that. She is really a very amiable person. Lars is going to be a very happy man, just as I'm going to be."

Janelle didn't answer. She cocked her head toward the door to the hall and listened intently.

"What?" Ross asked.

"I don't hear the guard moving around. You don't think he fell asleep, do you?"

"No, I don't. They only have three-hour shifts, Honey. Anyone can stay awake for that short a time."

Janelle shivered and pulled her robe closer, "I know we're supposed to be safe, with the guards and all, but I don't feel safe. This hotel is so big. A person could easily waylay one of the guards when he goes to the bathroom or to get a cup of coffee."

"What about the other guards? They'd notice if one of the guards didn't return or if a different person came back in place of the guard they were expecting," Ross argued.

Janelle nodded, her eyes searched Ross' face for comfort, "You're right, but I'm still worried."

He pulled Janelle into his arms and kissed her lightly. He had intended to ask her if she wanted to make love, but the look in her eyes and the pressure of her body against his, was answer enough. Ross kissed her again, his passions instantly on fire.

His lips brushed the soft skin of her face and traveled down her throat and back to her lips, while his hands roamed over the thin silk of her robe, stopping at the tie that bound it to her waist. His fingers fumbled with the knot that held it closed and finally released it. He gently pushed the robe free of her shoulders and tenderly lowered her to the bed.

Janelle's arms locked around him and pulled him close. In his arms, she finally felt secure, secure and loved.

The strangeness of the hotel room and their fear of Baxter disappeared as they joined together with a love and hunger that consumed them.

Baxter finished breakfast and picked up his package at the desk. He returned to his room, removed his newly acquired policeman's uniform from its wrappings and put it on. He turned slowly in front of the full-length mirror in the bathroom. *Fits like it was made for me,* he gloated. *Now for the beard and mustache.*

Removing the rented uniform, he carefully hung it up in the closet and quickly dressed in sport clothes. Locking the door behind him, he hung out the 'Do Not Disturb' sign. *I certainly don't want a maid to see that uniform in my closet,* he thought, *although I really don't think the cops would be smart enough to connect the uniform with my plans for Delphine and her brats, but no sense taking chances. If the maid did report the uniform after the murders, the cops would have a description of me and, since Delphine would definitely have reported his presence in the city, it wouldn't take them long to put a name with the description.*

His expression darkened at the thought of Delphine's brat reporting seeing him in Duluth and his lips compressed in a tight line. He could actually feel his muscles tightening in rage. *Thank God I haven't had any problems with the cops in Florida. There's no reason they should have kept track of my movements after I finished my parole and no reason for them to go snooping around in Miami.*

I have to go back and wipe out all evidence of my business. Kidnapping is a federal offense and carries a stiff punishment. I would end up dying of old age while I'm still in prison, he fumed.

I'm not going to spend the rest of my life worrying about the possibility one of my employees will decide to blackmail me or will have a pang of conscience and go to the police with testimony about the way I made my millions!

Baxter shuddered at the horrible thought of being returned to prison. No amount of trouble in destroying the evidence of his crimes would deter him from his objective; he would not allow that threat to hang over his head.

He took the elevator to the underground parking ramp and drove to the only other store, listed in the Duluth phone book, that carried costumes. He picked out a bushy mustache and a short thick beard that almost completely covered his face, starting from high on the cheekbones. Glancing along the counter, his eyes fell on the prominent display of many colored wigs. He smiled with confidence, a wig of blond hair would make the deception complete.

Jack and Ivy hurriedly worked on finishing their meal in the truck stop, both of them now anxious to return to Duluth.

Ivy's face lit up with joy as she listened to Jack explain his reasons for going back. "I figure Baxter wants the murders—if he manages to finish the girl and her mother off—to be blamed on me. Well, he's not going to get away with it. I've decided we're going back. We'll make sure the girl, and her mother, because the mother saw us, too, are dead, and then we'll lead the cops to Baxter," Jack grinned at Ivy with delight. "And here's the best part of the whole deal! After Baxter's out of the way—if the cops don't get him, we'll kill him, too—we'll start our own kidnaping ring. We'll be the ones taking in all the big money! What do you think of that idea?"

Jack had entirely forgotten his intentions to get rid of Ivy. The fight in the motel, her pulling a knife on him and his fears she would one day attack him in his sleep, were pushed from his mind in the excitement of having money in the large amounts that Baxter had it.

He would have the world by the tail, Jack told himself. And he could still have the fun of picking up stray girls, raping them and murdering them for the pleasure of seeing them die, that is if he still wanted that kind of fun. Having money in unending amounts would make a big difference in his wants and desires. He would be able to go anywhere he wanted, do anything he wanted. Maybe, just maybe, he wouldn't want to take the chance of murdering girls anymore. *I'll have a lot more to lose if I get caught after I have all the money in the world,* he reasoned.

Well, I'll think about that later, he thought, *right now, I need a plan for catching up with Baxter.* He frowned, so deeply concentrating on his strategy, that he missed Ivy's next words.

"We'll be partners," she declared. "Half for you and half for me!"

Jack bounced back to the present with a thump, "What?"

"You're not listening again! I said, we'll be partners."

"Oh, yeah," Jack said, sure as God made little green apples that he was not going to let that happen. Let her have half? No way! No way on God's earth was that going to happen. I'm the one who's going to be taking all the chances and making all the plans. No half-witted trollop was going to share half and half with him. Of course, he'd give her some money, lots of money, but half? No! "We've got a long way to go before the money starts rolling in, Babe. There are a lot of details to clear up first."

"Sure," Ivy agreed. "But that won't take us long and it doesn't hurt to dream. How are you going to find the people to buy the kids?" Ivy's thoughts flew to the vast number of girls, along with their boyfriends or husbands that she would be able to buy. With money, you could talk people into anything.

I could offer them ten thousand dollars to house sit for me, she planned, *I'd get a house way out in the country and set it up with a secret torture room. Course, I couldn't give the girls an address, because they might tell someone about their plans to house sit. If they disappeared the police would be sure to check out the address of the house-sitting job. I'll have to be careful not to bring the police down on myself.*

As they drew near Duluth, Jack said, "We need a car again. I'm sure that girl is not still at her mother's house. The cops probably have her hidden out in a hotel or motel. We'll have to stop at all of them and we can't do that using a taxi."

"But before we start with the hotels, we'll check the mother's house. We might find a clue to where they are and there might be evidence of a murder. Maybe the girl is dead."

"We've been over that, Jack, there was nothing on the radio."

"Not everything gets on the radio, especially if the cops don't want it on the radio," Jack argued.

"Okay, okay. Let's get on with it, I want that girl," Ivy said. Ivy had been picturing the girl in her mind's eye ever since seeing her at her mother's house. The girl was too pretty for Ivy to give up on getting her.

"You sure are a blood thirsty loser," Jack commented.

"Don't call me names!" Ivy's voice was low, but the menace it contained was perfectly clear to Jack. He suddenly remembered their fight in the motel and his plans to get rid of her. Well, he'd wait a little longer. He enjoyed seeing her joy in murdering someone, and besides, he could blame her if they were caught. It wouldn't get him off, but he'd probably get a lighter sentence.

Trying to soothe her, he apologized for the first time in their relationship, "Okay. Okay. Sorry, Babe."

Ivy was shocked at his apology and immediately suspicious of his motives, though she said nothing. She needed Jack, more now than ever, for he would be her means to money and the house in the country she had just been dreaming of.

Jack pulled the big rig into the empty parking lot of a deserted warehouse on the outskirts of Duluth.

"Why did you stop here?" Ivy asked.

"Because we don't want to be showing this truck around town. Did you forget it's stolen?" Jack's voice was sarcastic and dripped with venom.

"No, I didn't forget," Ivy shouted, "but there are no cars here. There are not even any houses."

"Then we'll just have to walk a ways, won't we?" Jack set the brakes, turned off the motor and jumped down from the Kenworth. "You can wait here if you want to," he called up to Ivy, who had not moved from her seat.

Ivy quickly lunged out of the truck. If Jack was really leaving the truck here, she had no intention of being left behind. Jack might not come back for her and there was no way she was going to miss out on the fun of catching up with Janelle Richardson.

The sun was well over the horizon and already becoming warm as they started down the street toward town. Jack hoped he would spot a car parked in an alley behind a house where the residents were still asleep. He wished now that they had never left the city. *I should have listened to Ivy,* he thought, *although I'm not going to tell her that.*

Stealing a car was always a danger, but stealing a car in broad daylight could be disastrous. There was no way of knowing if the people whose car he was stealing were watching him from the window. The cops could be on him before he could hot wire the ignition and get away.

Jack shrugged his shoulders. They didn't have much choice, they had to have wheels and they couldn't afford to buy a car; even a cheap car. The injustice of the situation made him furious with frustration. He yelled at Ivy, "Hurry up! We haven't got all day."

Ivy jumped at the sudden venom in his voice and stared at him. "What's the matter," she breathed quietly.

"That vile Baxter has money coming out his ears! Money we made for him. And we didn't get our fair share," Jack grumbled, suddenly remembering to keep his voice low.

When they finally reached the area where the houses started, he stomped down the first alley he came to, with Ivy close on his heels. Halfway down the block, they came to a three-car garage. Jack tried the door, it was unlocked. He whistled softly in glee.

Fifteen minutes later they were cruising down the street in a late model dark blue Chevy sedan. Jack took the car past Delphine's house, where he spotted a police stakeout team parked a half block away from the front of the house and another team at the back of the house.

"Not taking any chances, are they? No way we're getting in there without being seen," he growled. "That tells me Baxter didn't finish the job. Maybe he didn't kill any of them. If they were all dead, there would be no reason for the police guard."

Ivy didn't respond, but she looked at Jack with a new measure of respect. Quickly turning back to the window, she hid her look from him. *No sense giving him a big head,* she thought, *but that was pretty smart of him.*

Jack took the car around the block and headed back downtown. "There's only three big hotels in Duluth, we'll cruise past them and see what we find out. We'll forget the motels; they'd be too hard for the cops to guard. If there's nothing to see, we'll get something to eat and then drive past them again," he said, looking at his watch. "It's almost nine, but it'll be another hour before the stores open and people start getting around."

"Why wait for the stores to open?"

Jack sneered at her, "I'm waiting for the crowds, Idiot. We don't want to make ourselves a target for the cops. They happen to know my face."

Ivy flushed with fury, "Don't call me names!"

"Alright!" Jack turned away and frowned to himself. *She'll have to go. Soon.*

The hotels gave them no news. No cops were in sight. The downtown area was nearly deserted at this hour on a Saturday morning. They drove around until they found a small restaurant that was open and Jack sent Ivy in to get some food. He still wasn't willing to show his face around this town. His features had become too well known.

Should get a disguise, he grumbled to himself. *By the time Ivy gets the food out here and I get to someplace where we can eat it without being too conspicuous, it'll be cold.*

Jack carefully observed the pedestrian flow while he waited, noticing that the few patrons who stopped at the restaurant parked close to the door. He decided they would be safe eating right where they were, in the back of the restaurant's parking lot. Few people would even notice them and those that did would be indifferent to their presence.

Ivy came out ten minutes later, carrying the food in white Styrofoam boxes. They finished their meal quickly.

Jack glanced at his watch, "Let's catch a couple hours of sleep. There's nothing we can do right now anyway."

Ivy looked around at the growing number of cars coming into the parking lot, "We can't stay here."

Jack frowned. He had been so busy eating, he hadn't noticed how full the lot was becoming. "We'll go to one of the hotel parking lots."

Ivy shrugged, slid further down in the seat and closed her eyes.

Jack started the car and glanced in the side mirror, checking for traffic coming from behind them. A man and woman had parked behind their car and the man was coming up beside them on Jack's side, while the woman was advancing toward Ivy's side of the car. The man glanced at Jack in the slightly curious way people looked at strangers, turned away and then turned sharply back, walking quicker and staring at Jack for a long moment.

The man and woman came together in front of the car and the man whispered urgently to the woman, who turned abruptly and stared at Jack. The man whispered to her again, took the woman's arm and hurried her toward the restaurant.

Jack was furious. "Those two recognized me!" he raged, slamming his fist against the steering wheel. "Everyone must watch television these days! A person doesn't have an ounce of privacy anymore." He pulled out of their parking spot, wanting to floor the blue sedan, but knowing he had to act casual. If he flew out of the lot with spinning tires, the man would be sure to call the police. As it was, he had no way of knowing if the man would report his suspicions or not.

"Change of plans, Baby. We'll have to trade cars, just in case that guy calls the cops."

Ivy watched the man and woman enter the restaurant. "I could follow them and see if they make any phone calls," she suggested.

"No. We'd just be wasting time. Might give the cops time to get here before we're gone," Jack disagreed. He turned right at the street, drove three blocks and turned off the street they had been on. Zigzagging around after every three or four blocks, Jack hoped they appeared to be tourists. He had no idea in which direction the police might be coming from, if the man called them, but he was sure the man would have given a description of the blue sedan and probably the license plate numbers, too. No one followed them and no cop cars were in sight. Jack headed for the lakeshore area where they had left the Kenworth.

The man and woman hurried into the restaurant and followed the signs to the restrooms, where a public phone was located between the men's room and the women's room. The man reached for the phone book.

"Can't you call 911?" the women asked.

"I don't know. I thought that number was just for emergences."

"Why don't you try it? If you're not supposed to use that number, the operator will let you know, and besides, I think this is an emergency. If that was really Jack Thomas Huxley, he's a murderer and that's an emergency in my book," the woman said. She backed up a few steps and looked out the wide glass entrance doors in time to see the dark blue sedan drive past. "There he goes! He's driving away."

"Oh no! Get the license number! Watch which way he turns." The man punched out 911 and the operator answered immediately, "Duluth Emergency Operator 60. Can I help you?"

"We need the police. We...," the man had started to explain his need when the operator interrupted.

"I'll connect you, Sir."

A split second later a man's voice came on the line, "Duluth Police Station. Can I help you?"

The man was suddenly flustered and he stuttered in his hurry to relay his message, "We're at a res...restaurant. We jus...just saw Jack Thomas Huxley! The mur...murderer!"

"Okay, take it easy. Are you in danger?" the policeman asked.

The man took a deep, steadying breath, willing himself to remain calm, "No. No, he was in the parking lot, but he just drove out."

"Okay," the officer said again. "Where are you located?" The officer must have realized he was speaking too formally to the distressed man, for he added, "What restaurant are you at?"

"We're at Dave's Cafe. It's on Marion Street."

"Okay, I'm dispatching a car, hold on." The line went dead.

The man looked at his wife, "Which way did they go?"

"They turned right. I wrote down the license number," she said, handing a small slip of paper to her husband.

The officer came back on the line, "Did you get the make of the car, or the license number?"

"I've got both. He's driving a newer dark blue Chevy sedan, I don't know what model or year, and the license number is: 200-BWK. I didn't notice what state it was from. They just drove out, about two minutes ago. They're heading North on Marion Street."

"Okay. I'll give that information to the men headed over there. Please hold on the line, I want to get your name so the officers can talk to you."

A mile from the truck, Jack parked along a quiet residential street and got out of the car. Ivy quickly followed him. They walked five blocks before Jack found another unlocked garage.

This time the car inside was an old, rusted eighty-one Ford, with the keys hanging in the ignition. *The owner probably figured no one would want to steal a heap like this,* Jack thought. *And he's right, no one does wants to, but beggars can't be choosers.* He eyed the decrepit old car and disgustedly spat a huge blob of saliva against the dented driver's side door. Muttering under his breath, he pulled open the door and climbed in.

Ivy scurried around the car and repeatedly jerked at the passenger's door. It refused to budge. Jack sighed with frustration and shook his head. *Can't she ever figure anything out for herself?* he wondered. He pointed at the back door and Ivy finally gave up on the front door, pulled open the back door and fell into the car just as Jack started it rolling.

"Give me a chance to get in!" Ivy stormed, throwing him an evil look.

"If you weren't so extraordinarily stupid," Jack fumed, rage flushing his face a bright red, "you'd have figured out that door wasn't going to open. We can't hang around here all day!" Jack liked to tell himself that Ivy was stupid—perhaps in hope that when he decided to get rid of her, she wouldn't figure out what he was up to until it was too late for her to retaliate—but in truth, he knew she was smarter than she was letting on. *Maybe even a match for me,* he grudgingly admitted to himself, *I'll have to be very careful of her.*

Ivy muttered under her breath, but kept her thoughts to herself.

Jack drove out of the garage without a glance at the house, but Ivy watched the house until they turned the corner, blocking off her view. No one came out of the house. No alarm was raised.

Back in the downtown area, Jack swore again, "We can't drive into the parking lot of a classy hotel with a garbage heap like this." He glared at the street in front of him and swore steadily for a long moment. Ivy wisely remained silent and still. Suddenly his face lit up and he started for the outskirts of town again.

"Where are you going now?" Ivy asked.

"There's a ritzy area along Lakeside Drive where there's a lot of townhouses. Most of them don't have garages. I don't know why I didn't think of that before."

Ivy wanted to tell him he wasn't as smart as he thought he was, but she was sure he would completely lose control of his temper if she did. She needed him. He was going to help her get the girl and her boyfriend. Ivy ran her tongue over her full lips and swallowed nervously. It had been a long time since their last rape and murder. She was still furious with Jack for murdering a girl when she hadn't been along to enjoy it, too.

Forty-five minutes later they were back in the hotel district, driving a black, Lincoln Town car. Jack pulled into the ramp at the first hotel they came to.

The attendant rushed out of his office holding a parking ticket. Jack lowered the power window and called, "Thanks, Bubby, but I'll take care of it myself."

The young man opened his mouth to protest, seeing a tip go down the drain, but Jack drove past him without another word.

Ivy gaped at Jack in astonishment. He was acting exactly like the rich, sophisticated men she had seen in movies. She knew nothing of Jack's background, but suddenly a very pleasing picture played across her imagination. She saw the two of them rich. When they had a business like Baxter's of their own, they would be rich. They would be riding around in brand new luxury cars, wearing designer clothes, going to fancy hotels, watching Broadway plays, eating in elegant restaurants or flying to any part of the world they wanted to. Basically, doing anything and everything they wanted, including living in a secluded mansion with a hidden torture chamber. Ivy smiled dreamily in anticipation.

Jack circled through the entire ramp, not knowing what he was looking for, but keeping his eyes peeled just the same. At this time of the morning, the ramp was nearly full. He pulled into a spot on the lowest level and turned off the car. The day had grown warm, but the underground ramp was as cool as an air-conditioned room.

He looked at his watch, "It's eleven o'clock. We still have time to sleep here for a couple hours and then we'll cruise around again. Maybe there will be some activity at the old lady's house."

"And if there isn't?" Ivy asked.

Jack thought a minute, "Then you'll walk around inside the hotels. Maybe you'll spot Baxter."

"We've got to think of something better than that," Ivy argued. "Baxter could be back in Florida by now."

Jack lowered the reclining seat and lay back. "I'll think of something," he said, sounding more confident than he felt. *How are we going to find him?* he wondered silently. *She's right, he could be gone already. But if he's still here, he'll be at one of the three big hotels. Baxter's too spoiled by luxury to stay at any of the less expensive places.* He shrugged and put the worry out of his mind. *If he's here, we'll find him and if he's gone, we'll find out if the girl's dead. If she's not, we'll find her and finish Baxter's job.*

CHAPTER FOURTEEN

Jack and Ivy had been sleeping for almost two hours when Ivy awoke to the sound of a heavy door closing with a solid thump. For a few minutes she was disoriented. She remained still on the reclining seat of the luxury Town car, but her eyes slid to the tinted windows. A man walked between the car on their left and the white Pontiac parked next to it.

Ivy watched the man, seeing only his mid section as he unlocked the car and opened the door. His face came into view as he climbed into the car and started the engine. The man had not even glanced in her direction, but his profile was distinctly visible.

Ivy jerked with shock. Baxter! Surprise brought her body flying part way up before she gained control. She dropped back; afraid Baxter would notice any movement she made. She didn't want Baxter to look their way. The white Pontiac was backing out when she shook Jack awake and barked in a low voice, "Jack! Baxter's in that white car. Follow him!"

Jack awoke with a start and sat up quickly, levering the seat to an upright position. "Where?" he demanded, his head swiveling back and forth.

"There," Ivy was now sitting up, too. She pointed to the swiftly disappearing Pontiac. Jack started the Lincoln and shot out of their parking place. As they came up the final ramp before the street, they saw the white Pontiac turn to the right.

Ivy was ecstatic with joy, "How could we be so lucky as to find him that easily?"

"It wasn't that easy," Jack said. "We had to steal three cars and drive out to that girl's mother's house and back into the city again. And we sat in the hotel ramp for two hours." He fell in behind the white Pontiac, but left two cars between their car and Baxter's. "Where did he come from?"

"He must have come down in the elevator, but I didn't see him come out the door, I just heard the door slam. That's what woke me up. I didn't know the guy was Baxter until he climbed in that white car."

"So he must be staying at the Central East," Jack surmised. "And since he's still in town, that must mean he didn't kill the girl yet."

Ivy nodded, growing excited at the idea that Janelle was still alive. She was going to get her chance at the girl and Baxter would be an added pleasure. *He'll pay for all the times he shortchanged us,* she thought, *and he'll pay dearly.* "What are we going to do?"

"Follow him. See what he has planned. He must know where the girl is. We'll let him take care of killing her and then we'll kill him," Jack planned.

"No! I want the girl," Ivy argued hotly. "You know that Jack Thomas Huxley."

"Yeah. Well how do you plan to find her, Smart Aleck?"

Ivy thought for a long moment, "We can follow Baxter until we know where she is and then we can kill him before he gets to her."

Jack was silent for so long that Ivy thought he was going to agree with her. She watched as the Pontiac pulled in to a parking spot a half block ahead of them.

"It might work," Jack finally agreed. "We can try it, but if it doesn't work out, don't blame me and don't give me any trouble. The main thing is to get rid of the witnesses. There's plenty more girls." He pulled into a parking spot that was just being vacated. They were three cars behind Baxter's white Pontiac. "That was a lucky break," Jack breathed.

They watched Baxter go into a small shop part way down the block. Jack ducked down to see the name of the shop through the windshield of the car. He laughed softly, "Just what I was thinking of."

"What?" Ivy asked, trying to read the name of the shop from her position. She was too close to the store fronts to read it.

"A costume shop. Baxter must be getting a disguise," he laughed again. "Not a bad idea for us, too, if we had the money." The smile fell from his face and a grim ruthlessness took its place when Jack remembered the state of their finances, which he blamed entirely on Baxter. Their inability to spend wisely and budget their money had no bearing on the case as far as he was concerned.

Baxter emerged from the store ten minutes later and returned to the Central East Hotel, with Jack and Ivy close behind him. They watched as the elevator indicator rose to the fourth floor.

"What now?" Ivy asked.

Jack scratched his head in indecision, watching the elevator indicator go back down to the first floor, "I guess we'll have to wait here and hope he uses the car when he leaves again. There's no sense following him into the hotel. We can't ask what room he's in because I'm sure he's using an alias and we don't want him to see us. He probably has something planned for tonight. We'll wait here. And we're not going to take the chance of leaving, not even for eating. You better go and get us some food right now. It's a pretty safe bet he won't leave again right away. Bring plenty, we might have a long wait."

By eight p.m., Jack and Ivy were bored silly and beginning to get on each others nerves. The food was nearly gone and they were almost out of cigarettes.

"I'm going to get some more food and some cigarettes," Ivy announced, opening the car door.

"You better hurry. If Baxter comes out before you come back, you're going to get left."

Ivy hesitated. She didn't want to get left behind, but she knew that if they ran completely out of cigarettes, their arguments would turn mean. Jack could be a real mean mother and she didn't want to be bruised up again.

She climbed out of the car, telling herself that Baxter wouldn't come out until after dark. They had an hour and forty-five minutes until it was dark.

By ten p.m., Jack and Ivy had decided to take turns sleeping and watching. Ivy took the first watch.

Two hours later she woke Jack, thankfully lowered her reclining seat and closed her eyes.

Jack was tired. The two hours of sleep had only made him want to sleep more. He decided to take a short walk. He needed to empty his bladder.

He had walked to the corner of the ramp and just finished urinating against the cement wall, when the ding of the elevator bell brought him up short.

Baxter slept away the early evening hours and arose at twelve thirty a.m. Sunday morning. He carefully spread glue on his upper lip, cheeks and chin and attached the mustache and beard. Meticulously patting them into place, he examined himself critically in the mirror. He grinned at the picture he presented with the longhaired blond wig completely covering his own black and gray hair.

Baxter eyed his altered reflection with stunned amazement. *I wouldn't even know myself,* he thought, thoroughly satisfied with his disguise.

He donned the policeman's uniform and checked his watch. He'd be early, but no problem. He threw his regular clothes in a paper bag, placed his uniform cap at a jaunty angle on his now blond head and quietly left his room.

A policeman with blond hair came out of the elevator. Jack dismissed the man, but definitely decided to stay out of sight. He quickly crouched behind the closest car. He didn't want to be recognized by the cops now. *Or ever,* he told himself. He watched as the man approached the white Pontiac and stuck the key in the door lock.

Baxter in disguise. It had to be him!

Jack was furious with himself. *Why didn't I stay in the car?* He could just see himself reaching the street and finding Baxter was already out of sight. All these hours of waiting! He seethed silently as the white Pontiac backed out of its place. *Thank God I backed our car into its spot,* he thought, *that'll save a couple seconds.*

I've got to wait until Baxter turns the corner, he told himself, his muscles tensing impatiently, *if I don't, I'm taking the chance of Baxter seeing my movements in his rear view mirror.*

The white Pontiac had barely started its turn, when Jack sprinted for his car, praying Baxter wouldn't look over his shoulder.

He slammed into the car and threw the door closed with such force that Ivy, awakened abruptly, screamed in fear.

"What? What happened?" she asked, her eyes going to the spot where the white Pontiac had stood.

"Baxter came out while I was taking a leak."

Ivy gasped. "Don't let him get away!" she screamed, panicked at the thought of losing her one small link with Janelle Richardson.

Jack sworn under his breath and demanded, "You think I want to lose him?"

Ivy clamped her mouth tight and didn't answer. She gripped the edge of the dash as the heavy Lincoln swerved around a corner of the ramp. And then they were passing the ramp attendant and the street loomed ahead of them. The taillights of only one car glowed softly from the distance.

"That's got to be him," Jack muttered, swinging the car into the street. Fifteen seconds later they were close enough to see the white Pontiac. Jack immediately let the Lincoln fall back and sighed in relief.

A half hour later Baxter was parking the white Pontiac in the underground parking ramp at the Claremont Hotel. Turning off the engine, he slowly and carefully surveyed the area. One car had entered the ramp ahead of him, but the car had parked in the first available spot and Baxter had proceeded to the lowest floor of the ramp.

There was no movement of any kind and only six or eight other cars were on the same level as he was. Baxter slid out of the car and carefully locked the doors. Moving at an ordinary pace, he approached the elevator and pushed the call button. Seconds later the elevator slid noiselessly open, revealing an empty room.

Baxter took a deep, steadying breath and entered the lift. As the elevator rose swiftly to the fifth floor, he smiled in satisfaction, congratulating himself on his choice of times. At almost two a.m., the majority of the hotel patrons were cozily settled in their rooms.

Exiting the elevator, he contentedly patted the pockets that contained his gun, knife and the small bottle of ether. Delphine and her girls would be oblivious of their final moments.

Baxter frowned as he entered the staircase to the sixth floor, wondering if he would have the stomach for cold-blooded murder. He had thought he was going to enjoy murdering Delphine and her daughters, but now, in the final minutes before he would kill them, he suddenly doubted his decision to carry out this mission alone.

He had never directly killed anyone, except the policeman outside of Delphine's house. And that man had been a complete stranger to him. In the dark, and even with his powerful binoculars, he hadn't gotten a clear look at the man's face. Baxter felt no remorse for that death.

Also, two or three of the children he had ordered kidnapped, had died at the hands of his employees. Baxter did not consider these rare incidents as his crime. He had not ordered the killings; therefore he was not responsible for their deaths. In point of fact, he had been disturbed and angered by the deaths, feeling a sincere sorrow for the loss of the kids, over and above any loss of fees. Baxter loved kids, all kids, but especially very young girls.

At the door of the sixth floor, Baxter quietly turned the knob and opened the door a minute crack, totally unaware that he, the stalker, was being stalked.

Jack and Ivy followed Baxter to the Claremont Hotel ramp. They drove slowly down the ramp levels, letting Baxter stay two floors below them.

When Baxter parked on the bottom level, they quickly parked where they were, not wanting him to hear their car approaching. They walked swiftly, but quietly, to the bottom level.

They reached the bottom as the elevator closed behind Baxter. As they watched the elevator ascend to the fifth floor, Ivy said, "What are we going to do now? We can't follow him. He'll see us."

"We're going to have to take that chance," Jack replied, pushing the elevator call button. "If we don't follow him, we won't know where the girl is and we won't know if he kills her or not. All we can do is hope he's too absorbed in his plans to notice us."

Jack and Ivy reached the fifth floor in time to hear the click of the stairway door closing on the sixth floor. Jack quickly pulled open the door leading to the fifth floor and glanced up and down the hall. Seeing no sign of Baxter, he assumed Baxter had been the one going to the sixth floor.

They silently hurried up the steps. Jack cracked the door open and saw the disguised Baxter talking to another policeman outside the closed door of one of the hotel rooms.

"So that's his game plan," he whispered, watching closely as the two men conversed.

"What?" Ivy asked, unable to see around Jack. Jack kept his eye to the crack and didn't answer.

Bob Kelly sat on a chair next to the closest room to the stairway. He held a magazine in his beefy hands, but his eyes were focused on the doorway where Baxter would appear. This deal was making him more and more nervous. *I should have told Ellen to start packing,* he thought, *but if someone from the station should stop at the house and see the suitcases, it might give us away. They'd know I would have said something if we were planning a vacation.*

When the door cracked open, Bob dropped the magazine and jumped to his feet. He looked around quickly. No one else was in sight.

Bob was paralyzed with fear. He wished he hadn't gotten himself in this mess. He had a bad feeling about the whole plan.

Baxter pushed the door wide and advanced to Bob's position. He held out his hand for the key Bob offered him, delighted to discover only one key lay in his hand; a master key to either the entire hotel or at least the sixth floor. *Wonderful,* he thought, *I won't have to search for the correct key to each room*. He turned back to Bob and nodded toward the slowly closing stairway door, signaling him to leave.

Bob took two steps toward the door, still looking at Baxter/Florida and then turned back. If he didn't clue Florida in on the changes, Florida would probably get caught and if Florida got caught, he would probably rat on Bob. "There's been a change. I didn't hear about it until I reported for duty. There are three guards now. Apparently the boyfriend of one of the daughters showed up. Detective Dena Lark assigned another guard to the third room."

Baxter nodded, "Any other problems?"

"The two on that side take turns getting coffee. After you rotate at three a.m., it will be the other officer's turn to go. The guy over here doesn't leave at all. If the guard on this side needs to go to the bathroom, he has to wait until he's rotated to the other side."

"Okay. Anything else?" Baxter asked.

"No."

"Do both guards know your story about being sick?"

"Yes. They're both expecting the new guy on the force to take my place." Bob Kelly confirmed. He took a couple steps toward the stairs, hesitated and then added, "I would guess they'll be over here within ten to fifteen minutes to introduce themselves and welcome you to the force."

Baxter smiled and sighed silently in relief, hoping Bob didn't see the relief he felt at learning this piece of news. He had planned to enter the room as soon as Bob was gone. "I'll report that important conveyance of information to my boss. I would bet you've just earned yourself a bonus." He made a mental note to add a thousand dollars to the original fifteen thousand he had planned to pay Bob.

Bob turned away, sure that the bonus would make his wife, Ellen, happy. That was another thing he sometimes wished he could change; he wished he hadn't told his wife about his little indiscretions. But of course, if he hadn't, he wouldn't have been able to use any of the money he was illegally receiving. As it was, he had to be careful how he spent the money and leave the impression with the guys at work that he was deep in debt.

Ellen saw his paycheck each week and she was smart enough to realize they couldn't live as high on the hog as they did on just his paycheck. And she paid the bills, she knew what they owed and to whom. There had been no way to fool her, so Bob had told her the truth. What was the use of having extra money if you couldn't use it?

He hurried toward the stairway, shaking his head and wondering why he had gotten himself into this mess in the first place. The money was nice, but was it worth the fear that someday he would be found out?

Jack put his finger to his lips, warning Ivy to silence. The second cop turned toward the stairway door and Jack quickly pushed Ivy up the stairs toward the seventh floor.

They waited silently, just around the corner of the landing, but the door didn't open.

"Wait here," Jack whispered to Ivy. He had started back around the corner when the door below him opened with a swish. He ducked back out of sight, barely missing being seen by the man entering the staircase, and listened to the footfalls going down the steps.

He nodded and smiled, telling Ivy confidently, "Now Baxter's the guard."

"How do you know?" Ivy asked innocently, smirking to herself. Any dummy could have guessed Baxter's plan.

"Because Baxter was wearing a policeman's uniform. He's counting on his blond wig, mustache and beard to keep the cops from recognizing him," Jack whispered importantly. "Stay here. I'll see what's happening." He silently went back down the stairs to the sixth floor.

Ivy waited impatiently for five minutes, and then she followed him. Jack gave her a dirty look when she came up behind him, but allowed himself to be pushed out of the way so she could see through the tiny crack of the door.

She saw the policeman sitting in front of the door, "That's Baxter?"

"Yup, sure is."

Cussing silently, Baxter seated himself on the chair Bob had vacated and picked up the crumpled magazine from the floor. Fifteen minutes was not enough time to complete his objective, especially since he now had another room and another person to eliminate. Both girls and their mother had to be killed. Baxter knew how much the girls looked alike; he didn't want to make the mistake of killing only Allison and leaving Janelle, the witness, alive.

With the guards alternating positions every hour, waiting ten to fifteen minutes for the two men to introduce themselves to him would also cut into the time allotted for him to be inside the rooms. *It'll still be enough time*, he reassured himself. He could only kill Delphine and one of the couples the first time in the rooms. He would have to wait until he was stationed around the corner and the other guard had left to get coffee before he would be able to enter the third room.

He cursed again, two more men would now have the opportunity to observe his disguised face; two men who had been specifically trained to scrutinize every detail of every situation. Baxter didn't know one of the officers was a woman, or he would have worried a lot more. Women were often more tuned into personal appearances than men were.

Baxter debated the possibility of eliminating the two police officers. His chances of success would be slim, if not totally non-existent. Overpowering or tricking one policeman might work, but with two men.... Baxter discarded the idea immediately. He would have to rely on the good quality of his disguise and hope that neither man recognized the wig, false beard and mustache for what they were.

Baxter glanced at the door he sat next to. He wondered which couple he would find in the room. Not that it mattered one way or the other, they all had to go.

"There's another cop coming!" Ivy jerked back, letting go of the door. Except for Jack's quick reflexes, the door would have clicked shut with enough sound to alert the two men in the hallway.

He sworn at her under his breath and glued his eye to the small opening. He watched and listened as Baxter shunned the friendly cop. *He's a cool one,* Jack thought, wondering if he could have remained so calm. Ivy knelt on the floor and watched the scene from under Jack's position.

No more than thirty minutes passed before the first man came around the corner. Baxter's lips thinned with annoyance. Now he would have another wait, after this man left, before the second man made his appearance.

The officer moved quickly to Baxter's position, while Baxter rose slowly to his feet and faced the man, giving him a hard stare. No sense being friendly, the man would stay longer if he was met with a friendly co-worker. In fact, if he was cold enough, maybe the second officer wouldn't come over at all.

Officer Tom Sutherland ignored the chilly welcome he was receiving and smiled broadly. He stuck out his hand to the new officer, "Hi. I'm Tom Sutherland. I hear we're going to be working together."

The man nodded and shook hands. He did not remove his driving gloves and he said nothing.

Tom was temporarily at a loss for words. He was very aware of the slur intended when the man did not remove his gloves. The man was an ice cube. He didn't crack a smile and his eyes didn't move a flicker as he inspected Tom. Tom shivered involuntary. The guy's stare was so cold and blank.

"Are you new to Duluth?" Tom Sutherland asked, finding his voice in a rush. He smiled, trying to break the icy indifference of the other man.

The man shook his head, but still didn't answer. He continued to stare until Tom was so uncomfortable that he backed away and muttered, "Well, hope you like our department." At the continued lack of response from the new man, he abruptly turned away and started back to his position.

At the corner, Tom glanced back. The man stood as he had left him, staring after him.

Tom turned the corner and walked slowly toward the third guard. He didn't see Baxter hurry silently to the corner, wait a few seconds and cautiously inch his head forward until he could see around the corner.

Tom passed his station and proceeded directly to the other officer's position, shaking his head as he walked. "That new guy is a cold one," he reported to Officer Alcott, their voices carrying to Baxter's position. "I introduced myself and he didn't say a word, just nodded and shook my hand, not even telling me his name. And he didn't take off his gloves." He shook his head again at the explicit slur. "Then, to make conversation and break the ice, I asked him if he was new in Duluth, but he just shook his head no. I was embarrassed. I felt like I was forcing myself on him. I left. You don't need to bother trying to make friends with him."

Officer Peg Alcott frowned, "Wonder what his problem is?"

"I don't know and I don't care. He doesn't need to worry about me making any more attempts to get to know him. You should have seen his eyes," Tom grunted in defeated resignation and threw up his hands. "Cold, I tell you, real cold."

Peg shook her head and her red curls bounced lightly on her shoulders. "Sure hope I never have to have him for a partner," she exclaimed.

"That's a big ten four!" Tom agreed wholeheartedly. He turned and started back to his position, keeping his eyes on Peg's beauty as he walked, "It's your turn to get the coffee."

"Right. I'm going to stop at the bathroom while I'm down there so I'll be gone an extra couple of minutes."

"Okay, no hurry," Tom replied.

Baxter ducked quickly away from the corner when Tom Sutherland headed back toward his position. He was pleased with the way the conversation of the two officers had fit right into his plan. He knew he didn't have to worry about being disturbed again. He congratulated himself on his acting abilities.

He hurried back to his position and quietly slipped the key in the door lock, already wondering how long he was going to have to wait before he could gain entrance to the third room; the one that was not connected to these two.

Jack and Ivy watched Baxter enter the hotel room. They held their breath in anticipation of a scream and were surprised when no sound came from behind the closed door.

"We've got to follow him," Ivy exclaimed, jumping to her feet and pushing on the door. "I bet he's killing the girl right now!"

Jack roughly pushed her back, "Are you crazy? Do you want to get us caught?"

"Baxter's out of sight and there's no one else around! You've got to stop him, you promised me I could kill the girl."

"Forget it! I'm not going in there and take a chance on being caught. And neither are you. We'll wait and see what happens," Jack ordered.

"You're not the boss," Ivy argued, beside herself with impatience and a lust to kill.

"Okay, go ahead, but you're on your own. If you go out into that hall, I'm leaving."

Ivy studied Jack's determined face. *He's not going to change his mind,* she decided. She scowled at him, but backed down, resigning herself to waiting for their next victim, which would be Baxter.

Slipping silently into the room he was supposed to be guarding, Baxter quietly closed the door behind himself and quickly removing the bottle of ether from his pocket. He grinned as he poured a small amount on his handkerchief, keeping the sleep-inducing drug as far away from himself as possible.

The overhead light in the bathroom had been left on and the door was cracked open, spilling a dim light into the bedroom where Baxter stood. The room was big, with two queen-size beds, but only one was occupied. His sharp eyes easily picked out the sleeping form on the occupied bed, but the dim light did not reveal the identity of the sleeper.

Silently moving forward until he stood next to the bed, Baxter recognized Delphine. She was lying on her side with the blankets tucked snugly under her chin. He smiled; suddenly sure his long nursed hatred of the woman would ensure his ability to snuff out her life without any regrets.

Reaching out, he held the ether soaked rag close to her nose without touching her. Delphine stirred slightly and rolled to her back. Baxter had again placed the hankie under her nose, still without touching her, when Delphine opened her eyes.

Dulled by sleep and the first effects of the ether, she was slow to realize the dark form hanging over her bed was real and not just a carryover from her nightmares. Her lack of response gave Baxter the time he needed. He lunged forward with enough force that the bed rolled sideways, almost making him loose his balance. He clamped the hankie over her nose and mouth with his right hand and used his left hand to lock her left shoulder to the bed, effectively pinning her to the bed.

At the force of his attack, her eyes widened in terror, but she gave no hint of recognizing Baxter behind his disguise. Her arms came up swiftly, her right one sweeping across the nightstand and dislodging the heavy lamp that stood there. It fell to the thickly carpeted floor with a weighty thump. Her fingers clawed at her face in a desperate attempt to dislodge the sweet smelling rag from her nose and mouth. Her struggles lasted no more than ten seconds before her eyes slowly lost their brightness and slid sideways under her lids.

Baxter stiffened in alarm as the lamp struck the floor, but held the hankie in place for another thirty seconds, until he was convinced she was unconscious. His ears strained for any sound from the connecting room. Nothing. He relaxed slightly, but felt a burning need for haste.

The room was dimly lit, but seemed menacingly dark and silent when Janelle awoke with a sudden start. Terror gripped her with a vise like hold. Her heart pounded with fear and her breath came in small gasps, making her feel she was suffocating. She held her breath, listening intently. Nothing stirred. No sound reached her straining ears, but Janelle was certain some threatening sound had awakened her. She was afraid to move, afraid to turn on the light, almost afraid to breathe.

Ross was silent and still beside her. She couldn't hear his breathing, but she knew he was a sound sleeper. She did not think her sudden movement, when she was startled awake, would have woke him.

Suddenly knowing beyond a doubt that Ross was awake, Janelle whispered, "I heard something."

"So did I," Ross whispered back.

Janelle was not surprised to hear his voice come out in a whisper. Somehow she knew he had awakened to the same feeling of danger that she had. "What did you hear?" she whispered.

"I don't know," Ross's voice was barely audible in the silent room.

Long moments passed while neither of them moved, each straining their ears for a hint of what had awakened them.

Baxter had intended to suffocate Delphine with her pillow, there by blocking out his sight of her and insuring his ability to actually kill her, but he abruptly changed his mind. Regardless of his very real desire to have her dead, he had not wanted to be looking into her face when she died, but smothering took too long, and in her unconscious state, he would not be sure she was dead.

His hand shook slightly as he reached under his uniform jacket, trying to retrieve his knife from its scabbard. Cursing his cowardice, he took a firm grip on the butt of the knife and unsheathed it in one quick jerk.

Raising his arm, ready to strike the fatal blow to Delphine's unconscious body, Baxter's eyes inadvertently fell on her peaceful face. His face blanched and a sudden cold ripple flashed down his neck. Cold sweat poured from his brow, dripping in his eyes. He pulled his hankie from his pocket and mopped at his forehead, dislodging his wig from its seat on top of his head. It slid down his face and fell to the floor, slightly under the bed. The hankie fell unnoticed from his shaking hand as he dropped his knife on the bed and retrieved his wig, hastily realigning it on his head and twisting the cap until it felt comfortable and in place again.

He grabbed the knife, took a quick, desperate breath and pulled the pillow from under Delphine's head. Her head rolled sluggishly from the pillow and plopped onto the bed. Baxter quickly covered her face with the pillow, effectively blotting out the sight of her face. His troubled conscience immediately ceased to plague him.

Steadying his wildly pounding heart with another deep breath, Baxter raised his arm and plunged the sharp blade directly into Delphine's chest, piercing the artery next to her heart. Moments later she was dead. Baxter withdrew the blood coated knife from its hole.

He carelessly wiped the blade across the fluffy white bedspread that was quickly turning a bright red. He grabbed the either soaked hankie from the bed and jammed it into his pocket. His eyes slid quickly over the bed, looking for anything he might have dropped that would give the police a clue to his identity. Satisfied, he pushed the bed back to its original spot and turned to the adjoining door that led to the room Janelle and Ross shared.

Still shaky from his ordeal with Delphine, he released the doorknob before it was clear of the latch, causing it to click lightly. He froze, listened intently for no more than four seconds and then abruptly moved forward, telling himself that the click had only sounded loud to his overwrought nerves and could not have awakened Janelle or her boyfriend.

Suddenly a faint click broke the smoldering darkness. Janelle tensed with fear, clutching at Ross' hand. "The door to Mom's room...," she croaked.

No further sound followed the slight click. Unable to bear the terror that could lurk in the dark unknown, she reached out and flicked on the bedside lamp.

Time was short, Baxter reminded himself. Before the three a.m. guard change, these three had to be dead and he had to be calmly sitting on the guard chair with the door to Delphine's room locked behind him. If this chance got away from him and he didn't manage to eliminate all the people who were able to identify him as the man at Delphine's house on Friday evening, he may not get another opportunity.

He stepped into the silent, dark room and was immediately aware—without knowing how he knew—that Janelle and her boyfriend were awake. Rage overtook him; he couldn't afford to lose this opportunity. He lunged forward just as the light flashed on, temporarily blinding him. Moving on instinct, he slashed at the spot where the fuzzy figures had lain on the bed.

A dark clad figure was moving swiftly into their room. Janelle's terrified mind registered a police uniform but she was too traumatized to hold back her scream of fright.

The man's right hand was curved tightly around the butt of a large bloodied knife that was directed at their bed.

Janelle screamed again as the figure lunged toward them. Ross grabbed Janelle and rolled swiftly away from the descending knife blade, pulling Janelle to the floor on top of him.

Janelle's shrill screams shocked Baxter from his blind rage. He had missed his targets, but there was no time for another attempt. The sound of a key being inserted in the door lock stabbed into his brain. *Hurry!* he told himself. The other two guards couldn't capture him.

He jerked his knife free of the entangling sheets and fled back to Delphine's room. Shaking with weakness and fear, he waited until he heard the door of Janelle's room slam against the wall and then carefully cracked open the door that led to the hall from Delphine's room.

Janelle screamed again as the door to the hall flew open and crashed against the wall. Relief flooded over her as the guard from the hall rushed into the room.

The intruder had turned at the sound of the key in the lock and ripped his blade free of the mattress. Spinning away from the bed, he had disappeared back into Delphine's room a split second before the door to the hall burst free of its lock. The connecting door stood slightly ajar, but the man was gone.

Ross and Janelle scrambled clear of the tangle of bedclothes that had rolled with them to the floor and rose shakily to their feet, pulling the loosened bedclothes around their naked bodies. Ross held one arm in front of Janelle—whether to restrain any movement toward the door or only an instinctive gesture of protection—Janelle didn't know.

The guard, Officer Tom Sutherland, had drawn his gun and shouted a warning into the hallway behind him. He entered Janelle and Ross's room quickly and threw himself to the floor at the side of the doorway, anticipating gunfire being directed at him. His eyes flew around the room, while his outstretched arms, with his hands frozen tightly on his weapon, followed the movement of his eyes. His young, inexperienced face was a mask of barely concealed fear. Ascertaining there was no one in the room except Ross and Janelle, his worried eyes came back to rest on them.

"The middle room," Ross shouted an alert to the officer. "He went back into the middle room!"

Baxter saw the redheaded female officer rush down the hall and charge into Janelle's room seconds behind the other officer. He quickly made his escape. Swiftly darting past Janelle's room, he decided the best place to hide was in the least expected place, another room. If he raced for the stairs, he would be intercepted long before he reached the parking ramp. The elevator was out of the question for the same reason.

The first officer cautiously approached the door to Delphine's room as another officer entered behind them. Janelle wanted to yell at them to hurry, but she realized the need for extreme care. No sound came from the room as he slid into the darkness and positioned himself along the wall a few feet from the still open door.

Officer Peg Alcott quickly covered the short distance to the doorway Tom Sutherland had disappeared into. Bursting into the room behind Tom, she called out loudly, "Police! Freeze!"

There was no answer, no sound at all.

Janelle had tossed on her robe and was staring at the empty doorway when she suddenly realized there had been no sound from her mother. A scream of terrible anguish tore from her throat. Forgetting all caution, she raced across the floor and sprinted into her mother's room; throwing on the light switch as she plunged through the door.

CHAPTER FIFTEEN

Jack and Ivy waited ten minutes before Janelle's shrill scream cut through the peaceful night.

"Come on! We've got to get out of here," Ivy whispered frantically. They hurried down the steps, ignoring the elevator, and emerged in the ramp a few minutes later.

Back in their car, Jack said, "We'll wait to see if he gets out of there. If he does, we'll follow him. Now that we know where the girl is, we don't need Baxter anymore. We can get rid of him, if he makes it out of there."

Ivy lips spread in a wide grin before she remembered the length of time that had passed before the scream, "How do you know she's still alive?"

"I don't know for sure. But dead people don't scream. We'll have a talk with Baxter before we kill him. Think you can make him tell us the truth? If you can't, I can. Before he dies, we'll know if both the girl and her mother are dead or not.

Ivy relaxed against the seat. She hoped at least one was still alive. That was a girl's scream. Maybe they're both still alive. That would be fun. We've never had a girl and her mother before. And before them, there was Baxter.

Baxter rounded the first corner past the rooms Delphine's family was occupying and stopped at the first door he came to. He quietly inserted the key in the lock and turned it slowly. He nearly shouted with joy when the key turned with ease and the lock clicked open. His presumption about the key had been correct. At the very least the key would most likely open all the doors on the sixth floor.

Slipping silently into the room, he softly closed and locked the door. He stood still while his eyes adjusted to the semidarkness of the room. This room—unlike the windowless room Delphine had—had a large picture window, which was uncovered by drapes, making Baxter hopeful that he had picked an unoccupied room.

Fastening his eyes on the king-size bed, which dominated the luxurious room, he sighed with relief to find it empty. He quickly searched the room for any signs of occupancy. Finding none, he relaxed slightly and took a long, deep breath, hoping to calm his badly frayed nerves. Returning to the locked door, he placed the chain lock in its latch, securing himself a precious minute or two if a security guard or policeman decided to check the room.

Moving more slowly, he examined the room again. He needed a place of concealment if the room was searched, which he very much doubted, but greatly feared. The bathroom was equipped with both a shower and a bathtub. The shower curtain was pulled closed; leading Baxter to assume this was the normal procedure of the cleaning staff. *It might work,* he thought, but if the curtain were pulled back, he would be trapped.

He shook his head, rejecting the spot, and returned to the bedroom. Five places presented themselves to his imagination; under the bed, behind one or the other of the two large easy chairs, which graced the room, in the closet or behind the door. Baxter stuck his head under the bed and then got down on his stomach and wiggled himself under the bed.

He immediately felt a sense of doom and a sick claustrophobia overcame him. Frantic, he pushed himself free of the bed, totally convinced that this tight little crack would not be one of his choices.

He crouched behind one of the large chairs, but discovered that the chair was not large enough to completely conceal him.

The closet was eliminated for the same reason as the shower; Baxter did not want to be trapped in a small area, unable to move quickly to defend himself.

The last available place was behind the door. Baxter knew most people conducting a search would look there first, and a lot of searchers slammed the door against the wall with force, which is what the police who had stormed into Janelle's room had done, eliminating the possibility of a person being hidden there or, if a person was concealed there, slamming the door into the person, temporarily disabling them. He finally chose behind the door as his hiding place, simply because he would not have been able to tolerate the other places.

I've still got my gun, and the silencer, he reminded himself. *If I'm found, the finder will just have to be eliminated.* He patted the solid comfort of the firearm and then decided to be prepared in case of an emergency. He removed the gun, swiftly attached the silencer and stuck the gun in his waistband.

Baxter crossed to the large picture window, where the light of the moon, along with the lights of a few late night people, filtered into the room, allowing him to move comfortably around the room without the use of the electric lights. His eyes scanned the side of the massive brick walls of the hotel. There were no outside fire escapes, the building was too new.

He suddenly wondered how much chance an occupant of one of the hotel's rooms had in case of a fire. State ordered sprinkler systems were not always as effective as they were designed to be and did nothing to eliminate the killing smoke. Elevators became firetraps, stopping at the floor where the fire was located, regardless of the buttons the rider chose, and stairways became a roaring chimney for the hot flames of destruction.

Collapsing in the plush easy chair closest to the door, Baxter turned his mind to the problem of the remaining witnesses, Janelle and Allison. Both girls had seen him at Delphine's house, but Janelle was the only one who could identify Jack Thomas Huxley as the murderer in Ohio, therefore she was the most crucial witness.

Now what? What would the cops do? Would they move the witnesses to another hotel? Well, it would be no problem finding out which hotel; Bob Kelly was too money hungry to stop now and Baxter now had a big advantage. If Bob suddenly decided not to cooperate, Baxter would threaten to connect him to the murder of Delphine.

Bob has no idea what Florida really looks like, Baxter thought, *and he has no reason to suspect Florida was the person who took his place on guard duty.* The only thing Bob could report to the cops was the sound of Baxter/Florida's voice.

Baxter was blissfully unaware of the fact that Bob had taken just such a precaution. Bob had recorded Florida's voice each time Baxter/Florida had called him, starting way back twenty years ago. In fact, every deal he had made at home, Bob had recorded and placed in a safe deposit box at a local bank. He had decided at the onset of his illegal deals that, if he was caught, he would not go down alone. And, the recordings were the perfect life insurance, should they ever be needed.

Baxter worried the problem back and forth in his mind. When Janelle and Allison were moved to a different hotel—Baxter was sure they would be moved—the security in the new spot would be so tight it would be next to impossible to gain entrance.

He could try impersonating one of the room service boys, or, he could set up a bomb.... Baxter winced at the thought of all the innocent people who would die. Chances were high that the innocent would also include a number of kids. He frowned angrily; absolutely hating the idea, but if there was no other choice....

Light flooded Delphine's room. Janelle stopped two steps inside the door. She saw her mother, the pillow over her head, the snowy white bedspread covered with blood, but her mind refused to believe the truth her brain was trying to tell her. Her hands flew to her mouth and she froze, halfway into the room. "Mom?" Her eyes stared incomprehensibly at the silent figure on the bed. "Mom?"

Ross was right behind her. He knew immediately that Delphine was dead; that much blood meant an artery had to have been cut and too much time had passed for Delphine to survive the loss of blood. *How did this happen?* he wondered helplessly, *the police were right outside the door.* He couldn't believe it. Then he remembered the man, the man who had rushed into their room and stabbed at them. The man had been a policeman! Ross distinctly remembered the blue uniform and the badge on his chest as he lunged toward their bed. He shook his head in confusion. *Why would a policeman want to kill them?*

He wrapped his arms around Janelle from behind and tried to draw her back into their room. "Don't look, Honey," he whispered, grief making his voice unsteady.

Janelle pulled away from him, as though his voice and movements had released her from a trance. She rushed toward the bed and threw the pillow off her mother's face before she knelt on the floor and wrapped her arms around her shoulders. "Mom? Mom?" She put her hands on either side of her mother's face and gently shook her. "Mom? Wake up. It's Janelle. Mom?"

Ross fell to the floor behind Janelle. He reached out and put his arms around her waist. He gently held her as she struggled to absorb the image before her.

Janelle resisted his hug, tugging to free herself as tears poured down her pale face. Like a small child who was being ignored, she repeated the same thing over and over, "Mom? Mom....?

"Mom? Talk to me Mom. You've got to talk to me. You can't be dead. I can't lose you, I love you too much. Life will not be worth living without you Mom. Please! Talk to me!" Janelle buried her face against Delphine's unmoving shoulder, murmuring soft words of love and longing.

Ross' arms remained around her, but suddenly she felt lost, cast into a world without light, adrift in an ocean of sadness.

Long minutes passed while the room remained silent and still.

At last Ross tenderly moved his arms to her shaking shoulders. He drew her head away from Delphine's shoulder and tucked her into the comfort of his embrace.

Janelle didn't resist but she continued to sob and she didn't return his hug. Ross silently held her tight, letting her draw on his strength and love.

Behind them, Officer Tom Sutherland had blinked rapidly in the bright light when Janelle had flipped on the overhead light. His eyes searched the room quickly, but found no one. He moved to the bathroom and pushed the door wide open. The shower curtain was pulled open, exposing the empty bathtub, and no other hiding places presented themselves. Tom hurried to the open hall door.

Covering Tom from the adjoining doorway, Officer Peg Alcott watched as he checked the bathroom and hurried out into the hall. She immediately called for the paramedics and the homicide squad.

Assured help was on the way, she moved silently around Janelle and Ross and checked Delphine's carotid pulse. No pulse moved rhythmically under her searching fingers, though she spent long moments at the head of the bed; suddenly doubting her expert knowledge as to the exact spot to locate the pulse she sought.

Finally dropping her hand in resignation, she backed away from the bed and whispered, "I'm so sorry."

Leaving Delphine to Janelle's tender administrations, she swiftly searched Janelle and Ross' bedroom, and hurried into the hallway. Tom was just coming back from the stairway door at the end of the hall.

"I looked down the other way, too. Nothing. I didn't hear the elevator and there was no one descending the stairs, at least I didn't hear anyone."

Peg nodded. She hadn't expected him to find anything. Too many minutes had passed since the initial alert, which had been Janelle's scream of terror.

Both Officers hurried back to Delphine's room. Peg was torn between conducting a thorough search and the danger of leaving the remaining two women unprotected.

Tom and Peg had been informed which woman was the primary witness to the crime in Ohio and both of them wanted nothing more than to see Jack Thomas Huxley put away for murder. All past murder cases against him had been based on circumstantial evidence and in each instance, Huxley had been acquitted. The courts had managed to convict him on a rape charge and he did an eighteen-month prison term for that charge, but so far there had been no witnesses to the suspected murders.

They still had their witness and if Tom and Peg could help it, they weren't going to lose her.

"I'll get the sister and her boyfriend," Tom whispered to Peg, watching as she carefully locked the door between the two rooms.

"Okay," Peg said. "Try not to be gone too long. This isn't the best situation for an officer alone. I don't want to leave the room and that leaves the door to the connecting room unguarded."

Tom eyed the locked door. The battering weight of a man would most likely snap the lock, "You're right. I'll lock the hall door to the other room and I'll be right back." He left the room and Peg locked the outside door behind him, throwing the dead bolt at the same time.

In the distance, the mournful wail of sirens reached the ears of the people in Delphine's room. Janelle raised her tear stained face from Ross' shoulder, "I have to get Allison."

Ross rose to his feet and helped Janelle up. She leaned against his strength as they turned toward the door.

"You better stay here, Ms Richardson. Officer Sutherland is waking your sister. They should be here in a few minutes."

"I want to go to her," Janelle cried. Her eyes were desperate looking.

"It isn't safe for you to leave this room, Ms Richardson. We haven't found the person that broke in here yet. He, or she, could be anywhere. I don't want to see you hurt," Peg Alcott insisted—gently, but firmly. She stayed at the closed doorway and lowered her arm to her side. The weight of her service weapon was tiring. She allowed the gun to point to the floor.

She had holstered the gun briefly after they found the body, but had taken it back in her hand a few minutes later, unwilling to take a chance on being surprised by the murderer. Her eyes flicked to the locked door that led to the room Janelle and Ross had occupied. *This is not a safe place to be,* she thought again, mentally hurrying Tom, *there's too many doors for one guard.*

Her eyes came back to Janelle as Ross led her to a large, comfortable looking easy chair in the corner of the room. Sitting down, he pulled Janelle onto his lap, cradling her like a baby.

Sympathetic to the shocking loss the girl had just suffered, Officer Alcott had as yet asked no questions about the break in.

Watching the girl now, Peg decided to wait for Tom's return, although she knew there would be another delay while the sister absorbed the loss of her mother. Also owing to her decision to delay was the fact that Peg didn't want to divide her attention between questioning the young couple and guarding them from harm.

Peg's mind returned to the question that had been bothering her since the beginning of this ugly business; where was the new guy? Had Officer Sloan Berg been murdered, too? When they had time to look, would they find his body hidden away in a closet or an empty room?

Or...was he involved in this mess? Peg instinctively veered away from this thought, knowing her loyalty to the force was not shared by everyone, but unwilling to think the worst of a fellow officer, even if that officer was a most unlikable person. But where was he? Where had he disappeared to?

Officer Tom Sutherland knocked on the door and called out to Peg, "Peg? It's me, Tom."

Peg breathed a deep sigh of relief and cautiously unlocked the door, quickly backing away from the door immediately after releasing the locks. Peg knew this maneuver looked cowardly to the untrained eye, but it was a very necessary move. More than one officer had been surprised when he opened a door to a familiar voice and found the friend accompanied by the murderer.

Allison and Curt rushed into the room, followed more slowly by Tom Sutherland, his eyes running up and down the deserted hallway one more time before he stepped in the door. Peg turned away from the sorrowful scene taking place between the two sisters and whispered to Tom, "Let's wait outside. We can guard the doors better from out there anyhow."

"Right." Feeling himself close to tears, Tom was not anxious to remain in the room with the mourners. "I'll just check the other room one last time." He unlocked the door to Janelle and Ross' room and carefully advanced into the room, half expecting the murderer to jump out at him. It was entirely possible the man had backtracked and entered the room while he was waking Allison Richardson and Peg was inside the other room. Tom wasn't taking any chances.

The two officers met in the hall and advanced to a position at the corner of the hall, where they could see down the hallway to Delphine's door and watch the door to Janelle's room, too. They turned their backs to one another. This position afforded their backs protection, while each had a clear view of anyone approaching their position. Their extreme caution caused both officers to feel a little foolish, but considering the enormity of the crime already committed, they were leaving nothing to chance.

"Where do you think the new guy is?" Tom asked, keeping his eyes trained on the hall in front of him.

"I wish I knew," Peg said, unwilling to express her fears.

"Do you think the guy that broke into Mrs. Kipp's room killed him?"

"I think it's a definite possibility," Peg responded, her grip involuntarily tightening on her weapon.

The elevator bell pinged and the door glided open to reveal the paramedics and a backup unit from the police force. Peg heard Tom's sigh of relief as her own pent up breath escaped her lips. Tom held his position as she quickly moved forward to unlock the door to Delphine's room.

A second elevator arrived and Officer Dena Lark led two other officers into the hall. She stopped by Tom Sutherland, "What happened?"

"Someone broke into Delphine Kipp's room," Tom replied. He didn't immediately add that Mrs. Kipp was dead, aware of the close friendship between the two women.

Dena voice was sharp with anxiety, "Was she hurt?"

Tom's look of anguish gave Dena her answer before the words came from his mouth, "I'm sorry, Dena, she's dead."

Dena Lark turned away quickly and rushed toward Delphine's room. She realized her distraught emotions were unprofessional, but her friendship with Delphine had become closer than the friendship of two sisters and she could not control her sense of loss.

The two women hadn't spent as much time together as they both would have liked, owning to the time consumed on their separate professions, but Dena could not picture the future without Delphine to consult in times of trouble. Many times Delphine's uncanny ability to see directly to the core of a problem had helped Dena to solve more than one difficult case.

Dena was not married, having lost her husband of five years to divorce. She had one son, Wayne, who had joined the Marines at the age of eighteen.

He had decided, after his first tour of duty, to make the Marines his career and he was currently stationed in Japan. Dena rarely saw him, leaving her with no family in the immediate area.

Over the years she had met several men whom she might have married, but her dedication to her career had blocked the road to a happy relationship, just as it had with her ex-husband. Dena had more or less made up her mind that she would remain single.

Delphine had filled the empty spots in her life. The women had shared their innermost secrets. Delphine was someone, outside of Dena's working colleagues, to share meals with, see movies with, go bowling with, or just to sit and reminisce with. Dena couldn't count the morning coffee breaks they had shared over the years.

Tears rushed to her eyes and her hands shook with fear as she burst into Delphine's room. She had not accepted Tom's word as gospel and she prayed desperately for him to be wrong. Delphine couldn't be dead. It was impossible. There had been three police guards on duty! Impossible.

One look at the motionless form on the bed, and Dena knew her worst nightmare had come true. She moved slowly to the bed and stood silently looking down at her friend.

Long minutes passed before the sounds in the room broke through her grief. She turned toward Janelle and Allison with a low cry of despair.

Both girls rose to their feet and moved toward Dena. Allison hesitated briefly, but Janelle moved with the assurance of knowing she was headed for a deeply caring person. They wrapped their arms around each other and stood huddled together in profound grief, murmuring consoling words to each other. A stranger watching the three women would have thought they were a mother and her two daughters.

The paramedics had examined the body and left, leaving the police to their work. Sterling Templeton, the officer who had been first to arrive at Delphine's house when Jack Thomas Huxley, Ivy and Baxter had tried unsuccessfully to murder Delphine and Allison, had also been among the first backup team to arrive at the hotel. He had called the county corner and was now standing guard over the crime scene, making sure none of the evidence would be lost before the detectives could start their work.

Twenty minutes passed before Dena could pull herself together and return to her job. More officers had arrived and she outlined search duties for the men before she returned to question Delphine's family.

She escorted Janelle, Ross, Allison and Curt into the room Janelle and

Ross had occupied; noticing as she left Delphine's room that the detectives in her squad had arrived and were painstakingly putting together evidence against the murderer.

"I have to ask you some questions," she said, her voice catching on the words. "I'm sorry I have to do this now, but it's necessary if we're going to catch your mother's murderer. And we are going to catch him. I promise you, if it takes the rest of my days here on earth, we are going to catch him." Her voice choked off and she had to clear her throat before adding, "Delphine was a wonderful woman and my dearest friend."

Janelle and Ross sat next to each other at the round table in the corner of the room, while Allison and Curt were across the room in the easy chairs. Since Allison and Curt had not arrived on the scene until Delphine had already been dead, they could offer no clues to the killer's identity. Dena sat down across the table from Janelle and Ross.

Allison sat slumped in her chair, limp and dejected, but clinging tightly to Curt's hand. Tears still streamed down her cheeks, to plunk unchecked onto her robe. She had her bare feet tucked under herself and she looked like a child whose mother had deserted her.

On the other hand, Janelle's tears had dried up and a fierce determination was stamped across her pretty face. She felt as Dena felt; whoever had murdered her mother was going to pay for his crime. If the police were unable to find him, she would find him herself. He was not going to get away with it, not if she could help it.

Ross had his arm on the top of her chair and was gently rubbing her neck and shoulders, feeling the tightness of tense muscles beneath his fingers. He sensed the thoughts that were going through Janelle's mind and he hoped he would be able to turn her away from her troubling hopes for revenge against Delphine's murderer. It wasn't that he didn't want to see the person punished, he did. It was only that he felt it was a job for the police. And if they were unable to find the murderer, he didn't want Janelle to feel driven to find the man herself.

Unfulfilled visions of revenge could ruin a person's life. Ross understood Janelle's motives, since she held herself totally responsible for this entire horrid situation, but he didn't want to see her become obsessed with revenge.

Janelle's thoughts were following the same path as Ross', except she was just as determined to find her mother's murderer as Ross was determined to steer her away from that very revenge. Her love for her mother had increased over the years. Instead of following the normal pattern of becoming less and less dependent on her mother, Janelle had relied more and more deeply on her as the years had passed.

The psychiatrist she had seen after Baxter's abuse—and had continued to see periodically over the years, until she met Ross two years ago—had told her this feeling was not unusual in cases of a father's (or step-father's) abuse. She had gently explained to Janelle that she and Delphine had exchanged roles when Janelle had so desperately tried to keep her mother from finding out about Baxter. In Janelle's sub-conscious mind, she was the mother and her mother was the child she was protecting.

"It's only natural," the psychiatrist had said, "that you are now seeking the protection that was unknowingly denied you in your time of need. I am not saying your mother was to blame for this lack of protection. She was completely ignorant of the situation Baxter forced you and Allison into. She did not know you were rejecting her protection. If you had not believed Baxter's threats to kill your mother, if you had told her about Baxter's abuse, she would then have provided the protection you so desperately needed, which is exactly what she did when she found out about Baxter.

"Baxter was the only one responsible for the acts he committed against you and your sister. You were not responsible, not in any way. His threats against your mother brought on your desperate longing to protect her, thereby reversing your roles."

Janelle understood the reasons for her feelings, but until Ross came into the picture, and captured her heart, she had continued to grow more and more dependent on her mother, not leaving home until the age of twenty, when she guessed that Delphine wanted to marry Frank Kipp and was holding him off because of her fear that the same thing that had happened with Baxter could happen again.

For months she had been devastated, hopelessly lonely and lost, by her move to an apartment, but eventually she had made the adjustment and had begun to grow emotionally, finally maturing into womanhood. With the help of her psychiatrist, she had redeveloped the principles and teachings her mother had instilled in her and had become the striking, confident young women she now was.

"Did you see the person who broke into your room?" Dena asked, frowning at the remembrance of no broken door or lock. Did the murderer have a key?

Could one of the hotel employees be the murderer? But why? Was it possible that Baxter had paid a hotel employee to murder Delphine and her daughters? *Yes*, Dena decided, her face grim, *that possibility is entirely possible.*

Janelle and Ross both nodded and Ross said, his voice still betraying his disbelief of the uniform he was sure he had seen, "It was a policeman."

In spite of her many years of hearing the unbelievable, Dena was shocked. Her mouth dropped open and for a moment she was unable to respond. Swallowing the lump in her throat and licking her dry lips, she asked, "A policeman? Are you sure?"

Ross nodded again, "I'm positive. I distinctly saw his uniform and his badge."

"So did I," Janelle said.

Dena was silent for a minute, her eyes staring at the tabletop. She raised her head slowly, "Did you recognize him?"

"No. We only had a very hurried look at him, but I don't think I've ever seen him before," Ross said. Janelle shook her head.

"It wasn't one of your guards?" Dena asked.

"None of the ones that I've seen, but I didn't see the men who came on in the middle of the night," Ross replied.

"Janelle? Did you recognize the man?"

"No. I've never seen him before either," Janelle was shaking her head as she spoke, "but I didn't see all the guards either."

Dena was worried. Was it possible one of the trusted officers on the Duluth police force was responsible for this heinous crime? Her mind immediately went to the new man that had been hired two weeks ago. His reputation and recommendations had been above reproach, but....

"Can you describe him?"

Ross looked at Janelle, but she shook her head, "All I remember seeing was a beard and mustache. I think his hair was blond. I was too terrified to think about remembering what he looked like. At the time, I didn't think I was going to be around to make any identification."

Ross turned back to Dena, "He was short, five ten or eleven. And stocky; or maybe just overweight. But it was his eyes I remember the most. They were black, midnight black, and he was furious. His eyes flashed, or maybe I should say sparked. He looked like he was madder than a rampaging bull."

"What did he do?" Dena asked.

"He charged at us with a knife!" Janelle cried, her voice nearly hysterical with remembrance. "I screamed and Ross pulled me off the bed and rolled on top of me. I was so petrified I couldn't have moved on my own." She reached out and grasped Ross' hand, clinging to him as she would cling to a lifeline being thrown to her while she was drowning.

"He didn't hit either of you, did he?" Dena was horrified at the turn this case could have taken if Janelle and Ross hadn't woken up before the man charged into their room. Janelle and Ross could both be dead too. And as far as that goes, he might have broken into Allison and Curt's room, after he had finished with Janelle and Ross, and killed them too.

"No," Janelle said, her voice shook, "but his knife stabbed into the bed right where Ross had been laying." Her hand tightened on Ross' hand until he winced.

"What woke you up?" Dena wanted to know. If you rejected the distinct possibility that the murderer was one of the guards, something wasn't right. The man didn't break in, so he had to have had a key. The guards each had a key to the rooms. Dena had felt that was a necessary precaution; each man was able to enter the room he was guarding with the greatest of haste, if the need arose, but now she wondered. *Might the crime have been avoided if the guards had not had keys? Had the man killed one of the guards and taken his key? Was the killer one of the guards?* Dena shuddered at the thought. She didn't know who had been scheduled to work what hours, and she hadn't yet talked to either Officer Tom Sutherland or Officer Peg Alcott, so she had no idea if anyone was missing or not.

Janelle and Ross both shook their heads. "I don't know," Janelle said. "All I remember was being suddenly awake and terrified. I didn't know why I was so scared and I don't know what woke me up." She trembled and her eyes went to Allison, who was sobbing into a Kleenex.

"Ross?"

"I don't know either," he shook his head again. "It seems like the bed might have jerked."

"I jumped a little when I first woke up," Janelle remembered.

In spite of herself, Dena's face fell. She had not wanted her face to show her disappointment, but she had hoped Janelle and Ross would have a clue to the killer. "Okay.... I'm going to talk to the guards. Can I bring you anything? Coffee?"

All four young people refused the offer and Dena reluctantly turned back to Delphine's room. For the moment, she wished she wasn't in charge of this investigation. She would have liked to stay with the girls, offering whatever support she could.

Baxter stood looking out the window of the room he had hidden in. Suddenly he noticed the bright light that seeped around the drapes in the room around the corner from his position. Calculating quickly, he determined the room was the one Janelle and her boyfriend were in.

He slammed his fist on the windowsill in excitement. If the police left them in the rooms they were in now for the rest of the night, he would still be able to reach them.

He thought about his early days as a mountain climber. For a number of years, in his youth, mountain climbing had been his greatest thrill. He had learned all there was to learn in books and then had begun to climb mountains. He moved to Colorado and joined a mountaineering club, where he progressed quickly through the relatively easy climbs used to teach new climbers.

Baxter's one hang-up was his need to work, as his parents were not rich people and he had been on his own since he graduated from high school. He took part-time jobs as a waiter and worked only enough to finance his climbing.

After a year of climbing in the Rocky Mountains, he joined a group of mountaineers who were headed for Mount Everest, the highest mountain in the world. Baxter fell from a cliff while on that climb and broke his leg in three places, which required steel pins to repair the extensive damage. His mountain climbing days were over.

But scaling the side of this hotel will be easy, he thought. His excitement rose to a fever pitch at the thought of using his mountain climbing skills again.

The hardest part was going to be getting a rope and a pick. He would have to make do with tennis shoes, but this didn't worry him. Tennis shoes would work fine on the rough brick of the hotel.

Baxter stared at the roof of the hotel. Suddenly it came to him. A grappling hook! And who would have a grappling hook? And a long sturdy rope? A police station of course. Grappling hooks were used to fish bodies out of lakes or rivers. It would make the perfect tool to anchor his rope to the top of the hotel. Baxter laughed out loud, Bob Kelly was going to make an amazingly fast recovery from his illness and he was going to be making a previously unscheduled stop at the police station's equipment room.

Now to get out of this hotel without being detained by the police, he thought. He quickly stripped off his uniform jacket, shirt and tie. Clad only in the blue uniform pants, which he hoped would pass for mere dress pants, shoes and a white undershirt, he inched open the door to the room he was in.

Two policemen stood talking at the corner leading to Delphine's room. Both men had their backs to Baxter.

Leaving the door cracked open—to avoid the noise of closing it—he casually walked out and headed away from the policemen. His gun, with the silencer attached, was stuck in his waistband and his knife, in its scabbard, was nestled snugly against the bare skin of his chest. The bottle of ether was safely tucked in his pants pocket. He had pulled his undershirt loose from his pants to hang over the weapons. He looked a little lumpy, but he hoped the policemen would not see the bumps from a distance. Of course, Baxter reassured himself, if they came after him, he would be forced to shoot them.

Holding his breath, not daring to look behind himself, Baxter walked slowly toward the stairs at the end of the hall, expecting at any moment to hear the shouted, 'Halt!'

The policemen either had not seen him, or they supposed him to be an innocent hotel patron, because Baxter was not challenged. He reached the steps and quietly opened the door, casting a quick look in the policemen's direction; neither man had moved and neither man was looking his way.

He noiselessly closed the door behind himself and raced silently down the steps, laughing under his breath. Janelle and Allison would be seeing him again...and sooner than they thought.

CHAPTER SIXTEEN

Detective Dena Lark softly closed the door between Delphine's room and Janelle and Ross' room; she wanted to spare them as much as possible.

The lab crew had finished their examination of the crime scene. They were quietly packing up to leave.

"Please stay a few minutes," Dena said. "I need to talk to the guards on duty, but I'll be back in a few minutes." The men nodded and she hurried out the door, finding Tom and Peg right outside. She glanced at the other officers in the hallway and then asked, "Were you two on guard here tonight?"

Peg and Tom both nodded.

"Who was the third guard?" Dena asked.

Peg answered for both of them, "Bob Kelly was here until two a.m., but he was sick. The new man, Sloan Berg, took his place."

"Where is Officer Berg now?"

Peg lowered her head and Tom answered Dena's question, "We haven't seen him since before the murder."

"Did he say he was leaving for some reason?" Dena asked, already knowing the answer to her quest.

Peg and Tom said in unison, "No."

Dena searched their faces, "And you don't know where he is? You have no idea where he might have gone?"

They shook their heads.

Dena thanked them, "Thank you. Please stay here. I have to talk to the lab crew before they leave and then we'll go into this in more detail." Both officers nodded again.

Dena returned to the death room and addressed the lab crew, "What did you find?"

"Not much," Harland Galeson, the senior lab technician, replied. "A few fake blond hairs, which will probably test out as having come from a wig, a few black hairs, which are probably from one or both of Mrs. Kipp's daughters and a few auburn hairs which I'm sure are Mrs. Kipp's. There are plenty of fingerprints, which we'll need to check against all the people who had a right to be in the room. Grady found a hankie," Harland believed in giving credit where credit was due. He hadn't found the hankie and he wasn't going to let Dena Lark think he had. "It was under the edge of the bed and was slightly damp, probably with sweat. That's our only real hard evidence right now. A person's perspiration is like his fingerprint. If you find the person who did this, we can prove he was in this room by his sweat on the handkerchief," he paused and then added, "I'm hoping the coroner will come up with more than we did."

Dena nodded, "Okay, thanks Harland. The handkerchief is a big plus. We'll need every shred of physical evidence we can get."

She turned to the three detectives in her squad, Grady Walker, Ed Marshall and Alex Hall, and started with her partner, "Grady?"

"Near as I can figure, the murderer had a key. There are no signs of a forced entry and no one heard any unusual noises. The windows are sealed shut and the seal hasn't been disturbed. There's a sweet odor by her face that I would guess was ether, but that will need to be confirmed by the coroner's office. The first officer on the scene," he checked the notebook he held in his strong hand, "Tom Sutherland, said there was a bed pillow over her face when they first entered the room, but I don't think the woman died of asphyxiation. I'm quite sure the coroner will confirm the knife wounds were the cause of death." He stopped and looked at the body. "Can't figure the reason for the pillow. Presumably the woman was already unconscious from the ether. Maybe the guy had an attack of conscience?" Grady's stocky body held a position of surprise, perhaps surprised that this thought had popped into his head. He frowned, making the small scar on his cheek—that he had received while playing college football—stand out and turn a dull red.

"Just a minute," Dena said. She leaned out the door and called to Tom Sutherland and Peg Alcott to join them, noticing that there were still four officers left in the hallway. "You guys keep your eyes peeled," she called to the other four officers. "We want to question anyone who approaches or leaves the area."

The men nodded and the two at the corner of the hall belatedly turned so they could see down the hall past the doors that led to the rooms where Janelle, Ross, Allison and Curt had been, never guessing that they had already missed seeing Baxter leave the room he had hidden in.

The arrangement of the room doors had been the one objection Dena had had to the placement of her guests. The room that had been Delphine's opened in one hall and the connecting room, where Janelle and Ross had been, opened in the hall around the corner. The room Allison and Curt had shared opened a short distance down the hall from the door to Janelle and Ross' room.

The rooms the police usually used for witnesses in protective custody were on the fifth floor. On that floor there were three connecting rooms, with the doors all opening into one hallway, in plain sight of each other.

Tom and Peg joined Dena and the other detectives in Delphine's room, where the coroner was just removing the body. Dena stood silently watching as the sheet covered body was lifted and carried from the room. Her face betrayed her deep grief. The men, and Peg Alcott, remained silent, eyes cast anywhere but on Detective Dena Lark.

Long moments passed with the room in complete silence. Dena rubbed her forehead and then shook her head as if to clear it. Her voice was soft when she murmured, "I'm sorry." No one said anything and she briskly turned to Tom and Peg, "What does Officer Sloan Berg look like?"

Tom answered, since Peg had not even seen the man, "He's rather short, about five ten and slightly overweight, about a hundred and ninety. His hair is blond, dark blond, and he has a full beard and a mustache. Black eyes." Tom suddenly looked puzzled, "Black eyes, real black eyes, and blond hair? I think that's the first time I've seen a black eyed blond."

Dena was immediately suspicious, "Could he have been wearing a wig?"

Tom frowned in thought, "Maybe. I didn't look real close at his hair, I was too embarrassed."

"Embarrassed?" Dena questioned.

"Well," Tom confessed, "I went down to say hello and welcome him to the force—I hadn't met him before tonight—and he was very unfriendly, in fact, I would call him a very cold man. He embarrassed me."

Dena thought a minute. Tom's description matched Ross'. Could the man have been disguised? Could he have been trying to chase Tom away with his cold manner? She voiced her thoughts, "Did you get the feeling he was trying to get rid of you?"

"Yeah, I mean yes, Madam. I did get that feeling," Tom replied. A look of anger and disgust filled his face. "But I didn't put any importance on it until right this minute."

Tom's use of madam was unusual. She had known Tom for more than five years and this was the first time, and probably the last time, he had ever called her madam. It was testament to the confusion and sorrow they were all feeling.

Her heart burned in her breast, feeling as though it had fallen away from its perch between her breastbones and was being sliced to pieces by her ribs. If only Tom had been suspicious of the new man's motives in rejecting Tom's friendly advances! Delphine might still be alive. Dena shook her head, knowing that she herself, in the same situation, might not have been suspicious. Hindsight was always twenty-twenty.

She abruptly realized that she now thought of the new man, Sloan Berg, as the murderer. Was it true? Had one of their own men murdered Delphine? Why?

"Could the man have been an imposter? How soon did you go down to introduce yourself after Officers Bob Kelly and Sloan Berg changed places?" Dena asked.

Tom answered the last question first, "Bob said Sloan Berg was coming at two thirty a.m. and I went down there about twenty five to three. I don't know about being an imposter, I guess he could have been."

Dena and the men pondered this information. "Not enough time for the murderer to get rid of Sloan Berg and take his place as guard," Grady Walker remarked.

"Maybe the murderer changed places with Sloan before they came into the hotel. Maybe Sloan's body is outside, in the parking ramp or the lot across the street," Ed Marshall put in. He pushed back the thick tumble of gray black hair that had fallen across his forehead and dropped his six foot two, two hundred and ten pound frame into one of the room's easy chairs. He had arrived home from a late night case at twelve a.m. and had slept for a short three and a half hours before the call had come to join Dena at the hotel. He was bone tired and disgusted with the guards for not preventing this latest tragedy. He, above all others, knew of Dena's deep friendship with Delphine Kipp.

He and Dena had occasionally shared an evening together and Ed wished he could convince her to marry him. He was sixty, to her fifty-two, but if she didn't want to quit working and keep house, he was willing to do it. He was tired, tired of police work, tired of the constant human misery he was continually coming in contact with; human misery and suffering which he was unable to alleviate. He was ready to take it easy, do some fishing or just plain relax around the house.

"I suggest we get Bob Kelly down here. Maybe he can clear up this mystery. In the mean time, we better start looking for Sloan Berg and questioning the patrons in the rooms close by. Maybe someone heard something," Dena said, adding, "I'll call Bob."

The men split up and moved down the hall. Detective Ed Marshall stopped at the door next to Allison and Curt's room. He eyed the open crack of the door and then drew his revolver, calling Detective Grady Walker back from the door he had approached.

Ed kicked the door open, slamming it hard against the inside wall. Nothing moved. He reached in and flipped on the overhead light, stepped quickly into the room and moved in a crouch to the side of the doorway, keeping the wall behind him.

Grady had also pulled his gun, covering Ed from the doorway. Their eyes traveled quickly around the room. A few pieces of clothes lay on the bed, but no one was in sight and there was no sound. Ed advanced toward the bathroom while Grady moved into the room, covering Ed's back.

Ed entered the bathroom and pulled back the shower curtain, nothing. He slowly turned back to the bedroom, noticing that the bathroom was clean and sanitized, apparently unused.

He looked around the bedroom more closely. The room did not seem to have been used, except that the clothes lay in a heap on the bed. He picked them up and whistled in surprise. "A policeman's uniform jacket," he told Grady, who had already identified the uniform for himself.

The two men looked at each other and Grady mumbled, "Looks like the boss was right. But how did the guy get out of here without someone seeing him?"

Ed shrugged and eyed the clothes again, "Everyone was pretty relaxed. I know I didn't have the faintest idea the murderer could be right around the corner from us, if these clothes are actually from the murderer."

Dena called Bob Kelly's home. The answering machine came on after the fourth ring. She replaced the phone and turned to Officer Peg Alcott, "Peg, take Tom with you and run over to Bob's house. He's not answering the phone, but he's probably sleeping and just doesn't hear it. Bring him over here."

Ed Marshall returned to Delphine's room, "Found something you should see, Dena." Dena followed him around the corner without questions, knowing Ed would show her what he wanted her to see or explain when he was ready. "The door was unlocked and cracked open when I got here," Ed told her. He showed her the policeman's clothes on the bed. "It looks like your theory was right, Boss," he said, repeating what Grady had said.

Dena frowned playfully and punched him in the arm, thankful for the brief reprieve from the grief of Delphine's death. "Don't call me Boss," she said, mock anger in her voice.

Ed smiled at her, his face softening with emotion, "Sorry, I was just teasing."

Dena turned away from his open look of adoration and examined the coat on the bed. She looked around the room, "We better get the lab guys back here and have them go over the room. Maybe they'll turn up something useful."

"Right," Ed reached for the phone, all business again, wiping from his mind the memory of the way Dena always turned away from him. He called the lab while he watched Dena carefully search the room for clues to the person who had left the clothes.

When Ed hung up the phone, Dena asked, "Anyone see the guy leave?"

"Nobody reported seeing him. I'll check with the two guys who were watching this hall." He left Dena still examining the room.

Peg and Tom returned to report that Bob Kelly wasn't at home. They had banged on the door until his wife, Ellen, had stumbled out to the door. "She said Bob came home about quarter to three and went to bed shortly thereafter. The phone rang before he was asleep and he told her he had to run out for a few minutes, but he didn't say where he was going. We told her we had called, but she said she had fallen asleep again before Bob left the house and she didn't hear the phone ring again."

Dena didn't answer. Bob Kelly? Was it possible he was involved in this mess? *No*, Dena thought, *Bob has been on the force for twenty-five years and there has never been the slightest mention of anything bad since he had accidentally killed that Asian boy.*

But who had called him? And more important, where had he gone? Dena thought about the times involved. Janelle's scream had come at two forty five, about the time Bob had arrived home—according to his wife. This put

Bob in the clear, as far as the actual murder was concerned.

Tom had talked to the new man on duty at two thirty five and Bob had been gone at that time, collaborating Bob's wife's report. How much time had passed after Bob had returned home and before he got the phone call?

"Did Bob's wife say what time the phone call came?" she asked Tom and Peg.

Peg answered, "We asked her, but she said she hadn't looked at the clock again. She had only looked when Bob came in the house and that was at two forty five. She says she was groggy, half asleep. I told her to have Bob call the station the minute he returned home and I made sure she understood it was very important. I told her it was an emergency."

"Good," Dena nodded and glanced at her watch. It was three forty five a.m. Sunday morning. Delphine had been dead an hour. "Will you two help search the rooms? We need to find Officer Sloan Berg."

Peg and Tom both nodded. Their shifts of guard duty would be over in a short time, but both officers knew the need for extra manpower in a situation such as this.

The lab technicians arrived back on the scene and Ed Marshall showed them to the room where the clothes were found. Grady returned to the task of questioning the hotel patrons and Dena went back into Delphine's room.

There has to be something I'm missing, she thought.

Baxter emerged on the ramp and walked sedately to his car. He saw no one moving, but did not want to draw attention to himself if someone was watching him. He did not see Jack and Ivy sitting in their car, studying his every move.

He drove three blocks before he found a public telephone and pulled into the curb. He fed the telephone and dialed Bob Kelly's number.

Jack turned the corner behind Baxter's position at the curb, quickly made a U turn and parked close to the corner, but out of sight of Baxter. He hurried to the corner and watched Baxter place his call, wishing he could hear the words being spoken.

Bob answered on the third ring, having delayed his answering in order to activate the recorder to record the phone call.

The voice he heard was brief, "Florida here. My man was unable to complete his mission. I need a grappling hook and a long rope. I am sure these can be found in the evidence room at the police station."

Bob's mouth fell open in surprise. Surely Florida did not expect him to go to the police station after he had said he was sick. His appearance there would look very suspicious.

Florida continued, "I want you to get them for me."

Bob hesitated, knowing that if he went to the station, he would be observed and questioned as to his reasons for being there. "I won't be able to get those things without signing for them, at least not before eight o'clock in the morning."

"I don't want you to sign for anything. You must know where the key is kept?"

"Yes...but I can't get in the station without being observed. If I'm seen, anything that is missing will be blamed on me."

Florida was silent for minute, "I'll send a guy to distract the duty sergeant. How soon can you be there?"

"Twenty five minutes." Bob didn't tell Florida about the camera at the station. It might be to his advantage to have a picture of Florida— or Florida's man, if he really did have a partner—and he'd think of some reason he had to return to the station, something to explain his appearance on the camera's tape.

"Make it five a.m., at the station," Florida instructed. "I have to call my man."

"Right," Bob confirmed. "I'll wait across the street until I see your man go in."

"Where should I have my man meet you afterward?"

"There's a theater parking lot two blocks south of the station. I'll wait there for him," Bob said.

"Okay. My contact authorized me to tell you this will be worth twenty thousand to him," Bob heard Florida say. His heart jumped with excitement, no way was he going to turn down this job; risk or no risk. "It will be deposited in your account."

Bob didn't answer and the connection was broken. He returned the phone to its hook and turned off the recorder. Now what? What had really happened at the hotel? Why did Florida need to sneak back into the hotel? Bob was sure that was why Florida wanted the grappling hook and the rope. Bob also suspected Florida didn't have 'a man' or 'a contact'. He was quite sure the man at the hotel tonight had been Florida himself and the man's image was firmly planted in his mind's eye.

Suddenly Bob smiled. *If I'm seen by the duty sergeant and fired for being in the evidence room without the guard, it will be my excuse to get away. There's no reason for anyone to suspect I'm involved with Florida. I'll make up some story to explain the grappling hook, if they see me with it.* Bob couldn't imagine what the story would be, but he'd worry about that if the need arose. *By tomorrow night Ellen and I will be long gone.* Bob smiled again. *We'll be able to live like kings and I won't have to work anymore.*

Bob was suddenly glad Florida had shown up again. It had been many years since he had heard from the man and Florida paid very well for small favors.

He went back to the bedroom, told Ellen he had to leave for a few minutes, and started to get dressed.

"Who was on the phone?"

"It wasn't too important, but it means more money for us. I'll tell you about it in the morning," Bob said. Ellen was asleep before he left the bedroom.

Jack watched Baxter return to his car and, guessing where the man was headed, raced the big Town car around him and parked on the street in front of Baxter's hotel, knowing Baxter would go to the ramp. At this time of the morning there was no traffic on the street and no doorman to monitor their comings and goings.

He and Ivy hurried to the fifth floor. They posted themselves by the East bank of elevators, knowing which elevator Baxter had taken on his last trip to his room.

They stood close together and Jack whispered his plan to Ivy. If a passerby had approached their position, they would only have thought the tall man was escorting his date back to her hotel and the couple was reluctant to part company. Natural enough.

Baxter double parked by the East elevators on the bottom floor of the ramp. He swore at the full ramp. He didn't have time to search for a different parking place.

He dashed to the elevator, forgetting, in his haste, that he hadn't wanted to draw attention to himself. He punched the call button and when the elevator door didn't immediately open, he continued to punch the button, growing more aggravated by the second. *I should have given myself more time,* he fumed to himself. *I've got to get out of these clothes and put on a suit.*

He planned to distract the desk sergeant at the station by saying he was a lawyer and his client, who was a prisoner in their jail, had called him and told him he was going to commit suicide. That should get the sergeant moving. He only hoped there were a number of prisoners in the jail and the desk sergeant wouldn't know the names of all of them.

The elevator finally arrived and Baxter pushed the fifth floor button. When the door slid open on the fifth floor, he saw the couple standing by the elevator, but he completely ignored them.

Jack and Ivy were on him before he had taken ten steps out of the elevator. Ivy jabbed her knife into his side with enough force to break the skin. Baxter yelped in pain. Fear flooded his face as he recognized the pair.

Trying for control and dominance over the two murderers, Baxter blustered, "What are you doing here? I told you to return to Florida."

Jack laughed softly, removed the key from Baxter's limp hand and guided Baxter toward his room. His voice was grim and threatening when he spoke, "Not another sound, Baxter, or I'll let Ivy have her way with you."

Baxter didn't know for sure that Ivy was a murderer, but a deep seeded gut feeling told him she was not only a murderer, but a sadist as well. He didn't argue with Jack.

His mind was racing. What did they want with him? Why hadn't they left Duluth when he told them to? Had they guessed that he had planned to point the police in Jack's direction? And why had he left his gun and knife in the car? he fumed. His knees shook as he preceded Jack and Ivy to his room.

Baxter was completely terrified of their intentions.

Jack unlocked the door of the luxury suite. He took Ivy's knife, shoved Baxter inside and followed him in. Ivy stayed outside and closed the door behind the two men.

Jack crossed the room to the elegant oak table by the bay windows, pulled the drapes across the windows and unplugged the phone from the wall. He moved to the phone beside the bed and unplugged it from the wall. He could have just sliced the wires, but he wasn't sure if that might alert the switchboard. Watching Baxter's face, he sliced the two cords in half. Baxter's face had drained of blood and his hands shook visibly.

"Okay, Baxter, let's hear you scream," Jack said. Baxter stared at him. Jack's arm flicked out, neatly slicing a long gash in Baxter's already injured arm. Baxter screamed with pain.

Jack went back to the door and pulled it open. Ivy stepped in. "Well?"

Jack demanded.

"Did he scream?" Ivy asked. "I only heard a very small sound, I thought you were talking."

Jack laughed out loud, "He screamed, Baby. Loud enough that it would have brought the cops if we were in a cheap motel or a cheaper room at this hotel. Okay, Baby, he's all yours, but we'll have to make it fast." He looked Baxter up and down, "Nice disguise you have there, Old Man. Never would have recognized you if we hadn't seen it before." He laughed at the mixture of expressions on Baxter's face, of which the paramount one was fear.

Ivy took her knife back from Jack and turned to Baxter. Baxter quickly backed away from the gleam in her eyes.

"What do you want?" his voice trembled with terror and his hands rose in front of him, as if to ward off Ivy's advance.

"We want to know," Jack said calmly, "if Janelle Richardson and her mother are dead."

Baxter tried to regain his authority over Jack and Ivy, "All you had to do was ask. There's no need to threaten me."

Ivy moved closer and Jack demanded, "Well?"

"Her mother is dead," Baxter quickly reported. "But I didn't get the girl or her sister yet."

"Her sister?" Jack asked.

"There's two girls. They look so much alike, you couldn't tell them apart. I think the girl at Delphine's house, the night you were there, was Allison, but I'm not sure. They both have to be killed, because the girl at the house saw me and Janelle saw you in Ohio. If we don't kill both of them, we can't be sure the one we kill is Janelle," Baxter explained. His mind jumped from one thought to the other as he spoke. He had to get out of here. But how? He was sure Jack intended to kill him.

"Okay, we kill both of them," Jack agreed.

"We have to kill the boyfriends, too," Baxter hurried on, hoping to gain the time he needed to find a way out of this crisis.

"Why?" Jack asked.

"Because one of the boyfriends came in the door with one of the two girls before I could get out of Delphine's house. I didn't get a good look at him, but he saw me. He may be able to identify me and I'm not going to take that chance." Baxter was frantic with worry. His mind could not come up with a plan to escape these two.

"Okay, we wipe out the whole group. What is your plan?" Jack asked.

Baxter was far from stupid. He immediately knew what Jack and Ivy had in mind and now a counter plan quickly formed in his mind. He had to make Jack and Ivy want him to help them. "I'm supposed to meet a guy. He's getting me some equipment."

"Equipment for what?"

Baxter didn't answer. He glanced at his watch, "I'm supposed to meet the guy in ten minutes. As long as you guys are here, you can be a big help, but we'll have to hurry."

"We're not going anywhere until we know the whole plan," Jack said, sitting in the big easy chair in the corner and stretching his long legs out before him.

Bob Kelly arrived at the police station ahead of schedule. He parked his car two blocks away, in the theater parking lot, and walked slowly back to the station on the opposite side of the street. He searched each doorway and alley for signs of anyone lurking in the area. Ordinary drunks and vagrants avoided this area of the city, not wanting to come in contact with the police.

Bob saw nothing, save a dirty, scavenging alley cat, which caused him to jump with alarm when it tipped a loose garbage can lid off its precarious perch atop the overfull can.

His heart still thumping from the scare the cat gave him, Bob concealed himself in a doorway across from the station. He would not move from his position until the duty sergeant was gone from his desk. If he was seen by the duty sergeant, there would be no way to erase the scene from the man's memory, short of murder, which Bob would never resort to. He considered himself a small time crook, only stealing from people who were also dishonest.

Bob knew—after twenty five years of working at the station, he should know—that a camera recorded everyone entering or leaving the station house, front or back, day or night. The tape was changed automatically every two hours. If Florida, or maybe it was Florida's man, came at the time they had agreed on, a new tape would have just been inserted in the camera.

Bob intended to take the tape out of the machine while he went to the equipment room. Finding a grappling hook and a rope would take no more than a minute. They had used four of the ten hooks the station possessed just last week and Bob knew exactly where they were. He could be in and out of the station house in less than five minutes, maybe three. He would insert a new tape in the camera before he left and hope no one would notice the tape was missing a few minutes of the hour. Activating the tape was like playing a home VCR; it took a few seconds after the tape was inserted in the camera before it started to film again. In those few seconds, Bob would be out the door again. The tape with Florida, or Florida's man, on it, would be in his pocket and his own arrival and departure at the station would not be on their tape.

The minutes passed slowly. A police cruiser pulled up in front of the station house and Bob flattened himself further into the concealing doorway. The officers entered the station house and Bob watched them disappear in the direction of the coffee room. He waited.

Ivy took a few steps toward Baxter.

"Alright," Baxter said, his eyes on Ivy. He quickly decided to give them some of the plan. "I have a guy getting me a grappling hook and a rope. I'm going back into the hotel where the girls and their boyfriends are as soon as most of the police leave. I'm going to go over the roofs and down the outside wall to their rooms.

"I don't think the cops will move Janelle and Allison tonight. This may be our last chance to get them."

"Where are you meeting this guy?" Jack asked.

Baxter looked at his watch again. He had to get Jack and Ivy to want to hurry to the meeting with Bob. "At the police station and we have to hurry. The guy might not wait for us, he's nervous."

Jack's eyebrows shot up in surprise, "At the police station?"

"Yeah. I have to be a decoy for the guy and distract the desk sergeant. He'll come in to get the grappling hook after he sees me go in." Baxter was getting more and more nervous. He had already given Jack and Ivy most of the plan. The only things they didn't know were the time and the meeting place to collect the hook and rope. "Let's get going! I have to change, I'm going to pretend I'm a lawyer and lawyers are always dressed in a suit and tie." In his fear, Baxter found himself babbling.

"Don't get excited," Jack said. "What time are you picking up the rope and where?"

God, Baxter thought, *he knows almost the whole plan.* He glanced at his watch again, four a.m. He thought of lying to rush them along, but if they fell for it and took him with them, they would arrive ahead of Bob and have to wait. Suddenly he made up his mind. It was worth the chance if it worked. He would be alive and he could make up more lies to explain. "Four thirty, at the theater parking lot, two blocks from the police station," Baxter said, forgetting he had said earlier that he was meeting the man in ten minutes.

Jack's eyes narrowed, he had not forgotten Baxter's earlier statement. *He's lying, but how much? Just about the times, or about the whole plan? Well,* he thought, shrugging his thick shoulders, *I don't have a better plan.*

He looked at his watch. Two minutes after four. He knew where the police station was and they still had enough time to get there for the meeting, but how was he going to pass for a lawyer in his dirty work clothes? Maybe they should take Baxter along. Let him get the hook and rope. Maybe even let him be the one to scale the hotel wall, he wasn't sure he wanted to attempt it. They could get rid of him later.

Jack scratched his head. How would he and Ivy get into the hotel unseen? They would have to enter the same way Baxter planned to enter and that meant three ropes, Ivy would never agree to stay behind. Could she climb a rope? Would she want to climb a rope? Jack could already hear her complains if she was afraid to go over the wall.

Jack suddenly realized he had no idea which window was Janelle Richardson's window. He wondered if Baxter knew for sure. They would have to take him along. Jack did not trust him to tell them the truth.

And how would they get back out after the murders? Go back out the window and up the rope? Jack didn't like that plan. He wasn't sure he could muster the courage to climb over the roof and let himself down the side of the building with only the help of a rope, but he was quite sure he would never be able to pull himself back to the roof, especially if the cops had somehow discovered they were there.

He went back to his first thought; he and Ivy could go through the halls. But even if they did manage to get in without being seen, they would have to murder the guards outside at the girl's rooms and at that point they'd still be *outside* the rooms.

Baxter would never unlock the doors and let them in. Jack was sure Baxter knew they planned to murder him, he might even find a way to alert the police to their position. Baxter could kill the girls and their boyfriends and then call the desk and tell them the girls had been murdered. If he climbed back out the window, he could be long gone before the cops realized how he had escaped. *And if Ivy and I are anywhere in the vicinity, we'll get caught and we'll get the blame for all the murders,* Jack thought.

Suddenly Jack had the answer. They'd let Baxter carry out his plan and they'd be waiting for him when he finished. Baxter would have to come back to the roof if he planned to escape unseen and that's where they'd be waiting.

He glanced at Ivy. She would have a fit. He had promised her she could carve Baxter up all she wanted after they had the information on his plans. And she also had her eye on the girl and her boyfriend. Well, she would have to wait to carve Baxter up and there would be other girls.

"What are you going to tell the cops to distract them?" Jack asked Baxter, wanting to know the whole plan.

Baxter was silent, he was quickly losing hope. Finally he found his voice and muttered, "I don't know yet."

Jack nodded to Ivy and she advanced toward Baxter, her eyes gleaming and a thin smile curving her full lips. Baxter felt his knees go weak as he backed up against the edge of the bed and he sat down hard. "I...I'm," he stuttered, his eyes following Ivy's every move, "I'm going to say one of my clients in their jail has told me he's going to commit suicide. I think the sergeant will come with me right away, leaving the desk empty."

Baxter didn't try to lie, he was too terrified to think up convincing lies...Ivy had her knife under his chin. He tried to turn his head toward Jack, but the knife pricked his neck and he spoke without turning his head, "You need me, Jack. You can't pass for a lawyer." He heard the pleading in his voice, but he couldn't help himself.

"Tell me again what time you're supposed to meet this guy and make sure it's the truth."

Baxter didn't hear Jack's command. He had abruptly remembered his millions and millions of dollars. Maybe Jack could be persuaded to leave him alive if he promised him a large amount of money. "I am a very rich man, Jack, I have a very, very large amount of money. I can make you and Ivy very rich," he stopped, letting the thought sink in, and then added, "But you won't see a penny of it if you kill me."

CHAPTER SEVENTEEN

After Dena left the room, Janelle slumped with dejection. How was she going to find her mother's killer? What chance did she have if the police, with all their scientific resources, failed?

Allison jumped from her chair and rushed to Janelle's side and threw her arms around her sister. "I can't stand the thought that I might have lost you, too!" she cried. She raised her streaming eyes to Ross, "Thank you for saving my sister!"

Ross turned red at the reference to his quick thinking action. Seconds later the color drained from his face as quickly as it had appeared, leaving him deadly pale and sick looking. He shuddered at the thought of what might have happened had he not instinctively pulled Janelle off the bed. He remembered the stiffness of her body as he had grabbed her, she would not have moved on her own. The killer's knife had accurately struck the spot he had been aiming for, Janelle would have been dead or gravelly wounded.

Janelle watched the emotions run across Ross' face and her own face suddenly grew alarmed, "What? Ross! What's wrong?"

He shook his head, trying to clear the horrifying image from his mind, "I was just thinking what could have happened...."

Janelle began to tremble with reaction and delayed shock. "I would have been dead...," she whispered, horror written in every line of her expression.

"But it didn't happen," Allison stated forcefully, regaining her composure in the face of her sister's fear. "You're here, and you're fine, thanks to God, and to Ross' quick thinking." Janelle's eyes went to Ross and Allison released her sister and moved back to Curt.

Janelle laid her head on Ross' shoulder and his arms came around her, holding her as though he would never free her again. Janelle forcefully pushed away the thought of her own possible death as her thoughts returned to the loss of her mother. *How am I ever going to live without her?* she wondered. Her arms tightened around Ross, *thank God I have Ross. If this had happened before I met him, I know I could never have survived her death.*

Her head resting snugly against Ross and his arm cuddling her close with love, Janelle wondered how her mother had endured the losses and terrors of her life. Death had stolen two loving husbands from her and Baxter, her second husband, had stolen both her daughter's innocence. Janelle didn't know how Delphine could have stood all that and still remained the wonderful person she had been. She had not become bitter; she had become stronger and more wonderful as the years had passed. And her faith in God had never faltered. *What a wonderful, wonderful woman she is,* Janelle thought, unaware her thoughts of her mother were still in the present tense. Without being conscious of them, fresh tears began to trail forlornly down her cheeks.

Ross gently wiped away the tears. "It's going to be alright, Sweetheart, everything's going to be alright. It's just going to take time," he murmured softly.

Janelle straightened up and lifted her face to Ross. "I know, but I loved her so," she said, a sad smile traced lightly across her lips.

"I know you did, Honey. We all did. And none of us will ever forget her and how incredibly loving and giving she was. We have the consolation of knowing she's supremely happy with God."

Janelle smiled again and this time the smile reached her eyes. Ross lowered his lips and kissed her tenderly on the cheek.

Dena prowled around Delphine's room, searching for something, anything, the lab technicians might have missed. She walked slowly around the room, her eyes going up and down the French provincial walls. *The rough texture of the walls might have caught a thread from the killer's clothes,* she thought, though she saw nothing on the walls.

She moved her examination to the floor. Partitioning it off in her mind, she moved slowly back and forth, back and forth. When she reached the bed, without finding a single clue, she pushed the bed against the wall and searched the area that had been concealed by the bed.

Her eyes fell on a group of about four or five hairs laying about a foot in from where the bed had stood. She scrutinized them closely, without touching them. Three of the hairs were coal black, while one was gray, almost white.

Going to her purse, she extracted a pair of tweezers and a clean hankie from her cosmetic bag. She carefully picked up the hairs and deposited them in the hankie, loosely wrapping the ends around the hairs. She laid the hankie on a dresser and resumed her search.

Finished with the bedroom, she moved to the bathroom. An ivory handled comb, with hairs attached to the teeth, lay on the vanity, but Dena knew the lab guys would have already taken samples from it. Nothing else presented itself to her close inspection.

She glanced at her watch and was surprised to see she had spent more than an hour on her search. *The crime scene should be preserved for further examination,* she thought, *but not this time. We'll have to hope we've found everything there was to find. I don't want to move the kids.* She knew that taking them out into the street would give the murderers another opportunity to kill them. She turned back to the adjoining room and rapped softly on the door.

Ross' voice answered her summons, "Come in", and Dena opened the door. She was not surprised to find the two young couples still in approximately the same positions as when she had left.

She tried to smile, but the smile felt forced and fake. "I had thought I was going to move you guys to another hotel, but I think this one will be just as safe as any other one...unless you want to be moved? Will you be uncomfortable staying in your mother's room?"

The sisters looked at each other and though neither spoke, their eyes said volumes. They were hurting and Dena knew they would continue to hurt for many months to come; just as she would. Janelle slowly turned back to Dena, "I don't know, Dena. I guess it doesn't matter to me either way. We have to accept Mom's death and the sooner we can do that, the better it will be for us." She was trying to sound matter of fact, but her voice quivered on her brave words. She turned to look at Ross and Curt, "What do you guys think?"

They shrugged and Ross looked at Dena, "Whoever it was wouldn't dare come back here tonight."

Dena hesitated. It was not unheard of, a criminal returning to the crime scene, but generally a murderer left the scene of his or her crime as fast as he or she possibly could and went as far away as possible.

But in this case, the murderer had been stopped before he finished his objective. Obviously he would want to finish what he started, but he would probably wait for a more opportune time. He or she had to know that the guard would be doubled and security harder to crack than an oversize walnut.

"I don't think he'll come back tonight," Dena said. "I don't want to scare you, but I do think he'll be back, sometime in the near future, and I want all of you to be on guard. I'm going to have the guard doubled and if you want, I'll have an officer stay in each of your rooms."

Janelle quickly shook her head, "I wouldn't be able to sleep if I knew someone was watching my every move. I can't forget waking up to find Baxter watching me, lusting for me."

"Me either," Allison inserted, an apprehensive look flitting across her sad face.

"Okay, no man in your room, but are you sure you want to stay here, or should we try in sneak you into another hotel?" Dena still didn't want to take the kids outside. She knew there was little chance of keeping a move a secret and therefore no reason to move them except if they were terribly upset about being in Delphine's room, which didn't seem to be the case. Four people, plus a small army of guards, could not be made invisible. Even if the murderer didn't see them, someone—Dena hated to admit it, but 'the someone' was probably a policeman—had told the murderer where Janelle was.

The four young people looked at each other. Ross answered for all of them, "We'll stay."

"Okay," Dena said. She moved to the window, wishing this room was windowless, like the one Delphine had been in. She opened the drape and inspected the window. It was sealed tight. It was not designed to be opened, preventing the hotel patrons from wasting the air-conditioned, or, in the winter, heated, air. She put her head as close to the glass as possible, but she could not see the brick wall below her that dropped six stories to the cement sidewalk and she could not see the wall above her either.

She shook her head. *No ordinary person could get in through here*, she told herself, *it would take a skilled mountain climber. And even then he couldn't get in without breaking the glass. If anyone tried that, the noise would wake the heaviest sleeper.* She nodded with satisfaction. Janelle, Allison and their boyfriends would be safe here.

Dena had no way of knowing that she had just contemplated the very way Baxter anticipated entering the room.

Dena intended to take the one remaining night shift of guard duty herself. She wasn't going to place Delphine's girls in the protection of someone she was not sure would protect them. *I'm being overly cautious now,* she told herself, *none of the men on my crew are corrupt. I'm absolutely sure of that. I could have one of them guard the kids and be perfectly sure they would do a good job.*

Dena frowned and moved restlessly back to the middle of the room. She felt the worried looks of the four young people following her every move and she knew she was increasing their anxiety with her unsettled movements, but.... But how did the murderer find out where Janelle was? Someone was an informer. And where was the new man, Sloan Berg? *We've found no body,* she thought, *and thank God for that. But where has he disappeared to and who was the betrayer?*

"Okay," Dena said again, forcing her body into a semblance of relaxation, "but I prefer that you use these two rooms. It will make our job a little easier and be a lot safer for you." The girls, Ross and Curt, nodded their agreement.

Dena's slight smile was closer to a frown than a smile, "Goodnight. I'll see you in the morning."

The young people nodded again and Allison and Janelle got up to give her a quick hug before she left.

Dena picked up her hankie with the samples of hair from Delphine's room and quietly left the room. A frown furled her face. Why didn't I call Sloan Berg's house? It's entirely possible he went home.

Closing the door softly behind her, Dena sent one of the officers on duty to find Ed Marshall and have him remain on guard until she returned; confident she could trust one of her own crew. She turned to leave, and then, with a look at the other three men on duty—all of whom she knew only slightly—decided to wait until Ed arrived. Impatient with the delay, she paced back and forth in front of the door leading to Delphine's former room and wished, not for the first time, that the doors to the rooms were both in the same hall.

Ed arrived within five minutes, puffing slightly from his exertions. Dena hurriedly took him aside and explained her reasons for wanting him on duty. "Someone told the murderer where Janelle was to be found and I don't as yet know who that someone could be, so I'm leaving you in charge until I get back."

Ed frowned when her eyes slid sideways to take in the officers posted next to the door, but he asked no questions as Dena turned and rushed off. She could be right. Policemen had been known to take bribes and do atrocious things to receive kickback money.

Dena turned away from Ed, wishing she didn't have so many things to check on, wishing she could stay on guard right this minute. "Take care," she murmured under her breath.

She took the elevator to the main floor and entered the manager's office, which the manager had kindly offered the police as a base for their investigation. Two uniform patrolmen were in the office, monitoring the incoming calls.

"Anything new?" she asked. She checked her watch, 5:15 a.m.

The men shook their heads.

Dena picked up the city directory and found Sloan Berg's number. She dialed the phone quickly. It was answered on the fourth ring by a woman's voice. Dena knew Sloan wasn't married, but after all, this was the nineties.

The voice was slurred with sleep, "Hello?"

"This is Detective Dena Lark. Is Officer Berg there?"

There was a moment of silence and then a deep voice answered, "Officer Berg speaking."

Dena was taken by surprise. She really hadn't expected Sloan to be there. "Detective Lark here. We have a small problem here. Did you agree to replace Officer Bob Kelly on guard duty at 2:30 a.m. this morning?"

"What?" Sloan's voice was confused, drowsy with sleep.

"Did you...," Dena began again.

"I'm sorry, Detective Lark, I heard you, I just don't understand."

"Officer Kelly was ill this morning and he told his fellow officers that you were replacing him on guard duty," Dena explained. "Did you replace him?"

"No. No one called me. I haven't heard from Bob. I didn't know I was supposed to replace him," Sloan said. "Do you want me to come now?"

"No, it's alright, forget it. We're covered. I'm sorry I woke you. Go back to sleep." She slowly replaced the phone, her mind whirling, and turned to one of the patrolmen, "Where's Officer Peg Alcott?"

The patrolman checked the log lying in front of him. "She's on the third floor, interviewing hotel patrons."

"Thank you." Dena pulled out her two-way radio and asked Officer Alcott to join her in the manager's office.

Within minutes Peg Alcott rapped on the door and entered quickly, pushing the door closed behind her.

Dena decided to hear her report before telling her about her talk with Officer Sloan Berg. "Anything new?"

"We've worked our way down to the second floor. None of the patrons have heard or seen anything. They all claim to have been sleeping."

Dena nodded, she hadn't expected any help from the patrons.

"We haven't heard anything from Bob Kelly yet," Peg Alcott continued. "I called his wife again at 5, but she says he hasn't returned home and he hasn't called. She wasn't happy I woke her again."

"I don't suppose she was. I wouldn't like it either." Dena replied absentmindedly, her mind jumping ahead to the problems surrounding her. Where was Bob Kelly? Other than being called in for extra duty, where would he go in the middle of the night? Dena didn't like the implications of the middle of the night phone call shortly after he arrived home from work after saying he was sick. No one at the station had called him, so who had? Was Bob the traitor? Dena shook her head firmly, no, not Bob, he had been with the force more than twenty years.

"I called Sloan Berg's house. He was at home and had not agreed to take a shift of guard duty for Bob Kelly," she told Officer Peg Alcott. "No one called him, not Bob and no one from the station."

Peg's eyebrows rose in wonder, "Bob lied? Or is the new guy lying?"

"I don't know, but I'm sure going to find out." Dena turned to the two patrolmen, "Let me know the minute Bob calls in."

They both nodded and one man murmured, "Yes, Madam."

"You can go back to your search, Peg, and you and Tom can both go home when you're done. I'm going to the lab. You can reach me there or on my car radio if anything turns up."

"Okay, and thanks, the bed will really feel good tonight, or I should say this morning." Peg laughed as she left the office and Dena found herself envying the young woman. Although Delphine's murder was terrible and Dena knew Peg felt bad for her loss, it was, in actuality, just another case to Peg.

Jack's eyebrows rose in astonishment when Baxter offered them his bribe money. *Why didn't I think of that?* he wondered. *We'll get all, or at least a big portion, of his money and then we'll murder him. Why should we work for a living when Baxter's willing to give us all the money we'll ever need? Money we helped him make,* Jack fumed, *and money of which he didn't pay us a fair share.*

Besides, there's always the chance the police would discover what we're doing for a living and then we'd end up in jail or executed. Jack wondered idly if Florida had the death penalty and he shuttered involuntarily.

Of course, he considered, we couldn't let Baxter live. Everyone knows that a blackmailer is either eventually murdered or caught by the police. In this case, since Baxter would never go to the police, we can figure on being murdered, unless we kill him first.

Jack looked at Ivy. Her eyes were shining with greed. And something else...a gleam? *That's the gleam that comes into her eyes when she knows she's going to get to torture someone,* Jack decided. He wondered again if he should get rid of Ivy. He liked killing people, too, but he wasn't as crazy about it as she was. Ivy was obsessed with torture and murder.

If I was rich...if I could do anything on earth I wanted to, Jack thought, *I'm sure I could give up the killing.* But he was just as sure that Ivy couldn't give it up. Having money would only make her worse. *She'll figure out a way to buy the girls she wants,* Jack guessed, *just as Baxter's customers are buying the boys and girls they want. Yup, she'll have to go,* he mused. *I'll find myself a decent girl, someone with some class. Someone I won't be ashamed to be seen with. Someone I won't worry about turning my back to.*

"What do you think, Ivy? Should we take his offer?" Jack didn't want Ivy to guess he was planning to get rid of her. He wouldn't be able to sleep if she found out he was going to kill her. She'd stab him to death while he was sleeping or she'd get him while his back was turned, maybe even in the shower. He didn't trust her as far as he could throw a horse.

"Sounds good to me," she said. "But we still have to get rid of those girls and their boyfriends," she stopped short, but Jack could read her mind. She meant, "Baxter, too."

"Right," Baxter inserted forcefully, drawing a long silent breath of relief. *At least I'm safe for the minute,* he thought. *These idiots will probably try to kill me as soon as they get their grubby hands on my money, but they're in for a big surprise. I can be dirty too and there's no way they're going to get all my money. They're not even going to get a small portion of it!* he promised himself.

"Alright," Jack said, standing up. "Let's get on with this. We're going with you. I want to make sure those girls are dead this time."

"And I want to help kill them!" Ivy exclaimed, the gleam bright in her eyes.

"Shut up, Ivy. We aren't going to have time for your games," Jack snorted at her, "And besides, since when did you become a mountain climber? Or did you figure on just walking in the front door of the hotel? We'll be waiting on the roof for Baxter to finish the job he started and if we're going to make it back out of the area, we're going to have to hurry."

"You don't have to come along," Baxter argued. He wanted to be free of these two sadists as soon as possible. "One person will have a much better chance of getting in and out again without being seen. I'll come back here when I get done and let you know how it went."

"Sure you will," Jack sneered. He was through taking orders from Baxter and he wasn't going to let the man out of his sight, not until he had to. Jack still didn't like the idea of letting Baxter go down that wall and into that room alone, but he could see no alternative.

Jack suddenly tensed. He knew that Baxter, with all his money, could have a hit man hired in less than a minute. What about the time Baxter was alone in the police station, and later, in the girl's room? At the station, the desk sergeant would be with Baxter, but what if Baxter killed the man? And in Janelle's hotel room Baxter would have all the opportunity he needed.

"I will come back. I promise," Baxter's promise broke into Jack's alarming thoughts.

Jack shook himself free of his morbid thoughts and decided he'd cross the bridges as he came to them, "We're going along and that's the end of the discussion," Jack said. "Get changed."

Baxter moved to the bathroom, with Jack two steps behind him, still pondering on his latest problems. When Baxter tried to close the door behind himself, Jack forced it back open.

"I just have to take a leak," Baxter protested weakly.

"Go right ahead," Jack leered. "Ivy won't look." His eyes roamed around the luxury of the bathroom, taking in the phone that stood on a small oak table between the sink and the bathtub. He smiled and congratulated himself on his foresight, although a phone in the bathroom was the last thing he had expected to see. Jack admitted to himself that he had a lot to learn about the luxury lives of the rich.

Baxter threw Jack a dirty look when Jack followed him into the bathroom, but he didn't argue further. He ignored the telephone, praying Jack wouldn't slice the cord. He'd get his chance later, maybe here and maybe after he killed the girls and their boyfriends. If all went the way he wanted it to go—and fervently prayed it would go—there would be no alarm raised when he murdered the kids. He'd have plenty of time to make his call before he rejoined Jack and Ivy on the roof.

Baxter didn't think Jack would follow him down the rope and into the hotel room. He shuddered at the thought of Jack and Ivy on the roof while he climbed down the rope. If they decided they didn't want the money, all they had to do was wait until he was on the way back up and cut the rope. No one could survive a six-story fall to unyielding cement. Baxter hoped and prayed the promise of money had persuaded them to hold off on killing him. He knew Jack still planned to kill him. The man would have to be a complete fool if he didn't...and Jack was a lot of things, but he was no fool.

And if Jack did follow him into the room, he'd find a chance later. The longer he could keep himself alive, the better chance he had of staying that way.

Baxter hastily ran a comb through his fake hair and beard. He was relieved he still worn his disguise. He would never have been able to enter a police station as himself. He was sure Delphine still had the restraining order, against his being in the city, in effect. And he had told Jack his appointment with Bob Kelly was at four thirty. He wouldn't have had time to reapply the disguise without making Jack suspicious. He returned to the bedroom, changed into his suit and moved to the door. Trying again to take control of the situation, he ordered, "Let's go. You've wasted so much time, we're going to be late. I have to stop at a drug store and get some more adhesive tape."

"What for?" Jack growled, his anger again provoked by Baxter's tone of voice.

"The windows of the hotel don't open, so I'll have to break the glass. I don't have a glass cutter and there's no place to get one at this time of the morning." Baxter's face showed the victory he felt at having thought of the tape.

"What is the tape for?"

"To muffle the sound of the glass breaking. Now let's go!" Baxter replied, still smug, but a little worried about Jack's obvious anger.

Jack grunted, but didn't react to Baxter's order. He and Ivy followed Baxter to his car.

Baxter drove around the block and stopped at the all night drug store where he had bought the gauze and tape for his gunshot wound. Ivy followed him into the store, but Baxter had expected this and he made no comment.

His mind was whirling on the drive to the police station. Suddenly an idea occurred to him. He would be going into the police station alone—Ivy wouldn't dare follow him in there—he'd find a reason to explain his use of the phone to the officer at the desk and he'd have to hope the officer would give him some privacy. A phone call to a contact, who was well equipped to set up an ambush for Jack and Ivy, would only take a minute. He could make the phone call on the way back from the cell block, after Bob Kelly had had a chance to snatch the grappling hook and rope and be back out the door.

Abruptly he remembered that he didn't have a good excuse to feed the desk sergeant for his 'client' not being in the cellblock, the client who had supposedly just threatened suicide and called his lawyer from his cell. The excuse was going to have to be a very good one.

Baxter was so involved in his problems that he drove right through a red light. Jack's shout of anger caused him to slam on the brakes in the middle of the block.

"You stupid fool!" Jack screamed. "If you're trying to get us stopped by the cops, forget it. Ivy is very fast with her knife. You'd be dead before the cops reached us."

Baxter cringed against his seat, his horrified eyes finding Ivy in the rear view mirror. He hastily put the car back in motion, though his legs were shaking so bad that the car jumped erratically ahead. "I wasn't trying to attract the cops," he stammered, his voice cracking with fear. "I have just as much to lose as you do."

Jack didn't answer him, but his threat had made Baxter more nervous. His hands tightened on the steering wheel while at the same time he was telling himself to relax, everything was going to come out fine. His eyes jumped back and forth between the windshield and the rear view mirror and his panicked mind suddenly refused to concentrate on his problem.

Baxter reached the theater parking lot and parked beside the only other car in the lot, which he guessed would be Bob Kelly's car. He had still been unable to form a plan of retreat that would satisfy the desk sergeant.

Bob was waiting across from the police station. He was surprised to see the couple with Florida's man and shocked when in no more than two seconds he had put a name with Jack's face.

This is the last thing I'm doing for Florida, he promised himself. *Florida must be a murderer or his contact wouldn't be keeping company with a murderer. As soon as I get home, Ellen and I are packing and leaving. I'll draw out all my money. I'm not even going to wait for this latest payment.*

The guys are getting too close to discovering my little indiscretions, Bob worried, *I've known that for sometime now and this looks like a very good time to get out.*

Baxter stopped by Bob and said, "Well, here we go, ready?"

Bob nodded silently.

Baxter started across the street. Halfway across he looked back and jerked with fear when he found Ivy two steps behind him. He stopped and whispered, "You can't go with me! The desk sergeant won't move if there's two of us."

Ivy sneered at him. She had a story ready for the desk sergeant, "You don't think we'd be dumb enough to let you go in alone, do you? Tell him I'm the guy's wife and I came along to talk him out of committing suicide."

Her story made sense to Baxter and he was sure the desk sergeant would fall for it. His shoulders slumped. There goes my chance to make that call and I still don't have a story ready for when we're ready to leave.

He turned back toward Jack and Bob. He hated to admit to Jack that he couldn't think of anything to say when they didn't find the prisoner they came to see and were ready to leave. But his nerves were completely shot, with Ivy so close to him, and his mind refused to concentrate. His retreat story was now more important than ever. He couldn't allow himself to be questioned by the cops, not with Ivy right next to him. He had no doubt Ivy would lose her patience and kill the cop. He knew she liked to kill and she would be quick enough to overcome the unsuspecting guy. If she killed the cop, it would be a nightmare of trouble for all of them. He himself would probably land back in prison and most likely on death row.

"Where are you going?" Ivy asked.

"I've got to talk to Jack," Baxter muttered. Afraid of startling her and causing her to use her knife, he moved slowly and deliberately. Ivy followed him back across the street, never more than two steps behind him.

"I need a story to tell the desk sergeant when he finds out the guy I came to see isn't there," Baxter confessed.

"Why didn't you say so?" Ivy asked. "Tell him you went to the wrong Precinct."

Jack and Baxter both looked at Ivy with a gleam of new respect in their eyes. She saw the look and actually laughed at them. "You never ask me for my opinion," she explained, which puzzled Baxter more than no explanation would have, but Jack had had his suspicions about Ivy's supposed denseness for quite a while. Baxter didn't know Ivy faked a big share of her supposed 'dumbness'.

Ivy wanted them to think she was dumb. It suited her purpose. For example, she gloated inwardly, *Jack would be more on guard if he knew I had already guessed he planned to kill me and then killing him would be more difficult.*

When Baxter's money is in our hands, she promised herself, *Jack is going to die.*

Baxter and Ivy rushed into the police station and confronted the half asleep desk sergeant so abruptly that his hand went instinctively to his service revolver and his face was nearly comical in its shock.

"One of my clients just called me. He's going to commit suicide!" Baxter yelled, his fake story holding truth in his very real terror of the moment. The desk sergeant stared at them, his mouth hanging open in surprise.

"Hurry! He's in your cell block!" Baxter took a few hurried steps toward the back hallway.

The desk sergeant turned and pulled a ring of keys from a drawer behind him. He lifted the hinged counter and led the way to the cellblock. "Follow me. What cell number is he in?"

"I don't know. I haven't had a chance to talk to him since he was arrested."

The desk sergeant stopped with his key in the lock leading to the cellblock. Baxter had said the wrong thing. "We haven't had any arrests in the last twenty four hours," his voice held a question. All prisoners were allowed to see their lawyers within their first twenty-four hours of imprisonment.

Baxter groaned inwardly at his dumb mistake. If the man refused them entry now, they would return to the front desk before Bob had had a chance to finish his job. "He was arrested three or four days ago. I was out of town and he wouldn't see my partner," Baxter quickly improvised.

The desk sergeant hesitated and his sharp eyes searched Baxter's face. He slowly turned back to the door, unlocked it, held it open for Baxter and Ivy to pass and let it slam shut behind them. Baxter cringed as a morbid feeling of claustrophobia washed over him.

Walking briskly, the desk sergeant led them toward a long row of dimly lit cells.

Baxter stopped when they reached the first cell and stared through the bars before slowly moving forward again. He stopped at each succeeding cell door, pretending to check each prisoner, until Ivy grew impatient with his delaying tactics.

"He won't be in bed! He's tried to commit suicide before and he'll be pacing the floor," she shouted.

Baxter tried to ignore her, but she grabbed his arm and dragged him forward. Baxter recoiled from the strength he felt in her long, thin fingers. If he had had any doubts about her abilities, they quickly fled. He followed her without question.

"He's not here!" Ivy cried when they reached the end of the row, she sounded very distraught and the illogical thought crossed Baxter's mind that she would have been a good actress. Before he could say a word, Ivy continued, "You've brought me to the wrong place! This isn't the Precinct he was taken to."

The desk sergeant's eyes flicked between the two people, but no suspicion showed in his eyes.

"Isn't this the eleventh Precinct?" Baxter asked the officer.

The man shook his head, "This is the fifth."

"Darn it!" Baxter muttered, turning to find Ivy halfway back to the front of the station. Momentarily he considered stopping, letting her get out the door, but Ivy was too smart for him.

"Hurry!" she called urgently, stopping short of the cellblock door. Baxter hurried after her, the desk sergeant close behind him.

With Bob gone and the grappling hook and rope on the seat between them, they were soon stopping at Baxter's hotel, where he quickly changed into a dark sweat suit that allowed him freedom of movement and would conceal his presence from any prying eyes at the hotel.

Seeing his attire, Jack ordered him to take them to the truck he and Ivy had stolen. The two changed into the dark clothes they had used when stalking Delphine's house.

Forty minutes later, Baxter parked two blocks from the Claremont Hotel, within shouting distance of Janelle, Ross, Allison and Curt.

Allison tried to hide her sigh of relief when Janelle volunteered to take the room where their mother had been. She had been worried that Janelle wouldn't want to go into their mother's room, but if she was honest with herself, she realized Janelle was stronger than she was. Janelle had always faced up to her problems. When they were young, she had been the one to finally make the decision to run away from Baxter. She had also been the one to see a psychiatrist when the memories of Baxter's abuse had begun to resurface after so many years.

Allison admitted to herself that she had needed to go back to a doctor for many years, but she had been terrified that someone would find out she was going. She couldn't face her friends if they knew she was going to a psychiatrist and she was afraid she would lose her job if her boss found out about the visits. Accordingly, she had buried her problems deep in the recesses of her mind.

She rose to her feet and kissed Janelle on the cheek, whispering, "Thanks."

Janelle hugged her and whispered back, "We'll be okay, Allison, it's just going to take some time. They'll find Baxter and Jack and lock both of them away for life. We'll never have to worry about them again."

Allison nodded. Tightening her arms around her sister, she murmured, "Are you scared?"

Janelle hesitated. She was scared, but she didn't want to alarm Allison further by admitting it. Finally she said, "A little, but I trust Dena. She'll take care of us."

Allison pushed back from Janelle and tears began to slide down her cheeks, "I don't want to be mean, and I know Dena means well, but she was in charge when Mom was murdered."

Janelle searched her sister's face, wishing she could deny her charge against Dena. Allison never knowingly hurt anyone, but Janelle knew they were both very upset. Hoping to remove some of Allison's fear, she said, "But Dena thinks someone, probably a policeman, told the murderer where we were. The man who was in our room was a policeman, or I should say he was wearing a policeman's uniform. I think the murderer is either Baxter or Jack Thomas Huxley disguised as a policeman. But there's no way Dena could have predicted that. She'll be a lot more careful now."

Allison nodded, "You're right. And she said she was going to double the guard, but I'm still scared."

"I am, too," Janelle unwillingly admitted.

With a deep sigh, Allison slowly turned back to Curt. Janelle and Ross said goodnight and turned to their room. When they entered the room, Janelle noticed that the bed her mother had slept in was gone. She was both relieved and frustrated by the discovery, feeling the absence of the bed had taken away her last link with her mother.

"I wish they had left Mom's bed," she said.

Ross was astonished before the reason for Janelle's statement dawned on him. "You have your memories, Sweetheart."

"I know, but it just seems like now that the bed is gone, Mom's really gone...," Janelle's voice was low and dejected. Ross pulled her into his arms, desperately wanting to take away the loss and hurt, but knowing he could do nothing but try to comfort her in the best way he knew how.

"I'm so sorry, Honey. Your mom was a very special person. It's going to take us a long time to accept her loss." Ross' own mother, Cheryl Page, had remarried three years after his father's death, when Ross had been twenty. She and her husband lived in Cleveland, OH and they saw her quite often—stopping whenever their loads took them within a hundred miles of her home—but Ross still missed having her close. She had been very upset with the reason Lars' wedding had had to be postponed, but she loved having an excuse to stay in Duluth for a much longer length of time than she had originally planned. She hoped to convince her husband to make Duluth their summer home after he retired.

Her husband, Alfred James Page, or AJ, as everyone called him, had to return to his business on Monday, but Ross and Lars' mother was staying until after the wedding. Ross had never thought of AJ as his stepfather, although he realized that was what the man was, and since he had met Janelle and heard her account of her stepfather, he definitely did not want a stepfather.

Ross knew that Janelle was very fond of his mother—and she liked AJ, too—but Cheryl Page lived too far away to help Janelle with the loss of her mother. A sudden sinking feeling invaded his stomach at the thought of having to tell everyone of Delphine's death. Everyone had loved Delphine Kipp, he could not think of a single person who had not liked her.

He moved to the bed, threw back the covers and pulled Janelle down beside him, cuddling her close in his embrace. "Try to get some sleep, Honey." He wanted to tell her things wouldn't look quite so grim in the morning, but he knew Janelle would not believe him. He held her close and said nothing.

"I can't sleep, I'm scared," Janelle moaned softly. "Did you hear what I told Allison about Baxter?" Ross shook his head and Janelle repeated, "I don't think the man who killed Mom was a policeman, I think it was Baxter.

Or maybe it was Jack Thomas Huxley, but Jack is bigger than the man in our room. Anyway, I'm sure he's coming back. Aren't you scared?"

Ross admitted that he was worried, but not really scared, "We're well protected, Honey. There must be three guards on each door. No one is going to get past that many policemen."

"He got past them before," Janelle needlessly reminded him.

"I know, but they weren't really expecting anyone to break in here then," Ross argued.

"They should have been," Janelle whimpered, her voice bitter.

Ross had no answer for her reasoning. He could feel her tremble in his arms and tears plopped wetly on his chest. He tightened his hold on her and murmured comforting words in her ear.

Janelle was silent for a short time and then moved to sit up. "I'm going to take a hot bath. Maybe that will relax me enough so I can sleep. Will you sit with me?"

Ross immediately sat up, but his face was puzzled when he answered, "Of course."

"I'm scared to be in the bathroom alone," Janelle explained. "I guess I've seen too many movies where unsuspecting girls are murdered in the shower or the bathtub. And now, with Jack and Baxter after me, it seems too close for comfort. I'm sorry."

"It's alright, Sweetheart. You have every reason to be scared. I'm scared, too. These guys are playing for keeps. I'll keep you company. Can I join you in the tub?" he eyed her with mock lust, making his eyebrows jump up and down comically.

Janelle removed her robe and headed for the bathroom, rewarding his banter with a small smile and shaking her head at his silliness. Ross moved from the bed to the table in the corner. He poured a cup of water in the small coffee machine that the hotel furnished for their guests and sat down, lighting a cigarette and watching the coffee began to fill the cup.

"Will you come in here when that's done?" Janelle whispered.

"Sure. I'll be right there." Ross sobered at the fear in her voice.

Janelle started the water in the tub and stood in the bathroom doorway until Ross joined her. As she slipped into the tub, Ross moved to the side of the tub and perched on the ivory enamel.

Janelle looked at him, unconcealed apprehension causing her eyes to jump between him and the open doorway, "Can you pull a chair in by the door? You can't see out into the room if you sit here."

Any other time, Ross would have laughed at her paranoia, but he could see Janelle didn't need laugher. She needed sympathy and comforting. Besides, Ross agreed with Janelle. He too thought the murderer was Baxter, and that man was smart and very devious. If there was any chance at all of someone, anyone, getting past the guards, Baxter was the man who would think of a way to do it.

Neither Janelle nor Ross had the slightest idea that Baxter had already conceived a way to get into their rooms and was, at that very moment, parking his car two blocks away from them.

CHAPTER EIGHTEEN

Bob Kelly arrived home to find his wife awake and waiting for him. Seeing the lights on, his heart dropped like a large stone thrown in a deep lake. His breath came in gasps as he hurried into the house.

"Why are you up?" he gasped, before Ellen could say a word.

"Something's wrong," she said. "Two policemen were here over an hour ago. They asked all kinds of questions about where you were and why you had left in the middle of the night. And then, when I had just fallen asleep again, a woman officer called and asked again if you were home. She said to have you call the minute you walked in the door. She said it was an emergency. What's happening?"

Bob began to shake. He ignored Ellen's question and asked, "What did you tell them?"

"Just that you had received a phone call and left. That you had an errand to do for someone."

Bob stared at her, "Why did you tell them about the call?"

"I don't know. You said it wasn't anything important...."

Bob rushed to the attic, with Ellen close on his heels, mentally kicking himself for not taking the time to tell Ellen about Baxter's phone call. If he had told her what was happening, she would have made up a story for the cops and not told them about the phone call.

"What! What's wrong?" she begged.

"I don't know. All I can think of is that they've discovered what I do for extra money." Bob pushed through the twenty years of boxes that had collected in the attic and pulled out their suitcases. "We've got to get out of here. Right now!"

Ellen didn't argue. She grabbed one of the three suitcases from Bob and hurried back to the bedroom.

Dena asked the lab technician on duty for a rush job on the strands of black hair she had found under Delphine's bed.

"I'll need some of the hair from the person you think this is to make a comparison," he said, positioning the hair under his microscope.

Dena was prepared. She had stopped at the station and taken a strand of hair from Baxter's file. She produced the hair for the technician. Harlan Galeson was not surprised at her foresight, he had expected no less from her. He knew Dena to be a very accomplished and intelligent detective.

Several minutes passed while Harlan kept his eyes glued to the microscope lens. Dena fidgeted anxiously.

Finally he raised his eyes, admiration in his gaze as he looked at Dena and reported, "A perfect match."

Dena forgot herself in her fury, "That monster! Hadn't he already hurt that poor women enough?"

"Who?"

"Baxter Perry!" she shouted.

Harlan was not upset by her anger, knowing it was not directed at him, "Who's Baxter Perry?"

Dena took a deep breath to calm herself and looked at the man, "I'm sorry. You couldn't have known the pervert. He was arrested and convicted long before your time." She sat down, afraid her legs would no longer support her as the rage slowly drained from her body. "He's the ex-husband of the woman who was murdered tonight. And he's the murderer! There's no other way his hair could have been in that room unless he was there tonight. At least now I've got some physical evidence against him. The important thing is: where is he? And does he plan to return to the hotel tonight? I know he'll come after Janelle again, I just don't know when," she sighed.

"If you're that sure the man's coming back, I'd make darn good and sure that girl is well protected. I haven't seen such a vicious murder as that one tonight for a long time."

Dena nodded, "The worst part is, I'm pretty sure one of our officers was involved in this."

Harlan was shocked, "You can't be serious!"

"Oh, but I am," Dena replied, her face set with determination. She was quickly seeing a clearer picture of the processing events of the night as she talked, "and I'm moderately sure I know who the traitor is. Without his help, Baxter would never have known where to find Janelle and he wouldn't have had an easy time of the break-in. I'm going to get that cop and put him away for as long as humanly possible! He's as much a murderer as if he had done the job himself." She rose to her feet and hurried to the door, calling, "Thanks for the rush job, Harlan." She was out the door before Harlan could answer.

Dena headed for Bob Kelly's house. She would have liked to use the siren to make better headway through the few Sunday morning early risers that got in her way, but she didn't want to warn Bob of her approach.

She reached for the car phone and called the manager's office at the Claremont Hotel. It was answered on the first ring and she ground out, "Has Bob Kelly called in yet?"

"No, he hasn't," came the answer.

"Thanks," Dena said. She had reached Bob's street and immediately saw his car parked at the curb. She thumbed the two-way radio, praying Bob did not have a scanner in his home, "Send a back up unit to Bob Kelly's residence. No sirens."

She pulled up behind Bob's car and sat for a minute in the car. She knew she shouldn't approach the house alone. But would Bob guess the reason for her presence? And if he did guess why she was there, would he try to use force to escape? Would he pull his service revolver?

At that moment Bob emerged from the house with a suitcase in his hand. If she stayed in the car, he would immediately guess why she was there and there would be a stronger chance he would pull a gun. Dena pulled her gun and, keeping it under the folds of her skirt, stepped from the car, calling out a friendly, "Good morning, Bob," as she started around her car.

Bob dropped his suitcase and reached for his gun. Dena dove behind the protection of the car and rapidly brought up her own gun, training it on the surprised man. "Don't do it, Bob!" she shouted. Bob hesitated and she continued, "You'll just make matters worse for yourself."

Long seconds passed as Dena watched the conflicting emotions that flicked over Bob's face. Finally his hand dropped slowly away from his gun and he stood silent as she cautiously approached him. "Pull it out with two fingers and carefully lay it on the sidewalk," she instructed, wishing the back up unit would arrive. She knew she was taking a big chance allowing him to even touch the gun, but she would be taking a bigger chance if she relieved him of the gun herself.

She prayed Bob would not make an attempt to escape or overpower her.

Regardless of his supposed part—due to his reaction to her presence, Dena was now quite sure that Bob had been Baxter's informant—in Delphine's murder, Dena did not want to kill the man whom she had called friend for more than twenty years. *Besides, killing is too good for him,* she thought. She wanted him to pay for his part in Delphine's death by spending the rest of his life in jail. She also needed the information she hoped to gain from him.

Bob gingerly removed the gun from his holster and was bending to place it on the sidewalk when the back up unit arrived. He hesitated, looking at the patrol car with fear in his eyes.

"Come on, Bob, lay it down," Dena softly commanded.

Bob glanced at her, started to raise the gun back up, and then moaned aloud as he slowly placed it on the cement.

Dena took a deep breath, "Back away, Bob." He followed her directive and she carefully moved forward, not taking her eyes off Bob. Kicking the gun sideways, she sent it spinning into the grass.

The men behind her advanced to retrieve the gun, puzzled looks on their grim faces.

Ellen Kelly opened the door and stopped in surprise at the gathering on the sidewalk. She dropped the suitcase she held and rushed toward Bob, crying bitterly.

Dena had wondered if Ellen knew what Bob had done; she wondered no more. Ellen Kelly would be prosecuted beside her husband, as an accomplice to his crimes.

Bob and Ellen were read their rights and taken to the police station, where Dena questioned the two.

She didn't know if Bob knew Delphine was dead, but she didn't tell him, figuring if he didn't know a possible murder charge hung over his head, he would talk more freely. "I know you helped the man at the hotel get into Delphine Kipp's room, Bob." Bob's eyes widened in surprise at this revelation, but he didn't deny the charge. "Who was the man?"

"I don't know," Bob said, admitting by his statement that he was responsible for letting the man in the girl's room. "I take orders from a voice on the phone that calls himself Florida," Bob said, staring at his feet. His shoulders were slumped forward and his hands hung loosely by his side. He looked and acted like a totally broken and disheartened man; someone who had lost every reason for wanting to live.

"You must have seen the man when he changed places with you at the hotel."

"No. Or at least I don't know if the man who came to the hotel was Florida or not. He said he was sending one of his men."

"How do you get a hold of this Florida if you need him?" Dena asked.

"I don't. He calls me. I have no way to reach him."

Dena searched his face and finally admitted to herself that she felt he was telling the truth. She nodded and changed directions, "What did the man at the hotel look like?" She wanted to confirm that Bob had seen the same man Officer Tom Sutherland had seen when he went to welcome the supposed new man on the force.

"He was short, five ten or eleven, blond hair, mustache and beard. Black eyes."

Dena nodded again. The description fit the one Tom had given. It also fit the description Ross had given of the man who attacked him and Janelle. "Okay. Did you give this blond man your key?"

Bob lowered his head and nodded, misery etched in every line of his kindly looking face.

"And then what happened?"

"I went home," he raised his face to Dena.

"Why did you leave home again?"

"Florida called. He wanted me to...." Bob suddenly stopped in the middle of his sentence. A look of caution came over his face. He had stolen from the police station, compounding his already numerous crimes. Not only had he stolen the grappling hook and rope, but he had taken the video tape with his, Florida's (or Florida's man) and that woman's (they had called her Ivy) pictures on it.

"To what?" Dena spoke softly and gently.

Bob stuttered, "I..it wa..was..it wasn't Florida. He only called once. I was thinking of someone else."

"Come on Bob, don't start lying. You have valuable information that could help us catch this guy. We need your help."

"I am not lying," Bob insisted, not meeting Dena's eyes and thereby confirming her suspicion that he was lying. "He only called once. The second call I was thinking about was Ellen's mother."

"In the middle of the night?" Dena's eyebrows rose in question, before her eyes fell to her watch.

"Yes...she a...she was sick and she wanted me to pick up some medicine for her."

Dena saw the look of relief flash over Bob's face as he came up with this fabrication. She decided she might get more cooperation from Bob if she told him that Delphine had been murdered. She could then appeal to the man's basic sense of decency, which she knew he still possessed. "That's not true, Bob. If you don't come clean with us, I personally am going to see that you are prosecuted as an accomplice to a murder!" she threatened, thinking that that was what she was going to do anyway, regardless of whether Bob cooperated with them or not. He had made a very serious mistake when he decided to peddle department secrets to criminals. Dena's personal feeling was that a lot of the crimes that were committed around the world would have been abandoned in their infancy if the criminal had not found an inside person to assist him or her in their efforts.

Bob sat up with a jerk, his face incredulous, "Mur...der?"

"Yes, murder!" Dena asserted forcefully, not surprised at the look of total shock in Bob's eyes. "Delphine Kipp was murdered in her bed and the murderer tried to kill her daughter, Janelle Richardson, too."

Bob's face had turned a sickly shade of gray and his mouth worked convulsively as he stared at Dena in shock. His hands fiercely gripped the arms of the straight-backed chair he sat in and his right leg twitched nervously. Dena waited.

"He...said he...was only going to scare the girl," he finally mumbled.

"Who, Bob? Who was the man?"

"Florida."

"Come on, Bob. You must know more about this guy than just Florida," Dena implored.

Bob sat looking at the floor for a long drawn out minute. Shaking his head, he raised his eyes to Dena, seeming to have come to an unwanted decision. Dena breathed a prayer of thanks as he began to talk. "I have a tape of Florida's voice and another tape with a picture of either Florida or the man Florida hired to do his dirty work for him," he confessed.

"Where are the tapes, Bob?"

Bob reached in his pocket, pulled out the videotape he had taken from the police station and handed it to Dena, knowing it would further incriminate him. "The tape of his voice is at home, in the drawer below the phone."

Dena stared at him a long moment and then asked, "How is Ellen involved in this?"

"She isn't! She had no part in any of this."

"Ellen knew what you were up to, Bob. That was evident in her reaction to seeing us at your home."

"She's innocent. She had nothing to do with any of this," Bob insisted forcefully.

"But she knew, Bob."

Bob slumped in his chair and didn't answer.

Dena watched him and then softly asked, "Why, Bob? Why did you do it?"

Bob's eyes fell to the floor and he mumbled the one word that could make millions of people do just about anything in the world a person wanted them to do, "Money."

Dena turned away from in him disgust, leaving him to be booked and locked away.

She went to the break room and pushed the tape into the VCR the department furnished for the force, wondering how Bob had gotten the tape. The voice tape was easy to figure, any home recorder could record a telephone call.

Seconds later the videotape's origin was clear to her. She watched the blond, bearded man and a woman rush through the doors of her own Precinct. Their voices, as they talked to the desk sergeant, were loud and distinct, although she could no longer see the two people.

Since Bob had said nothing about the theft of the grappling hook, Dena wondered what the man and woman wanted in the station house.

She heard them explain their reason for being there to the desk sergeant and shortly the slam of a door told of their entrance to the cellblock. Dena stiffened in surprise when Bob's imagine came on the videotape. His worried face blurred as he walked directly up to the movie projector and a second later the tape went blank.

Dena jumped to her feet. She caught up with Bob while the arresting officers were still fingerprinting him. "Why did you come to the station?" she questioned.

Misery flooded his face as Bob looked up at her, "Florida wanted a grappling hook and a rope."

"And you took them for him from the store room," Dena guessed.
Suddenly she straightened with petrifying fear, "A grappling hook!" She turned and immediately broke into a hard run. She reached her car in split seconds.

No longer worried about warning anyone with a siren, she flipped it on and raced toward the Claremont Hotel. *I hope those devils do hear the siren*, she thought, terror making her shake like a leaf. *Maybe they'll panic and run*

TAKE CARE

before they reach Janelle's room.

Her fingers shakily jabbed the two-way radio, "Patch me through to the Claremont. Get me Ed Marshall."

The radio crackled. There was a long pause. A pause that to Dena seemed interminable and much, much longer than it actually was. She was frantic with worry and dread.

Ed's voice came clear and calm, "Dena? What's up?"

"Get in that room, Ed, NOW!" Dena ordered. Ed didn't ask questions, the radio abruptly went dead. Dena pressed her foot harder on the accelerator and prayed harder than she had ever prayed in her life.

Janelle soaked in the hot tub for fifteen minutes, keeping a running dialogue with Ross going the whole time; more for her own sanity than because she had anything important to say. Ross sat on the chair in the open bathroom doorway and occasionally nodded in response to her chatter.

"Ross?" Janelle said softly. "Are you falling asleep?"

A long moment passed before Ross' head jerked in surprise as the room became silent. "What...?"

"You're tired," she said, "and I think maybe I might be able to sleep now, too." She climbed from the tub, while Ross returned the chair he had sat on to its original place.

Climbing into bed, Ross was asleep before his head touched the pillow. Janelle tiptoed to the door of Allison and Curt's room, where she flattened her ear against the wood panel and listened intently. There was no sound. She noiselessly opened the door to find Allison and Curt both in bed and deep in slumber.

She crossed quietly to the hall door and silently inched it open a tiny crack. Ed Marshall swung his head around in astonishment at the faint creaking as the door opened. The other two officers immediately straightened away from the wall, where they had been quietly conversing.

Janelle blushed, "I...I was just checking to see if you were awake. Goodnight." She quickly locked the door and quietly crept into bed. As anxious as she had been, she had not realized she was so tired. She was asleep in less than two minutes.

Baxter, Jack and Ivy left Baxter's rented car and moved silently down the street. Still a block from the hotel, but in the same block as the hotel was on, Baxter turned into an alley that ran the length of the block, exiting into the next street beside the Claremont hotel. In their dark clothes, they appeared as shadows in the still predawn darkness.

"How are you going to get to the hotel roof?" Jack questioned in a whisper.

"We're going in a different building and we'll jump across to the hotel's roof," Baxter mumbled, privately hoping both Jack and Ivy would fall to their deaths in the jump.

Ivy blanched with fear. Few things scared her, but heights were a complete terror to her.

Jack felt a lump rise in his throat, but he was far from terrified. In fact, he was tremendously excited by the danger and risk involved in their deadly caper. He wasn't sure if the lump in his throat was in response to the impending danger or the thrill he was experiencing. One thing he did know, he had never felt this element of danger while he was kidnapping a child or killing a terrified, helpless woman.

The building next to the hotel was considerably older than the hotel building. They reached it without being seen and Baxter pointed out the outside fire escape to Jack and Ivy. "We're in luck," he whispered, advancing to the steps. He reached up and grasped the lower rung of the steps, tugging at the long portion of the steps that was suspended above the head level of innocent passers-by. The rusty hinges refused to budge.

Jack fastened his hands beside Baxter's and both men pulled until the steps came way from their perch with a blaring shriek of un-oiled metal. Baxter and Jack dropped their hold on the steps and flung themselves against the side of the building, their eyes quickly searching the night for signs of spectators. Ivy had disappeared against the building. Eerie, silent minutes passed slowly as three pairs of eyes searched the street and buildings for signs of discovery. Nothing moved, no heads appeared from the windows surrounding them.

With the initial rust hold broken the steps made only small squeaks the second time Baxter pulled on them, quickly bringing them within reach. Minutes later the three murderers were on top of the building, staring across the four-foot space that separated them from the hotel roof.

Ivy gasped with fear, "I can't jump that!"

"Then you'll just have to stay here, won't you?" Jack sneered, knowing his implied insult would gloat her into making the jump. He glanced at the narrow alley below them, thinking, *it would save me some trouble if she falls.*

He chuckled to himself, allowing the smile to curl his lips faintly. Ivy threw him a terrified look and backed further away from the opening.

"I'll go first," Jack said. "Keep a close watch on this scoundrel, Ivy. We don't want him playing a disappearing act on us." He backed ten feet away from the fissure, ran forward and vaulted across the gap, easily clearing the open space. "Okay, Baxter, your turn," he called softly.

Baxter followed Jack's example and seconds later was standing beside Jack on the hotel roof.

"Come on, Ivy, there's nothing to it," Jack jeered.

Ivy backed away, stopped, took a deep breath and ran forward. At the crevice, she suddenly stopped short, gasping with fear. Jack laughed. She swore at him and again backed up. This time she jumped, but she fell short of her mark up a slim, but deadly, three inches. A long scream burst from her plunging body, seeming to last for an eternity and bouncing hollowly off the walls of the buildings before ending abruptly as she crashed into the unyielding cement of the alley, six floors below.

In spite of his plans for Ivy, Jack felt a stab of sorrow. He took a swift step forward, but stopped himself in time. Out of the corner of his eye he saw Baxter move ahead quickly, preparing to push Jack over the edge. He swung around and struck the surprised Baxter in the stomach, causing Baxter to crumple to the tar roof with a snort of pain.

"Try that again and you're a dead man," Jack threatened, his face distorted with fury. He pulled his own knife from his pocket and switched the blade open with a flick of his wrist. Baxter cowered away.

Suddenly Jack heard voices far below them. A woman screamed and a man's voice called out, "Call 911!"

"Let's get out of here," Jack said.

Baxter lunged to his feet and raced for the space between the buildings, Jack close on his heels. *He's right*, Baxter thought, *this place will be swarming with cops in a matter of minutes.* Minutes later they piled into Baxter's car.

"Go slow and easy," Jack warned. "We don't want to draw attention to ourselves."

They rode in silence until they reached Baxter's hotel. "What now?" Jack wanted to know, watching the day brighten as the sun found its way over the horizon.

"I don't know," Baxter muttered, "but I'll think of something. Those kids have to be killed, one way or another."

They rode the elevator in silence and entered Baxter's room. "One thing's for sure, we'll have to wait for night. I'm not going to take the chance on being spotted in the daylight," Baxter seethed. "We might as well get some sleep."

"Good idea," Jack agreed. He pulled a thin length of strong nylon rope from his pocket and advanced on Baxter.

Baxter backed away from him, "You don't need that. We're in this together. Those kids can identify both of us."

"In this together? Yeah...like on the roof? Don't get the idea that Ivy was the only one with brains in this enforced truce between us. And I know that the kids have to be killed, but I'm not giving you a chance to wipe me out, too," Jack said. "Get on the couch, unless you prefer the floor, and put your hands behind your back."

Baxter did as he was told and lay down on the couch while Jack securely hog-tied both his hands and feet. "Get your evil mind working, I want you to have a plan ready by evening," Jack ordered, plopping down on the king size bed and closing his eyes.

Ed Marshall was in Janelle and Ross' room, his gun drawn, within seconds of Dena's phone call. He was not quiet with his entry, but Janelle and Ross did not wake up. He saw no one and charged to the connecting door, knowing the other two officers on guard covered him from behind.

Allison and Curt did not stir as he rushed into their room. No one moved. He slowed down and quietly searched the bathrooms and closets of both rooms. Nothing. He sheepishly peeked under the beds, although he was sure an adult could not fit in the small space there. These were Dena's dearest friends, and he was leaving no stone unturned.

He pushed the curtain away from the window in Allison and Curt's room. Nothing. No broken glass, no movement in the street. His heart slowly resumed its normal rate. He scratched his head in bewilderment. What had Dena learned? He had not misread her panic. Something had happened to put her in such a state of terror. He shook his head, slowly returned to the hall and resumed his post.

He had the dispatcher patch him through to Dena's car and reported that the kids were fine; no one had been in their rooms.

"Thanks, Ed," Dena said, a sigh of relief escaping slowly.

"What happened?" Ed wanted to know.

"I'll explain when I get there. See you in a few minutes."

Baxter awoke at six p.m. His legs and arms were stiff and cramped. He wiggled himself to a sitting position. Jack was snoring on the big bed and Baxter immediately began searching for ways to kill the man.

Suddenly he remembered the phone in the bathroom. Jack had not damaged the cord on that one. The phone was still in working order. He could call one of his contacts and Jack would be dead in an hour. He slithered to the floor and quietly began to crawl laboriously toward the bathroom.

He had reached the doorway when, for no reason that Baxter could fathom, Jack abruptly woke up. His eyes found Baxter on the floor and his snarl of anger truly resembled the snarl of a dog with distemper.

Baxter stopped in his tracks and swiveled to stare at Jack's lumbering approach. "I didn't want to disturb you," Baxter whined. "I have to take a leak."

"Sure...," Jack drawled. He left Baxter on the floor and entered the bathroom. Baxter heard him relieving himself before he reappeared in the doorway with the phone in his hand. Baxter gritted his teeth with frustration, but kept the look hidden from Jack. "Help yourself," Jack laughed. He untied the rope that bound Baxter's feet, but left his hands tied behind his back.

"How am I supposed to go to the bathroom with my hands tied behind me?"

"Ah...good question. Want me to get it out for you?" Jack sneered.

"No! Untie my hands." Baxter felt himself blush.

"Alright, but remember, I always have this knife real handy." He swished the knife within inches of Baxter's face.

Baxter closed the bathroom door and Jack laughed again, plugged the phone into the wall beside the bed and ordered supper for the two of them.

When Baxter reappeared, Jack demanded, "What's your plan?"

Baxter was ready for him. "I'll call my contact in the police department. We'll find out from him where the kids will be tonight and make plans from there."

"What if the cops have your contact? They have to have guessed that someone helped the murderer find the witnesses."

Baxter shrugged, gaining confidence in his control of the plans, "I'll think of something else."

"Okay. Make your call, but be sure I can hear every word your contact says."

Baxter dialed the phone and Jack grabbed the receiver from his hand, holding it close to both his and Baxter's ears. He pushed his knife against Baxter's flabby neck and whispered, "Just in case you get any ideas."

The phone rang four times before a man's voice answered, "Hello."

Baxter stopped with his mouth open to respond. He wet his lips nervously and asked, "Who's this?"

"Bob's brother. Who's this?" the voice countered.

Baxter ducked away from the receiver and whispered, "Hang up."

Jack depressed the phone button.

"That was not my man. We better get out of here right now. It was probably the cops and they have ways of tracing calls within minutes of the call," Baxter said.

Jack frowned. Get out? Supper was on the way and he was starved. Was Baxter right? Was it the cops? Jack stared at Baxter and then made up his mind. *It's not worth the chance,* he thought, starting for the door. He pointed his knife at Baxter, "Okay, we're going. But you better not make any unexpected moves, because I'm even faster with a knife than Ivy was. And you know the old saying, 'The hand is faster than the eye.' You'd be dead before you saw it coming. And leave some money for the hotel bill; we don't want them after us, too." Baxter quickly dropped four hundred dollar bills on the table beside the room key and grabbed his suitcase on the way out the door.

Jack cursed to himself. Now what? Eat in a public place? Suddenly he remembered that Baxter was a hunted man, too. He would not attempt to summon help and thereby place himself in as much danger as he would be placing Jack in. Jack relaxed.

They ate silently in a small restaurant a mile from Baxter's hotel. Baxter had been thinking while he ate. When they were back in his car, Baxter said, "I've got a plan, but we need a disguise for you and a different one for me. We'll have to go to the shop on the west side of town because I used the one on the south side for this disguise."

"What's your plan?"

"We'll go to the hotel where the kids were—you'll need a suitcase; hotels are suspicious of patrons without luggage—and rent a room right next to theirs. If the cops are still on duty, we can be pretty sure the kids are still there," Baxter explained.

"What if they're not there? What if the cops keep the guards there as a decoy? What then, Smart Man?"

Baxter was insulted and his voice sprayed with sarcasm, "Have you got a better idea?" He knew how he'd find out if the kids were there, but he wasn't ready to spill all his secrets to Jack.

Jack sneered, "Not yet. Okay, let's assume they're there, what happens then?"

"We plant a nice big bomb in our room and get out of there."

CHAPTER NINETEEN

Dena arrived at the Claremont Hotel to find the street full of police cars and ambulances. She had heard the radio calls on her way to the hotel and already knew that the woman who had died in a fall from the apartment house next to the hotel did not resemble either Janelle or Allison. Ed Marshall had called and told her that nobody had been in either Janelle or Allison's rooms and that the kids were all sleeping peaceful when he left them. Dena still wanted to be in the hotel and on guard.

She stopped at the scene of the woman's accident and viewed the body. The woman was still unidentified, but Dena immediately recognized her as the woman on the tape Bob had stolen from the police department. She wanted to assume the death had been an unrelated accident, but the entire incident had happened too close to her witnesses and she was now sure the woman had been on the roof with Baxter and Jack. Had they been up there with a grappling hook? Maybe the woman's fall had caused Jack and Baxter to run before they made it to the hotel.

Officers were busy interviewing the apartment house occupants, but so far they had found no one who had seen the woman before the accident.

She checked with the dispatchers in the hotel manager's office. There had been no new developments.

Why had Florida wanted the grappling hook and rope? She didn't think Bob had lied about his involvement in the theft. Bob knew he was in more than enough trouble. Florida had to have had a definite plan that involved the use of the hook and rope.

Dena entered the elevator and pushed the sixth floor call button, rubbing her forehead in frustration and exhaustion. Ed was still sitting outside

Janelle's door when she arrived on the sixth floor.

"Anything new?" she asked.

"Nope. Everything's quiet," he reported.

"Okay, Ed. Why don't you head home and get some sleep. I'm going to need you again in a little while."

"No rest for the wicked," Ed smiled. "What did you find out that scared you so much?"

Dena wanted to check the kids again; just to be sure they were all right. "Just a minute, I have to have a look."

Minutes later she was back. She told Ed about Bob stealing the grappling hook and rope. She explained that the woman who had either fallen or been pushed from the roof of the next-door apartment house was the woman that had been keeping company with Jack Thomas Huxley. "I figured Baxter—Bob calls the guy Florida, but I'm sure it's either Baxter or Jack, most likely Baxter because of the height—had come through the window and was already in the kids' room." She looked at Ed and tears glistened in her eyes, "It was terrible, Ed, horrible, the pictures that flew into my mind." She shook her head, "I'll never forgive myself if something happens to those kids. They're very dear to me, like my own daughters."

Ed reached out and squeezed her hand, "We won't let anything happen to them, Dena. But your theory about the grappling hook makes sense and may also serve as a lesson to us. I would never have thought of them coming down the wall from the roof." Ed stood thinking a few minutes and then shook his head, "I can't figure the connection between Baxter Perry and Jack Thomas Huxley."

"Neither can I, but I'm sure they're associated in one way or another. Coincidences don't stretch that far."

Ed nodded in agreement. His face was lined with weariness, "Well, I'll get some sleep and be back at eleven. Okay?"

"Fine, have a good nap." Ed disappeared into the elevator and Dena sat on the chair he had vacated, her mind in turmoil. What was Baxter's connection with Jack Thomas Huxley? They had both invaded Delphine's house on the same night. That had been no coincidence. The two men were somehow associated with each other, but Dena could not comprehend how. And why, after thirteen years of silence, would Baxter want to come back and kill Delphine?

Baxter had murdered Delphine, of this Dena was sure. The few strand of black hair she had found in Delphine's room were his and proved he had been there. Allison and Janelle had both seen him at Delphine's house the night before, when he had almost murdered both Delphine and Allison. And Allison and Delphine had seen Jack Thomas Huxley and a woman called Ivy. She was sure the woman on the tape, who was killed in the fall from the apartment house, was Ivy, but she wanted Allison to verify her findings.

Dena made a mental note to have Allison look at the body as soon as the autopsy was finished.

She shook her head in remorse. If only she had foreseen Baxter's use of a disguise. Delphine would still be alive. Her spirits dropped further as another terrible thought plagued her. Except for Janelle and Ross' unexpected arrival at Delphine's house, Allison might be dead, too.

But how were the two murderers connected? Was Baxter Perry here because Janelle had seen Jack with the young girl in Ohio? Dena shook her head in frustration, wishing the pieces of the puzzle would fall into place.

Janelle awoke a little before nine. Ross was sleeping like a young puppy, legs and arms spread over the entire bed. She crept silently to the bathroom and closed the door. She showered, washed her hair and brushed her teeth. Fifteen minutes later she softly opened the bathroom door.

Ross sat up when she came in and admonished gently, "You should be sleeping."

"I can't sleep any longer. I slept for about three hours."

"That's not long enough, Sweetheart. You'll make yourself sick," Ross' voice was worried.

Janelle shrugged and asked, "Are you hungry?"

"I could eat something," Ross answered, not wanting to admit that he was starved.

Janelle conceded to herself that she was hungry, too. She immediately felt guilty for thinking of her own comfort when her mother was dead.

"I'm going to see if Allison and Curt are awake." Quickly turning away from Ross' searching eyes, Janelle wiped the tears from her eyes and wrapped softly on the connecting door, opening it when Allison softly called, "Come in".

"Are you guys ready for breakfast?"

"Whenever you are," Allison replied, a lost look in her eyes.

"Let's order and then you guys come in our room, we have a bigger table than you do."

"Okay. We'll be over in a few minutes," Allison said.

Half an hour later they gathered around the table in Allison and Curt's room. As they finished the last of their breakfast, Janelle said, "How are we going to find Baxter?"

Allison's mouth dropped open in shock, "I don't want to find him! And I don't want him to find us."

"He already knows where we are, Allison, and we can't let him get away with this," Janelle said. "I have an idea." Ross stiffened, alarm evident in his eyes. "I'll be a decoy," she stated firmly.

"No, Janelle! I won't let you put yourself in danger. I can't lose you, too," Allison shrieked.

"I wouldn't be in any real danger," Janelle argued. "I'll get Dena to help me set it up and protect me."

Ross was shaking his blond head, "You'll get hurt, Janelle. Decoys are usually found out by the murderer before the police can get there to protect them, even if the police are only across the street."

"I don't agree, Ross. I've seen a lot of movies where a decoy works to catch the crook or murderer. Anyway, I'll be very careful and I'll do whatever Dena tells me to."

"Let's give the police and Dena a chance to do their job first. They'll catch them...they just haven't had enough time yet," Ross declared.

Janelle slowly nodded in agreement, "Okay. I'll give them a week. And in the meantime, I'm not going to miss Mom's funeral. And Lars and Kate's wedding is only three weeks away. I don't want to have to ask them to postpone it again. I don't think Dena will want us to go to the wedding if Baxter and Jack Huxley are still on the loose." She looked down at the table and a long moment passed before she returned her eyes to Ross, "You don't think Dena will say we shouldn't go to Mom's funeral, do you?"

"Dena will let us go to the funeral and she'll see that we are well protected. But a wedding is a lot different. Too many people are wandering around all over the place at a wedding."

Ross didn't like Janelle's compromise on the decoy idea, but he decided not to argue about it now. If Baxter wasn't caught in a week, he'd think of a way to persuade her to change her mind. One thing he knew, he did not want her to take the chance of being a decoy to attract Baxter or Jack. He agreed with Janelle...Baxter and Jack Thomas Huxley knew exactly where they were and were actively looking for a way to get at them and not get caught.

At nine forty five a.m., Janelle opened the hotel room door to find Dena on guard. "Haven't you been home to sleep?"

"I'm not tired," Dena lied. "This whole thing has got me totally baffled and I won't be able to rest until I figure it out."

"No new clues?"

"One. A woman fell, or was pushed, from the roof of the apartment house next to the hotel. There's a chance the woman was the same woman who was with Jack Thomas Huxley at your mother's house." Dena did not tell Janelle she had seen the same woman with Baxter on Bob's tape, she did not want Allison's identification of the woman influenced by this information.

Janelle frowned, "What was she doing on the roof, if it was her?"

Dena bit her lip. She should have known Janelle would ask just that question. She looked up at Janelle and decided to level with her, Janelle and Allison had the right to know the danger they were in. "One of the officers on the Duluth Police Department was responsible for helping Baxter get into your room," she hesitated, then continued, sorrow in her voice, "This is not an excuse, but the officer thought the man was just going to scare you, make you not want to testify against Jack Thomas Huxley.... Remember when you were a kid and I explained to you about the system?"

Janelle nodded, but didn't speak. She had never really understood what Dena had meant, all those years ago, by telling her and Allison about the system and how sometimes the system worked against innocent people, but now, in learning an officer had helped Baxter get into their room and kill her mother, she finally understood.

"Anyway," Dena continued, her face sad, "this was one of those times that a man who should have been helping you and other innocent people was instead helping the bad guys. That same officer stole a grappling hook and a rope from the police station and gave them to Baxter, or I should say to a guy the officer calls Florida, but I'm pretty sure is Baxter. I think they were planning to come into your rooms from the roof and through the window...."

Janelle was horrified. She sat down quickly on one of the chairs next to Dena. "And you think that because the woman fell, Baxter and Jack took off."

"Yes," Dena breathed. "They had to know the area would fill up with police and emergency vehicles within a few minutes after the accident, or whatever it was. I want Allison to look at the woman's body after the autopsy is completed. She saw the woman with Jack and Baxter at your mother's house."

Janelle's eyes grew big and a fear worse than the fear of death invaded them. "Allison won't go! She'll be terrified."

"I know she will and I wish I didn't have to put her through this, but.... Will you try to prepare her? If she identifies the woman as the same one who was with Jack and Baxter, it will help us establish that Baxter and Jack were most probably on the roof with her. We'll be better prepared to protect you."

"Why don't you move us to a different hotel?"

Dena looked pained as she admitted, "The same thing could happen there, Janelle."

"Then what are we going to do?"

"We'll get more guards. We'll watch the roof too," Dena reassured her. "I don't think we have to worry until nightfall. Baxter won't take the chance of coming in here in the daytime. If they make another attempt tonight, we'll be ready for them. In fact, I hope they do try to get in again, then we'll catch them and this nightmare will be over."

Janelle hung her head. She had wanted to be a decoy and now Dena was telling her that they were all decoys. Suddenly being a decoy didn't sound like such a great idea.

"How was breakfast?" Dena asked, changing the subject.

"Fine...," Janelle answered indifferently. She looked up at Dena with compassion, "I really wish you'd get some sleep."

"I will, Honey, later. I had the dispatcher tell Alex Hall to report for guard duty. He's one of the guys on my squad and I trust him implicitly. He'll be here in a few minutes and then I'm going to go over everything again. Maybe I missed something. Maybe I'll discover something that will tell us what Baxter and Jack are planning next."

"Okay," Janelle murmured. She gave Dena a fierce hug and returned to her room. She told the others about the officer who had helped Baxter get into their room and had stolen a grappling hook for him.

"Who was the officer?" Allison asked.

"I don't know. Dena didn't say his name." Janelle didn't want to know what the officer's name was; she couldn't believe there were men who would do things like that for money.

They all knew what a grappling hook was and Allison asked, "What does Dena think Baxter wanted a grappling hook for?"

"To come down from the roof and in the window of your room," Janelle admitted.

Allison gasped with fear, "Did they try it?"

"Dena thinks they were going to, were on the way to, but then a woman fell from the next door apartment and was killed. Dena thinks the woman was the same woman you saw with Jack Thomas Huxley. She wants you to look at the body, Allison, and let them know if it was the same woman."

"She wants me to look at a dead woman?" Allison was astounded, her face paled and she unconsciously backed away from Janelle.

Janelle held her eyes and nodded sadly. "If it's the same woman, Dena hopes that knowing that will help her discover what Baxter has planned."

"I can't do it, Janelle," Allison whispered, fear thickening in her voice.

"Yes you can. Just think of Mom and how you'll be helping catch her murderer."

"I can't," Allison burst into tears.

"You might also be saving one of us, Allison. Maybe yourself, or Curt." Janelle suddenly felt like a traitor. She didn't like the responsibility Dena had placed on her shoulders.

Allison hesitated and then whispered, "Will you go with me, Janelle?"

Janelle looked up in surprise. She had not expected Allison to ask her to go along. Maybe Curt, but not her. She didn't want to see a dead body either, but she sighed in defeat, "I'll go with you."

Dena stopped back in at noon. She had no new developments to report, except that the autopsy was over and would Allison come and identify the woman.

Allison slowly nodded her head, "Janelle can come with me, can't she?"

Dena frowned, "I'll be with you, Allison."

"But I'd really like Janelle to be there, too," Allison was close to tears again.

"It's okay, Allison, don't cry. Janelle can go with you," she wrapped her arms around Allison and gently patted her back. "I'll be back in a few minutes. I have to round up an escort."

Forty minutes later they arrived at the county morgue. They were surrounded by officers, some of whom had followed their car.

Allison shivered. Janelle put an arm around her, hoping to fortify both herself and Allison for the ordeal to come. Hanging on to Janelle, with Dena on her other side, Allison started up the steps.

Neither Janelle nor Allison had ever been in a morgue before. They entered a narrow room where the walls were covered with shelves filled with varying sizes of sealed glass jars. Janelle's first thought was of her mother's fruit cellar. She was afraid to ask what was in the jars.

An open doorway led to a brightly lit room where a stainless steel table dominated the room. A white sheet draped the form of a body on the table. A man dressed in the white blazer of a doctor stood beside the sheet-covered body. Janelle noticed the conspicuous absence of the stethoscope doctors usually had hanging around their necks or sticking out of their pockets.

Dena led the girls to the head of the table and the doctor silently lifted the corner of the sheet, revealing the battered face of the blond woman who had been with Jack Thomas Huxley at Delphine's house.

Allison took one quick look, swayed and swiftly turned her face away from the gruesome sight. She assured Dena that the body had been the woman Jack had called Ivy. Dena nodded, satisfaction on her face.

Allison wiped tears from her eyes and moaned, "I hope I never have to go through anything like this again."

Ten minutes later it was over. Janelle felt she would never again be able to put the image of the dead woman out of her mind. Outside, in the bright sun of the June day, Janelle breathed deeply of the fresh air and pushed away the light headed sensation that was threatening to plunge her into darkness.

They returned to the hotel to find everything quiet, but the guys had been pacing the floor with worry. Both men went straight to their woman and wrapped their arms around her with a sigh of relief.

Janelle, Ross, Allison and Curt spent the afternoon making phone calls to arrange for Delphine's funeral, which was to take place on Tuesday. By the time everything was arranged, they were depressed and beginning to feel the pressure of being confined to a hotel room; the guys more so than the girls.

Janelle looked around the table and suggested they ask Dena if they could eat in the hotel's restaurant. The guys perked up and then slumped with rejection. Ross said, "We can't ask her that, Janelle. It would take too many men to protect us. And just because we're getting stir crazy."

"But I've seen their restaurant and there are private little rooms where we can eat and the guards would only have to watch one door," Janelle argued.

"That would be the same as eating in our room," Allison sighed.

"But we'll get to walk through the dining room," Janelle declared.

"It's not worth the risk, Honey. What if Baxter or Jack is in the dining room with a gun?"

"They wouldn't do that," Janelle stated flatly. "They don't want to get caught."

"Well, maybe they wouldn't," Ross agreed, "But it's still too dangerous."

Janelle subsided graciously, "Okay. It was just an idea."

Baxter no longer worried about the innocent people—including children—who would be hurt by a bomb, he was too worried about his own life and breath. Janelle, Allison and their boyfriends had to be killed and he had to figure out a way to tip off his contact that he wanted Jack killed before the kids were dead and Jack had his money.

"Where do we get the bomb?"

"I have connections," Baxter boosted arrogantly. Forgetting for a moment that he was this man's prisoner, he allowed his outrage and resentment to show on his face and in his voice.

Anger darkened Jack's face and he swung his meaty fist, connecting with Baxter's windpipe. Baxter choked and coughed for a full minute.

"Be respectful," Jack smirked. "And don't think I really need your help to wipe out those kids. I've killed plenty of kids."

Baxter nodded, keeping his eyes down. He knew that the actual planning of the murders was not what was keeping him alive. Jack wanted his money.

"Let's get going. We have a lot to do before we check into that hotel," Jack ordered.

The disguises and a suitcase for Jack were quickly and easily purchased. Against Jack's wishes, Baxter insisted on a suit for him. "We need to look like respectable business men," Baxter argued.

"I don't like those monkey suits."

"Fine, but the police will be suspicious of you the way you're dressed now."

Jack backed down and allowed Baxter to purchase the suit.

Baxter became a redhead and Jack a blond. Baxter wore a fake mustache and beard, but Jack refused to shave his face, preferring to keep his own beard and mustache. They had included an artful scar for Baxter's cheek.

An hour later they checked into the Claremont Hotel, using assumed names and dressed in conservative, well cut suits. Both men carried a briefcase along with their suitcases.

Baxter requested adjoining rooms on the east side of the hotel's sixth floor. The clerk looked at him in surprise and Baxter suavely explained, "We're early risers and we like to get right to work. The morning sun inspires energy and alertness. And the sixth floor has become our lucky floor. We've made it a tradition for all our business meetings."

The clerk nodded, lowered his head to the registration book and rolled his eyes. *Boy, we sure get our share of creeps in here,* he thought in disgust, privately guessing the men were queers. He searched the diagram of the hotel. The sixth floor was completely full, except for the area not rented due to the group of witnesses the police were guarding. "I'm sorry, the sixth floor is full, but we have a nice set of rooms on the fifth floor."

Baxter pulled a hundred dollar bill from his pocket and slid it across the desk, "Please check again. We want the sixth floor, east wing."

The clerk slipped the bill into his pocket and returned to the diagram. *Fine,* he thought, *the witnesses will most likely be leaving today anyway, and a hundred bucks is not to be sneezed at.* "Oh, here we are, I missed this one," he smiled at Baxter, pushing a registration form across the desk.

The room they received was across the hall from Janelle and Allison's rooms. Baxter swore under his breath, wrong side of the hall. He needed to be right next to the kids.

The guard at the kids' door glanced up as they approached. Baxter silently swore again, now he's seen us. We'll have to pretend we're curious as to why he's here. Baxter knew most hotel patrons would be too curious not to ask the cops some questions and he didn't want the cops to remember them as being different.

He stopped in front of Janelle's door and asked politely, "Are we going to be in danger if we stay here, Officer?"

Ed Marshall shook his head.

"What's happening?" Baxter persisted.

"It's confidential," Ed said, dismissing the man and turning his eyes back to his novel.

"Okay, thanks, Officer," Baxter said. Turning away, he deliberately kept his voice loud enough for the cop to hear when he told Jack, "Let's get a different room, we don't want to take any chances."

Ed Marshall didn't look up from his book.

They started back toward the elevator and Jack demanded in a whisper, "Why did you say that? What's wrong with across the hall from our targets?"

"I'll show you in a few minutes." Baxter rushed back downstairs, Jack on his heels, and complained softly—he didn't want to attract undue attention to himself—to the clerk. "The room you gave us is on the west side of that wing.

I very specifically asked for the east side." Baxter slipped him another hundred.

The clerk's eyes gleamed with greed as he quickly slipped the bill in his pocket and searched the diagram of the hotel's rooms. "We don't have a double room available on the east side of the sixth floor, but we do have a large single room with two beds."

Baxter nodded and looked at Jack, "I guess that will have to do. We won't settle for the west side." The clerk rolling his eyes went unnoticed by the two men.

They returned to the sixth floor to find the room they had attained was the same one Allison and Curt had shared the night before. Baxter was delighted. Jack closed the door behind them and shouted, "This is worse than the other one. Now we're around the corner and can't even see the doors of the kids' rooms."

Baxter calmly laid his suitcase on one of the beds and opened it. "I'm talking to you," Jack shouted again, advancing on Baxter and pushing him away from his suitcase. "What have you got in here? A gun?" He rummaged through the suitcase, but found nothing to use as a weapon.

"Relax, Jack, I'm going to show you why I wanted this room. We're right next to the girls." Baxter reached around Jack and pulled a stethoscope from his suitcase while he spoke. "Just one of my many standard tools of the trade."

Jack eyed him suspiciously.

Baxter moved to the wall separating them from their victims and held the stethoscope against the wall. He listened silently for a few minutes and then shook his head. "Either no one is in the room, or if someone's there, they're sleeping," he reported.

"Are you sure you'd hear them?"

"Yes. If someone talks or bumps something in there, we'll hear them with this," he held up the stethoscope.

Baxter suddenly held up his hand. "Someone's there, but not in the room right next to this one. They must be in the next room, but I can hear the faint murmur of their voices and someone just closed a door." Baxter handed the stethoscope to Jack, "You listen while I call my contact."

Jack placed the stethoscope against the wall and Baxter hoped he would be so involved that he would give him time to whisper to his contact. It would take only a couple words.

Jack smiled and looked pleased, "You're smarter than I thought you were."

Baxter took a small black telephone address book from his suit pocket. He moved to the phone, turned his back to Jack and began to dial.

"Just hold on there a minute. Who are you calling?" Jack demanded, wrenching the phone from Baxter's hand.

"I'm ordering a bomb," Baxter explained.

"Okay," Jack handed the phone back to him. "But hold it away from your ear so I can hear, too, and don't try anything funny."

Baxter dialed again and held the phone according to Jack's order. He had tried to think of a way to alert his contact without Jack guessing what he was doing, but no safe plan had come to him. Jack watched him like a hawk.

When this is over, Baxter thought, *I will devise a code to let Jim know what I want when I can't be specific. I should have thought of it before, I wouldn't be having this problem with Jack.* Baxter was worried, but he was sure he could out-smart Jack and come out the winner in this battle, especially with that blood thirsty Ivy out of the way.

Jim answered on the sixth ring, after Baxter was sure the man was not at home. "Florida here. I need a bomb that will take down a large building. It's six floors tall and covers half a city block. And I need it delivered by nine-thirty tonight."

"Right," Jim answered with no hesitation. "Where do you want it delivered to?"

Baxter glanced at Jack but didn't ask his opinion. "Bring it to the Claremont Hotel. Go to the bottom floor of the parking ramp. There's a white, ninety-three Pontiac parked there. License number," Baxter pulled out his wallet and checked the rental receipt of the white Pontiac, "218-BWW. Leave it in the car. Set it to explode at ten p.m. tonight. Your fee will be deposited in your bank tomorrow morning."

"Right." There was no discussion on the amount of the fee. Baxter's contacts knew the amount was always more than generous. It was this fact that kept them ready and willing to drop anything to fulfill one of Florida's orders.

The phone went dead in Baxter's hand and Jack looked at him in surprise. "It's that easy? God, it sure is going to be nice to have money." B a x t e r looked away from him, not wanting Jack to see the murderous look in his eye.

"How are we going to be sure the kids are killed in the blast?" Jack frowned at Baxter.

"The bomb will be big enough that everyone in this hotel will be killed, plus a few people in that apartment house next door."

"And how will we be sure they don't leave before the bomb goes off?"

"With this," Baxter held up the stethoscope. "We'll stay here until five minutes before the bomb is set to explode and listen to be sure they're still there."

For the next half hour they took turns listening at the wall. Finally Baxter held up his hand, "They're in there. I can hear them as plain as day."

Jack was curious, "What are they saying?"

Baxter listened for a moment and then reported, "They're planning what to have for supper."

"They aren't leaving, are they? We'll have to hurry!" Jack exclaimed. "Let me listen." He grabbed the stethoscope out of Baxter's hand and jerked the earplugs from his ears.

"They're not leaving. They're ordering from room service. All we have to do is move the car to the bottom ramp and wait for our package," Baxter said, rubbing his ear and gritting his teeth in fury.

At seven p.m., Dena came to the kids' room. "We have one small lead that should have been a lot bigger, considering the man-powder required to turn it up. A man answering Baxter's description is checked in at the Central East Hotel. We checked the room, but it was empty. We have a man watching his room and we're hoping he'll show up there. The clerk says when the guy arrived, he was being chauffeured around in a black limousine, but he later rented a white Pontiac. We have the license number and an all points bulletin out on the Pontiac. There's been no sign of Jack Thomas Huxley, but if we find Baxter or his car, we'll probably find Huxley, too.

"I stationed a couple of men on the roof and I've decided that we're going to put a man in each of your rooms, too. I'm sorry, but I'll feel safer that way." She looked at Janelle and Allison with sympathy, "If you want, we can hang a blanket around your beds."

They looked at each other and both girls shook their heads. "We'll get used to having someone watch us sleep," Janelle said, "And after hearing about Baxter trying to come in the window, I'll feel a lot safer with an officer in the room." Her mind skittered away from the thought that only the freak accident of the woman's fall had saved them from death.

"Me, too," Allison agreed.

"Well, I'm going to catch a few hours sleep and I'll be back around eleven. I don't think they'll show up before that, there are too many people around early in the evening." Dena hugged the girls, said goodnight to Ross and Curt, and left.

On the other side of Allison and Curt's room, Baxter smirked and told Jack, "The cops found my room at Central East and they know what car I'm driving. We'll have to change license plates and call my contact with the new number.

"They've doubled the guard on the kids and they have men on the roof. The woman that was talking to the kids just now says she doesn't expect us to show our faces before eleven p.m.," he snickered and added, "By then, this place will be nothing but a pile of burning rubble, with bodies everywhere."

CHAPTER TWENTY

Jack and Baxter immediately left to change license plates on the Pontiac and move it to the bottom level of the ramp. They encountered very few people on the brief trip.

An hour after his second conversation with his contact, Baxter and Jack ordered a room service supper. When finished, Baxter said, "We'll have to rent a different car for our getaway. Do you want to call or should I?"

"Go right ahead, you're the boss. At least for the minute." As Baxter dialed the phone, Jack moved close and held his ear near the receiver.

Fifteen minutes later they left the hotel and walked to the car rental, two blocks from the hotel. Having secured a gray Ford Thunderbird, they parked it at the bottom of the ramp, a short distance from the white Pontiac. Positioning themselves halfway down the ramp from the target car, they hid behind a support pillar of the ramp and awaited their delivery.

Jack grew weary with the wait, "When's he supposed to be here?"

"Nine-thirty."

"Haven't you ever seen this guy?"

"I've seen him, but he's never seen me. And that's the way it's going to stay," Baxter replied.

Jack filed this information away for further reference, knowing Baxter was smart not to have face-to-face meetings with his contacts. *Clever idea to follow when I'm rich,* he thought.

At nine-thirty on the dot a maroon Ford circled into view and slowly approached the Pontiac. It stopped behind the Pontiac and a tall, thin man of about fifty emerged from the Ford, carrying a small package. He opened the door of the Pontiac, placed the package on the front seat, locked the doors and quietly left.

"Mission accomplished," Jack grinned, already anxious to witness the blast when the bomb exploded.

Baxter and Jack retrieved the bomb and nonchalantly made their way back upstairs. They examined the bomb in the privacy of their room and found that Baxter's contact had left detailed instructions on setting the clock on the bomb if they changed their minds as to the time of the blast. A second note informed them that the bomb could be set to double time if they pleased; making the clock run twice as fast as normal.

Jack went to the stethoscope and Baxter eased the bomb to the floor beside the wall closest to Janelle, Ross, Allison and Curt, leaving the timer set for ten p.m. He had no desire to muddle around with the bomb, in spite of Jim's precise instructions.

He checked his watch. Nine-forty p.m. Twenty minutes till blast off time. He sat by the table in the corner and watched Jack's facial expressions in response to the kids' conversation on the other side of the wall. His mind drew a blank when he tried to visualize a plan to eliminate Jack and his frustration showed on his face. If Jack had been paying attention to him, Baxter would have had to watch his expressions.

Fifteen minutes passed slowly. "Someone just came into the room," Jack exclaimed in a whisper.

"Who?"

"I think it's that woman cop you were talking about." Jack listened intently and then jumped up from his perch on the floor. "A snitch told the cops about our bomb! That cop is taking the kids out of the hotel!"

Baxter didn't wait to hear the rest of Jack's explanation. He flicked the switch to speed up the clock on the bomb and started for the door. "We've got less than three minutes to be out of here." He disappeared through the door, with Jack close on his heels.

Dena quickly explained the call from the snitch to Janelle, Allison, Ross and Curt. Ross' mouth dropped open, "They wouldn't blow up a hotel full of people just to get Janelle, would they?"

"According to our snitch, I'm afraid that's just what they plan to do," Dena confirmed, gently but firmly pushing the girls toward the door. "I've warned the hotel security force. Let's get out of here!"

All four young people had already changed into pajamas. "We can't go out in our pajamas," Allison exclaimed, looking down at her skimpy short pajamas, which she had covered with a sheet to protect herself from the eyes of the two guards in their room.

Janelle wrapped her sheet closer around her thinly clad body, shouting, "We have to, Allison! That bomb could go off at any second!"

The blast of the hotel's fire alarm caused everyone in the room to jump in terror. Dena glanced at her watch. Nine-fifty six p.m. If the bomb had been set for ten p.m., as the informant had reported, they had four minutes to be clear of the hotel. She grabbed Allison's arm and began to pull her toward the door, "Let's go! Right now! Follow Ed, he knows the quickest way out."

Ed motioned the kids to follow him. In the hallway, he headed for the stairs and Allison protested, "Won't the elevator be faster?"

"No! The elevator may never make it to this floor with everyone trying to escape at once!" Ed shouted over the shrill beeping of the fire alarm. He ran for the steps. The kids, Dena, and the guards from the hall were close behind him.

People were pouring out of every room, dressed in a variety of different clothes. Some were not dressed at all and held sheets or blankets around their nude bodies. Their eyes were wide with terror and panic. Screams of horror vibrated from the walls.

The stairs from the sixth floor to the fourth floor were still relatively clear, but before they reached the third floor landing the stairs were a mass of human flesh scrambling over each other in their haste to escape the building. Smaller people were being trampled by bigger people and screams of anguish joined the chaos of noise.

Dena was grimly determined to see her charges to safety, "Hold hands! We don't want to be separated!"

Ed reached back and grabbed Janelle's hand. She drew comfort from the firm steadiness of his grip. Ross was already holding her other hand and he reached back to grip Allison's hand just as a big man rammed into him from the side, breaking the momentary contact they had achieved. Allison was left behind as the man forced his way between them, pushing and shoving.

Ross pulled back on Janelle and screamed, "I've lost Allison!"

Janelle hung back and Ed turned around to encourage her to hurry.

"Ross lost Allison!" she shouted at the detective, her words nearly lost in the turmoil surrounding them.

Ed flattened himself against the wall, allowing the burly bully to pass him, and waited while Ross pushed himself back toward Allison, who

TAKE CARE

was now separated from them by four or five other panicky people.

Ross finally reached Allison and grabbed her hand, pulling her, Curt and Dena with him as he forced his way back to Janelle. They joined hands and Ed Marshall again began to drive his way forward.

Dena checked her watch when they bulldozed their way through the doorway to the first floor. "Hurry!" she shouted to Ed, "Our times nearly gone." It was nine fifty eight p.m.

The hotel lobby was a congested mass of frenzied people all running for the exits. Dena, Ed and the kids had about forty feet of space to cross before they would reach the front doors of the hotel. Ed hollered at the people around him, encouraging them to hurry, but the mob of people seemed not to move. His eyes fell on the huge glass of the display window ten feet to their left. Making a snap decision, he turned to the window.

The crowd pushed past them toward the door, but it still took them precious seconds to reach the window. Ed grabbed a straight-backed chair from a small grouping beside them, threw all his six foot two inches and two hundred ten pounds of strength behind his thrust and sent it crashing through the plate glass of the window. The safety glass crumbled around them as they jumped through the opening and ran for their lives.

They raced across the street, where the traffic had jammed so tight that it was no longer moving at all, and headed up the next block.

The blast from the bomb threw them off their feet. Debris flew in all directions, while they lay on the cement of the sidewalk and covered their heads with their arms.

The hotel seemed to have grown wings and a thick covering of dust and smoke mushroomed around the disintegrating building. Chunks of walls, broken pieces of beds and chairs, mattresses, patron's clothes and thousands of other unidentifiable pieces of material flew past and around where they huddled on the ground.

Bodies and pieces of bodies fell out of the sky, causing Janelle and Allison to scream with fear and cry with pain for the hundreds who were murdered by Baxter and Jack.

Baxter and Jack flew out of their room into the hall, but they were more than a hundred feet further away from the stairs than Janelle, Ross, Allison, Curt, Dena and the detectives had been. They headed for the elevator and Baxter impatiently and repeatedly punched the call button. After less than a minutes wait, they both ran for the stairs.

As they turned from the elevator, the hotel's fire alarm suddenly started its ear splitting howl and the hall was immediately packed solid with people—in terrified bunches—pushing their way toward the stairs.

When they reached the staircase, Baxter turned away from Jack and headed for the door that led to the roof, praying Jack would not be paying attention to where he went; if Jack was blown up with the kids, all Baxter's problems would be over.

Jack noticed Baxter's change of direction and followed him, shouting, "Where are you going?"

Baxter clinched his teeth in frustration, but decided he better answer. Jack was sure to have his knife in his pocket, if not in his hand. "We can jump across to that apartment house and be out of here long before the bomb goes."

A woman next to Jack heard the word bomb and began to scream with renewed magnitude, "A bomb! Someone put a bomb in the hotel! Run!" She tried to follow her own advice, but the word bomb had caused the people around her to react with a delirium worse than they had been feeling from the threat of a fire. People began to club other people over the head and run over the fallen bodies when they collapsed on the floor. One man picked up a young girl and used her screaming body as a battering ram, pushing the people in front of him down the stairs; they fell like dominos and he climbed over their bodies.

Jack and Baxter turned away from the frantic flow of people heading down the stairs and opened the door leading to the roof. They pulled the door closed behind them and raced up the steps. At the top, they found a locked steel door, with a reinforcing steal bar padlocked across it. Neither man had tools with him to pick the lock or batter the door open.

"We've got to go back!" Jack screamed. Baxter had already turned around and was pounding back down the stairs, no longer worried about Jack's wishes or his switchblade knife. The stairs from the sixth floor had cleared, but at the fifth floor landing they once again came up against the screaming crunch of people trying to force their way out of the doomed hotel.

They had reached the third floor when Baxter checked his watch for the fiftieth time. "We have less than a minute to go!" he screamed in panic.

Jack's eyes widened in terror and he gave the horde in front of him a powerful thrust, causing some of the people to fall screaming to their knees, but not making a break in the solid wall of humanity.

"Go out the door and on to the floor. We can jump from a window!" Baxter screamed, forgetting he didn't want Jack saved. They both pushed and shoved, but they were now going against the stream of people and they made no headway at all.

"It's time!" Baxter screamed, his face contorted with fear. "We're not going to make...."

His words were cut off in mid sentence when at that second the bomb exploded with a horrifying blast of sound that did not have time to reach the ears of the people trapped in the stairway before they were catapulted off their feet—along with the walls, stairs, ceiling and floors of the building surrounding them—and hurled into the night.

Janelle and Allison shared a hospital room. Four hours had passed since the bomb had exploded. Neither girl had been seriously hurt, miraculously escaping with a few cuts and bruises, but Dena had insisted they spend the night in the hospital. Police guards were again posted outside their room, as there was no way of knowing if Baxter and Jack had been in the hotel when it exploded.

Ross and Curt had been given the room next to them. Ross had received a slight concussion when his head cracked against the unyielding cement of the sidewalk and Curt had broken his leg when the explosion had violently thrown him against the curb of the sidewalk.

Incredibly, Dena had not been hurt. The other detectives, like Janelle and Allison, had small cuts and bruises, but none had needed hospitalizing.

The death count at the Claremont Hotel had not yet been completed. The dozens of fires the bomb had started through out the rubble of the hotel were hampering rescue teams. It would be days before all the dead were identified.

Janelle and Allison were visiting Ross and Curt. The girls gingerly sat on the edge of the men's beds and held their hands. Allison was tempted to lie down beside Curt and snuggle into his comforting embrace, but she was afraid a nurse might walk in on them.

Janelle sat softly, trying not to jiggle the bed. She knew Ross had a bad headache and she didn't want to make it worse. She shook her head sadly, "I still can't believe there are actually people as vicious and demented as Baxter and Jack Thomas Huxley."

"You're lucky you weren't at Mom's house the night they were there with that woman, Ivy. Baxter and Jack are horrible people, but I think that woman was the worst. You wouldn't believe the look on her face when she thought she was going to get to kill Mom and me. She had pale blue eyes, but when she looked at us, they glittered and actually seemed to throw sparks. You could tell she couldn't wait to start cutting us up," Allison's eyes filled with tears. She sniffed and wiped her tears away with the corner of the sheet on Curt's bed. "That woman was truly insane."

"Don't think about it," Curt murmured softly, caressing her hand.

"I can't help it," Allison groaned. "I can still feel the terror that clawed at me when Ivy advanced on me and Mom."

"My Doctor says you need to think about things that happen to you. I don't mean dwell on them, but you should think them through and talk to someone about them. She says that's the way to put bad things behind you for good. If you don't talk about them, they could still bother you years later," Janelle said.

Allison nodded, "That's what happened with Baxter's molesting. I never could tell the doctor everything that happened, I was too embarrassed."

"But you shouldn't have been embarrassed, Allison, you didn't do anything wrong," Janelle consoled her.

"I know that now, but at the time, I wasn't sure if somehow the whole thing wasn't my fault."

Janelle was shocked, "I didn't know you felt that way. I felt the same way, but I told the doctor about it and she convinced me that there was nothing I could have done to change the way Baxter acted."

The sisters talked on and their men marveled at the way the two girls appeared to have become closer to each other than they had been before the tragedy.

Monday afternoon, when all four young people were well rested and recovered from their ordeal, Dena moved them to another hotel. Curt was on crutches, but the other three—except for their continuing sorrow over the loss of Delphine—were well on the way to becoming their old selves again.

At five p.m. Monday the bodies of Baxter Perry and Jack Thomas Huxley were positively identified when they were removed from the wreckage of the Claremont Hotel. One hundred and sixty innocent people had died in the disaster that Baxter and Jack had activated. Authorities had been amazed that the amount of dead was not higher, considering the enormous measure of destruction the bomb had caused and the large amount of people registered at the hotel. Two hundred and five people had been seriously injured in the blast, not counting the dead.

Janelle, Ross, Allison and Curt told Dena they would like to leave the hotel and return to Delphine's house immediately. Dena escorted them home, thanking God that their ordeal was over and they had not been seriously injured.

Delphine's funeral was Tuesday morning. She was laid to rest beside Janelle and Allison's father, Fitzpatrick Lanley, and her head stone read, 'Delphine Mary Lanley', as was her wish.

Janelle and Allison took comfort in their shared belief that their beloved mother and father were reunited and happy with the Lord.

The story of Duluth's Claremont Hotel bombing and fire was televised nationwide and the night after the news became known around the world, Dena received an anonymous long distance phone call.

"The guy who put that bomb in the hotel in Duluth had a business here in Miami," a girl's voice said. "His name was Baxter Perry and the other guy, Jack Thomas Huxley, worked for him. The company is called Caretaker's Trucking and his business was stealing kids to sell for pornography and to those demented people who like to have sex with kids. He also sold kids to guys who like to torture and murder them.

"Now that Baxter is dead, I'm no longer afraid to tell you about this, but I don't want to get involved. I also don't want to see the business started up again and that could happen if one of Baxter's evil accomplices decides to take over where Baxter left off." The phone clicked and went dead in Dena's hand.

Dena immediately called the FBI and reported the call. A week later a friend of hers from the Federal Bureau of Investigation called. "We've rounded up the whole gang that worked for Baxter Perry. It seems Baxter had called for a meeting of the whole group. They were all in town waiting for the meeting. And we've found forty of the kids Baxter and his bunch of goons kidnapped. They've been returned to their parents.

"That's so far. Baxter Perry left very complete records of every client he ever did business with. Names, addresses and telephone numbers and if you can believe it...videotapes of his perverted sex games with some of the children.

"As you can imagine, we don't want this to get out yet. We've arrested thirty five people so far, and that doesn't include the truck drivers he had on his payroll."

Dena was horrified by the devastating amount of human anguish Baxter had caused in his lifetime. She was happy the man was dead and gone. He was one of those people who should never have been born.

Officer Bob Kelly was convicted for his crimes and sentenced to ten years in prison. Ellen Kelly was also convicted as an accomplice, but was given a suspended sentence. She disappeared from Duluth and never once visited her husband in jail.

Lars and Kate's wedding was over. Janelle and Ross had been subdued during the wedding mass and the celebration which followed, although they tried not to let their sorrow show.

Allison and Curt were still in Duluth, having decided to make their old hometown their home again. Janelle, Allison, Ross and Curt had spent the week following Lars and Kate's wedding planning their own weddings, which would be a double ceremony and would take place in April of nineteen ninety four. Dena and Ed Marshall helped with the wedding plans and had happily agreed to give the girls away.

Janelle and Allison both observed Ed Marshall at different points in the wedding planning and both girls saw the deep love he had for Dena. They hoped Dena and Ed would someday join the ranks of all the happily married couples in the world.

Seven weeks had passed since Janelle had seen Jack Thomas Huxley at the Ohio rest area with Penny Davis, the young red haired girl Jack had brutally murdered. She didn't think she would ever want to stop at a rest area again.

Printed in the United States
22271LVS00002B/208-213